THE UNHOLY SM

Her body was wracked
lay naked, vulnerable u
hideous Devil figure th
inconceivable to her th
could be filming such bar
whirled on and the Black Mass continued as
celebrants called to their Satan.

'I say Satan's will be done! Come now to the violation of the virgin.'

With the crash of yet another organ chord, Judith struggled to free herself. But hands held her tightly as the gigantic Satan figure pranced closer . . .

She tried with all her will to see Satan as only an actor, but everything was too complete, too authentic.

Now, the moment of her ravishment was inescapable!

She would die, she thought, or maybe worse . . .

By Gregory A. Douglas, and published by New English Library:

THE NEST
THE UNHOLY SMILE

THE UNHOLY SMILE

Gregory A. Douglas

NEW ENGLISH LIBRARY

First published in the USA as *The Rite* in 1979 by
Kensington Publishing Corp.

First NEL Paperback Edition March 1986

NEL Books are published by
New English Library,
Mill Road, Dunton Green,
Sevenoaks, Kent.
Editorial office: 47 Bedford Square, London WC1B 3DP

Printed and bound in Great Britain by
Cox & Wyman Ltd, Reading

British Library C.I.P.

Douglas, Gregory A.
The unholy smile.
I. Title
813′.54[F] PR6054.083/

ISBN 0 450 05833 6

The author is indebted to the writings of J.K. Huysmans for an account of Baron Gilles de Rais. Thanks also to American novelist Eli Cantor for suggesting a contemporary horror story based on one of the darkest and least known villains in history. —G.A.D.

From
Encyclopaedia Britannica, 1969 edition

"RAIS, GILLES de (1404-1440) . . . satanist, and murderer, the central figure of a 15th-century *cause célèbre*, whose name was later connected with the story of Bluebeard. He was born in Anjou in 1404, the son of Guy de Laval, baron de Rais . . . (who left him) great wealth and possessions . . ."

"He kept a more lavish court than the king and dissipated his wealth . . . To redeem his fortune Rais turned to alchemy . . . He resorted to necromancy, satanism, and finally the torture and ritual murder of kidnapped children, perhaps as many as 200."

In June 1440, Baron Gilles de Rais desecrated the celebration of Mass at a chapel in Brittany. "This desecration led the bishop of Nantes to investigate all Rais' activities. Arrested . . . Rais was condemned for heresy . . . and sentenced to death for murder . . . His confession and repentance, and his resignation at his execution . . . were acclaimed at the time as an example of Christian penitence."

CHAPTER ONE

Ominous thunder crashed over lower Manhattan just as Judith Bradford dropped her knapsack on the SoHo doorstep. The blond young actress hastily checked the crumpled address in her hand as she huddled away from the downpour. The deluge broke over the art quarter like the sudden storms of the girl's home in Iowa, but here in New York City the lightning lit up forbidding, looming rooftops instead of inviting fields. To Judith's travel-weary eyes, the flashing sky above the deserted street seemed filled with cabalistic signs.

Was it a warning that she should not have come to this door, so distant and different from her life at home? For a dismal moment of irresolution Judith's shoulders sagged. She thought of turning and going back to the bus terminal. But home could never be the same again! she reminded herself sternly. She had been right to run off. Of that she was unalterably certain, no matter what might lie ahead.

The slim girl straightened and lifted her chin. She pressed the bell determinedly as gusts of wind drove the rain against her back. Her thin cotton blouse was already soaked, plastered against her skin.

Still no answer. Perhaps this silent reception was what she deserved, Judith thought hollowly. True, the movie company advertisement had said "Open Audition" but now, actually standing on the threshold of the famous Werner Christed "Film Loft," Judith had a sinking sense of how meager her high school and summer stock experience would appear among real professionals.

Her confidence wobbled again. If she hadn't needed to leave Iowa for the other, sickening, reason she would never have dared to answer the ad. It was cheeky of her to think that an important film director like Werner Christed might give her a second glance, even as an extra. But here she was, and desperate, and she might as well try her luck. Nothing ventured—

Hoping to see a light in some window, Judith squinted up against the cloudburst. There was only the gathering darkness and the pelting rain. Then she noticed the man across the street—a gaunt-looking figure in filthy overalls watching her narrowly from a dilapidated garage. She couldn't tell the man's age, but she felt his eyes like snake's fangs flickering at the back of her neck. Judith shivered with a cold chill although the New York pavement was steaming in the heat of late June. Impatiently, she told herself not to be childish. The man had made no gesture or motion of threat. He was dirty and ugly but no menace, no reason for her heart to be pounding beneath her drenched breasts. If his eyes gave her the creeps—well, she was bone-tired and her nerves were shot.

Judith turned to look up at the windows again. They were prison-like and begrimed with dirt and soot. To Judith they seemed eyeless sockets staring forbiddingly from a hulking skeleton. The bleak structure was certainly not what she had expected. It appeared more like a haunted, abandoned warehouse than the glamorous movie studio famed throughout the youth culture as the Mecca of avant-garde cinema. Judith forced herself to recall the rave reviews of Werner Christed films in the *Village Voice*, the *Berkeley Barb*, the *Rolling Stone*, and the other with-it papers her friends sent on from Chicago. There were few hayseeds among the youth of the country anywhere any more.

If there were any hayseeds left in her own hair, New York was where she would shake them out, Judith pledged to herself once more as she pressed the recalcitrant bell again. Grimly she told herself that someone had to be inside. Knowledgeable kids in Chicago, where she had stopped over, had assured her that travelers were always welcome at the Loft, could stay the night at least. Werner Christed kept open house, they said. Judith now prayed they were right. She had counted on it, had no place else to go, and she felt the huge metropolis sprawling around her in an increasingly unfriendly and alien way. The spying man in the garage did not take his gaze from her, and she could not control her shivering reaction to his reptilian eyes. Maybe she wasn't as much of a pistol as she had reckoned, the girl thought miserably as the studio door remained shut and silent before her. As if to underscore her self-doubt, a speeding taxi splashed Judith from her blond topknot to her soaked sandals. Maybe she should have stayed with her Chicago friends, and tried the Goodman Theatre, she thought morosely. But that would be the first place her mother would check. Judith considered that she could lose herself safely in New York for the three months until her eighteenth birthday. Then she would contact her mother, not before.

But her plan seemed to be failing before it got started. True, it wasn't her fault that a bus breakdown had made her a day late for the Christed film auditions, but now she blamed herself. If she was taking responsibility for her life, she should have anticipated unexpected difficulties—that was the difference between a child and an adult.

With a sigh of resignation, Judith turned from the unfriendly door, to find that the garageman had come up behind her, unheard in the pelting rain and thunder. Judith's fist went to her mouth to stifle an involuntary scream. Looming over her close up, the man was even creepier than she had judged. His face was pasty white, like a corpse's, and the pallid contrast with his sunken, bloodshot eyes made them more evil-seeming as he stared hungrily at her. Judith shrank from both his sight and his smell. A stench came off him that seemed to be carried by the rain over the whole street. It was a pungent, unfamiliar odor that reminded Judith of the noxious stink of sulphur in her high school chemistry lab. It suffocated Judith like a sack over her head.

She moved to slip past the man, but his hand clawed out and grabbed her arm. She felt as if her skin were splitting beneath the iron grip of his bony fingers. "What you want here?" came rough words. The man spoke with a thick foreign accent Judith had never heard before.

Matching her fright, Judith's temper flared. "I don't see it's any of your business! Take your hand off me!" she demanded. She might be in a strange city, and lost, but she wouldn't let herself be bullied.

"I am watchman for here," the man grunted importantly. "Nobody go in!"

"Fine," Judith said. "I'm just leaving."

But the man did not let go her arm. His lips parted in a lascivious smirk that revealed broken, dirty teeth. He gestured meaningfully toward the garage, all the while holding Judith fast. "You come in from rain with me. Dry off. I make you coffee. Nice cup of coffee, eh?"

Revolted, Judith cried, "No, no!" Quick panic filled her breast as she read his lecherous expression.

His clawlike fingers seemed stitched into her muscles so that she could not tear away. He started to pull Judith across the street. Judith looked about wildly for help, but the storm had swept the place clear of people. Desperately she swung her knapsack at the man. He gasped and grunted with sharp pain as it slammed heavily into his ribs, but with a fierce curse he grabbed the bag and flung it easily away into the gutter. He might look like a scarecrow but he had the strength of an ox. Judith squirmed wildly in his grasp, slipping helplessly along the street as the man dragged her relentlessly toward the open garage. He kept making a gurgling sound in his throat, an inner cackle of lewd glee that seemed pure insanity. Judith felt she was doomed. She screamed out as loud as she could, though she knew there was no one to hear. In a fierce effort to free herself she tried to swing her arm up to scratch at the man's eyes. She tried to disable him by twisting to knee him in the groin. She could be savage in self-defense, but he was too quick for her each time. Like a beast pulling its captured prey into its cave, he was dragging Judith through the garage door when, suddenly, a woman's voice called loud and commandingly from the door that had been locked and silent.

"Leave her! At once!"

The claw fell away from Judith's arm. The man stood blinking in the wet night, his mouth working with frustration, a spittle of fury dripping from his lips.

The woman called again, sternly, with angry, strong authority. "Do you want me to report you to them again?"

Judith, panting with relief, saw the hard light click out of the man's ugly eyes. He seemed to shrink and bend in half. He slunk quickly out of sight like a whipped cur. Judith stood on the sidewalk wishing to call out her thanks to the woman, but she could only shake and weep, grateful and terrified and furious all at once.

"Now it is all right," the woman's voice was saying, close by. A gentle, comforting arm was across Judith's heaving shoulders. "You come inside with me."

Later, wearing a dry smock and quieted by a cup of tea the woman had prepared, Judith began to take in the loft where they were sitting. Her heart quickened—with a rising expectation replacing the horror of the street. Plainly, she was in the sanctum of Werner Christed's movie studio. The high ceiling was crisscrossed with metal catwalks and grids for spotlights. Scenic canvases, a cyclorama, flats, and platforms of every shape and color were stacked along the brick walls. Eye-filling posters advertising Christed's many films were everywhere—a promise and an inspiration that caught at Judith's throat. But otherwise, to Judith's surprise, the huge stage set was echoingly empty. There were none of the cameras, microphones, booms, electric apparatus she expected, none of the complicated paraphernalia of a functioning film studio.

As if reading Judith's unspoken question, the woman explained, "Everything has been moved from here to location. I am Lena Ludovici. My husband is the assistant director of Werner Christed." In the woman's voice Judith made out the same accent of the garageman, though much fainter. She could only wonder what their relationship might be. Certainly this woman was the man's opposite—kind, caring, motherly. Judith found herself admiring the round, pleasant face. Although the woman was stout, she moved with the poise of the dancer she had once been, with a natural grace, and Judith was drawn to her at once. The good earth. A Maillol sculpture. The woman's wide-set eyes and broad cheeks came across with an inviting foreign attractiveness. A slight hint of a mustache made Lena Ludovici more appealing, not less.

For a long moment, the two so-different women took each other in. Lena Ludovici saw a young girl whose shy violet eyes were begging for help though they tried to appear self-sufficient. Lena felt a pang of her own private pain. This girl's transparent vulnerability to life reminded her of her daughter, now dead a year in a horrible auto accident. It was the girl's spiritual innocence that was the same. Physically, there was no resemblance. Robina had been dark and only passably pretty. This girl was stunning. She had everything—an actress's genuine beauty of high cheekbones and sparkling eyes that drew one in, coupled with a model's perfect nose, silken hair, and a generous mouth quick to smile pleasantly—soft lips that should be laughing carefree on some campus, the older woman thought, instead of trembling nervously in this Manhattan loft.

"Where are you from?" Lena asked conversationally, wanting the girl to feel at ease after her ordeal on the street.

"Oklahoma," Judith fabricated. She hated to lie to this woman who had helped her so dramatically, but it was best to be supercareful and not trust anyone too quickly. With just one clue, her mother would be down after her with police in tow.

Lena did not have to be told that Judith Bradford came from a country place. The girl had a golden airiness about her, and the glow in her face reflected strength and hope taken from the natural order of prairie seasons. In the girl's open awe at the Christed posters the woman saw the dewy beauty of horizons she too had dreamed in past dawns in her own, distant country.

The sympathy in the woman's manner seemed to Judith a permission to speak the question burning within. "Is it really too late to audition for Mr. Christed?" she asked pleadingly. She went on quickly, with a pressing need to explain. "My bus broke down. I thought there might still be time. Please! Couldn't I still see Mr. Christed on location?"

The woman quietly searched the misty eyes before her. Lena had seen at once that this girl was a runaway. But she also perceived that this wasn't one of the cop-outs she despised, those who came looking for kicks, drugs, and sex because they had been given too much of everything too soon. This girl was clearly running *to* something, worth helping. And she was unusually beautiful, with the particular qualities Werner Christed was looking for. It was truly too bad the audition was over. It would be complicated to open everything up, even though Lena now considered Judith Bradford more promising than the girl Werner Christed had finally selected and taken out to the company. Yet, Werner himself might be the first one to wish to see this girl. Perhaps, Lena considered silently, she should discuss it with her husband, who would be coming in from the location in a few hours.

Judith rose and put her teacup down on the paint-flecked table between the two women. She took Lena Ludovici's silence to be her answer—nothing could be done. "Thank you for the tea," she said. She tried a smile, to show the woman that she understood. "I have to find a place to stay tonight. Do you know where I might try?"

"Why, yes," Lena Ludovici unexpectedly returned the smile. "Right here." Then, "There is no sense your getting wet again. I am here alone until my husband comes in from location later. With the company away, our dormitory floor is closed upstairs, but there is a cot in one of the property rooms you can use."

All at once, Judith felt her bone weariness. The woman's sympathy reached her with an irresistible ache for motherly support. It had been such a miserable trip. She felt like a mangy stray cat. The only bright spot was this decent woman, who was asking unexpectedly, "Do your parents know where you are?"

"Oh, yes!" Judith declared. The Oklahoma lie did not make this one easier, and Judith's eyes dropped under the woman's appraising look.

Lena Ludovici went on quietly. "You have run away from home, haven't you?" If she was going to follow the plan taking shape in the back of her head, she needed to know more about this proud and obviously distressed young person.

For the first time since leaving Iowa, Judith Bradford felt truly homeless. The hustled planning and traveling had buoyed her up against all her trepidation and doubts; now those supports were gone. Despite herself, she could not stop the tears that welled up. In a quick motion of compassion, the woman drew the girl close, stroking the soft hair, and making comforting sounds in her throat. "It is not an easy time, I am sure. Here, sit by me and tell me."

The two held each other in a mutual need that dissolved the age difference between them.

Lena encouraged, "Maybe I can help you."

In her despair, Judith made up her mind. She did not know this woman but she trusted her. The warm arms holding her expressed a tenderness she had not known from her own disturbed mother for many years now. And it was true, as someone had said, that it was easier to talk to strangers than to friends, for strangers will soon be gone and do not hurt you or reveal your secrets in the end. It would be a relief if she could share her pain at last instead of continuing to bottle it up.

The story came in a rush once Judith began. "My father died two years ago, a heart attack." The girl did not try to mask her bitterness. "My mother kept pushing him to sell our farm. A resort company wanted the land, but he loved it too much. He was stubborn, and my mother fought him day and night. It was awful—and all for nothing, because after he died the company decided not to go ahead, and we were poorer than ever.

"Then last year my mother married again. He is a contractor, and we moved into town into his big house. I tried to like him but I couldn't, even after he got me a job in a summer theatre. And then—" Judith faltered. "One night when my mother was at her club meeting, he got drunk and he—"

"I understand." Lena nodded with a surge of womanly compassion.

Judith whispered, "I managed to stop him, but you see why I can't go back."

The woman said at once, "Tonight you will stay with me." Her mind was made up. "Tomorrow I will talk to my husband. I will try to persuade him to take you out with us." As Judith's face kindled with quick hope, Lena cautioned, "I doubt he will agree, except maybe for you to help me with props and costumes and so on. Would you be willing to do that?"

"Oh, yes! I'll sweep floors, wash dishes, anything!"

"I will try, then." Lena stood up. "Now you need to get some rest." She led Judith to an unpainted plywood door. "You won't be too comfortable here, but it is better than the rain." She pointed across the hall. "There is a bathroom here. I will bring you linens for the cot."

Judith thanked the woman genuinely. Her adventure might not be ending with a whimper after all. Yes, she would wash dishes, scrub floors "on location!"—magic words!—if that's what it took to join Werner Christed's company. Once she was with them it would be up to her to make the most of the opportunity. She could not ask for more.

The woman brought sheets and a towel for Judith. "I don't even know your name," she smiled.

"Judith Bradford." It wasn't a lie. Judith did not explain that she was using her real father's name rather than her stepfather's, which was Wayne. She vowed she would never call herself Judith Wayne.

The woman held out her hand formally, saying, "I have already told you I am Lena Ludovici." The two laughed self-consciously to be shaking hands this way after the embrace and the confidence they had already shared. It seemed to Judith that she had known Lena Ludovici for years. It seemed to Lena that Judith Bradford had come into her life to be a consolation and palliation. Hugging the girl close, she hoped her husband would accept her plan. He could be difficult, her Gregor Ludovici—a proud man, a strong-willed man, in many ways a man inscrutable to her even after more than twenty years of marriage.

Lena frowned as her mind unwound a troubling thread. Not just Gregor but so many things on Gomay Island were turning out to be unanticipated and difficult. For a moment she wondered if the girl would not be better off looking elsewhere. Then she impatiently shut the thought away; the start of a new film project was always a nervous time for everyone. Yes, there had been the unfortunate accident on the island, the terrible accident that had left them without the leading girl, so that they needed the last-minute auditions—but accidents happen all the time, as with her own Robina. It was no reason to turn Judith Bradford away from what might be a heaven-sent happenstance for everyone.

"Ludovici," Judith was repeating. She liked the

foreign sound. As long as she could remember she had been captivated and intrigued by anything hinting of distant places and other ways. Second only to acting, she wanted more than anything else to travel, to be a part of the picturesque scenes of exotic places, bizarre ways, colorful costumes, strange foods and manners.

Lena recognized the girl's interest, and chuckled. "My husband and I are from a tiny country nobody knows, except in Dracula movies!"

"It must be terribly exciting making movies with Werner Christed!" Judith couldn't keep her imagination from sparking.

Lena shrugged. "It is at first. You grow accustomed." She laughed. "Sometimes I think they are all insane, especially Werner Christed."

With an edge of sharpness, Judith observed, "He's a genius! Everyone knows how great he is!"

Lena laughed again, a friendly, accepting sound. "Yes, everyone knows he is a great genius, especially Werner Christed."

"His work speaks for itself!" Judith was a little surprised that it should be *she* defending the director.

"Of course," Lena Ludovici answered, genuinely and loyally. "It is just that you must be prepared for a man who knows his own worth."

"What kind of picture is he making now?" Judith asked eagerly, unable to restrain her growing curiosity.

There was a moment's silence. Lena seemed to move away, though she did not stir. All at once her tone was conspicuously and uncharacteristically curt. "I am not permitted to talk about this film," she said. "All I may tell you is the name." She hesitated for another moment, then spoke the title brusquely: "*Baron of Darkness.*"

She added at once, "But if it turns out that you do not come with us, you must not mention it to anyone. Werner would be furious if it got out before he is ready."

"I understand," Judith promised.

"Good. Now get some rest." The woman turned down the corridor leaving Judith standing before the plywood door holding the linens for her bed. The movie title echoed in her ears. *Baron of Darkness.* What might the picture be about with that name? It had not escaped her that Lena had been evasive. The title and Lena's manner were both intriguing and provocative, even mysterious—as everything Werner Christed did was intriguing and provocative, and in its own way of art, mysterious.

Opening the plywood door, Judith could only pray that Lena's husband would agree to take her to the director. For now, she needed badly to sleep, to look her best in the morning.

But, with her first step into the room, Judith was staggered. A cry of disbelief curled from her throat. What house of horrors had she been trapped into! Was Lena Ludovici a madwoman, as crazy in her way as the garageman who had attacked her? In the unlit chamber, a swarm of eerie animals was revealed by flashes of lightning through the narrow window. Vile-looking rats crouched on the floor ready to leap at her. Black ravens stared at Judith with villainous eyes. Most gruesome, scores of bats were spreading their ghoulish wings to fly at her face, their needle-like fangs hungrily bared.

Judith hopped back into the hall, slamming the door against the sinister shadows. A new scream ripped through her as she bumped into an unseen figure in the now-darkened hall. It was Lena, reassuring her at once, with loud apology. "Oh, I am so sorry. I should have warned you, of course. The animals inside are props for our picture. We have raided every taxidermist in town, as you see." With that, the woman opened the door and pulled a light cord. A harsh, swaying bulb set the gruesome animals to dancing in a grisly way. Judith's breath came back. *Stuffed specimens!* But her heart was still thumping with deep-rooted revulsion.

"I—I'm all right," Judith managed to say, feeling ashamed. It was plain to see that the animals were lifeless and harmless. Still, they charged the room with a dismal echo of death too near for comfort. What kind of weird picture was *Baron of Darkness* that it required these revolting corpses for props?

Lena Ludovici was speaking quietly. "So I will say goodnight once more." The woman turned into the hall's shadows and left Judith alone again.

For a moment, Judith stood undecided. She thought of sleeping on the floor in the big studio. Then, annoyed with herself, she observed that stuffed animals couldn't hurt her—she could think of them as the stuffed toys she had had at home. They weren't all that different when you came right down to it. Judith made her way gingerly across the floor. Now the cot looked inviting. Her fatigue was greater than any remaining disquiet. Her body felt leaden, her eyes were closing. She had slept only fitfully for two days. She dropped down. The animals didn't matter. The thunder and lightning outside didn't matter. The detectives her rich mother had hired by now didn't matter. The rain was a comforting, lulling sound on the window, and Judith was deeply asleep before she could undress.

She came awake in the first light of morning with a knotted feeling that she was being watched. Could the garageman have found her?—he had said he was the watchman, he would have a key! She bolted upright fearfully, to find giant insect eyes glaring malevolently at her. With a gulp of terror and disgust, she scrambled from the cot, only to be stunned by the threat of huge snakes coiled on the floor to strike at her.

One part of Judith's brain tried to tell her immediately that the monster insects were ordinary stage spotlights, the "snakes" nothing but heavy electric cables. But at her core, Judith felt them come alive, reaching for her. The insect antennae were squeezing her throat—she felt her neck muscles snapping and ripping. She gagged and coughed, unable to draw breath. At her ankles Judith felt sharp fangs sinking into her flesh, and hot blood dripping from the slashed wounds. The woman had lied, she was no samaritan. These were no props. She was in a torture chamber. She was being sacrificed in this terrible way for some awful dark purpose.

At the same moment, Judith Bradford knew that all of the horror was only in her brain—her head now wrapped in the too familiar yellow mist that always announced an hallucinatory attack. Judith moaned in new misery. She had thought and hoped and believed she was free of the devilish mind-tricks, but apparently she was still subject to false visions. The doctor had warned that tension and stress could bring back the effects of the drugs, with fantasies and phantoms more real than real. God knew she had been through tension and stress the past days.

Sinking down on the cot, Judith fought for air, battled to clear her head of the yellow fog. She mustered her sanity to cry silently that she must not give way to this seizure. Her good new friend outside was going to help her get to Werner Christed. She needed to be clear, and dressed, and fresh to impress the woman's husband, the assistant director of the movie! But the fog pressed Judith down despite her efforts. The animals were alive and attacking her mercilessly.

To herself, Judith again cursed the day she had gone with "the wild kids" in Chicago. She had never suspected they were dealing dope. She had certainly never suspected that the innocent-looking cigarette had been spiked with Angel Dust and that, worse, a "purple pill," LSD, had been dissolved in a drink she was given. The double effects were disastrous. She had been hospitalized for a week before she could be taken home, and then her mother would not believe she was a victim.

Right now, Judith scolded herself vehemently, she needed to hold on to what Dr. Willoughby had promised. The attacks would fade with time, he had said, would become less frequent, less intense. Clenching her fists, Judith strained harder to dispel the yellow swirl. To her grateful relief, the cowl seemed to be thinning, lifting a little. The animal squeals she was hearing in her delusion began to fade, then whimpered into silence so that she could hear her own panting breath. Then, as suddenly as her brain had been seized by the lingering chemical imbalance, it was free and recovered. Judith fell back on the cot, emptied with her effort. The room took quiet shape. The insects were harmless spotlights again, the snakes were plastic cables, the animals were inert. The storm was past.

Rising from the cot, Judith made a small sound of thankfulness that Lena Ludovici had not seen the attack. That would surely have ended any chance of joining Werner Christed. Perhaps, Judith thought, she should not even have shared as much as she had about her stepfather. In any case, she resolved that she would keep her drug problem to herself, her own private affair. Indeed, Judith encouraged herself, hadn't she just overcome a tough episode? It proved she did have enough strength to win out if she tried hard enough. She could depend on herself. She could in good conscience ask to work with Werner Christed. If she were positively involved in a film production, she was sure her unfortunate, unsought vulnerability would dissolve once and for all.

Feeling a surge of new confidence, Judith hurried to get dressed. Humming, and lugging her knapsack, she crossed the hall to the bathroom. A shower, fresh clothes, some makeup, would wipe out the nastiness of the past days, and the future was opening up with new promise. Her humming grew louder and more tuneful.

In the bathroom, Judith's eyes were caught by her image in a broken mirror with a zigzag fracture down the middle. It slashed her erratically in two with a livid wound. A frightening echo flashed through her head—was this another omen, like yesterday's lightning, like the disgusting animals? She chided herself for an impressionable fool. She had to stop spooking herself. She did not realize her hand was making a gesture she used whenever she was disturbed—her little finger at the back of her neck, rubbing in little circles beneath her hair.

The mirror showed Judith her body filling out with nubile maturity. Standing in this peculiar bathroom, she could fantasize becoming a Christed star, famous over the world. An irrepressible impulse made Judith wrinkle her nose at herself in the mirror. She grinned, feeling like the kid she had been when she played actress in her grandmother's attic. Then she frowned at herself. It had better be the grown woman in the mirror who took charge of her life now. The Big City and the Christed company were no place for a starry-eyed schoolgirl.

Looking for a shower, Judith tugged at a door in the corner of the bathroom. It stuck. She pulled harder, and shrieked in new shock. She was gaping at a soiled coffin lying in the bathtub. It did no good to tell herself it was obviously another prop. Spasms of disgust pumped through her blood at the gory, cobwebbed sight.

Lena's voice came from behind, quick with concern. "Oh, dear, I forgot to tell you that these things are all over the place. I am so sorry you were frightened again."

Judith reached for the woman's fingers, grateful for their roughness and strength. They reminded her of her grandmother's hands, and reassurance flowed from their touch. She took a deep breath and smiled. "I did realize it, but it will take me a while to get used to the idea, I suppose."

The woman patted Judith's shoulder encouragingly. "I put a tray in your room. Hurry now. My husband is here and I want him to interview you."

When she was dressed, Judith walked down the corridor anxiously. She stopped and listened to voices coming from the studio. She did not want to eavesdrop; at the same time, she considered, it might not be wise to interrupt Lena at this point. She held her breath and waited.

Lena's voice was persuasive. "Gregor, I tell you this girl has what Werner wants—the face of an angel and the body of a Lorelei."

The man's sound was gravelly. "That may be, but you know the part is filled."

"I think Werner will change his mind."

"Let's leave well enough alone, eh? There are too many complications . . ."

"What is the harm in taking her to him?"

The man was irritated. "You are aware of the rule made by both Werner and Dr. Gomay. Nobody who comes on the island now may leave before the shooting is finished."

"I am sure the girl would gladly stay. She has no place else to go."

"Werner and Dr. Gomay are not running a home for strays!"

"She can play an extra if Werner doesn't like her for the lead. She can help me in my work . . ."

"You know the other qualification they insist on!"

"Yes. I am sure the girl is—pure." In the corridor, Judith blushed. Being a Christed actress was not so simple.

"How can you be sure?"

It was the woman's voice that sharpened with impatience. "Frankly, I must say that is nonsense to me! How can it make a difference on the screen?"

The man's voice took on a tone of professional authority. "Leave that to Werner, eh? There will be scenes when an innocent girl will react differently than someone who is not chaste! It is precisely these subtleties that make a difference between Werner's genius and the Hollywood butchers. In any case, it is Dr. Gomay who insists."

"Well, the old man is mad, but I suppose it is not for the likes of me to say so."

"Exactly! Since it is Dr. Gomay's script, his money, and his island! We do not second guess Felix Gomay!"

"Do you expect me to *ask* the girl if she is a virgin?"

"Of course not. Werner and I depended on your sensitivity with the other one."

Lena said firmly, "Well, I believe in her."

There was a coarse, male laugh. "Two virgins in New York City—it's hard to believe!"

Embarrassed, Judith took a soft step backward, but heard Lena replying with spirit, "There are still girls everywhere with old-fashioned ideas about getting under a man!"

"You put it so delicately, my dear."

"There are still women who consider it a delicate matter!"

"Have it your way, Lena." His tone was dismissive.

His wife would not be stopped. "Werner will thank you for bringing her to him! You will see."

The man must have turned back. "You seem to have your heart set on this girl."

"I do!" There was a pause, then Judith heard the woman softer, and sadder. "It is almost as if—" The words stopped.

The man answered, with some sympathy now, "I understand how it is with you, Lena. I am not a monster, you know. I have my own feelings about what happened to our Rubina."

Judith did not understand what they were discussing, but she sensed that Lena was winning her husband over. She listened with growing hope. Lena was saying, "Oh, Gregor, you are a good man!"

"Well, let me think about it."

"Ah, I knew you would not disappoint me!"

There was a pause in which Judith imagined Lena was embracing her husband. She heard the man speak again.

"Let me see this paragon of yours before I decide."

Excitement mounted in Judith. She had a chance! She patted her hair hurriedly, straightened her dress, ran her tongue over her lips. If ever she looked attractive, she implored the gods, let it be now!

The man was speaking again, with emphasis. "Lena, be very sure the girl understands that there will absolutely be no way for her to leave the island!"

In her anticipation, Judith wanted to call out that the prohibition, strange as it sounded, didn't bother her a whit. Werner Christed and "Dr. Gomay"—apparently the person backing the production financially—must have their own good reasons for the restriction. They would have no problem with her wanting to leave!

Lena called her name, and Judith hurried into the studio. The man's booming voice had prepared Judith to expect a large figure but nothing like the giant who was standing on the empty movie set. He had the bulk of an Olympic weight lifter. His great round face was pitted, but there was a broad smile for Judith that gave the man a half-handsome cast.

His size alone gave him importance, and an animal magnetism. Judith could see how Lena Ludovici might be taken with him, but she herself was put off by a pomposity of manner, and above all she did not like his eyes. They were small and close set—she did not want to say piggish. They seemed to be searching through her clothes. What might be intended for a suavely devilish European gleam of appreciation for her pulchritude came to Judith as an unpleasant touching of her body.

Gregor Ludovici was indeed taking Judith in with an assurance that amounted to rudeness. He openly assessed her firm breasts and her narrow waist widening attractively to hips he could call nothing less than youthfully voluptuous. He took clear pleasure in the shapeliness of Judith's long legs and the ripe promise of her inviting thighs. "The face of an angel, the body of a Lorelei." His wife was correct. The other girl, Emily, was a good choice, but this Judith Bradford was more exciting by far. The contrast between her flowering body and her open, prairie face was stirring, no question. Werner would be interested in this girl without doubt.

Lena's husband began pleasantly enough, "My wife tells me you are an actress." Closer to the man now, it seemed to Judith that there was a wheezing breathiness in his chest as he spoke. Like someone buried alive and gasping for air, she thought, feeling cold. His skin gave off a dank, earthy odor she found unpleasant. It came to her that he smelled a little like the garageman, and it put her off even more. She answered formally in a feeble tone that wasn't hers. "Yes." She almost added "sir," but it would sound less adult, and unprofessional.

"And you want to work with Werner Christed?"

"Oh, yes!" Her voice rose with the intensity of her ambition.

Gregor Ludovici turned to his wife and nodded. "I think you are quite right, Lena." He gave Judith his most attractive smile, and she rebuked herself for her unpleasant reactions. She now assured herself that if the man had stared at her it wasn't callously, but professionally.

"You would like to come with us for a screen test then?"

"Oh, *yes!*" Judith exclaimed. Her dream might be coming true!

The man pinched his fat chin. He repeated what she

had overheard about the island, adding, "It is an isolated place, you understand. There is only our film company there. Even some of our own people did not come with us. They found the prospect of being locked in too unpleasant."

Judith nodded eagerly. "I have no other plans!" Rockets of joy went off in her head. The man was nodding to Lena, her benefactor. She was going to be a part of Camelot!

"Good, then," Lena's husband said crisply. He rubbed his oversized hands together. "My wife and I will be your sponsors and vouch for you." He turned to the woman. "Now I have some work in the office. You two start packing. We must clean everything out by tonight," he ordered. He went off briskly. Lena hugged Judith silently and happily.

Judith smiled against Lena's shoulder. It was a miracle that she was finding not only Werner Christed, but this largehearted woman she was coming to love as a mother.

Lena led Judith back to the prop room where she had slept. "Let's begin here." She pointed to cartons and then to the animals. "Handle them carefully, they are very expensive, Judy."

"Judy." Not Judith. The room held no gloom for her now even when Judith had to pick up a great, lifelike rat whose tail felt slimy and cold as death on her arm. With gritted teeth Judith wrapped the sickening rodent in newspaper, packed it into a carton with care she didn't feel, and reached for another loathsome body. They would find there was *nothing* they could ask of her she would not do—any of them: Lena and Gregor Ludovici, and Werner Christed of course, and the mysterious Dr.

Felix Gomay, whoever he might turn out to be.

As they worked, Lena brought Judith up to date on the current Christed project. The crew had been on location for a month preparing the sets. The acting company had joined them on Gomay Island just now. There were many different types in the troupe. Lena was sure Judith would like them, and they Judith. Most of the crew and the actors were long associates of Christed, a few were newcomers during the recent auditions. All were joined by devotion to Werner Christed and his artistic creed. If Judith wasn't familiar with the director's philosophy, she would learn it quickly enough on the island.

When they stopped for lunch after hours of packing—not only the animals, but curious black candles, electrical equipment, and other props from various rooms in the Loft—Judith felt she could ask Lena a personal question. "Have you and your husband been with Werner Christed a long time?" She had been under the impression that the Christed company was made up of young people.

Pouring coffee, the woman smiled reminiscently. "It is so strange how things work out, yes? Some years ago my husband was making movies in Europe. I helped, mostly wardrobe and such. Gregor was not commercial, and we needed funds. Gregor remembered that a distant branch of his family, the Gomays, had taken early root in America. They were very wealthy in the old country, but were driven from their lands, for reasons I do not know.

"It was a Count Ludvig Gomay who purchased much land here shortly after the American Revolution. He resettled the Gomay family near the end of what is now Long Island. To this day they own a large stretch of the shore, including a small village called Gomayville, and of course, the Gomay Island that we have been speaking about so much.

"That area became a prosperous fishing and farming settlement, but through the years the Gomay descendants took heavier and heavier tithes until most of the people moved away. There are also tales that the Gomays practiced strange rituals. It is true that the family maintains its old European traditions, as you will see, but of course the stories are exaggerated.

"The village of Gomayville on the mainland still has some local population, mostly fishermen, but Gomay Island is deserted except for the Gomay estate—and now, of course, the film company. The estate is called Urwolde. Nobody seems to know what Urwolde means, even Dr. Gomay, but you will see that it is a beautiful, beautiful place. The actors are very content there." Lena laughed heartily. "We have seldom eaten so well."

She went on. "As for Gregor and me, we learned some years ago that the only remaining descendant of the family was Dr. Felix Gomay, now a very old man. He is the owner of the estate today—a medical doctor, but he turned to an interest in folk remedies. His research took him back to the old country for many years, but mostly he now lives on Gomay Island with his servants and retainers, doing his experiments in chemistry, alchemy, and sorcery."

Judith could not help interrupting. "*Sorcery?*"

Lena laughed charitably. "Nobody takes the old doctor seriously. A bit dotty in the head, you know. He puts on costumes and boils up horrid-smelling brews, but it is all a game with him. He is a kind old man. He welcomed Gregor and me as kin and invited us at once to his island.

It turned out that he himself had in mind a film project which he had been discussing with, of all people, Werner Christed! He believed that only Christed had the artistic concepts and creative techniques his story required. So instead of financing Gregor's plans, he brought us together with Werner, and that is how we are all in this arrangement."

Lena paused. There was a limit to how much she wanted to reveal. She explained further only that it had taken two years to reach the point of actual production. Felix Gomay kept demanding his scripts back to rewrite, insisting the story must be absolutely perfect.

"In the meantime," Lena concluded, "Gregor and I have worked with Werner on different projects. We admire and love him, and I think I may say he shares our feeling. I believe you will, too."

"Amen!" Judith smiled brightly. *Gomay Island!* The name was fascinating in itself. Judith particularly liked the fact that the island was apparently isolated and little-known. Surely her mother could never trace her there. In fact, no one she knew in the world would have the slightest idea where she was. It would be as if she had disappeared off the face of the earth—exactly as she wanted it for the time being! It would be sufficient later to let them all know—mother, and friends, and old teachers who had encouraged her—let them know what they could never guess in a million years. That she, Judith Bradford of Lomis, Iowa, had been making a movie! And with Werner Christed! How lucky could a person get?

CHAPTER TWO

It was nearly night by the time the packing of the props was completed. Outside, scudding clouds were brewing another storm. Judith and Lena helped Gregor stack the filled cartons in the freight elevator. They were about to descend when Lena cried out in dismay. She had to go back for a bracelet she had taken off while they worked.

Gregor grunted impatiently. "We are late, Lena! I will pick it up when I come again next week."

Lena shoved at the door furiously. "*You know I go no*

place without my bracelet!" There was such heat in the woman that Judith hardly recognized her. Wide-eyed, she watched Lena hurtle down the hall.

In the elevator, Gregor eyed Judith. She pressed against the cartons with a fear of the huge man she could not define. His eyes appeared somehow inimical, as the stuffed animals had seemed. But there was nothing of harm in what he was saying, softly. "Did my wife tell you about our daughter?"

Surprised, Judith shook her head.

"It was a terrible loss. Our dear girl, Robina, was in a car smashup. It was a year ago, but for my wife it is still as if yesterday." He sighed heavily. "It is hard for me to forget, also."

Judith recalled the conversation she had overheard that morning. Now she understood, and was touched that she reminded the Ludovicis of their daughter. What she had taken for a lust in Gregor Ludovici's eyes was, she now realized with remorse, his sorrow, his tears unshed as he remembered the untimely death. Once again she had jumped to a false conclusion. She would have to curb her mercurial judgments. For one thing, it was certainly no way to win friends and influence people in the world she was about to enter.

"I am sorry, Mr. Ludovici," Judith murmured, genuinely contrite.

"Please," the man said quietly, "you call my wife Lena, call me Gregor." He went on, with another sigh. "It has been harder for Lena. I have more work to keep my thoughts from Robina. You see how my wife would not leave without the bracelet—Robina gave it to her on the last Mother's Day. Now Lena treasures this bracelet beyond life, she would rather die than leave it behind."

He paused, looking upset. "But there is a time to stop mourning."

Not knowing how to respond to his evident pain, Judith nodded ineffectually. She now better comprehended Lena Ludovici's quick offer of motherly friendship. She was sorry it sprang from unhappiness, but she was grateful. If she could be some solace to the good woman, and this man, her own new experience would be even richer.

When Lena returned, they rode down silently. Out of the corner of her eye, Judith studied the bracelet. It was made of elephant's hair, with a silver triangle carrying the initial "L." It was distinctive. Judith was glad that Gregor had explained the bracelet's significance.

She saw, too, that Lena was now wearing a ring. Like the bracelet, it was an unusual design: a golden serpent swallowing its tail. The scales were engraved with startling clarity, and the snake's eyes were two sparkling red jewels. Seeing Judith's interest, Lena volunteered with a smile, "Gregor gave it to me, it is my wedding ring . . ."

"We did not eat for six months afterwards," Gregor laughed. He patted his wife's shoulder. "Thank God and Werner Christed, now we eat every day."

The elevator banged to a stop with a metallic clatter, and they walked out to the street. In her exhilaration, it took a long moment before Judith realized, with a physical jolt in her chest, that "the truck" waiting for them at the curb was a black hearse.

Her mouth dropped open in surprise. Her first reaction was to turn away. Her little finger went to the back of her head as Gregor started to lift cartons into the death wagon. But Judith collected herself quickly, pretending nothing was out of the ordinary. She should not be so skittish—what should anyone expect from the eccentric genius, Werner Christed, but that HE would of course have a hearse for a delivery van!

Judith held to that thought grimly when she next noticed a coffin pushed back in the gloomy interior. No doubt it was the prop she had seen that morning. No doubt it was empty. Instead of knocking her knees together, Judith instructed herself, she should be kneeling with thanks that she was going to be a part of all these colorful cinematic doings.

But the hearse was not taken for granted by a group of four young men who stopped on the sidewalk to watch. Gregor and Lena were in the building, Judith was keeping watch on the van. The men were an oafish band, glassy-eyed on marijuana. One with a red beard stumbled toward Judith, mouthing, "Hey, foxy lady, give us a ride!" His friends laughed uproariously. The red beard leered at Judith. "You don't want to go in that meat wagon, baby. We got some real fine Gold down our pad." He put soiled fingers on Judith's arm confidently, and she pulled away with disgust.

"Beat it!" She spoke with all the self-assurance she could muster.

The man brought his face so close she could smell his fetid breath. He grinned nastily. "You don't wanna go nowhere with these creeps, kid." He gestured at the hearse. "They are *witches,* man!" He bobbed to his companions and they supported his accusation. One said, "Oh, it's well known in the neighborhood. They eat cute chicks like you for breakfast!" Redbeard grasped Judith's arm again. "We'll protect you from the baddies . . ."

Judith cried angrily, "Get lost!" What did these clods

know of Lena and Gregor and Werner Christed and *Baron of Darkness?* She was ready to shout for Gregor—one sweep of his great arm would scatter the four of them—when a police car appeared. The man moved away quickly. "Too bad, foxy lady," the red beard called back, then in a mocking sing-song, "You'll be sor-ry . . ."

The police car stopped. "Those fellows bothering you?"

Judith shook her head quickly. The last thing she wished was attention from police, who might have a missing-person's report on her for all she knew. And what was she to complain about if she wanted to? Complain that idiots had called her friends "witches"? She would have to be more strung out than those fools to take such claptrap seriously.

When all the cartons were loaded on the truck, it was full dark and drizzling outside. Judith was anxious to be away from the hot city, to be starting her adventure. But Gregor delayed. After slamming the rear door of the hearse, he did not join Lena and Judith in the front seat but strode across the street. Judith's fists tightened. Had Lena told him about the garageman? Was Gregor going to punish him?

It turned out quite differently. Gregor reappeared almost immediately, carrying a small cage with—to Judith's open delight—a lively white rabbit.

"Another prop?" She laughed. "I'd like to hold *this* one." Lena and Gregor both smiled fondly as Judith gentled the rabbit out of the cage and cuddled it. "He reminds me of a pet I had one Easter," she told them happily. "I called it Jimmy until I found out he was a girl." The rabbit nestled in Judith's arms, its pink nose wriggling hungrily for the lettuce she took from the cage to feed it.

The van glided away from the curb smoothly. Judith thought they must make a curious picture, the three of them and the rabbit in the black hearse. Even with Lena's motherly arm around her shoulder, and the warm, lovable animal in her lap, Judith felt chilled. She could not banish from her mind the image of other passengers who had been conveyed, to their graves, in the dark vault just behind her head.

Stroking the rabbit, she focused instead on the exciting promise of Gomay Island and a bright new chapter in her life. By the time the hearse was passing the cemeteries that stretched alongside the road as if waiting for them, Judith was sound asleep against Lena Ludovici's shoulder.

CHAPTER THREE

Exhausted by the pace of her experiences, Judith slept through the rest of the trip. She was awakened hours later by the barking of dogs, a strange clanking of chains, and a rough racket she couldn't identify. She peered through the hearse's windshield. It was still raining. The long black hood of the van was spotted with drops glittering like the rodent eyes that had horrified her in the Film Loft.

Judith bit her lip with annoyance. She was at Gomay

Island! "On location!" She should be on top of the world instead of remembering animal corpses.

The hearse had stopped on a small pier extending from the narrow mainland dirt road on which they had traveled. Dense trees stretched in both directions as far as Judith could see. The rattling sound was coming from—yes, she was right, amazing and improbable as it seemed!—she was looking at a medieval drawbridge being lowered for them over what appeared to be a deep, wide moat. The water was roiling in the gusting wind, howling as loud as the disturbed guard dogs on the other side. To Judith, the uninviting channel before them looked like the treacherous currents and blowholes of the Nishnabotna River, near her home, where an unwary person could be sucked down and disappear in an instant.

"You slept like a baby," Lena smiled at Judith. "Now we will be across in a minute. Gregor and I have an apartment of our own in the manor house, and you will stay with us tonight until you meet Werner Christed and Dr. Gomay tomorrow."

The prospect of a real bed brought a yawn that Judith felt satisfying down to her toes. She was glad when the hearse started again; soon she could really sleep. But immediately across the bridge, Gregor braked beside a stone building at the water's edge. Judith made out an old caretaker's building. Two burly guards stepped from the ivy-covered doorway holding rifles. They greeted the hearse with raised hands. Across the road, Judith saw two huge dogs hurling themselves at a high fence, barking wildly.

To her surprise, Gregor got out on his side, and Lena on hers. It crossed Judith's mind that they had to present credentials to the guards. But a different ceremony was taking place. The guards moved to stand stiffly beside Gregor, and the three men faced the raging dogs. The men were lifting their faces to the sky, their eyes shut, speaking aloud in a gutteral language Judith had never heard. Unlikely as it might be, they seemed to be saying some kind of incantation. More unlikely yet, Lena was reaching into the van and taking the rabbit.

Spellbound now, Judith was completely unprepared for what next transpired in a series of tripping actions, like jerky stroboscopic photographs flashing on and off. Lena joined the men, with lifted head and prayer. Gregor seized the rabbit from her hands. The two guards pounded with their rifle butts at the dogs' gate, increasing the fury of the beasts. With a wild shout, Gregor flung the rabbit in a high arc over the fence.

The dogs swerved, leaped and dived like frenzied sharks. They were upon the small animal in a flurry of snarls, flying fur, spurting blood, and one high, piteous squeal of terror, of primal life protesting death just before the rabbit was torn apart. One dog jerked the crimsoned body up in its jaws and shook it madly as if to make it fly apart. Shreds of meat and bone shone through the air in the headlights of the hearse. The second dog lunged for its share and ripped the body in half, entrails hanging from the vicious snout in livid strands. Judith felt something clammy strike her cheek, saw blood smeared on her hand when she wiped at her face. A piece of the dismembered rabbit had flown in through the open door. Judith bent from the cab, vomiting.

When Gregor and Lena returned, the dogs were quiet, all traces of the rabbit devoured. Judith was cowering in the seat. She wanted only to ask them how she could get back to New York. Her revulsion was too great for questions about what they had done. But the drawbridge was being raised behind them, and Judith knew her die was cast. They had warned her that once she set foot on Gomay Island she could not get off.

The worst of it, for Judith, was that the woman, Lena Ludovici, was now smiling kindly, as before, as if nothing unusual had happened. Her husband was breathing deeply, his lips were moist, as if he had just enjoyed a delicious meal. What kind of people were these, Judith asked herself in inner agony. How could they relish the bestiality of the dogs wolfing down the living rabbit?

The woman realized the girl's distress. "It is our custom," she said quietly, and without a trace of apology. "A custom from the old country. The dogs guard us, and we repay them with food—a live rabbit when we return after being away. It is our way of thanking them for safety . . ."

Gregor interrupted, sensing Judith's numbness, rejection, and withdrawal. "They must eat, as we must eat."

But not *alive*, Judith protested silently. Yet, as the shock of her disgust diminished and the hearse made its way slowly along a narrow road between heavy trees on both sides, she had to accept the matter-of-fact explanation of the woman beside her—a woman who had never shown anything but decency and kindness until now.

But that was just it, Judith shivered. Clearly, there were depths and currents in these people of which she had only the slightest hints. What was she getting into? Was she in some nameless danger? *Was* there a movie being made somewhere in this forbidding-looking forest? Was Werner Christed on Gomay Island at all? Was Gregor Ludovici what he seemed? *Was Lena?* Could there possibly have been truth in the gibe about witches flung at her by the drug-stoned men on the street? How could anyone believe in such nonsense in this day and age?

Judith's head was whirling with her scorching questions. There could be only one answer, she told herself. firmly.

Everything might turn out to be unequivocally aboveboard, although alien in custom, but she was not going to dally to find out. It was more than she could handle, especially in the still-dangerous shadow of the Angel Dust. Somehow, some way, she would escape. She would be careful, very careful—of Gregor, of Lena, of the giant guards, of the devil dogs, of Werner Christed himself—but she would be leaving Gomay Island, and good riddance, at the first opportunity.

Satisfied in this decision, Judith allowed herself to be led into a small apartment that she hardly looked at. She fell into bed, drained by the shocking turn of events and the turbulent doubts that were putting an end, so distressingly, to all of her high hopes.

But the next day, in the brightness of a sun-glorious morning and a totally unexpected scene outside her window, Judith's questions began to seem less thorny and intractable. Under a vaulting, cerulean sky, benignly cloudless, Judith regarded a most pleasant scene. She was looking out at a doubles match on a manicured lawn tennis court and, just beyond, she saw attractive young men and women swimming and diving in an Olympic-sized pool. She could hear their lighthearted laughter. Judith savored the view. It was truly like a glittering Hollywood film colony, she thought with astonishment. Nothing Lena Ludovici had said had prepared her for this glamorous prospect.

A motion beyond the pool attracted her. In an

expansive, western-type corral within a spanking-white fence, there galloped—Judith blinked, unbelieving—a jousting knight on a milk-white steed. He wore shining armor and a plumed helmet. Although it was obviously an actor rehearsing for the film, the spectacle was out of a fairy tale!

Judith hugged herself happily. Fortune *was* smiling on her. She dressed hurriedly, impatient to be part of the tantalizing action outside.

Stepping into the air in a clean blouse and skirt, Judith breathed in deeply. Her chest swelled with the fresh breeze carrying the tang of the Atlantic Ocean. The salt air was unfamiliar to her prairie lungs. It was heady, and made her feel she was almost flying.

Blond hair blowing in the breeze, Judith relished everything she saw, heard, and smelled, but mostly she was drawn to the corral and the incredible knight. She felt almost sorry that she knew the mundane explanation. How wonderful it would be if this tall rider with the shining silver lance were not a movie performer but a medieval champion ready to joust for his lady's scarf on his magnificent steed. How fantastic if this island were truly an enchanted place inhabited by princes and princesses.

Judith restrained a giggle at her return to her schoolgirl's dreams. Her mother had always scolded that she read too many romances. But they had been an escape from the hard world of the farm, the daily chores, the too-often failed crops. She remembered the extravagant novels with a pleasure that had never faded. Even now she could recall purple passages she had memorized and recited to herself as she went about her farm work. Her favorites through the years, old and dear friends now, were the tales of the pale, innocent damsels trapped in the clutches of evil, beset by apparitions and ghosts, and saved in the end by the silent handsome heroes who had seemed indifferent and unreachable at first.

Reality asserted itself jarringly as, hurrying to the white fence, Judith tripped over a rock and sprawled on the ground with an exclamation of pain. At the noise, the white horse reared, dislodging its rider, who crashed unceremoniously on the other side of the fence in a heap of clanging metal. It was comical to Judith even while she flushed in consternation. What a way to introduce herself to the Christed troupe! For all she knew, the rider might be Werner Christed himself!

Men from the nearby stables rushed to lift the actor to his feet. Judith got up slowly, embarrassedly brushing off her clothes. Her eyes widened as she watched the scene before her. She *was* in a fairy tale! Taking off his helmet and stepping out of the armor, was the most handsome young man she had ever seen. He had the aristocratic face of a Renaissance prince, long black hair, knife-keen blue eyes, with a devil-may-care mouth above a strong, cleft chin. He turned a quick smile to Judith. "Nothing broken," he told her in a musical voice that sounded as engaging as he looked.

Could this be Werner Christed?

Judith felt at once she had met the man she might love. It was less a meeting than a recognition, and if it were too romantic to be true, as in the novels she loved, it held the same magical promise and prophecy. Somewhere, it seemed to Judith, she had known this man's face and voice, even his touch. Maybe it was only an echo of the pale old pages, but maybe, too, it was in the spirit that seemed to be flashing between the two, firming a bond out of the fragile meeting of their eyes.

Like every girl, Judith had wondered how love might come to her. The modern world seemed no longer a place for the kind of romance her book-tutored heart had yearned after. She had sadly come to believe that "love"—the wondrous transforming potion of poets—did not really exist, not if you looked honestly at the world. You saw good friendship, yes. And sex, of course. You saw fondness and accommodation, and comfort. But in real life you did not see what she was experiencing now—a high-voltage surge of happiness that made her feel it was the man before her and not the sun in the sky lighting up the day. She marveled at the encompassing emotion.

His voice came again, vibrant, shaking her to her core. "You're white as a sheet . . ."

"I'm all right," Judith managed to get out. *Could love overtake the heart so suddenly, so overwhelmingly!* Judith was grateful to see Lena coming up to them. It helped her gather together the tinkling pieces the man had sent spinning inside her.

Lena was smiling broadly. "Good morning, Judy! I see you have met the star of our picture. Rick, say hello to Judith Bradford. Judy, this is Rick Gilbert."

So it wasn't Werner Christed! Judith was almost relieved. Christed, of course, was in another world, another league. To fall in love with such a figure could only mean hopelessness and rejection in the end. With an impatient clearing of her throat, Judith chided herself for spinning a fabric of nonsense. This was no time for absurd fantasies, she scolded inwardly.

"I'm glad to meet you, Judy," the man said genuinely. He held out his hand, and she knew from his eyes that he too felt the electricity of their touch. This, at least, was no fantasy.

Lena addressed the actor with an easy familiarity. "Rick, do me a favor, please. Werner will give Judith a screen test tomorrow afternoon. I am tied up in work. Will you show Judith around the island?"

"Gladly!" His response came with genuine enthusiasm.

Judith's heart leaped in her breast. She was going to have the film test! And this handsome actor, Rick Gilbert, was to be her companion today!

On his part, the actor candidly showed his admiration for the girl standing shyly beside Lena.

Judith had put on a full poplin skirt and a yellow cashmere sweater over a crisp robin's-egg blue blouse with a wide collar. She had let her hair down. It fell golden to her shoulders and softly framed her now-rested face. She looked as if she had stepped off a magazine cover, a paradigm of wholesome loveliness. She was pleased at the approval she read in Lena's eyes; she did not want to disappoint her sponsor.

Rick was saying, "Let's start with breakfast, Judy. I'm starving!"

He led her away promptly. They headed to the green that centered the Urwolde buildings like a New England village common. Groups on the grass waved to Rick as he took Judith toward a large red barn-like building. He said to her, "We won't stop now. You'll meet everyone later." In his voice, Judith thought she detected a trace of the same accent she heard in Gregor and Lena. For all his youthful gaiety, there was a courtliness in the man's bearing that she would have expected in someone much older, and she wondered if he was European, too. She asked, "Have you been with Mr. Christed long?"

Rick said quickly, "Judy, don't ever let Werner hear you call him 'Mister'! It upsets him badly. To answer your question, I assume Lena has told you Gregor was a European film-maker in Europe. I used to work with him, though mostly I was in England. When Gregor teamed up with Werner, he asked me to join him. I was twenty-two and glad for the chance to come to America. Now I have been with Werner for a few years, and it has been the best time of my life!"

Judith remembered the Ludovicis saying the same thing. Werner Christed was central to so many people. Suddenly the thought of a screen test with him gave her butterflies.

The movie company's dining hall was a large, airy space in a building at the end of Urwolde Common. The busy room was decorated with posters that enchanted Judith at once: Mack Sennett! Cecil B. De Mille! Charlie Chaplin! Mary Pickford! The famous Jewish actress Molly Picon! As Rick held a chair for her at a table with a red-checked cloth, Judith looked around her with brimming interest. Most of the people she saw were young, few over thirty. Everyone seemed friendly, like a good-natured college crowd. Heads turned toward her with curiosity and, she sensed, with immediate respect because she was with Rick Gilbert. But Judith's interest was seized and held by the distracting waiters and waitresses.

Startlingly, the men wore monk-like brown robes with black cowls over their heads. The women were swathed in habits of light blue, with purple cowls. Strangest, all wore gray masks that hid their faces. Their eyes were just visible behind narrow slits for vision. They looked conspiratorial, or like robots out of a space movie, as they shuffled silently about their service. More like zombies, Judith considered again. There was something frightening, even repulsive, about them. But she remembered her self-pledge to avoid quick judgments. For all she knew, they might be actors costumed for a Christed scene. Still, it was a weird tableau, the melancholy figures contrasting in a warped way with the chattering breakfasters who were dressed in fashionable shorts, jeans, bikinis, crinolines, ginghams.

Rick Gilbert took note of Judith's bewilderment. "Everyone has the same reaction at first," he assured her, and explained. "The servants here are Dr. Gomay's personal staff. We call them 'the Gomays.' They live in their own quarters next to the Manor House. Their place is absolutely off limits to us. Please don't forget that. They also have their own section of the island for their recreation. It's up by an old abbey I'll show you later. If you ever do walk in that direction, don't go further than a stone fence you'll see there. Dr. Gomay's arrangement with Werner is that we obey these injunctions strictly, no exceptions."

"I understand," Judith breathed, although she didn't. There seemed to be some quite strange aspects to the production of *Baron of Darkness* on Gomay Island.

Rick continued, "You'll notice, too, that the servants don't speak to us, and we don't speak to them, except for routine things. It's the way Dr. Gomay wants it."

"Why?" Judith asked, feeling free to show her puzzlement.

"Nobody knows for sure. Actually, Dr. Gomay brought these people over and they have their own religion and their own language, an offshoot of Transylvanian." The actor shrugged. "They do their job and we do ours, and everybody's satisfied."

"Transylvania?" Judith picked up. "Is that a real country?"

"Certainly. Near the Carpathian Mountains close to Rumania."

"I thought it was only fictional, where Dracula was supposed to come from, you know . . ."

"It's real, all right. These people are a religious sect over there. You'll notice their dress is like some of the Christian orders."

"Why the masks?" Judith interrupted.

"It's their custom back home—and not so strange at that. Remember how Islamic women wear veils."

"I see." It was certainly curious, but in its way not unreasonable, and it appealed to Judith's abiding interest in things foreign.

A masked waitress appeared, deposited heaped dishes, and glided away. Rick spread a fresh-looking marmalade thickly on a muffin. "The Gomays use masks instead of veils and, as you see, the men cover their faces before strangers too."

The scene appealed to Judith's sense of the exotic. With her questions answered, she found it rather intriguing to have the alien figures all about. It was like being in a distant land. She regarded the servants with less disquiet, and began to eat. The food was delicious.

Rick drained his coffee, and a waitress appeared from nowhere to pour more. "It's sort of odd, I know," the actor went on, "but it's exactly the kind of thing Werner digs. He and Dr. Gomay are as different as day and night, but they hit it off perfectly. I suppose you know that Dr. Gomay is the producer of our film?"

Judith nodded. "The producer, the backer, and the author!"

"Yes. And we do not bite the hand that feeds us, so we follow his rules. Lord knows Werner needs the help. He has lost a fortune so far in his film work. I know he has been tempted to go back to his painting, where the money is for him. Do not get the wrong notion, though. All the gold in the world would not lead Werner Christed to make a movie he did not believe in."

Rick's intensity bespoke a fidelity Judith admired. "Everybody here feels the same way," he added. Judith surveyed the scene to which Rick Gilbert pointed. Outside on Urwolde Common, scores of people were sunbathing, reading, listening to portable radios. One group was in leotards doing modern dance. Another was practicing tai chi, the flowing oriental exercise that was like a dance itself. Everywhere came the sound of bantering voices, actors hanging loose, waiting for a picture to begin and—on Gomay Island—reveling in luxuries to which few were previously accustomed.

In the bright sun under the blue sky, the scene was idyllic, Judith thought. It reminded her of old French tapestries of handsome youths disporting themselves on some royal fief. The Urwolde estate was an oasis of bright green lawn surrounded by trees of imposing height. The island forest formed a literal wall encircling the buildings and fields Judith saw before her. Looking at the screen of trees, Judith had a sense of nature abiding patiently to encroach on the clearing and reclaim it to wilderness. The forest seemed to be waiting with a knowledge of time and destiny deeper than man's.

Judith shook her head. It was no time for philosophy. She turned from her unbidden notion to study Urwolde, which was to be her home for an indefinite time.

Urwolde Common was like a small park surrounded by an oblong path made of pebbles and crushed oyster shells. It ran north and south, and sported a central pavilion with classical marble statues of nymphs and fawns. The dining room where Judith sat was the only building at the south end of the sward. Following the circling path eastward to her right, Judith saw with an involuntary start the hearse that had brought her the night before. It was standing like an obedient dray animal under a shed beside a burial ground. The cemetery, in turn, abutted a spreading lawn beyond which rose, at the north end of the Common, an impressive Gothic church. Beyond the church, Judith could see an extensive, lush-looking vegetable garden being worked industriously by a squad of the Gomays. The garden was bounded by the ubiquitous forest.

At the top of the Common, its bordering path joined the black-topped road that led to the drawbridge. From where Judith sat, the church was to the right of this road. To the left was the Urwolde Manor House. It rose majestically from manicured lawns planted with every kind of ornamental bush. The structure dominated the entire scene, a spreading, chateau-like building with high round towers at each end. Even in the sunlight, the stark shadows they cast struck a heavy note.

The manor was turreted like an ancient castle. Judith made out small, jail-like windows in the towers. In the main section, however, the windows were high and spacious, gleaming invitingly in the morning sun. The glass was set in Gothic frames of stone, and the walls were decorated with classical pilasters. Scowling griffins, half-lion, half-eagle, stood guard at each side of massive stone steps that swept up to a regal, iron-gated entrance.

Altogether, Urwolde House exuded an air of lofty majesty that seemed almost to remove it from the summer reality of the green trees, the grass, the brilliant sky, and the carefree laughter of the film people. Somehow the manor seemed a structure of the night. For Judith it sent forth a somehow menacing aspect, as if those tiny tower openings held smoldering secrets. Indeed, Judith almost called out to Rick that she saw a glint of light from one window. She stopped herself in time. Clearly, it was only the sun reflecting off a pane of glass, and not a signal. She had to keep her imagination on a tight leash, Judith rebuked herself again.

At the same time, she recognized the source of her unease. It was the "Gomays." Despite Rick's explanations, they still seemed to her like mindless, creeping ants. She hoped Rick was right about getting used to them. It was true that none of the Christed company was paying them any attention—but what was it her grandmother had always said? "What you may be paying no mind, may be paying mind to you . . ."

Judith tossed her head impatiently. Rick spotted the uncertainty in her face. He repeated, "The servants will never bother you, Judy. Just follow the rules I have told you."

"It still seems odd," Judith observed, feeling stubborn.

"We simply respect their privacy," Rick smiled. "Nothing odd about that."

"I suppose not," Judith agreed. People were entitled to their ways, bizarre as they might be. After all, it was the Christed troupe that was the intruder on Gomay Island.

Rick dropped his napkin to the table and rose. "Come

on, then. I'll show you where everything is and introduce you around."

Judith got up, then held back. Something caught her eye. Had that light flashed again in the tower? Three times? Could that be only the sun, or a bird building a nest on the sill? She stared hard across Urwolde Common, but the window was blank. She turned to Rick, the light dismissed, and asked eagerly, "Do you know where I'll have my screen test?"

To Judith's surprise, Rick pointed to the church. "Over there, Judy."

"In the *church?*"

"Oh, it's been cleared out and done over. It makes a terrific sound stage. Moose will show it to you tomorrow."

Judith's eyebrows went up at the uncommon name. "Moose?" she asked.

"Moose is our crew boss," Rick laughed. "He is Werner's closest friend as well. The two of them go back to Alaska together."

"Alaska?" It seemed to Judith that she had nothing but questions or ejaculations.

"Alaska is where Werner comes from. Moose got his name when, one night on a hunting trip, he caught a cold. Werner says his coughing attracted every female moose in the vicinity. It must have been pretty funny to see moose muzzles poking romantically into your tent . . ." Judith laughed with Rick at the image.

Before they left the dining hall, Rick told Judith that the room was rearranged at night. "Musicians play for dancing. Game tables are set up. Upstairs are the bedrooms for our cast and crew." Rick stopped with a small frown. "I suppose it's where you should stay but we're chock-a-block, as London bus conductors say, full up." His smile returned. "Lena will find a place for you in the main house, I'm sure." His smile broadened. "It won't be one of the royal suites, of course, but you'll be too tired to care after a day with Werner. I can promise you that."

They walked outside. The air carried the fresh fragrance of newly-cut grass. It brought a touch of farm nostalgia to Judith, but she was too intent on Rick's words for it to last. "Now let me orient you to the island itself," her new actor friend was saying. He turned right past the dormitory building, on a path heading away from Urwolde Common in a southerly direction. Before following Rick, something made Judith turn for another glance at the tower window. She caught her breath sharply. There *were* flashes, she could swear!—unmistakably three separate, distinct flickers!

"Mr. Gilbert!" she called.

"What?" The man was startled by Judith's tone and her use of his formal name.

"A light from that tower! Someone signaling."

"I don't see anything."

The window was blank again. Judith spoke with frustration. "I had a record player that broke down regularly, and every time the repair man came it played perfectly!"

"The sun, I suppose," Rick Gilbert said casually, starting away.

"Three separate flashes," Judith countered.

Rick's eyes crinkled. "Maybe a flying saucer . . ."

She caught up to him. "Now you're making fun of me!"

"The last thing I would ever wish," the man said with

gallantry. "You see, Judith, those towers happen to be vacant and closed off. A long time ago they were elaborate apartments for the family, but Dr. Gomay is the only one left. Nobody stays in the manor except Dr. Gomay, the Ludovicis, and Werner. Of course, Werner could be shooting a scene over there . . ."

Judith bit her lips. Shooting a scene—that obvious possibility was one she had not remotely considered. How could she forget the only reason they were all on Gomay Island?

"Now here we have Dr. Gomay's formal garden," Rick was announcing.

Beautiful beds of flowers rollicked with brilliant colors in the blazing island sun. It seemed as if the salt crystals in the sea air gave the light a penetrating power that amplified the blaze of colors. Hedges of square-trimmed boxwood filled the air with a pungency new to Judith. Enclosing three sides of the garden ran stately rose arbors and colonnades with Greek columns and urns ornamenting the cool-looking trellised walks. At the garden's south end, where the forest began, the boxwood had been grown taller than a man. Judith had never seen a formal maze before, but she had often read how royalty played hide-and-seek in bygone days. The reality here was another delight for her.

Following Rick into the garden, Judith picked up a pebble in her shoe. She leaned against the sundial conveniently nearby. Two tall Gomays sprang from nowhere, making menacing noises at her through their masks. Judith shrank away, frightened. Rick pivoted at the sounds. He commanded the servants sharply, "Leave us!" The two figures moved off obediently. Shaken, Judith saw for the first time the inscription on the column: "NE TOUCHEZ MOI"—"Don't touch me." She wondered what there was about the quite ordinary garden ornament to stir the servant creatures to a rage. *Creatures!* Her misgivings about the Gomays rose again.

Rick was at her side, supporting her as she fixed her shoe. "I am sorry about this!"

"I'm okay," Judith said coldly. She felt withdrawn even from this handsome, obliging man. With the illogic of her youth, something in Judith blamed him for the shock she had suffered. And he had spoken to the Gomays although he had emphasized they must not be addressed. That had not escaped her notice.

She pointed at the dial, careful not to touch it. "What does this symbol stand for?" She was staring at a weatherbeaten design, like a double arrow with broken points, 

Rick seemed indifferent. "It is from the Gomay family crest. You will see it all over the estate."

Judith gestured toward the two Gomays now watching her in a sullen posture over their shovels. "They seem awfully touchy about it," she commented.

Rick agreed. "Their ways are strange but as I say, we have to respect them."

"They scared me half to death!" Judith complained.

"I should have warned you about the sundial," Rick apologized. He broke into a smile, trying to change Judith's mood. "There are no more booby traps on our tour. I promise."

"Thank goodness. Let's go on, please. I've never seen the ocean, you know." Judith started to explain about Iowa, but Rick interrupted, still smiling. "In the maze over there, we play our own game. The girl has a twenty-second start. If the man can find her within two minutes, he wins a kiss." His voice was half teasing. "Would you like an amusement?"

For a moment, Judith imagined Rick Gilbert's handsome lips seeking hers. In imagination, she could feel his bronzed arms holding her, his blue eyes half-closing as they embraced. She would enjoy it—too much. She was no prude, and she was strongly attracted to the man, but it was too soon. She had to remind herself again that she was no fair damsel ready to swoon in the arms of a fictional hero. "How do we get to the cliffs?" she parried. Her voice issued with an edge she did not intend, and Rick Gilbert's smile faded.

The way to the cliffs was a steep, winding path in an umbrageous forest tunnel. The forest floor was dappled with amber splashes of quivering liquid as the thick leaves shuttered the sun. In the calm, cooling twilight of the path, birds called sweetly. Judith glimpsed a young deer through the heavy underbrush. It would take such a little animal to penetrate these copses, she thought. She was glad it was daytime. She would never come to this intense forest at night. Its depths and darknesses would swallow her terrifyingly in minutes.

The incline rose steeply. Judith needed to stop for breath. The topography of the island was clearer to her now. The Urwolde clearing from which they had ascended was like the flat bottom of a saucer or basin. The lip, covered with trees, curved upward to the heights they were approaching overlooking the ocean.

Rick Gilbert came back to her. "Are you all right, Judy?"

"I thought I was in better condition," she smiled.

"It's a tough climb." As the man bent over her solicitously, Judith had an overpowering fancy of his lips on hers. It came without her will. In a sudden contradiction, his kiss seemed possible now. Each of the moments they had shared this morning was, by some magic, beyond her, taking her outside of time. Judith met Rick's ardent eyes, grave on hers in the forest shadows. Yes, she had known them always. Meeting this man was not finding someone new. It was as if his face was a dear photo in an old, locked album, unopened until this day. Judith was grateful for his sensitivity when Rick stepped away without touching her. She might well be lost and gone if he had held her then.

Judith exclaimed with rapture when they emerged onto a clearing above the sea. The arduous climb was worth it. The sight of the Atlantic Ocean electrified Judith. The closest she had ever come to such an eye-boggling expanse of water was Lake Michigan, and that never seen from a pinnacle like this cliff that rose sheerly from the waves one hundred feet or more. Standing at the brink of the precipice, Judith incautiously looked straight down. The plunging view was physically dizzying. She fell back with a gasp of wonder and fright, to find herself in Rick Gilbert's steadying arms. Whether she was light-headed with the elevation, or the invigorating air, or the gulls wheeling like celebrants in the shining sky, or the distant bellbuoys ringing over the waves like church bells at a wedding. Judith lifted her face in surrender to the man's seeking mouth.

Judith felt Rick hold her with as much tenderness as passion, and she knew in her heart she was safe. To Judith, it was as if the entangling trees she had passed through were her own entwined confusions, and the open cliff now was sudden certainty that she was miraculously and wonderfully in love with Rick Gilbert.

And he with her, it seemed, as he murmured a soft endearment with his lips in her hair.

Contentedly, Judith stayed against Rick's breast as she took in the rugged and glorious nature around them. "It's so peaceful here," Judith sighed, feeling the sea's vibrancy, and its evocation of eternal time and space.

"Today," Rick Gilbert said, "the waves are playing kitten, licking those rocks down there like catnip. But you will see what happens when the weather turns mean. The ocean becomes a thousand sharks tearing at the cliff with their wave-teeth, trying to swallow chunks of the island . . ."

Judith was impressed with another side of this man, his poetic sensitivity.

"They call this Balefire Bluff," Rick went on to Judith. "Pirates once used the island, and they flashed false signals up here to lead ships onto the rocks."

"Pirates!" Judith was back to one-word exclamations. Gomay Island held no end of colorful oddities!

Rick pointed to their right. "Down that way is the only beach on the island, but it is barb-wired. We all use the pool at the big house anyway. Dr. Gomay wants no trespassers. These cliffs help, of course. They are steep and unclimbable all around the island. I suppose Lena told you there is no way on or off except the drawbridge you came across . . ."

Judith uttered a little laugh. "When I saw that drawbridge I couldn't believe my eyes! Right out of the Middle Ages!"

"That's the way Dr. Gomay thinks."

"Rick—the girl who won Werner's audition in the city—do you think I have a chance against her?"

Rick smiled. "Emily? If *I* had the decision, she would

have no chance against you."

"Do you think Werner will like me?" Judith knew it was a fatuous question, but could not suppress her anxiety. Now that she had found Rick, she doubly wanted to be not just a nonentity in the troupe, not just a helper with props.

Rick's answer did not comfort her. "Werner is Werner. No one can predict how Werner will react to you or to anyone or anything else."

"He must be fascinating to work with."

"You will find out tomorrow."

Judith decided it was time to change the subject. She realized that in her newness she could easily seem a nuisance to the man beside her. His assurance was an unsettling contrast with her own continuing feelings of insecurity. She asked, "Is this the highest spot on the island?" Geography, like weather, was safe to discuss.

"No," Rick told her. "The highest peak is Death Point." He motioned to their left. "We'll be shooting a scene over there soon. But that can wait, Judy." Gently, he led Judith to a fallen tree that made a natural lover's seat from which they could enjoy the airy scene. "I come up here alone to watch the sunset," Rick said. "Tonight we will see it together." Whispering, he added, "This grove will be our own place." With a sense of great inner peace and contentment, Judith nodded.

Her eyes saw not the barren shelf of wind-ravaged rock before her, but a verdant grove of flowers and enchanting odors. She imagined a delicious perfume that stole through her veins. She sighed with her happiness, feeling new strength flowing through her. No longer need she feel an uprooted or rootless person. Neither need she be bothered by the strange proclivities of the Gomay group.

Rick Gilbert watched the girl with a faint smile as she fell trustingly asleep against him. A leaf had drifted down and rested on the scarf she wore on her golden hair. The breeze moved it carelessly to her cheek. The man gazed at Judith thoughtfully, gently lifting the leaf from her silken face. About this girl there was innocence and grace coupled with strength and ambition that intrigued him. She was a refreshing change from the women of the film company. Pleasant though most of them were, he was bored by their inner glaze of hard sophistication. He was ready for someone like Judith Bradford, Rick Gilbert mused, looking down at the girl with anticipation. She could bring to him all the passion of woman, yet refresh him with her innate youth, modesty, and reserve. It was a captivating change.

CHAPTER FOUR

When Rick brought Judith down to Lena from Balefire Bluff, the woman saw the radiance in the girl's face. Lena's glance at Rick was knowing. Indeed, why not these two? They made the finest-looking pair she had seen in a long time. And if Werner agreed tomorrow that Judith should have the female lead in the picture, they would be a team with splendid career potential for fame and fortune.

Judith's elation burst at Lena in a non-stop description

of all that Rick had shown and told her. She now had a clear picture of the island forest and cliffs surrounding Urwolde. There was the grove on Balefire Bluff, the higher pinnacle on Death Point some distance away, and on the other side the closed-off beach. Then, further along the cliffs, as Rick had described, there was the Gomays' restricted area on the site of the old abbey. Several paths ran like connecting ribbons among these ocean-view points, with trails like spokes leading from the Common back and forth.

Rick excused himself, and Lena took Judith in hand. She had arranged for Judith to stay in the main building. It was a small room on the top floor, old servants' quarters, but the room would be mostly for sleeping so it shouldn't much matter. Judith agreed without a second thought. As long as she had Rick Gilbert in her mind she would not be alone anywhere.

Approaching the imposing facade of the Manor House, Judith saw how it commanded the Common. It had great height but seemed to press heavily downward on the earth rather than lift and rise from its wide lawns. Its towers seemed driven like enormous stakes into the ground by some mighty engine.

Viewing the Gothic windows more closely, Judith noted that the stone frames were deeply carved with serpents twisting up to shields that keyed the arches. Each tablet was emblazoned with the alien mark of the sundial,  Remembering the mark and the episode in the garden, a chill dampened the inner glow Judith had brought from her hours with Rick.

When Lena took her into the manor through a side entrance, Judith felt almost cheated. She had expected to come upon stately rooms, noble tapestries, high balconies, suits of armor, imposing portraits, all the trappings of a family wealthy in both money and history. Instead, she was in a drab, narrow passageway of grayish stones that smelled musty and stale. She followed Lena up creaking, decrepit wooden stairs. Lena was saying, "You will use this entrance, Judy, unless Dr. Gomay invites you into the main hall. Follow me, please."

There was no sound except their own steps on the protesting stairs. The only light came from unshaded bulbs on each nondescript landing. The walls pressed so close that two could not climb abreast, and Judith found it stifling, almost cavelike and claustrophobic. Finally and thankfully she came up to a square landing from which a dim corridor ran in both directions. A door stood ajar, waiting.

Lena pointed down the dingy hallway to the left. "Gregor and I are at the other end, Judy, one floor down. You can come across to us if you need anything." She turned to the right, and her voice grew emphatic. "This way leads to the tower. It is off limits, absolutely! Dr. Gomay makes a special point of it, so be sure you stay away. The reason is that everything up there is in dangerous disrepair, and we want no one hurt. I am sure you understand."

There was no light where Lena was pointing, but Judith could vaguely make out a shadowy arch and through it a spiral staircase starting up into the gloom. Mentally, Judith took her bearings. The window with the flashing light would be in this structure, in some chamber reached by those spiral steps. She was strongly tempted to ask Lena about the flashes she had seen, but it seemed pointless. There was no sound, no hint of any presence, or of any mystery. If anything, this whole section of the great house was just dingy and ordinary—"back stairs." But she wanted to satisfy her curiosity, and asked Lena, "Were they filming in the tower today?"

Lena looked surprised. "No. I told you it is not used. Why do you ask?"

"Nothing," Judith replied. She didn't want to appear silly. She said instead, "I'm sure I'll be fine here, thank you," and opened the door to her new room. Thank the Lord, there were no menacing animals, stuffed or otherwise, to give her heart failure this time.

She saw that her bags had been transferred. Lena gave Judith final instructions about her schedule and went away. The girl unpacked and relaxed. She had made her new bed and was lying in it, she thought, largely with satisfaction. The bed was comfortable although the room was tiny. The walls were of a peeling stucco material. There was a scratched chest of drawers, an old-fashioned rocker, a small desk with a battered lamp, and a dormer-type window. The stone floor was partly covered with a threadbare rug long ago faded to an indecisive color. The bathroom was across the hall.

Judith did not mind the drabness of the room. Fortune was smiling on her in other ways, and she was grateful.

Still, there was inevitably a shadow of loneliness. Resting in what was to be her new home, Judith had an acute realization of the giant step she had taken. She wanted the escape and the adventure, without question, but she could not deny the tremor of uncertainty she felt now that she was by herself in this unfamiliar place. And she could not put the rabbit episode, or the strangeness of the Gomays, entirely out of her mind.

Her uneasiness wasn't helped when, turning, she

found a Gomay staring at her from the doorway. The ghost-like figure, appearing without a sound, gave Judith such a start that she could barely acknowledge Lena when she ushered the woman into the room. "This is Lilia," Lena said of the exceedingly tall, pencil-thin servant. Though robed and masked, the woman would be recognizable in any group. "It is permitted to speak to her here in the Manor House, when you need something. Lilia will be here every morning and evening, for cleaning and laundry and so forth. You may leave a note on the chest if you miss her."

The robed figure inclined its head like a robot, Judith observed again. Judith, feeling sandpapery inside, nodded in return. It was weird to have this apparition for a maid. The woman's eyes behind the mask-slits caught the late afternoon sun coming through the window, and looked like red marbles. Judith imagined spitefulness and malevolence in them, and at once checked herself. Lena would allow no harm to her, of that she was still sure. She said politely in a neutral tone, "I'll appreciate the help. Thank you." It sounded stiff, but she was too ill at ease to care. She wanted only for the Gomay to leave, and Lena too. She wanted to be alone to rest and digest the exciting events that had been happening to her so swiftly. Maybe too swiftly, she reflected.

When at last they were gone, Judith dozed. The kaleidoscope scenes of the day turned colorfully in her head, but the clearest and the shining remembrance was Rick Gilbert's sweet kisses on her mouth.

Best of all, Judith considered in her half-awake state, it was wonderful to be on her own two feet, her own free person, away from the misunderstanding of her mother and the importunities of her stepfather. Her room on

Gomay Island might be nondescript in contrast to her new lavish bedroom back in Iowa, but she was in Paradise. Her only wish now was finally to meet Werner Christed, and to have him approve her. Given his idiosyncrasies as a director, there was some chance, if small, that she might impress him enough to land the Big Role. But she would be satisfied with any part in *Baron of Darkness* that kept her in contact with Rick Gilbert . . .

The light faded at Judith's window and she slept. She had no awareness of the twilight's shadow moving like a silent hand, lifting a blanket of growing darkness along her reclining body. She did not hear the melancholy sound of piteous moans brought by a veering wind through her open window—coming plainly from beyond the dark arch of the corridor outside her door, from the keep everyone was forbidden to enter.

Judith had set her clock to wake in time to freshen for dinner. She hurried to the dormitory building with anticipation, all her emotions on Rick.

Dinner was plentiful and excellent, and then the transformed room came alive with dance music and games. The Gomays left to go to their own pursuits. To Judith's disappointment neither Werner Christed nor Dr. Gomay was present. Rick said they were making last-minute script changes. Lost in her swelling feelings for Rick Gilbert, Judith scarcely took notice of the many people who stopped to chat at their table.

A few stood out. One was Moose, Werner's intimate. He was a short but husky fellow, shiny bald, with a candid, jovial grin and hearty handshake. Judith's instinct told her she could trust this man. "I'll be helping with your screen test tomorrow," he informed her.

"Which side of your face do you favor?" Judith had never thought of it, but he needed no answer. His friendly grin broadened. "Don't worry about it. You're a knockout on both sides, darling."

"Darling." As with theatre people everywhere, the word was only a convention, not an endearment. Judith took it gratefully as a mark of acceptance.

The other standout person for Judith was, not surprisingly, the actress who had won the Christed auditions. The girl came to Rick's table with a hand outstretched to Judith. "I hear we're rivals," she said with a generous smile that offered immediate friendship. Judith responded to the girl's instant attractiveness as Rick said, "Judy, meet Emily Lawrence." Judith thought the only word to describe Emily was *saintly*. The girl was slim, about Judith's height, and seemed to float ethereally rather than walk. Her lovely face had a waif-like cast that made her look younger than her twenty years. Her gray eyes were doe-like and endearing.

Judith answered with unreserved admiration, "I can see why Werner chose you!"

Emily laughed. "I can see why he might change his mind! I hope we can be friends however it turns out."

"Me, too," Judith said genuinely. Emily's fingers felt frail in hers, though the girl seemed strong and was well-built. It was as if Emily had an inner illness she did not show, about which she did not even know, except in a hidden sadness Judith thought she glimpsed in the girl's almond-shaped eyes.

As an actor took Emily away to dance, the girl called over her shoulder to Judith, "I wish you luck to-morrow." Judith heard that Emily meant it. A truly generous heart. They would be friends, yes.

Rick was called away from Judith for his turn in an ongoing company pingpong tournament. Judith left the smoky room seeking fresh air and a chance to be by herself. She had much to reflect on. The cool of the night was welcome. The moon had been bright, but clouds were beginning to mask it.

Across the darkened Common, Judith clearly saw a flash of light. And again. And again. No trick of her imagination, no reflection of sun or moon, no nest-building bird! But even as Judith stared at the tenebrous tower, the small flares ended. She waited, breathless, watching intently. Nothing. It was her confounded record player again! There was nothing for her to call Rick to witness.

Of one thing she was certain. *Someone* was in the tower! And, it occurred to her, that someone was a not-distant neighbor of hers. Now she would ask Lena. There was probably a simple explanation, Judith insisted to herself—a workman, a night watchman—but she needed to check it out. And why shouldn't she?

Returning to the dance, Judith found neither Lena nor Gregor nor Rick. Emily answered her surprise: A Gomay had come with a message from Werner Christed, and the three had left at once for a meeting.

With Rick gone, Judith found it pleasant to sit chatting with Emily over a soft drink. It took her mind off the tower light, and she learned something no one else had mentioned. It happened when Emily asked, "Judy, did you think it strange when you saw Werner Christed's advertisement?"

Judith was uncertain about what the girl was driving at.

"Well, I mean, this production has been in the works

for quite a while. They wouldn't wait to the last minute to cast a leading part, would they?"

"You're right, of course!" It came to Judith that she had been too excited and preoccupied to ask the very obvious question.

"Nobody likes to talk about it, but I found out what happened . . ."

Judith leaned forward as Emily bent over the table, whispering. "There *was* another actress, of course. She took sick suddenly and died here!"

Judith shivered involuntarily.

"Dr. Gomay tried to save her, they say, but some think it was poison."

Judith was aghast. She searched Emily's face. There was no deceit in it, no effort to unsettle her before tomorrow's tryout. The girl believed what she was saying. "Why in the world would anyone want to poison her?" Judith asked.

"Why in the world would a perfectly healthy young person die suddenly?" Emily answered.

They were interrupted by two actors who tugged them on to the dance floor.

As Judith undressed for bed later, her question to Emily kept circling in her head. It was swept away, however, when she heard a muffled sound outside her room. Someone was climbing the stairs! Who? The Gomay servant, Lilia, had come and gone. There should be no one else in this part of the house. Judith's skin prickled. It had not even occurred to her to lock her door—she did not even know whether or not there was a lock. The steps came louder. Heavy. A man's. Judith swallowed hard. It might be a watchman passing on his rounds. At least there was no attempt at concealment.

Her small consolation at the thought evaporated in a puff of anxiety as a demanding knock came at her door.

Judith swallowed with rising fear, and scolded herself angrily. She was in no danger, and if she were she would only make it worse by responding with panic. She called out firmly, "Who is it?"

The voice was recognizable at once. "I. Gregor. Gregor Ludovici." Judith did not know whether to be alarmed or reassured.

"Are you decent?" he asked. It was the backstage question of the theatre.

She had to open the door, whatever the man's intention. To her surprise, he was carrying a gift of flowers. "For your first night in your new room." The man looked about, smiling. "It can use some brightening up, eh?"

Judith put the flowers on the chest, and drew her robe tighter around her body. Gregor Ludovici was eyeing her crudely as he had done at the Loft. Was this to be a casting-couch encounter? He would find she wasn't as naive a country cousin as he might believe!

He gave her his ambiguous smile again, but spoke straightforwardly. "I am here as assistant director, because you need to know about tomorrow. I regret I have been so occupied that this is the first moment we can talk."

Judith stood before the huge man awkwardly, only half relieved. The only place to sit was on the bed, and that would establish an intimacy to be avoided. Her head told her she needed this man on her side, but his appearance and manner still put her off in a way she could neither fathom nor deny. His features were somehow discordant. She wondered whether it was his bulk, his artificial-seeming airs of nobility, or, more likely, his wheezing breath. It reminded her again of the smell of dank earth.

He was explaining, "Your screen test will be in the afternoon, at the church, immediately after lunch. Werner wants you without makeup, and with no special costume. He does not wish you to know anything of what he will ask you to do, so you have no script to study, no lines to memorize."

Even for Werner Christed, it seemed strange to Judith, but she held her peace in deference to the director's reputation. Novices should be seen and not inquisitive.

Gregor continued, "By now you are quite aware that Werner works in his own special way. His key is one word—spontaneity. Remember that, and you will do well. You see, what Werner aims for on the screen is nothing less than life itself. Obviously, he expects you to possess technique, but he does not want 'acting' in the usual sense of studied reactions, stale rehearsing, and Hollywood posturing. He has as little patience with the actors who pick their noses and scratch their behinds as with those who melt in the moonlight and walk into tomorrow in a squirt of symphonic syrup . . .

"No. For Werner, when an actor is totally natural, then can come Artistotle's catharsis, the purification and purgation of the emotions through the expressiveness of art!" Gregor paused in self-appreciation of his rhetoric, then resumed. "For example, an audience that truly experiences a well-done murder on the screen is then cleansed of its own secret wishes to commit murder, which we all possess. Eh?"

Judith listened with all her attention. Dislike this man or not, he was trying to help her.

"You will meet Moose at the church at two o'clock,

right after lunch."

He was moving to the door. "My wife and I have faith in you, Judith Bradford. Do not disappoint us." Before she could answer, he was gone. Then just as suddenly he materialized in the room again. "The hall light has gone out," he muttered, annoyed. "I think there is a flashlight." He fumbled in a drawer. "Ah, good. And here is a candle if you should need it."

The talk of lights triggered a decision in Judith. "Mr. Ludovici . . ." she began.

"Gregor," he corrected her with his quick, heavy smile.

The interruption nearly untracked her, but she persisted. "Gregor, I saw a light in a tower window this afternoon, and again tonight!" She made an uncertain gesture toward the nearby structure. "It seemed to be a signal of some kind."

Did the man pale, or was it her imagination? "No!" he stated at once. "Impossible!" His voice was a rasping file. "You have been told there is nobody in the tower! You are mistaken, and I advise you not to speak of this further to anyone!"

"But I—" Judith protested.

The man cut her off roughly. "We did not bring you to the island to have an accident. The tower is unsafe. You are not to go near it, ever! Lena will come for you in the morning. I wish you good night and a good night's sleep." Gregor clicked his heels and was gone in the blackness outside the room.

Judith got into bed, shivering. Suddenly, the room was freezing. She had not felt cold before. It was as if Gregor Ludovici had brought an aura of heat with him, and taken it with his going.

That was impossible, of course. As it was impossible that she had not seen the flashes!

Why did everyone insist the place was unoccupied?

Judith turned over restlessly and pulled the pillow over her head. Why couldn't she mind her own business? She should be concerned about meeting Werner Christed at last, not having premonitions about mysterious windows! She was so scatterbrained that she hadn't even thanked the assistant director for his thoughtfulness in bringing her flowers. It was typical of her, Judith reflected, that she should be so quick to misread the man's intentions when he had announced himself at the door. At the same time, she considered, it was sensible to keep her guard up since she was now fending for herself.

When Judith fell asleep finally, the wind was from the west, and carried away from her window the mournful cries that issued, more weakly than the night before, from the nearby tower.

CHAPTER FIVE

Waiting for her appointment in the New York detective agency, Judith's mother could not keep her eyes off the sign behind the receptionist's desk:

BLAKE INVESTIGATION SERVICE, INC.
PROFESSIONAL SERVICE — LICENSED, BONDED, INSURED
DOMESTIC - RETAIL - SURVEILLANCE
FINGER PRINTING - ID CARD SYSTEMS - UNDERCOVER
MISSING PERSONS LOCATED
Local - National

Missing Persons Located! It still seemed impossible to Barbara Wayne that those words should have anything to do with her. Ungrateful children!—the world was falling apart these days. Her mood did not improve when, finally, she was ushered into the inner office. The New York detective recommended by her lawyer turned out to be not only a woman but blond, slim, and svelte, looking more like a fashion model or Hollywood actress than a private investigator. But Ursula Blake's manner was brisk and immediately to the point. Taking the photographs of Judith from Mrs. Wayne, she began her routine questioning.

"Did your daughter talk of suicide?"

The expensively dressed woman flared with antagonism. "Judith had a very strict Catholic upbringing!"

"Is she religious?"

"Until just last year she talked about becoming a nun . . ."

"I see." Blake wrote on her form.

Mrs. Wayne added at once. "But she's too sensible to fall for those Jesus Freaks and Krishna Hares or whatever they call those people . . ."

"Well, that's what we have to find out, isn't it?" Blake said matter-of-factly. "We have to be serious about every possibility, Mrs. Wayne." Blake moved down the form. "Did Judith have any boyfriend difficulties?"

"No, of course not!"

Ursula Blake spoke plainly; sometimes bluntness could not be avoided. "I mean might she be pregnant?"

"That is disgusting!"

"If you want me to try to find your daughter you'll have to answer my questions."

"Judith is not that type of girl!"

"Has she seemed despondent or depressed lately?"

"Distant, yes, if that's what you mean. She'd sit with us but she always seemed to be tuned in to something else."

"Like her name in lights on Broadway?" Blake smiled.

"Exactly! After her nun business, all Judy talked of was being an actress. She was *good* on the stage, too!" A note of genuine pride came into the woman's voice.

"Does Judith drink?"

"She's under age, you know. I suppose an occasional beer, certainly nothing more."

"Any history of mental illness?"

"Of course not! Judy's been just your average American kid—majorette, swimming team, cheerleader, you name it. And, of course her acting, and her eternal books."

"I see. What about drugs?"

Mrs. Wayne repeated the word as if she had never heard it. "Drugs?"

Ursula Blake waited. The drug answer always came slowest when there was something to hide.

The woman sighed. "Obviously you need to know about it. We had an awful episode this past Christmas vacation. Judy got into Angel Dust and LSD and God knows what else." Mrs. Wayne put a delicate handkerchief to her forehead. "It was the most terrible thing I ever saw in my life. The poor child—it was as if she were totally out of her mind. Dr. Willoughby told us it could keep coming back even if Judy never went near drugs again. He said some people were very sensitive, and could have—a trip—almost any time, with no warning. I hope she doesn't have another attack wherever she is!"

Blake continued her notes. One thing was obvious.

Drugs or not, she was dealing with a high-strung, sensitive youngster.

"I have to tell you," Barbara Wayne spoke again, "it seemed that more than Judy's imagination was at work. The time she had her nightmare at home, she said her bedroom was on fire. From *Satan's* breath! And I swear if she didn't look sunburned! Dr. Willoughby called it a fancy name . . ."

"A form of hysteria," Blake affirmed. The phenomenon was well-known to psychology and not as strange or rare as Mrs. Wayne believed.

Judith's mother shook her head. "I still can't believe that a person can see and hear things that aren't there!"

Blake answered, "Mrs. Wayne, I'm sure you've read about the scientific experiments where different parts of the brain are stimulated by electrodes. We know that the subject does *actually* smell a perfume, or taste food, or see an animal, and so on. The same things can happen with drugs like phencyclidine and LSD." Blake rose, saying, "I'll follow up the acting lead here in New York, and I'll alert my associates around the country. But, Mrs. Wayne, I want you to know this can be very costly, and I can't guarantee a thing. Your daughter could be with any of a hundred groups, some legitimate, some not." The detective did not want to remind Mrs. Wayne of the Charles Mansons who enslaved girls from homes like Judith's, or the Texas monster who had tortured more than twenty-five boys to unspeakable deaths. The daily headlines were filled with too many such horror stories.

Mrs. Wayne said, "I understand. Incidentally, you ought to know that Judith may be going under the name of Bradford. My husband has adopted her legally, but she may be using her real father's name."

"Yes, that's helpful."

She escorted the woman to the door, and saw genuine tears of worry as she shook Mrs. Wayne's hand. Beneath the confusion of this family's mixed-up relationships, there was a caring center. She would do more than her best for this case.

When Mrs. Wayne was gone, Blake sat studying Judith Wayne/Bradford's appealing photographs. A young, very vulnerable face, but a woman's grown body. Above all, a posture of self-confidence. How wrong this girl could be in her self-assurance, Blake considered. It was bad enough to see the thousands of youngsters being sucked down in the world's cesspools every day. A girl like this one, with her drug seizures, could be a pathetically easy victim of the many depraved, sick-minded degenerates who masqueraded under plausible fronts. Judith Wayne/Bradford could already be enmeshed in God knew what foul net.

Of course there was always the real chance and hope that she was meeting good people, but finding her would in any case be tough. These days it was looking for a needle in a haystack, and there were thousands of haystacks.

There was a great deal to do. Ursula Blake reached for the phone. It was another date she would have to break with her fiance, Police Lieutenant Carlos Rodriguez. "I'm sorry, I have a complicated runaway who could be in serious grief. Tonight I need to set up my contacts around the country . . ."

"I understand. See you tomorrow, then. Let me know if I can be of help."

"Thanks, Carlos."

CHAPTER SIX

Outdoors the world was beautiful and inviting. It was another morning of clear blue sky and bright sunshine. Urwolde Common looked more than ever like a luxurious resort. Among the relaxing groups on the green, Judith recognized many of the Christed company she had met the night before, but Rick hurried her along without responding to their greetings. He had packed a brunch and proposed a private picnic up on "their place" until it would be time for the screen test. Judith was delighted.

To wait alone for her meeting with Werner Christed would have been nerve-wracking.

As the two walked past the church, heading for the path through the forest, Judith heard heavy hammering and noticed for the first time a low shed with stacks of building materials alongside—obviously the production's workshop. She made out the easily recognizable figure of Moose directing a crew. He waved at her, and she returned the friendly gesture, beginning to feel like an old-timer.

Her attention was drawn to another motion. Driving up to the workshop was the well-remembered hearse. It stopped smoothly nearby. As several men went to the back of the van, Judith detained Rick to watch. The black door was opened and the men reached inside. Judith's eyes widened as a coffin emerged from the dark interior. It was plain from the men's effort that the box was not empty. She wondered what could be inside. Transfixed, Judith disregarded Rick's tug on her arm.

Then it happened that as the casket came free of the hearse, one of the workmen tripped. The box tilted and swayed. Judith heard mutters and curses as the men struggled to steady the load, but they could not hold its weight. The coffin crashed from their hands. The top broke open, swung for a moment on its hinges, and tore off with a grinding noise that was like a deathly moan. To Judith's unspeakable horror, the naked body of a woman thumped to the earth with a sickening thud.

"You bloody damn fools!" Gregor yelled, rushing to the scene.

The body kept rolling down the incline of the ground. The corpse slipped by reaching hands until it rotated grotesquely to a stop against Judith's legs.

Jumping back, with a spasm of abhorrence that choked her throat, Judith viewed an exquisite young girl, whose long black hair streamed dismally on the grass above a death-white countenance. The youthful eyes were wide open and staring up at Judith as if pleading with her for help. Frozen and faint, Judith heard Gregor's rude cry of fury again. "Damn you all to hell! Pick her up!"

"God Almighty!" Judith cried to Rick. She clutched at his shoulder with a terrible scream. *"Rick!"* He was her last hold on sanity on this island of bombshells.

She hardly heard his response. "Judy! Don't you see this is a dummy, a mannequin?"

"Oh, no!" Judith groaned. Had she been taken in by a prop again? But the girl's skin looked so real, so soft if she were to touch it. The lips seemed only just now to have spoken, to still be moist with a recent kiss. If it were a mannequin, the maker must be a genius of geniuses. She wanted to reach down and feel the girl's flesh, but Gregor and some men quickly lifted the body and were taking it to the shed.

"It looks so real," Judith moaned to Rick.

"That's the idea," he said reasonably. "Come along, Judy. We don't have too much time." He spoke as if nothing out of the ordinary had occurred.

Judith hung back, waiting until the doleful figure disappeared into the workshop.

Seeing her continued agitation, Rick spoke gently. "It's just a wax dummy, Judy. You've seen them in the wax museums, I'm sure. Of course they look more lifelike than life. It wouldn't make sense otherwise, would it?"

Judith could not return his reassuring smile.

"Werner has a little old man in New York who makes

these to order for us," Rick went on. "If you want to, we can go inside and you can see it closer. He is really a remarkable craftsman."

Judith shuddered. "No, thank you!" Just the thought of looking at the figure of death again made her stomach queasy. But it *had* looked human, no wax artifact! New dark doubts began to percolate in Judith's head. Considering Werner Christed's far-out ideas, might he not actually use a real corpse? Wild as it might seem, like the ghouls in mad-scientist movies, he might buy dead bodies for his "spontaneous reactions." Or rob graves!

Judith's head was whirling. What could she believe, who could she believe? If the figure in the broken coffin were really a dead person, who here would admit it, who among these strangers—after all, they *were* strangers—would tell her the truth? If uncanny things were happening—like flashing signals from a tower everyone said was empty!—she, the outsider, would not be informed. Not even by Rick. The truth was she was alien here, even to him. And alien to Lena, too, who could watch with relish as wild dogs tore a poor rabbit to pieces. And alien to Moose and Emily, for that matter, who might all be putting on an act on this island of acting and make-believe! And also to Werner Christed and Dr. Felix Gomay, whom she was now almost afraid to meet!

They might, all of them, seem fine and trustworthy on the surface, yes, but she recalled a lesson her grandmother had taught: The one sure bet about a swindler is that he never looks like one!

But another part of Judith's spirit could not accept her tacit accusations. The figure *could* be just wax. If she did not want to believe Rick, she should have accepted his invitation to go into the church and check for herself.

She turned to study the handsome face of the man waiting patiently beside her. She asked herself how she could feel what she did for this man if those candid blue eyes of his were a lie. No, Judith decided squarely, she was wrong to doubt him, and wrong to doubt what had already been proven to her so many times now—that she was on a movie location, with professional film-makers making a professional film. She ought to come to grips with her vacillations. If she didn't want to accept their ways, she ought to leave. If she wanted to remain, she ought to swallow her concern about dishonesty and the Gomay servants and tower lights and corpses and embrace what her new friends told her, once and for all.

And she *was* among friends, not enemies, she told herself forcefully. She was sure she would find a satisfactory explanation even for "the poisoned actress" Emily had not finished telling her about. Judith turned to Rick and gave him her hand again, with a newly trusting smile. "Come on," she said. "Now I'm the one who's starved."

Up on the cliff, Judith leaned back contentedly in Rick's arms after they ate. The wind was down, the leaves scarcely moved. The easy surge of the quiet sea below made a sweet cadence in the silence. To Judith, the sight of the endless ocean was a continuing inspiration. Even without Rick, she would be content to watch the waves for hours as they broke into foam and spray on the island's hem. Far breakers were writing white lines of poetic grace on the green-blue waters, creating an enchanting calligraphy in Judith's eyes.

The air was like a lullaby itself, with soft bird calls around them, and a faint peal of bellbuoys adding to the tranquility.

With Rick's gentle hand softly stroking her arm again, Judith had a sense of benevolence surrounding her, radiating from the sublime and powerful sea and the repose of the giant forest. This scene, Judith mused, was an impressive witness of God and Creation itself, a testimony of nature's grandeur and man's love.

At that moment, she felt Rick's hand touching her breast. His eyes were on her face, inquiring.

Judith lowered her head. She was not too surprised, not born yesterday. And she was quite sure of her deep response to this man, even though they had just met. But she was not sure of her feelings about herself. Most modern women would have no trouble yielding to the desire that rose in her undeniably. But she was not ready. Call her prude or prissy, it was not her nature to scorn the "old-fashioned" conventions as readily as so many of her friends. She had been scoffed at, at home and in Chicago, and she was not prepared to say they were wrong. In the end it was her own honesty to which she was accountable.

Deliberately, Judith moved away from Rick's embrace.

She half-expected him to be put out. Instead, with an understanding smile, he said, "You are an innocent, aren't you?" And went on after a pause, "You've never been with a man, have you?"

Judith felt herself blushing as she shook her head. At the same time, she felt some indignation. It was unfair that females were supposed to acquiesce to sex in the name of self-liberation. Rick and every other man should respect her right to her own standards. She intended to hold her belief that it was wrong to go to bed with any man but her husband!

Her resentment at his question grew so sharp that she was about to leave the grove when she heard Rick whisper, "I'm glad, Judy."

She studied him. His look was genuine, and accepting.

Judith sighed with a remaining inner confusion. Some sort of confrontation like this was inevitable, she supposed. She was thankful that Rick was a gentleman. She knew, at the same time, there were women below on Urwolde Common who would not answer this man as she had done. She would understand if he would turn back to them after this disappointment with her.

Meantime, she appreciated Rick's tact when he rose to walk about, and tactfully changed the subject. He talked about Werner Christed. "It will help you in your test this afternoon if you know more of Werner's background, and how he makes movies now . . ."

Judith was grateful. She observed, "Gregor told me some of that last night."

"Good. Did he speak about the Alaska days?" Judith shook her head, negatively. "It explains a great deal about Werner." Judith listened with quickened interest. "Before he was sixteen, Werner was painting like fury. He mixed Indian and Eskimo forms with a primitive force of his own. He was already developing the concepts he uses in his movie-making.

"As a young artist, Werner shocked everyone, as I'm sure you know. He used actual blood, animal gristle, furs, bones, teeth, eyes . . ." Judith's nose wrinkled. "He used innards that literally stank. His idea was to use art concussively, the way political activists use bombs, to awaken people out of their ruts. When he had a San Francisco show ten years ago, when he was only eighteen, he let a skunk loose on opening night." Rick smiled. "Werner calls it the 'shock treatment' in art."

It was a provocative concept, Judith reflected.

Rick resumed, "Werner hit it very big with his paintings. Most of his buyers were fad-followers, and the money rolled in. But Werner was unhappy. He became totally convinced that in an era of electronic and television communication, painting was outdated and ought to give way to movies entirely. Film gives him the chance to explore his basic idea—that to capture an audience you must alienate it!" Rick's face was alive with the shared conviction. "It may sound mad and paradoxical, but it works!"

Judith nodded enthusiastically. She badly wanted Rick to know that she was no Philistine, no "hick." She had pored over the advanced cinema magazines. She could enter this conversation confidently with her own observations: "It's something like what Herzog is doing in Germany, isn't it?—making the audience reconcile contradictions on the screen . . ."

Rick threw Judith a new appreciative glance. This girl might be an innocent, and puritanical about sex, but she was no unsophisticated rustic.

Encouraged by Rick's open approval, Judith added, "And there's Rosselini, who throws away the script and most of the dialogue and just lets the story happen in front of the camera. And a lot of others, like Fellini—I mean, when you know about them, you realize Werner's ideas aren't so outrageous at all."

"That's right," Rick said like a professor praising a bright student.

Judith had an almost schoolgirlish wish to impress Rick with her knowledge. "A genius like Werner is always ahead of his time. I always remember what

Charles Ives once said . . ."

"The composer who was an insurance man?"

Judith nodded. "When everybody laughed at his music, he asked, 'Are my ears on wrong?'"

Rick laughed with her. "I never heard that."

Judith added more, happily: "There was the composer Varèse who said that every generation has to find new ways of expression, new vibrations, new acoustics, new instruments. That seems to be what Werner is doing."

"Exactly!" Rick hugged Judith. "You're not going to have any trouble this afternoon, I can see!"

Judith was pleased the exchange had taken place. She felt less the apprentice and outsider. With new confidence, she let Rick take her back to their seat. She leaned against him quietly again, once more enjoying the scene before them.

Broken clouds were appearing. The gulls seemed restless in their flight as the morning wore on. They dipped and rose angularly instead of tracing the graceful, lazy circles of the earlier hour. The ocean took on a grayish cast, and there was a new coolness in the air though the sun was high. Judith snuggled closer to Rick when he tightened his arm around her. As if the change in weather brought an alteration in Judith's mood, she asked Rick now the question she had restrained as a newcomer.

"Rick, what is *Baron of Darkness* about? Shouldn't I know before my audition?"

The man's arm came off Judith's shoulder. "Believe it or not, I do not know."

It was incredible. If Rick Gilbert, the leading man and an intimate of Werner Christed, didn't know the story, who did?

Rick seemed to find nothing unusual in the situation. He said casually, "I'm sure you've heard of Dr. Gomay's hang-up with the script. So far, Werner has given out some bits and pieces that require special preparation, like my jousting scene." He grinned at Judith. "That armor weighs a ton, you know . . ."

Judith recalled his tumble and how it had seemed comical and frightening at the same time. "What's the mystery, though?" she pursued.

"No mystery. Dr. Gomay plans to read the final story to the company in just a few days now."

"That is correct!" A loud baritone voice boomed out behind Rick. Startled, Judith lurched to her feet. What new bolt was the island tossing at her now?

Bolt, indeed! A weird-looking character was stalking from the forest. The figure appeared like a phantom, a Merlin of an ancient man, clothed in a flowing multi-colored cape. A bobbing, bulbous head showed sparse gray hairs looping around a gnomic countenance of dried-out wrinkled parchment. A large patrician nose overhung a jutting jaw that quivered with age. Bulging eyes behind thick lenses reached for Judith's face like the fingers of some strange space creature trying to feel her skin. Her flesh crawled.

Judith identified the man without a word from Rick. Certainly it wasn't Werner Christed. It had to be none other than the long-heralded Dr. Gomay, owner of the island, the eccentric master of the masked Gomays. She had wondered how and when she would meet him. Given a peaked hat, she imagined, the man could have stepped right out of the pages of her old books. He was the court magician, the king's wizard—the coven's sorcerer!

The aged figure gave Judith a cryptic welcoming smile,

showing long, yellow teeth, and gray gums. "Yes, my dear Miss Bradford, I am rewriting my script yet another time. I know our great director will use it his own way, but it is my passion that it be beyond question or cavil!"

Judith was overwhelmed by Dr. Gomay's voice. In contrast to his wizened, feeble appearance, it was the tone of a virile, powerful young male. Thoroughly intimidated, Judith clung to Rick's arm and inclined her head. "I'm glad to meet you, Dr. Gomay."

To her amazement, there was no answer. The apparition had vanished into the trees as abruptly as it had appeared. Flabbergasted, Judith turned to Rick questioningly. He smiled at her obvious puzzlement. "That's the old man," he offered with an easy tolerance of eccentricity.

Judith thought of how long she had waited to see the fabled doctor, and how brief the encounter had been. She could only hope she would have more time with Werner Christed.

To Rick, she blurted, "For a minute I thought I was seeing things again!" She broke off in consternation. Rick was too bright not to notice her saying "*again*."

It did bring the response she feared. Rick asked alertly, "You see things, Judy?"

Judith debated with herself. Should she tell Rick about the Angel Dust and LSD? The bouts might be finished, why confess needlessly? On the other hand, if her growing feelings for Rick were genuine, he ought to know everything about her. Love wasn't the expectation of perfection, it was the acceptance of human weaknesses. It was early for a test of their just-budding relationship, but she would save herself grief later if she learned Rick's reactions now.

Her mind made up, Judith recounted her drug mishap in Chicago and its troublesome aftermath. She waited anxiously as the handsome actor stared at her silently when she was finished. Softly he said, taking her hand, "It makes no difference to me, Judy."

It did not escape Judith that Rick accepted the accidental nature of her experience without question. It was another positive sign of the faith that was flowering between them.

"If it should ever happen here," Rick said, "come to me, and I'll take you to Dr. Gomay. He is a very good physician with many old-country remedies that work wonders."

Judith could not escape a fleeting recollection of the actress Emily had described. Apparently, Dr. Gomay had not been able to save her life.

The notion of seeking help of any kind from the emaciated man she had just seen unsettled Judith. She could never bear the touch of those creepy-looking hands. But she was happy she had confessed the drug truth to Rick Gilbert, glad that shadow was removed. It might have come between them sometime. She wanted the openness and candor with him that promised so much.

Alone with Rick again, the vibrations of Dr. Gomay's intrusion faded. Judith could fancy the sound of the sea as a rippling stream winding through the sun-speckled lawns of her romantic volumes. Pairs of lovers strolled in bucolic scenes, in glades and avenues bordered by alabaster and marble statuary. A faraway harpsichord played sweet music for their pleasure.

A Camelot of the old days, Judith sighed, eyes closed. Its ramparts would be gilded by the golden sun, while stretching fields beyond bore every kind of fruit and blossom for the enjoyment of the gallant knights and lovely ladies. At the same time, there would be shadows, a lonely landscape and pathless forests, silent as tombs; and ruined abbeys would stand with haunted halls echoing vanished glories and tales of banished lovers. These were tales she never wanted to forget, Judith mused. Maybe one of the things wrong with the world today was that such romance was out of favor. The heightened prose in her memorized passages—call it purple—had been fanciful, but had cast a spell by its very excesses. Although here on Gomay Island in Rick's arms she needed no extravagant poetic flights, Judith was glad she remembered the very words. They told of a view of innocence and love that honored the spiritual as well as physical aspects of life. And in many ways, Judith considered, they reflected deep truths about human emotions—fear, lust, dreams, courage, and love—truths even deeper than the modern-day realists reached with all their frankness and bold confessing.

Rick murmured in Judith's ear, "What are you thinking?"

"How happy I am."

Rick breathed her name in an ardent whisper and leaned over her, his face a soft question. Luminous-eyed, Judith Bradford let herself drift into the magic of his kiss. Behind her half-closed lids she saw the delicate light of new dawns promising a lifetime of joy. She did not have to recall or imagine that enchantment now. It was not in books any longer for her. She held it in her own hands here on Gomay Island. She could let her heart go freely now because Fate had brought her to a man she could love and trust without reservation.

Then it was time to descend the path to the movie studio in the church and Judith's first encounter with the director, Werner Christed.

CHAPTER SEVEN

At the church entrance, Lena was waiting with Moose. "I have only a minute," she told Judith, "but I want to wish you luck with Werner." She lifted her wrist to Judith. "Rub this for good fortune," she said solemnly. It was the elephant hair bracelet, her daughter's gift. Judith was touched. Inwardly she frowned at herself for ever having entertained a negative thought about this woman who was so kind and supportive to her.

"Thank you, Lena," she said with gratitude. "I need

all the luck I can get!"

Moose took Judith's arm. "Not to worry," he offered. "Uncle Moose will see you through."

Judith was glad for his calloused hand steadying her. The prospect of coming into the presence of Werner Christed unnerved her, now that it was imminent.

Inside the church, Judith moved instinctively to make her Catholic obeisance but, except for the stained glass windows in the massive walls, there was no reminder of religion—no altar, no crucifix, no chapels, no pews. She was on a grand sound stage surrounded by every kind of film gear and rigging. Rick had prepared her for the building's transformation, yet viewing it brought a sense of blasphemy. Once a church, always a church—wasn't that true doctrine? A structure once dedicated to God could never be turned to other purposes without sacrilege. She wasn't "religious" any more, but a sense of disharmony echoed somewhere in her.

Judith reminded herself with impatience that she was an aspiring actress and not a religious novice. She recognized that her mind was meandering, not wishing to face the situation. *Could* this be real? *Could* she, Judith Bradford, farm girl from Lomis, Iowa, be standing here—albeit on trembling legs—in Werner Christed's magic domain, waiting actually to meet the director? It seemed to Judith that her dreams of this moment had been more real than the actuality itself. It seemed to her she must be dreaming now . . .

But the sound of Moose's voice was real enough. Beside her, the crew boss was looking to the ceiling, calling up to a high catwalk, "Okay, Werner?"

Puzzled, Judith stepped back. She could see no one overhead, but heard distinct steps. Apparently, Werner

Christed had been watching her from the high scaffolding since she had walked in! It was queer—yet so typical of Gomay Island!—Judith reflected, that her first contact with the great director should be a voice issuing out of an invisible presence. It had been that way with Dr. Gomay also.

There the comparison with Dr. Gomay ended. This voice boomed down like the disembodied injunctions of Greek gods rolling Olympianly over mortals below. This deep voice was one that entered not one's ears but one's whole being, a resonance once heard never forgotten, although only one word had been spoken—"*Yes!*"

The single sound reverberated through the church.

It was as if an organ had in one note struck the overtones of all the great chords the instrument held, a promise of mighty music.

Werner Christed, indeed!

Judith's little finger went to the back of her neck. How could she feel all that in one small syllable? It was unearthly, even as the voice of true genius. She half expected the yellow swirl of a drug episode around her head, brought on by the excitement and challenge of the moment. She wanted to turn and flee. She didn't belong here. She was a pretender, a usurper. Emily should keep the part, Gomay Island should keep its secrets. Everything had been a mistake—Lena's assistance, Rick's embrace, her ambition. She knew her face was crimson, her body shaking beyond control, her breath racing. She tried to reach toward Moose, but he had gone behind a camera, and every movement she made was clumsy and awkward. She had become a wooden puppet, her joints glued stiff. *A fine first impression she must be making on Werner Christed*, Judith thought miserably.

And then the director was standing in front of her.

He was even bigger than magazine photographs had led her to expect. She realized it wasn't his physical size, though he was tall, as much as the power that came from him. He was a force in himself, like a part of nature, a great tree. He held the natural dignity of the spreading forest all around them.

Black-browed and square-jawed, the director silently scrutinized Judith Bradford with his penetrating eyes. She sensed that even while he frankly assessed her, his gaze held humor, warmth, and respect. At the same time, there was an austerity in his face and manner—an aloofness—that bespoke the distance between them—an unbridgeable gap. Werner Christed, Judith divined at once, would always be beyond her, always privately distant in the necessary reserve of his art and his authority.

To Judith, he was a unique and uniquely compelling combination of power and grace—there was no other word for it.

Judith also felt a brooding spirit in the man, an engrossment in his own undertakings that was common to the heroes she so fondly remembered and had once dreamed of capturing her and stealing her away. Ah, the starry-eyed chimeras of childhood . . .

Yes, Judith bethought, this Werner Christed might have stepped out of the pages of her books, but she was grown up now, ready for a screen test and not a romantic legend.

Nor could Judith escape the marked severity and loneliness in the director's expression. Here was a man who called the whole world to account, with the passion of an artist dedicated to truth and beauty as he discovered it afresh. For all her youthfulness and inexperience, Judith strongly sensed the man's total integrity. She saw in an instant why Werner Christed had given up money and social lionizing for his offbeat films. He had earned the right to have his reputation for being impatient with fools and philistines. She would try to show him she was neither!

Werner Christed's dedication to his art was an inspirational power. It told her, too, that this man—unlike Rick and everyone else she had ever known—saw people not only as persons but like the colors on a palette, like clay on an armature, an actor on his stage. All were tools he used to express the endless restlessness and shifting Judith felt as a great crossing of tides in Werner Christed.

Those were deep waters in which she was not prepared to swim.

Judith Bradford stood in a silent awe no other presence had ever stirred in her.

Christed's dress added to the prodigious impression he made on the girl. He was wearing a soft white leather tunic fastened at the waist with a worn rope. Long jet-black hair fell to his wide shoulders. With his face burned by the island's sun and wind, Christed looked like a Viking, Judith observed. She was glad she had been told of his Alaskan days. She could fancy the literal look of eagles in this man's eyes—eyes that seemed to glow with ancient myths, forgotten wisdoms, forceful Northern rituals. Oh, this was a man not to be reckoned with easily, a man complicated and beyond her reach as, thankfully, Rick Gilbert was not.

Judith found it difficult to remember that the director was not, in fact, very much older than Rick.

Just before the director spoke to her, Judith had an impulse to curtsy. "Royal" was the word that summed up Werner Christed.

But the director, without ceremony, was grasping her shoulders, saying engagingly, "So you are Lena's girl . . ." Holding her at arm's length, Christed turned Judith about like a sculpture piece. "I can see why." In another quick, unexpected motion he drew Judith into his arms with a bear hug that squeezed out what little breath she had left. "I don't believe people can know each other until they touch." His laugh was hearty and unaffected. "Now that we're properly introduced, we can start."

Taken aback by the director's embrace, Judith suddenly felt her awkwardness melt away. His open, physical communication somehow reached directly into her, flushing away all her apprehensions. She could not know whether he would approve her acting or not, but she felt her natural self again. It was a good, solid feeling. She would be able to show her best. Then, if Christed preferred Emily, she would readily retire to sew costumes with Lena. She could not ask for more.

Judith moved and turned easily at Werner Christed's signals, and smiled bravely at Moose behind the camera during a close-up. She felt the test was going quite well, though she wondered why Christed was so undemanding. Until he stopped and turned to Moose, saying, "We can go downstairs now. Set it up for us."

With that, the director ushered Judith to a canvas chair and faced her with a clear expression of his interest. "Judith," Werner Christed began, in the resonant voice that sent thrills through her again, "I think you do have the possibilities that Lena and Gregor saw. Now there are several things you need to understand before I begin your real test . . ."

So the shots up to now had been only preliminary. Judith was ready, eager, for more. She was elated that he like her so far.

"First, my plan for *Baron of Darkness* calls for a very complex acting challenge. If you win the part, you will be playing several characters, not just one. You will have to range from a simple peasant girl to the heroic figure of Joan of Arc. It's an uncommon demand, and it won't be easy."

Judith was too rapt to try to speak. She knew of this Christed method; he used it to add subtle dimensions and comment to his film stories. She believed that under his tutelage she could satisfy any demands he made. Just sitting close to him was an inspiration that sent her blood pounding through her body with new resolution. It came to her that her very inexperience might be a plus—Werner Christed would be able to mold her to his own wishes and techniques the more pliantly.

"Second," the director said, with a note of emphasis, "you must say nothing to anyone about what happens in this audition! Aside from Moose, you are going to be the only other person in the world who will know of the machine I have invented downstairs. Moose and I completed it only yesterday, so your audition will be a test of the apparatus as well. It is a new kind of special effects equipment. Since I want its impact on the company to come as a total shock, they must be completely unprepared and have no inkling of what it does! That scene is going to be a major part of the picture. I want everyone absolutely thunderstruck, staggered, unable to believe his senses, as you are going to be. You will understand in a minute, when we go down. *But I must have your solemn promise not to breathe the slightest word or hint of what you see and hear!*"

Still unable to speak, Judith nodded her agreement, her eyes wide with the sincerity of her pledge. Christed was satisfied.

In the basement of the church, Judith observed Moose making adjustments on the most outlandish piece of machinery she had ever come upon. Werner Christed went directly to it, touching it as gently as if it were a beloved child. Judith beheld a fantastic array of metal pipes and gears, festooned with scientific-looking glass prisms, lenses, color wheels, rods of every size and shape. All surrounded a monster-looking projector with mirror panels that undulated like fun-house reflectors. The director said, quietly but with overt pride, "This is the apparatus you must say nothing about—Moose and I call it my 'Illusion Machine.'"

Even inactive, the instrument gave out a sense of eerie power. Its protuberances, tubes, and antennae were like the aerials of a spaceship or some outlandish flying saucer. Its glass knobs seemed like almost-human eyes regarding her inquisitively.

"You need to know what this is all about," Werner Christed instructed Judith, "or you won't be able to work with it. I won't be technical, but this machine is based on holography, laser beams, and electrophoretic screens." He stopped to see if he was over the girl's head. To his pleasant surprise, Judith contributed enthusiastically at once, "I know! They make incredibly three-dimensional pictures! I saw them in a museum in Chicago last winter. It was amazing! When I passed a photograph of a head, it seemed to turn and follow me! I couldn't believe my eyes.

There was one picture there where a woman's hand seemed to be sticking out into the room, right into the space, without a body!"

Werner Christed smiled at Judith's ebullition. "I'm glad you know about it!" Judith could see he was impressed with her, and thanked the stars that had led her to the unusual exhibition. "Check out the Museum of Holography in New York, too. And if you can ever catch the film called 'Holodeon,' don't miss it." Christed continued, "It isn't an illusion at all, really, you know. Your eyes do actually see things in the round, and in motion. In a nutshell, my machine stimulates the brain exactly as if the object were fully present!"

"Far out!" Judith enthused. She spoke the jargon to show Werner Christed she was "with it." Sharing her museum experience with the director made a special bond between them.

The director was obviously enjoying the chance to express his zeal for the machine, until now shared only with Moose. He regarded Judith with enlarged respect. This girl was uncommonly knowledgeable; it augured well for her audition and future in the Company. In any case, he could fortunately tell her more about the apparatus. It was extremely important that she understand and accept it, because the startling reality of its effects would throw her off balance otherwise. Werner Christed smiled to himself. He and Moose had been so successful that they could not quite believe the smashing success of the machine themselves. They did seem to have achieved the impossible—the creation of actual, rounded images out of thin air—images you would swear you could touch as well as hear and, yes, smell too!

To Judith's willing ear, the director started to explain

the scientific underpinnings of the apparatus, all solemnly attested in scholarly literature: "I give credit to the man who did the spadework in this photographic process called holography. His name should be better known, because ultimately everyone is going to be using this kind of thing one way or another. The man was Dennis Gabor." He repeated it. "Dennis Gabor. That was back in 1948, when he explored a process of taking and projecting pictures with three-dimensional reality. Technically, he—"

Moose interrupted, clearing his throat. "Why don't we save the nuts and bolts till later? I'm sure Judith has enough butterflies waiting to go on."

Christed went directly to the control board, signaling Moose behind a camera. "You're right!" he declared at once. And, "Judith, all you need to know for now is that I have this board hooked to a computer that is programmed to project any type of scene we want, on demand." He gave Judith a proud-father grin that made him look very young, and suddenly vulnerable, as great enthusiasm carries everyone to the verge of betrayal.

He continued, "So don't be surprised, Judith, if you suddenly find yourself in the middle of an earthquake, or a garden party, or a car smashup, or a bomb explosion. Do you get the idea?"

Judith inclined her head uncertainly. It was all coming too fast.

"What I want from you," the director said, his voice now crisp and forceful, "is just the way you react normally and naturally to whatever is happening. Don't try to act, don't put on a show for me. Just feel yourself in the middle of whatever turns up, and let yourself go. Right?"

"Right!" Judith answered. She did not know what she was in for, but this strange audition was her chance, her one chance. She had promised herself she could take Werner Christed's direction and she would, even though this was unexplored territory and completely unconventional for all of them.

"Lights!" Christed called out to Moose. Flooding spotlights blinded Judith momentarily. "Camera! Action!"

With that, the director flipped switches on his mammoth board and, to Judith Bradford, the world heaved up and turned over.

She was physically on a white sand beach along the clearest blue-green water she had ever seen. She could hear the waves. She smelled salt air scoured by a blazing sun. She could, indeed, swear she felt spray on her skin. It was uncanny. Although Judith knew in her head that it was the special apparatus at work, her mouth dropped open at the sheer miracle and marvel of it. All along the shore stood great palm trees, rising under a cloudless sky of the purest blue. The perfume of flowers and citrus came to Judith, filling her nostrils delightfully. The call of birds was so close she reached to touch them—hundreds just beyond her fingertips, a rainbow bewilderment of birds.

Glancing to the camera, Judith saw Moose at work, and Werner Christed enjoying her unconcealed bafflement. He made an encouraging gesture, and called, "You see, it's an ideal vacation spot—no mosquitos, no hurricanes, no crowds—unless you want them." The odor of delicious Caribbean food wafted to Judith as he talked. "One day everyone can have one of these in their living room! We'll call it 'Everyman's Dream Machine' and create Utopia!"

Judith thought with wonder that this man could do just that if it was his purpose. Talk about avant-garde! Werner Christed was pushing art into a totally new world. And she was a first witness!

"Or would you prefer Venice?" the director was asking her boyishly. The beach scene vanished and Judith was, unbelievably, in San Marco Square. The bells of the famous Campanile were ringing in her ears, more real than the bellbuoys heard from the grove with Rick on Balefire Bluff. That cliff was thousands of miles away! So was Rick and everything else on Gomay Island. The great bronze horses of the Cathedral lifted their beauty above Judith's head. The liquid sound of Italian was all around her. Judith forgot she was in a screen test. Suddenly, a sour smell assailed her nose, and she made a face. Werner Christed laughed aloud, and touched a button. "Oh, we can even clean the garbage out of the canals!" Then, before Judith could recover, his voice pealed out again: "Or would you prefer Moscow? Or Africa? Or the North? A snowstorm? Christmas? Fireworks?"

In a stunning series that left Judith breathless, she was everywhere the director mentioned, literally in the center of each new scene. And as suddenly, the machine shut off and tumbled her back into the basement of the church on Gomay Island. Around the world in thirty seconds! For a lapsed moment, Judith felt dizzy and had a foreboding of the damnable yellow mist. Was this entire episode a trip she was conjuring out of her own imagination? She could not find her voice.

It was as well. Werner Christed's attention was on his device, not on her. When he spoke, it seemed to be the machine he was addressing, and Judith had a chance to regain her composure and poise.

"This is just the start," the director was saying with fervor. "We will revolutionize the moving picture industry, bring people back to theatres! You see, instead of the cost and inconveniences of traveling, I can take people anywhere in a comfortable theatre seat! Greece or Timbuktu! We'll arrange for restaurants to serve the meals of the country! Souvenir shops, boutiques, marketplaces, all of it!" The man's ambition and energy flooded over Judith Bradford.

No wonder people said you could never keep up with Werner Christed, she reflected. He was like a child enthralled with a new toy. No, he was like a prophet—a prophet both solemn and joyous—he was years ahead of his time! What a privilege it was just to be able to be hear this man!

"Take the walls of a home," Christed was adding. "Why use paint? Why picture frames? I will project an entire scene! Live in Peru today, in Africa tomorrow!" His voice became a teacher's. "After all, everything is in the mind. Ultimately, everything is an illusion of the brain. Is there a true difference between the real and the synthetic? I suggest not. That is a semantic trap. There is only one bridge between the so-called real and so-called illusion, and that bridge is *art!* And, the greatest art is film, because film extends our capacity to go beyond reality both in emotion and time and space—when it is used to its potential!"

Without warning, the director grasped Judith's wrists and pulled her between the mirrors again. His tone was abruptly stern. "And that is what I want from my actors! All of your potential and more!"

Judith was taken aback by a sudden blast of hunting horns. Without warning she was in another world, encompassed in another reality. The machine had created the courtyard of a medieval castle. It was a boisterous Hieronymous Bosch painting come alive. Rearing horses and bellowing ruffians were milling all about. Judith smelled their rancid sweat with a grimace of distaste. She shrank from their coarse grunts as the men swilled from dirty gourds. Fierce curs snarled for food scraps. Judith frantically leaped away from their slavering fangs. Bawdy servant girls swung their hips sexily at the men. Their bosoms bulged out of tight bodices. Leering rogues clutched their crotches in obscene gestures at the swaggering slatterns and at Judith.

Despite Christed's explanations, the experience was more vivid and unnerving to Judith than even her drug nightmares. Again she thought she might be in the midst of a seizure, lost in a more terrible form of illusion than ever before. She fell to the ground as a black horse plunged directly at her, hooves rearing to strike at her trembling head. She quailed before a man clawing boldly for her breasts. She screamed aloud when his gaunt face came into focus out of the scene's turmoil—he looked like the garageman who had tried to rape her! But how could that be? Judith stared wildly about her for escape, then tried to quiet herself. If it was that man, he might well be an extra in a Christed movie—he had said he was a watchman for the Film Loft, so there was a connection. God knew he was grimy enough to be in this band of brigands with which the illusion machine was assaulting her. She could only hope he would never appear on the island in his evil-smelling flesh.

Her conjectures were blasted out of Judith's mind as a huge hound hurled itself at her throat. *This was no illusion!* Her skin felt raked by the savage claws of the beast. She jumped back from its dripping jaws in a panic of terror. A savage figure on horseback plunged to save her. His sword gleamed as it arced down on the feral dog. With one blow, it slashed the dog's head from its body. A geyser of hot blood shot out of the raw wound. The pulsing neck poured crimson as the severed head rolled gruesomely at Judith. The sword flashed again to cleave the twitching body of the decapitated animal where it lay. The belly ripped open with a foul bursting. Odious intestines and gore slopped out over the rough stones, oozing a slimy red pool around Judith's feet. A heaving wail of disgust burst from her as she buried her ashen face in shaking hands.

A howling shriek pried her eyes open—to witness another abomination. The dog had apparently belonged to another horseman, a giant of a man, who now lunged after the slayer. Sparks flew from his mount's hooves as he shouted curses that brought the first rider around. The crowd flew to the sides of the yard, eagerly bellowing incitements. The dog slayer lifted a lance and made for his challenger, who had only his sword. Ducking and weaving, the latter escaped the lance aimed mercilessly at his face. But his horse slipped and slid on the body of the butchered dog, and threw the rider. It was all the giant needed. Hot-eyed, with a roar of triumph he sent his horse full tilt at the stumbling man and drove his lance straight into his eye, piercing through the head and emerging bloodied from the back of the skull. It seemed to Judith that the gory steel would keep speeding right to her heart. She fell away, twitching convulsively with terror and fresh disgust. The murderer galloped at Judith with a roaring laugh of triumph. She dropped to her knees, praying.

Then suddenly there was total silence. Total, stunning quiet. Judith looked up apprehensively. Nothing! The scene was gone as violently as it had begun. There was no sneering garageman, no violent dog, no unspeakable evisceration, no stomach-turning blood and gore, no awful jousting match, no threatened abduction.

The director's voice came, calm and calming, from beside the camera. "You need to know, Judith, that this picture is full of this kind of violence—and worse. It is necessary, not only for the story we are to make, but to truly reflect man's nature—the vicious part of our nature we must all struggle to overcome. You see, I deeply believe the philosopher who said that man is the missing link between the ape and the human being. You will understand all this better when you know more about *Baron of Darkness.* Meantime, I can tell you that your reactions were exactly what I want. I think you can probably do the part splendidly, though we have to see a good deal more. But what I need to know right now is whether you think you can handle the violent scenes, the brutal material."

Judith swallowed, still sickened by the onslaught. But she was determined. "Yes," she answered Christed at once, thinking only that she had not come this far to quit now. After all, she told herself again, the muck and nastiness were only fantasy, laser figments, not real, not threatening unless she let her own pinball imagination light up with its sickly effloresence.

"I can do it!" Judith said to the director. Her voice was louder, without a tremor now.

"Good," Christed said in a pleased way that encouraged Judith. She felt more than better at once. She must be doing well! Christed could have stopped the audition right here if he did not find her promising. Her shoulders went back, her chin lifted. She was ready for whatever he might throw at her now.

Except his next direction: "All right, let's go on then—take off your clothes now, Judith." Werner Christed's tone was as uncharged as if he had directed Judith to do nothing more than turn her head left or right.

Judith stiffened. Her first reaction was a drilling disappointment. So even Werner Christed used the sex route! Her apprehension and confusion were sharpened when she realized his words had brought an involuntary, undeniable surge of female excitement. It seemed there was some way Werner Christed aroused her as even Rick Gilbert did not. It was a darker, more secret emotion than she had ever before recognized—and immediately to be denied!

Judith reproached herself at once. After all, she knew that most Christed films contained nude scenes. There was no sensible reason, in this day and age, why she shouldn't do as he asked. But she wished Lena had briefed her so it wouldn't have come without warning or preparation.

"I need to have nude shots of you now, Judy." The direction came again, cool and impersonal.

Judith wrangled with herself. This was no time to be a prude. Everything she wanted depended on pleasing Werner Christed. She could be sure that Emily had not balked or thought twice about taking her clothes off. Her own scruples were foolish and outdated!

But the director had turned the apparatus on again, and the ruffians in the courtyard were ogling her lasciviously. As she tentatively lifted her hand to unbutton her blouse, they cheered and nudged each other expectantly. Judith stopped, disgusted. Foul spittle dripped from their wine-stained scraggly beards. With panic, Judith was convinced these villains were real. Werner Christed had played a trick! He had turned off his crazy contraption and brought real actors in to assault her so he could film an actual rape! This unpredictable genius might be lost far enough in his "spontaneous art" to plan exactly such a shot!

Judith knew in the same moment that she was reaching for any wild excuse to evade what had to be her private moment of truth.

"Undress, Judy!" There was impatience now.

Judith didn't blame Werner Christed for being irritated. Hollywood pictures, even television shows, were showing everything but intercourse, and getting close to that. Christed was no pornographer. If this picture required nudity, she ought to give it or get out. It made no difference that she had never stood naked in front of a man before. Hectically, Judith declared to herself that it was no big deal. Certainly her body was nothing to be ashamed of! She lifted her hands to her blouse again, but at the last moment they fell helplessly to her side. Despite her resolve, something within stopped her from disrobing.

Tears of distress welled in Judith's eyes. "I am sorry, Mr. Christed! I have never stripped before!"

"Cut!"

Judith heard the words like a gunshot. As her banishment. Sobbing, she saw that the machine was shut off. She had blown her chance. All of her flying hopes were down the drain of her flaky prudishness. Tears flooded out uncontrollably.

But Werner Christed, miraculously, was smiling. He was nodding at her in a way that could only mean approval. "That was fine, Judy! The close-up of your face was terrific. Just the kind of purity I want."

Judith found it hard to credit her ears.

"I don't want a hooker or a burlesque queen. A girl like you *should* be as revolted and scared as you were among men like that gang." Christed repeated, "You were fine." He paused, then added, "But you realize the picture will have several nude scenes. If you can't manage that, I'll definitely use Emily—"

"I'll do it!" Judith cried out impulsively. If getting the part meant nudity, she would strip! She was too close to forfeit it now! Christed was giving her another chance. It was too good to be true.

"I want you to be certain." Christed's voice reflected an honest concern for her, for her ability to deal with nudity.

Judith knew now that she would do anything for this man. She reminded herself fiercely that she was an actress, not a dunce from Squaresville. She had to leave her horse-and-buggy qualms behind! She recalled Brutus's prophetic line from Julius Caesar when she had acted Calphurnia, the ruler's wife, in high school. Brutus had said to Cassius, *"There is a tide in the affairs of men/which, taken at the flood, leads on to fortune;/Omitted, all the voyage of their life/Is bound in shallows and in miseries."*

Maybe Emily would still deserve the part but, Judith vowed, she was not going to settle for the shallows and miseries if she could help it. She called out to the director with new determination. "I can do it right now, Mr. Christed!"

"Werner!" the director reminded her.

"Werner!" Judith felt old bonds snapping inside. It was as if she had been in a straitjacket and could breathe deeply for the first time. The air reaching the new spaces within was intoxicating.

"Good. If you're ready, we are."

"Got it!" Judith answered, her head high. She would show Werner Christed. She would show them all! She would win the director over no matter how good Emily might be!

She heard the magic words: "This is picture. Roll it! Action!"

Judith undressed, now without faltering, without hesitation. When she took off her blouse and undid her bra, she felt the air touch her exposed breasts like soft fingers. An image of Rick's hand flashed into her mind, then Werner Christed's, and both were gone, as she concentrated on what she had to do.

Slowly, Judith drew down her jeans, and the air was a stroking hand on her flesh. There was a fluttering like birds' wings between her thighs when, holding her breath, she slowly removed her panties. Heart pounding, fully nude, Judith straightened and deliberately turned to show Werner Christed and the camera every aspect of her proud female figure.

Judith's stomach churned even as she held her chin high. She felt the floor shake, and was afraid the strain of her stripping would bring the yellow dread. But she would not quit, until she was reprieved by Werner Christed's call to Moose, "Cut. That's a take. Get me prints of everything, right away!"

Exhaustion turned Judith's body to putty. She was drained physically and emotionally. Undressing, she had sharply realized that not only the director was watching. Moose was seeing her immodestly naked, too. There had been a new seizure of indecision, but at the same time her female awareness had asserted itself in a feeling of—what?—*exhilaration*, if she was to be honest with herself! She had uncovered not only her flesh but some primitive womanly depth into which her shyness and modesty sank soundlessly. She possessed unnamed emotions she had never confronted before.

Judith felt humbled. She recalled her scorn at school for girls who had "gone all the way." What a superior prig she had been! Not that those girls were right, or that she was ready to sleep with a man, not even Rick, but judge not lest ye be judged! Judith's groping thoughts grew more confused. It seemed that she would have to be prepared for surprises within as well as without in this new life she was starting.

Werner Christed was approaching her. There was admiration in his gray eyes. His close presence was a magnet whose force reached Judith palpably as he stood next to her naked body. As if it were happening, she could imagine his strong muscles pulling her to his rugged frame, bruising her with his power, with his virile yet sensitive lips. Gratefully, Judith seized the robe he held out. She silently gave double thanks—to the director for moving back without touching her, and to Rick for being her own new emotional center to which she could safely retreat.

Her feelings for Rick were familiar as her feelings for Werner Christed were not. Inwardly she knew she could deal with Rick as she could not deal with the director. Christed stirred storms in her she did not want to recognize, whirlpools in which she could only hopelessly drown.

Judith dressed hurriedly behind a screen. What she should be most thankful for, she told herself, was that no drug-sizzling had come upon her though she had just been through one of the most harrowing episodes of her life.

And now to hear the director's verdict! Judith could hardly breathe as she stepped to Christed. The man saw the question in her face before she spoke.

"You were excellent, Judy," the director told her at once, "but of course we have to see how you actually come across on the screen. You'll hear from me tonight after I get the print."

Judith made her way to the door with dragging steps. She had hoped to bowl Christed over, to evoke an immediate approval. Instead, she had been bowled over herself, and given a performance of uncertainty and amateur bungling. She wanted to weep. She wanted to find Lena. She wanted to be alone. She was sorry she had ever heard of Werner Christed and his film company. She would never survive until tonight.

The director called after her. "You have a very beautiful and lovely body, Judy."

As if that were any consolation.

Then she told herself fiercely to stop being a whipped child. She had many consolations. Werner Christed himself had taken her into his confidence about his magic machine—and it *was* the most wondrous thing she had ever experienced. She had Rick waiting for her. And Lena. She ought to remember the promises she had made so fervently at the Loft. Hadn't she vowed she would wash dishes, carry out garbage? If she didn't get the part, even the least task with the Christed company was better than anything else her flight from Iowa might have led her to. She ought to count her blessings, and thank the fates that had brought her to Gomay Island, Judith counseled herself sternly as she left the church, sobbing.

CHAPTER EIGHT

Judith looked for Lena at once when she came off the Christed set. She was told the woman had gone on city errands with Gregor. Rick was occupied somewhere. Only a few of the film company were on the Common. Judith guessed most were at the tennis court and pool. The day was blistering hot for the end of June. It gave Judith a start to realize they were approaching the weekend of the Fourth. She wondered if there would be fireworks. She wondered if Roman candles and pinwheels would get a rise out of the zombie Gomays she saw in the fields.

Restless, Judith thought she might walk up to the grove on the cliff, then decided she did not want to be there without Rick. She was still distracted; like the ocean after a storm, it would take her time to calm down. She missed Lena badly. She headed for the formal garden, then remembered the two Gomays who had startled her at the sundial with the strange family symbol. She was in no mood for silent eyes spying on her. She thought fitfully that the Gomays' robes and masks were stupid and presumptuous. Custom or no custom they were an anachronism here. These people were in the United States, not in Transylvania. They ought to accept the ways of the mainstream.

The Urwolde cemetery caught Judith's eye. It looked quiet and serene, the mood she required. Rick had told her the Gomays stayed out of the plot, so she wouldn't have to be concerned with them. She had wanted to examine the old gravestones anyway—she always enjoyed the carvings and quaint sayings in antique burial grounds.

Passing the hearse shed, Judith saw the van was gone. Of course. Gregor and Lena were in the city. Her mind went back to the scene of the falling coffin and the youthful corpse rolling out. She hunched her shoulders against the memory. Dummy or not, that poor body had been an awful sight to see. Today she could imagine what fantastic tricks Werner Christed's special machine would do to the mannequin. His sleight-of-camera would probably bring the wax figure to real life under their very eyes! Pygmalion of horror!

Judith entered the grassy graveyard, recalling childhood ghost stories with an indulgent smile. In those tales, the rusty gate would squeak protestingly. The sky would darken threateningly, and ghostlike lights would hover mysteriously among the headstones. But in reality the sun was radiant, and the only thing flying around was a prosaic small plane over the dwellings and shopping centers of Long Island not too far away on the mainland.

It was good to have the commonplace reminder of the outside world. It helped keep things in perspective. Gomay Island, *Baron of Darkness*, and Werner Christed were not the center of all existence.

Sour grapes! Judith told herself candidly as she stepped slowly among the graves.

To her surprise, she saw Emily rise from a stone where she had been kneeling. Emily said at once, "Judy! I hope your test went well!"

"Werner will let me know tonight." Judith found it hard to believe Emily's openheartedness, so obviously genuine. She was sure she herself could not be as charitable if the shoe were on the other foot. Especially now, she wanted to play opposite Rick. She had stripped naked for the part. She would have fought for it physically if necessary. She disliked herself for lacking Emily's unselfishness, but she had to accept the truth. Emily was just a nicer person. She could not talk about the contest between them. Seeking neutrality, and not very proud of herself at the moment, Judith said lamely, "I was just looking for a quiet spot . . ."

Emily spoke brightly, "I love it in here. I love the sayings on the stones. Let me show you this one, Judy!" She led Judith across a weedy path and bent over, reciting the grave's inscription in a hollow, dramatic tone:

"Reader
Keep Death and Judgment
Always in your eye
Non's fitt to live
But who is fitt to die!"

Emily's laugh tinkled. "They sure didn't know how to spell, did they?" More and more Judith appreciated the girl's fair humor. It would be so understandable if she were unfriendly and standoffish. Instead, Emily was pointing out another slab, where a death's head was deeply incised in the weathered stone. The skull's empty eyes seemed to stare accusingly at the young people as they knelt together to see the words.

"In midst of Great Prosperitie
Remember now that thou too may Die"

"Now that's a happy thought for the day!" Emily giggled.

Still, it's true, Judith reflected pensively. People do forget about their dying. Maybe living would be unbearable otherwise. Or maybe people would live more wisely, with more enjoyment of the gifts of life, and with more compassion for their fellows, who are all headed to the same end. In graves like these. All at once it seemed less important to Judith that she win the movie role. Whatever the decision, she would still be with Rick. Yes, a cemetery was a place for perspective.

Emily broke into Judith's introspection. "Judy, did Dr. Gomay ask if you were a virgin, too?"

Judith returned a startled look. "Dr. Gomay wasn't at my test."

"The old codger kept asking me," Emily frowned. "I told him I certainly was and he'd better not try to check it out!"

Judith enjoyed the girl's irreverence, and liked finding another "Victorian."

"At least if it was Rick," Emily teased. It came to Judith that the whole company must be aware of how she and Rick had paired off. Flushing, she asked, "Have you seen him?"

"There he is now!" Emily said in surprise. She was pointing to the Gomay quarters across the Common. Judith was flabbergasted to see a robed, masked servant letting Rick Gilbert into a side door of the off-limits house. Emily whispered uneasily, "*No* one of us is supposed to go there!" Her face was solemn for the first time.

Judith nodded. "I know. Rick told me that himself." After a moment, she added, "I suppose Dr. Gomay must have sent him there for some reason . . ."

Emily was dubious. "They impressed it on all of us!—It's the strictest rule on the island!"

"I know that," Judith repeated with a touch of annoyance. Emily didn't have to make a federal case out of it. Rick hadn't been slinking around or hiding. He had been standing there plain in the late afternoon sun for everyone to see. She repeated her surmise about an errand. What in the world else could account for *Rick* breaking the rules, and so openly?

Emily said, "Well, as you know, I just came to Gomay Island myself so there's lots I don't know. But it's a funny feeling to see Rick with those Gomays. They're certainly a weird bunch, aren't they?"

In a stubborn need to defend Rick, Judith found

herself also defending and explaining the Gomays. "It's their religion to dress the way they do!" she said with a conviction she did not feel.

"Yes, Werner explained all that." Emily still sounded skeptical.

"I suppose our customs seem just as strange to them," Judith lectured.

"Well, they give *me* the creeps," Emily said. "And I'd still like to know why the rules are different for Rick Gilbert!"

"What are you driving at?" Judith asked narrowly, feeling that Emily was in some way impugning Rick's honesty, his place in the Christed company.

Emily regretted the turn their conversation had taken. "Nothing," she said quickly. "I guess this island will give all of us the jitters a little until we get used to it." She offered her friendly smile again. "Anyway, what Rick does or doesn't do with the Gomays isn't any of our affair, is it?"

Judith considered that it might, indeed, be some of *her* affair, but she was satisfied with her own explanation of the episode, and accepted Emily's hand when the girl—her mood shifted back to gaiety—moved on to another grave. "This one once had a picture of Satan chiseled on the stone, they say. Of course, you're not allowed to do that in a Christian cemetery. See how the image is chipped away? Somebody must have played a prank. Back in 1796. How about that?" Without stopping, she added, "I know a joke about Satan . . ."

"Tell away." Judith wanted to sound affable. She felt friendly now, as if she and Emily were classmates relaxing carefree on some campus. It was more pleasant than seeing her as a competitor.

Emily told her story with relish: "There was this poor

young minister whose new wife was extravagant. She came home in an expensive coat. 'You should never have spent that much money!' her husband said. 'I'm sorry,' she answered, 'it must have been the Devil's fault.' The minister scolded, 'You could have said—Satan, get thee behind me!'

"'I did,' his wife said, 'but he called over my shoulder that it fit me beautifully in the back, too!'"

The young women laughed together with the enjoyment of people on the same wavelength. They strolled and chatted in the graveyard until, at the fence abutting the forest, Judith stopped short. She grasped Emily's arm. "That's a fresh grave!"

Emily assented sadly. "Yes. It's the girl I told you about—the one who had our part originally, and got sick . . ."

"Poisoned," Judith remembered Emily had conjectured. "Didn't they send her home?" Judith asked, shocked.

"It seems no one knew who she really was."

With a weak feeling in her knees, Judith stared dismally at the too-fresh wooden cross. All it said was "Roberta Leslie," and the year. It came to Judith that if she died here no one would know who she really was either. For the first time since leaving home, Judith knew an inner pang of loss. This Roberta Leslie—who knew her true name, her true story, the good or bad she had done? What mother and father had she left, alone and sorrowing? What a small cipher she was now in this anonymous grave where time and the nearby trees would cover her over, without memory, as if she had never existed.

A new quiver of uncertainty ran through Judith.

She, too, had chosen to be alone in the world, at least for this while. It could be cold, barren, and eternal loss. She thanked God there was Rick. And Lena. And Emily.

Emily was sighing, "Poor kid, whoever she was." She turned to Judith and spoke very slowly, as if choosing her words only after long consideration. "*If* it was poison, do you think whoever wanted her dead might feel the same way about *us?*"

Judith gasped. It seemed the spookiness of Gomay Island was getting to Emily. What a crazy thought! "You have to be kidding, Emily!" she declared.

Emily's answer came softly, almost a whisper. "Well, just think about it, Judy! It might have something to do with her playing the star role in the picture, mightn't it?"

"I don't see how," Judith dismissed the idea. "You have the part so far, and I might be getting it, but neither of *us* did anything to anyone, did we?"

"I suppose you're right," Emily said after a long moment. "I've been watching too many TV detective shows." She took a deep breath and made for the cemetery gate. "Come on, then! Last one out is a G-h-o-s-t!"

As they ran playfully from the graveyard, neither girl saw the light that suddenly came three deliberate times, still unanswered, from the tower window of the Manor House.

In her office, Ursula Blake was changing into her Greenwich Village clothes for another check of the bars frequented by unemployed actors. It was just a hunch that Judith Wayne/Bradford might hang out with that crowd, but it was all there was to go on at the moment. There had been no leads from her colleagues in other cities either. She could only hope the runaway girl was not in peril.

Blake hung Mrs. Wayne's gold locket with the girl's photo around her neck and headed downtown. This case could be a real loser, as she had told Carlos Rodriguez. His answer had been to declare that if she didn't set a wedding date soon, he was going to marry his new boss. She was an Amazon recently promoted to captain through women's lib pressures, he complained. He was only half-joking on both counts.

Today, Blake was headed for a bar where some Off-Off-Broadway characters hung out. A professional investigator didn't work on hope, didn't permit early leads to stir too much optimism, or a succession of nothing-days induce pessimism. A pro went doggedly about the unglamourous business of checking a hundred bars, as she and her operatives had already done.

Blake took in a group of drop-outs leaning drunkenly around a table in the rear of the place she entered. One fellow was picking aimlessly at a guitar. Where would the youth rebellion be without guitars, Blake thought sourly.

It was no trick to join them. The trick was to keep the red-bearded stud named Reuben Lintch from pawing her. For a while she had to put up with his vulgarity and with the jumble of pseudo-philosophy his friends were mouthing. "Shit, what's the difference? Everything's happened before, man."

"Only shittier now, man," the red beard contributed.

Blake understood their disgust with the imperfect world (her childhood in Hell's Kitchen had almost certainly been worse than theirs) but she could not accept their way of protesting. Millions of other young people would give their eyeteeth for the middle-class lives these cop-outs were garbaging. Fortunately, Blake reminded herself, the real youth of the world was learning, growing, doing. These people, too, would yet find that nobody can forever fly now, pay later. They, too, would come to want the security and amenities they so glibly despised while they had their parents' money. Meantime it was foolish to dignify their irresponsibility with her contempt.

Blake went to work by placing the gold watch-locket on the table ostentatiously, saying, "I have to go in a little while. I can't be late. . . ."

She had to use all of her self-control to hide her flush of excitement as she saw the hook take for the first time. *Finally!* The reward of professional patience. The man named Reuben was examining Judith's photo as if he recognized the face.

"She remind you of somebody?" Blake asked the question with a calculated air of indifference.

"I think," the man scowled. "Not as pretty as you, though," he smiled salaciously. Blake suffered his reaching hand on her thigh as the locket was passed around the table.

The fight happened so fast, it was over before the people at the bar took it in. With the locket in his fist, the man next to Redbeard leaped for the front door. Blake catapulted after him with one warning yell. The others watched astounded as the seemingly mild, slim woman tackled the bull of a youth and held him down as he tried to thrash free. When he pulled a fat fist to slam at her face, Blake slipped the punch expertly and banged the man's head on the floor, hard. It was his fearful cries and the cracking of his skull on the wood that brought startled eyes around from the bar.

Blake let the would-be thief go in an instant. It was the identification of the photo she wanted—the police could pick the goon up later. She returned to the table with the locket. "You were saying," she continued quietly with the red beard. The men looked at her with new respect. "Like wow," one whispered admiringly. "This dame is but *tough!*" They would have respected Blake even more if they realized how much restraint she had used with their pal, if they knew she had killed an attacker once with a single karate chop, breaking his neck with one blow. In her mind, she could still hear the awful snapping of his collar bones.

Blake nudged Redbeard. "You said you think you know her . . ."

The man studied the locket again—and no hand came toward Blake's thigh now. But there was avarice in his face. "Whadda you want with this chick? What's it worth to you?"

"I might just not hit you as hard as I did your buddy!"

The man blinked. "Well, if you find her or not is no skin off my butt either way."

"Could put some skin *to* you, man." Blake let the meaning sink in, took the locket, and stood up.

The talk of money clearly turned on Reuben Lintch. "Hey, I'd tell you, baby, but I honest-to-shit can't remember where I know this chick from . . ."

"Well, if it comes to you, let me know."

"Hey, how do I reach you?"

Blake indicated the watching bartender. He winked with understanding. She left in a hurry. Half a lead was better than none. She had primed the pump. Those dudes were remembering something about Judith Bradford; they might remember more.

Absorbed in the possible first crack in the Wayne case, tiny though it was, Ursula Blake started across Seventh Avenue without checking the traffic light. She hopped back just in time to avoid being struck by a black hearse that was trundling down the street. Lucky it was going slowly, Blake muttered to herself, or she'd have been a candidate for a trip inside.

Blake watched the death wagon sadly, marking how shabby it looked. It must serve a poverty area, she observed with the compassion that came whenever she recalled the struggling neighbors of her girlhood.

But Blake's high spirit returned in a moment. She had a hunch Redbeard would come through. She was getting close to the trail of the missing girl, the detective told herself confidently as she walked off in the opposite direction from the hearse driven by Gregor Ludovici.

CHAPTER NINE

Judith was brushing her hair before dinner when Rick came for her. She jumped at his voice outside her room. The afternoon had been endless. Was Rick bringing word from Werner at last?

He was.

And Judith saw at once that it was not good. Rick told Judith that Werner liked her very well on the screen, but there were certain things he preferred in Emily. Werner might try an innovation—having two actresses alternate in the same part, to use their different appeals. But it would be far out even for him, and he wanted another audition before he decided. The new test would take place the next morning, on a set just completed up on Death Point.

Judith listened to Rick in silence. Her hopes faded as he spoke, then rose again. Maybe she would do better on a normal movie set without the distraction of the Illusion Machine. She almost told Rick of her unsettling experience with its gory projections, but recalled her pledge of total silence.

"Will I have a chance to rehearse this time?" she asked.

Rick shook his head. "You know Werner's theory. To take the audience by surprise he takes his actors by surprise." He held Judith's shoulders tenderly. "It's the same for Emily. Werner will shoot you first, but Emily won't be on the set so she won't have any advantage when it's her turn."

"Will Werner be using costumes, makeup, this time?" Judith wanted to know.

Rick told her, "If you need anything, Lena will let you know. She will be back from the city with Gregor after dinner."

Dinner turned out to be a signal event—one the entire troupe had been anticipating with mounting, wondering impatience. In the dining hall, Werner Christed appeared unexpectedly, and stood on a chair to make his long-awaited announcement. That night, in the Great Salon of the Manor House, to which all were invited directly after the meal, Dr. Gomay would disclose the full story of *Baron of Darkness!*

The director left without further word. The company

erupted in a buzz of excitement. Judith felt her toes curling with the sparking electricity all around. At last her own curiosity about the movie was to be satisfied!—and in the morning she was to have another opportunity to prove herself against Emily! She would win the part, Judith vowed to herself again as she squeezed Rick's hand across the table.

In New York, the phone interrupted Ursula Blake just as she succeeded in affixing her eyelashes. She hurried from her dressing table in her elegant gown. It was Ralph, the Greenwich Village bartender, saying, "Your friend with the red beard wants to talk to you."

"I'll call him back tomorrow . . ."

"He says now or forget it."

"Put him on." Blake sighed. They all saw too many TV detective shows.

Redbeard's voice was higher pitched than she recalled; he was obviously in a state of great excitement. His words ran together in a taffy of greed. "Lady, I tagged the chick you want. But let me tell you upfront, honeysuckle, I want a hundred for this info or no play!"

"How do I know it's for real?"

"You have to take my word. Your Sappho trip ain't *my* busted valise!"

"All right. Tell the bartender. I'll bring the money in the morning."

"You bring the bread now, cunt, or freeze it!"

Blake considered. He might be conning her, but he might have something. She had her responsibility to her client. "I'll be right down."

Redbeard was alone this time. Blake showed him the money in an envelope. His eyes lit up. He leaned across the table like a television private-eye informant; Blake almost looked around for a camera. He whispered conspiratorially, "I saw your friend! Definitely!"

Blake kept hold of the envelope for which he reached. "How do we know that?"

The man showed an injured expression. "You never mentioned her name to me, did you? So if I tell you a name that rings your bell, that's it. Right?"

Obviously.

"So I heard this guy call your girl *Judy!* That fits, doesn't it?"

Blake handed over the envelope. Her own heart was beating harder. "What's the rest?"

Redbeard counted the bills avidly. "Your Judy was with this crazy dude we know around here name of Gregor."

"Gregor?" Not a common name certainly. This might be a genuine lead. Blake leaned closer.

Lintch continued, "I checked around and his second name is funny. Ludovici. He shows up once in a while. A weirdo."

Pots calling kettles black, Blake couldn't help thinking. "In what way a weirdo?" she asked.

"He's supposed to be into the real *wild* shit. Not just drugs and stuff. Like, he's supposed to be a warlock. For real. If you believe that crap." The beard quivered as its owner gave a superior but uneasy snicker.

Blake asked, "What makes him a warlock?"

"Like there's kids make candles down MacDougal Street, this Gregor orders big black sticks, special, by the gross. Tell me, what do you do with *hundreds* of big black candles if not spook stuff? Plus he buys out the voodoo store—all kinds of powders and skulls and puff stuff."

It seemed a possibility. The occult scene was very magnetic, attracted many runaways like Judith Bradford. In her experience, these groups were the most perilous of all the lunatic fringes. She could only hope her informant was wrong about the "warlock" while right about the lead. It was clearly worth pursuing. And, if it was a black magic cult, pursuing with dispatch!

"*Plus,*" her informant was going on, "this creep drives around in a spook-hearse. It's a sort of beat-up meat wagon."

Hearse! This could be a real door opening into a real room with a real Judith in it! Not every Tom, Dick, and Gregor rode around in a hearse!

"Have you seen this fellow lately?" Blake continued.

"Three-four days ago we saw the meat wagon, your chick was getting in it!" The man studied Judith's picture again and nodded heavily. "That I am sure of!" A hundred bucks was healthy bread and he would play level with this lady even if he didn't approve of her kind of hots.

Judith Wayne/Bradford riding somewhere in a hearse! Blake had the instinctive "glimmer" she got when a case was suddenly jelling. For a guilty moment she wondered if the hearse she had nearly walked into that afternoon might be the one she had to track down now. The red beard's description fit. Stupid of her not to have noted the plates. But then, she'd had no reason. Anyway, it should be no trouble—hearse conversions weren't that ordinary. Motor Vehicles would have it. The evening hadn't been wasted after all.

Blake went to phone Carlos Rodriguez for his help now. It might be time to bring the police into the Wayne case in any event.

*   *   *

Snapping winds hit the trees, and fitful thunder broke over the heads of the troupe racing through the sudden downpour to the Manor House. In the sodden darkness they made a bleak scene of bowed shadows bent and fleeing from some pursuing enemy, seeking the sanctuary of the torch-lighted Gothic windows at the north end of Urwolde Common.

When Judith entered with Rick, Lena, and Gregor into the marble foyer of the mansion, she felt like a shrunken Alice in Wonderland. Opening royally before her dazzled eyes was a grand salon. It was lit by immense iron candelabras standing along polished paneled walls, and by chandeliers of scintillating crystals on massive bronze links hanging from a ceiling so high it was lost in shadow.

Above the paneled wainscotting, the walls were of rampart-hewn blocks bearing regal tapestries. Their subjects echoed Judith's imagination, with scenes of medieval jousting, walled cities, conflagrations and battles, as well as idyllic interludes of shepherds and shepherdesses dallying in flowered glades. Impressive stained glass windows added to the magnificence of the vaulting chamber. Judith could imagine how sunlight must turn the glass colors to jewels on the Aubusson carpets, like sparkling pools of precious wine that never stained.

At the front of the Salon stood a throne, raised on three tiers of black marble steps. Judith's eyes rounded with surprise and wonder. She had never seen such extravagance, at the same time edged with an undertone of something somber she could not place. The elaborate seat seemed made of real gold. An aeruginous velvet screen stood behind, and there was a kermetic canopy above, on which opalescent reptiles formed a fringe of ophidian eyes. Perhaps it was the reptiles that struck the umbrageous note she felt, Judith mused. Screens to the side were of richly embroidered orphreys, gold-and-crimson on cerulean blue, with a thalo-green-silver braiding that looked like live snakes. Cabalistic designs were everywhere with, ubiquitously, the sundial's mark, . The still-mysterious symbol caught and held Judith's eye. *There it was again*—all over the estate, as Rick had said. Yet whenever she asked about it, she received no response or an evasive answer. She wondered again what meaning it masked. It seemed to cast an ill-omened shadow over the occasion, though the evening was an auspicious event—the actual start of the picture-making.

Judith reined in her speculation. Perhaps, she appraised, her quick uneasiness came from the corps of masked retainers moving ceremoniously around the throne, like a royal guard protecting the small figure seated above them in incredible splendor. Dr. Gomay was no Merlin now! Rather he was a Sultan out of Topkapi Palace—nothing less than a Margrave, a Satrap, a Nabob literally out of the pages of her romance novels of the East, richly-clad, gold-crowned.

Waiting for the company to be seated, Dr. Felix Gomay was surveying the gathering like an undisputed overlord, his manner majestic and imperial.

Judith wanted to esteem this magnate who was the benefactor of the company, but the potency he gave off had jagged vibrations for her. In her eyes, the tableau was like one of the early Renaissance portraits in which half-visible figures can be discerned hovering above the central subject. Sometimes the dim images are angels bearing blessings. Sometimes they are mercurial fiends and succubi, inviting temptation and damnation. Judith could not tell whether her imagination was conjuring angels or demons around the gleaming head of Dr. Felix Gomay.

She was off balance again, and on guard against a yellow spume. Dr. Willoughby had warned she must never relax her vigilance. With wind and thunder buffeting the manor windows outside she was glad she was sitting with Rick on her left and Lena on her right.

Nearby, Emily gave her a friendly wink. Other eyes on her seemed envious. She supposed it was because she, a newcomer to the company, was now so plainly Rick's clearly chosen favorite.

Her observation was cut off by Werner Christed's entrance. The director paced directly to the front of the throne. In striking contrast to Dr. Gomay's elaborate, embroidered robes, the director wore a plain white woolen sweater and blue jeans. He looked like any member of the film troupe, but even standing there waiting for silence his authority was clear. Not even the splendor of the Gomay pomp and extravagance could diminish the impact of the Christed personality. Tonight, very plainly, the granite of his purpose and determination showed in his expressive face.

The whispering in the hall sputtered and died away.

The director began, "We have all been waiting for this important moment. Before the reading of the script of *Baron of Darkness*, I want to thank Dr. Gomay on behalf of Werner Christed Productions and all of us here. We are fortunate. Dr. Gomay understands how I want to make this film, and his story has a signal message for our time, as you will see when you hear it out. And I urge you to hear it to the end without premature judgment, because this is not an ordinary script!

"Also, most of you know that even after you hear the outline tonight, you will not get all the details of the story until just before we shoot your particular scenes. In that way we will keep the freedom of reaction I want from each of you in your various parts."

A murmur of professional assent went around the room. Anyone, new or old, who did not know the director's distinctive cinema methods should not be present. Judith joined in with a sense of new, earned rapport. Before the camera that afternoon she had genuinely known the unrestraint Christed was seeking. Everything she had learned in school dramatics and summer theatre fell away—the false poses, the remnants of elocution. Despite her nervousness and trepidation, it had been a beautiful experience, as the unanimous response of the company to Werner Christed was inspiring to her now.

The director turned to the old man waiting on the throne with a script in his gnarled hands. "And we thank you, Dr. Gomay, for your hospitality on your island."

The company's grateful applause was matched by an enormous clap of thunder. It led the director to add a line that brought a laugh around the Salon. "The only thing Dr. Gomay cannot control is the weather—but that only proves there are powers greater than all of us—which our film will help the world remember! Now here is Dr. Gomay and *Baron of Darkness* . . ."

The audience rose spontaneously, applauding their host on Gomay Island. Judith clapped along with a full heart. She could understand their enthusiasm. It wasn't just the movie project, it was the comforts and the good time they were enjoying. Even though these men and women worked steadily with Christed in the Film Loft, they lived Spartanly for the most part. For many of them Gomay Island was Eden, with its gardens, sports, plentiful good food, and servants to cater to their needs. Suddenly the Gomays themselves were no longer ominous-looking to Judith.

The servants had risen with the company and, though they were not applauding, there seemed for the first time to be common bond between the groups. Live and let live, Judith thought. In the making of the film it was for the Gomays to do their job, the actors theirs, as Rick had said. And no more questions such as why Rick went to the servants' buildings when no one was permitted there! Judith was suddenly aglow with only good feelings and genuine anticipation as the audience settled down. The rustling ceased.

Staring expectantly at Dr. Gomay, Judith was once again surprised by the discrepancy between the ancient's skull-face and his commanding voice. Its power was different from Werner Christed's. Christed spoke as a leader, a man in charge. Dr. Gomay spoke in the tones of a priest or prophet. It might be the echoes in the vaulting chamber, but to Judith the voice from the throne sounded sepulchral, like some ancient shaman chanting. Dr. Gomay recited his words with the passion of fanatical commitment and Judith, like the others, was caught up in the hypnotic cadence of his introduction:

"Some years ago in my travels to remote places in Europe, I came upon an extraordinary account of an extraordinary man. His name was Baron Gilles de Rais." Dr. Gomay glared challenging around the room as if daring anyone to interrupt or doubt him. "At first I considered Gilles de Rais nothing but a creature of legend, a creation of superstitious folks, and no more true than the myths of witches, demons, and vampires, which have come from that same part of Europe.

"But as I studied the baron's story, I became convinced that this man had lived. A monstrous and astonishing life! Monstrous because of the evil and atrocious deeds he committed—deeds ignoble beyond imagination. And most astonishing because the baron's life, in the end, proved to constitute a most magnificent morality play! This is what Werner Christed referred to when he urged you to withhold your reaction until the end.

"Under Werner Christed's inspired direction, I can promise you a motion picture to stagger the imagination. Some critics will undoubtedly accuse us of pandering to violence and sex, but as you now hear the account of Baron Gilles de Rais you will see why I indeed truly view this movie as a morality play."

Judith felt some uneasiness again. Dr. Gomay's insect eyes were flashing about the room, and his words rolled on his lips almost coarsely. But Rick and Lena were leaning forward as raptly as the rest of the company, and Judith told herself she had no reason for misgivings. She had never expected that Werner Christed would be filming a Walt Disney sugar-candy scenario.

"To start, then, let me present basic documentation, since many of you will surely doubt that the events I am about to recount could actually have taken place." Dr. Gomay gestured toward the ornate, gilded library cases standing along one wall, and Judith stared at them as she listened. "First I refer you to a biography of Baron Gilles de Rais by a priest named Bossard. Also, the baron is described in de Viriville's chronicle of Charles VII. And you can check for yourself the record of the baron's trial at Nantes, as well as a petition made by the baron's heirs to the then King of France. For those of you who cannot read French, I refer you to the *Encyclopaedia Britannica*." The old man paused and stared out again as if to say that any skeptics should be more than satisfied. He would be telling the truth, the whole truth, and nothing but the truth, no matter how incredible it might seem!

The room was totally silent. Outside, the thunder was a rolling, insistent rumbling, as if the movie already had an eerie background score. It continued as Dr. Gomay resumed.

"This history is necessary because you will find it hard to believe that any human being could commit the atrocities ascribed to Gilles de Rais. The more so because as a young man he was associated with none other than the pure and saintly Maid of Orleans, Joan of Arc! Yes, for a time, the baron was the Maid's good right arm.

"This young baron placed his enormous wealth and talents in the service of king, country, and God. But the line between spirituality and occultism is thin. It has been well said that if you believe in saints, angels, and heaven, you then *must* believe in devils, fiends, and hell."

Dr. Gomay's beetling eyes dared anyone to argue his point. There was only the breathing of the fascinated troupe.

"No one knows just when or how the baron's evil transformation occurred, but somehow the handsome, cultivated nobleman became one of the most savage and merciless villains in all history. My script traverses all of the baron's debauchery. We will film all the ungodly rituals of ravishment and debasement performed by Baron Gilles de Rais in the dungeon of the remote chateau to which he retired from the French court.

"You will see that there was no outrage or abomination this abandoned man did not commit." Dr. Gomay bared his gums in a crooked smile. "You might say the baron was scrupulously wicked!"

There were a few obliging titters that faded quickly.

"Obviously, this is not a 'family picture' we will be making. Werner Christed and I wish it to be an accurate document of a true and horrible episòde in history from which the world may learn the horror of unbridled license."

Dr. Gomay lifted a book. "Despite my introduction, you will still find it difficult to credit the hellishness of Baron Gilles de Rais. Some of you may even secretly believe my own imagination is inflamed by some mental illness that conjures up this story." The old man lifted the book high and slapped it with his other hand, declaring, "No! I shall read to you from the book called *Down There* by the famous French author J. K. Huysmans, who spent years studying and researching the life of the man we will be filming."

Judith was relieved. Apparently, the baron *was* an historical figure and, although he was villainous rather than heroic, the prospect of hearing a new medieval tale intrigued her. Dr. Gomay began to read:

"At first there are no women in the baron's chateau. It seems that dislike for the feminine form came over him. He comes to be disgusted by the delicacy of the skin of women and by the odour of femininity which all sodomists abhor.

"He depraves the choir boys who are under his authority, but soon infantile pollution seems to him an insipid delicacy. The litanies of lust arise like the wind over a slaughterhouse. His first victim is a very small boy whose name we do not

know. Gilles disembowels him, cuts off his hands, tears out his eyes and heart, and preserves the blood of this child to write formulas of evocation and conjurements to Satan."

Dr. Gomay looked up. "I remind you that J. K. Huysmans, the distinguished scholar, has written this, not me!" He continued reading:

"From 1432 to 1440, the inhabitants of Anjou, Poitu, and Brittany walk the highways wringing their hands—for all the children disappear. Shepherd boys are abducted from the fields. Little girls coming out of school, little boys who have gone to play ball, return no more. Wherever the bloodthirsty Gilles dwells the women weep.

"At first the frantic people tell themselves that evil fairies are dispersing the generation, but little by little terrible suspicions are aroused. As soon as the baron traverses a countryside children are missing. He sends an old woman to accost children. Her speech is so seductive, her face so benign when she lifts her black veil, that all follow her to the edge of the wood, where the baron's men carry them off, gagged in sacks. Gilles himself takes to standing at a window of his chateau—"

Dr. Gomay interrupted his reading to say, with a wide gesture of his hand, "Which was much like my own chateau here . . ."

"When young mendicants come to ask alms, he has any who excite his lust brought in to him and thrown into an underground prison until, being in appetite, he is pleased to order a carnal supper.

"How many children did Gilles de Rais disembowel after deflowering them? The texts of the times enumerate between seven and eight hundred."

Judith could not help shivering. The word *monster* was taking on a new and more loathsome meaning with every quotation Dr. Gomay recited.

"At dusk, when their senses are enkindled by inflammatory spiced beverages and herbs, Gilles and his friends retire to a distant chamber of the chateau. The little boys are brought from their cellar prisons, disrobed, and gagged. The baron fondles them and forces them. Then he hacks them to pieces with a dagger, taking great pleasure in slowly dismembering them."

Judith tasted disgust in her mouth as she noted the relish with which Dr. Gomay read the passage. She plainly heard the quickening of his breath. It seemed to her that he was experiencing a form of carnal pleasure himself.

"At other times the baron slashes the boy's chest and drinks the breath from the lungs. Sometimes he opens the stomach also, smells it, enlarges the incision with his hands, and seats himself in it. Then while he macerates the warm entrails he contemplates the child's supreme convulsions, the last spasms. He says afterwards, 'I was happier in the enjoyment of torture, tears, fright, and blood, than in any other pleasure.'"

Judith glanced at Rick. Was she the only one whose stomach was twitching with revulsion? Rick's face was impassive. Judith turned to Lena. Surely she would be upset by the horrible tale and Dr. Gomay's salivating lingering on the gory details. But Lena was edged forward on her seat, taking the story in with her own quickened breath. Her eyes were coppery with what seemed lurid absorption. Judith's mind flashed to the gory incident with the sacrificed rabbit. Without doubt there was cruelty in Lena as well as kindness, salaciousness as well as motherliness. How complicated people were!

Dr. Gomay's expression, becoming more inflamed

with each incident, gripped Judith's attention despite herself. In a moment of both magnetism and abhorrence, she thought that the old man's voice was what a hissing serpent would sound like if snakes could speak. Was this nightmarish recital, holding this large audience in a spreading trance in the great room—was this, Judith asked herself, a kind of dark parallel to the Bible's reciting the fall of man when the serpent pressed the apple on Eve? For a moment, Judith fancied that Dr. Gomay's head had become a serpent's—his eyes tiny beads of reptilian fire, his teeth enlarged to fangs, his tongue into forked flickering needles. *Hold on!* Judith warned herself. Don't invite Angel Dust tonight. Dr. Gomay is unsettling enough!

Judith forced herself to take a deep breath, square her shoulders, and sit back firmly. It is only a story, she repeated to herself emphatically. It might be historically true, yes, but it was long, long ago—in the 1400's, hadn't Dr. Gomay said?—all over long, long ago!—and if they were making a film of it, that would only be make-believe, nothing to be so uptight about. She should be like Emily, sitting in the row in front of her, with a bemused smile on her lips, taking in Dr. Gomay's reading as if she were watching a television horror show at home.

Dr. Gomay was repeating, again with obvious, unconcealed savor: "I was happier in the enjoyment of tortures, tears, fright, and blood, than in any other pleasure."

Then he continued from the book.

"The baron becomes weary of these fecal joys. He heated himself with little boys, sometimes also with little girls, with whom he had congress in the belly . . ."

Dr. Gomay looked up, giving time for that image to

sink in.

"*. . . saying he had more pleasure and less pain than acting naturally. After which he slowly saws the throats of the children, cuts them to pieces, and the corpses, the linen and the clothing, are put in the fireplace, and the ashes are thrown into the latrine.*"

Judith sagged, pressing both hands to her middle. She would have to get out of here or be sick, she thought desperately. But Rick's hand reached for hers and pressed it firmly, helping her regain some composure.

"*Soon the baron wearies of stuperating palpitant flesh and becomes a lover of the dead. He establishes sepulchral beauty contests, and whichever of the truncated heads receives the prize he raises by the hair and passionately kisses the cold lips.*"

Judith found herself watching Werner Christed—both as a way of steadying herself, and in wonder as to his reactions. Beauty contests of corpses! That could be the purpose of the mannequin she had seen fall from the coffin. And what a field day Werner Christed would be having with his illusion machine, recreating these macabre doings. Yet, what a dismal use of his genius, Judith could not help but muse. What a weird cacophony of brutality they were going to picture.

Judith looked away from Christed to the rest of the company. She saw repugnance and frowns on many of the faces. That eased her a little. At least she wasn't the only one being turned off by the ugliness of Baron Gilles de Rais, the unholy bastard! Still, she counseled herself, she ought to be keeping an open mind, as both the director and script writer had asked. The story wasn't over. She sat back to listen again, her hands clasped white-knuckled in her lap unconsciously as when she had first sat nervously in school.

"Vampirism satisfied Gilles for some months. He even goes so far—one day when his supply of children happens to be exhausted—as to disembowel a pregnant woman and sport with the foetus . . ."

Oh, come on! Judith protested silently. No man, no matter how bestial, could commit a miserable act like that!

As if anticipating this reaction among his audience, Dr. Gomay raised a hand and looked out at the assemblage. "I know this is getting more and more incredible, and I am sorry to tell you that even worse is to come. But," he added quickly as if to brook no argument, "we must remember that we are dealing with not just a sex pervert, but a delirious sadist, an exquisite virtuouso in pain and murder. To quote Huysmans' final judgment of Gilles de Rais—'the Marquis de Sade is only a timid, mediocre fantasist beside him!' Along that line, consider this next amusement of the baron—which Werner Christed will also be filming as only he can do."

"One unfortunate child is brought into the baron's chamber and hanged up to a hook affixed into the wall. Just at the moment when the child is suffocating, Gilles orders him taken down. He revives him, taking the child on his knees, caresses him, rocks him gently, dries his tears, and pointing to his accomplices, says, 'These men are bad, but you see they obey me. Do not be afraid. I will save your life and take you back to your mother.' Then, while the little one, wild with joy, kisses him, Gilles gently makes an incision in the back of the neck and, when the head, not quite detached, bows, Gilles turns the body about and violates it, bellowing with pleasure."

Now Judith felt bile rise uncontrollably in her throat. She bent over, retching, and only Rick's quick, consoling hand on her head helped her bring control. Whatever the truth, Judith moaned to herself, how could a man like Werner Christed lend himself to film such inhumanity? She tried to get up, but Rick on one side and Lena on the other pressed her to her seat. "You have to hear the whole story!" Rick whispered hotly in her ear. Judith wished the two would free her hands; she would have slapped them over her ears to silence what had now become a menace as if Dr. Gomay's voice were a heavy, endless blanket unrolling from the throne to cover and suffocate her. It was going on relentlessly with Baron Gilles de Rais' awful biography:

"Plunging into new debauches, Gilles invents yet new deliriums of sick passion. He hurls himself upon a new child, gouges out his eyes, runs his finger around the bloody, milky socket, then he seizes a spiked club and crushes the skull. And while the gurgling blood runs over him, he stands, smeared with spattered brains, and grinds his teeth and laughs."

How could Rick, her kind and gentle and good-humored Rick, possibly play a part like that? Judith found herself agonizing. No wonder they were calling the picture *Baron of Darkness!* Baron of *Hell!* It was beyond comprehension, all of it, beyond not just belief but beyond imagination. She did not doubt that the Baron Gilles de Rais had lived, as Dr. Gomay swore. No one could make up such horrors. But if there had been such a beast, if such a pitiless, merciless savage had walked the earth, why not leave him buried where he had, thankfully, some day died? Why unearth his malevolent story now, why open his grave for the abominable stench of his perversions to poison the air? Why, indeed, give his execrable ideas to the all-too-sick degenerates stalking the streets of modern, not medieval, cities? She recalled, vividly, the news stories of girls who butchered innocent victims in cold blood. When the actress Sharon Tate, who was pregnant, pleaded with her attacker to save the baby, the girl answered icily, "I was not programmed that way!" Was that girl much different from the demon baron of the Middle Ages? And what about the unspeakable barbarisms of an entire nation gone insane in modern times—Hitler's Germany?

Judith became aware of silence in the room. Dr. Gomay had halted. People were absorbing the horrible biography, each in his own way. Most faces now were blank, as if the tale of Baron Gilles de Rais had penetrated to their most secret thoughts, and what they felt was private, not to be reflected in their expressions. Judith was numbed in the same way, glad only that the venalities seemed to be over. She heard only her own question echoing in her own ear: Why make a film like this at all?

It was as if Dr. Gomay knew the question was inevitable for all of them; he resumed by stating the very proposition: "Now I am sure you wish to know—and you have a right to know—why Werner Christed and I are so enthusiastic about making this film. Let me say at once that I agree that it should not be made!" The old man held his hand up in a dramatic pause. "Not if it were *only* about violence, bestiality, abominations, profanation and blasphemy. In that case I would rip up these pages this instant, indeed would never have taken my pen to them.

"But there exists a reason, an extremely vital reason, why *Baron of Darkness* should have been written, and should be filmed by you. That reason lies in the biography of the baron himself. The fact is that the life of Baron Gilles de Rais took a major and redeeming twist at the end! Difficult as it is to credit, all the documents agree that, at the very height of his dehumanizing debauches, the baron came to repent of his sins and prayed to God for forgiveness!

"The records of his criminal trial tell of the man's new and genuine dedication to God. They report that his renunciation of evil was so truly heartfelt that, believe it or not, he moved to tears even the mothers and fathers of the children he had ravaged, despoiled, and slaughtered!

"At his trial, Gilles de Rais asked for no forgiveness. Instead of clemency, he begged only for a chance to atone for his sins by making such amends as he could. It is in this transformation—and in the compassion with which his victims responded—that we find the lessons which make this a signal film, more than worthy to be made and seen around the world.

"For *Baron of Darkness*, taken in its whole, illuminates the worst *and* the best of the human spirit! That, to me, is the function of art. Tolstoy said it of literature, I say it of film. Werner Christed lives by that artistic creed, I know. Of all cinema directors, he is the one to undertake this challenge. Here his pathfinding and innovations have unlimited room to flourish.

"Now I hope this project excites all of you as much as it does Werner Christed and me. We have spent a long and arduous time reaching this point." With a sweeping ceremonious gesture Dr. Gomay rose and delivered a manuscript to the director. "Now I deliver the completed scenario of Baron Gilles de Rais to Werner Christed and—" he turned to the audience with a deep bow "—to all of you, with the greatest confidence that you will bring this morality play to life for the edification of people everywhere."

As the director took the script from the thin old hands

trembling with passion, the seated company started to applaud again. The hand-clapping was uncertain, only dutiful, at first. Dr. Gomay's scenario was a powerful dose for even this ultra-sophisticated group. But his final words and his adjuration had apparently reached them, Judith saw. The applause mounted and became enthusiastic. She herself still felt sick and dizzy. The climax of the baron's repentance had moved her, but she was repelled by the unmitigated ugliness and brutality of what went before.

The director was speaking, addressing Dr. Gomay. "Felix, your story is truly powerful, the more so for being true fact. It has a most crucial message for our times. I am proud and, as you say, challenged, to have this chance to make so provocative a film!"

From anyone else, the words would have sounded declamatory and hyperbolic. From Werner Christed's square-jawed face, they came through the Grand Salon as a solemn pledge. Judith felt chills up her spine, and her response to Christed confused her even more. Something within her wanted her to have no part in this picture, yet she wanted more than anything else to work with this man.

The director waved to the departing audience. "Rest well, everyone." He laughed with an enthusiasm that was like a shot from a race starter's pistol: "You aren't going to get much sleep beginning tomorrow!"

Moving toward the door with Rick and Lena among the chattering crowd, Judith saw Gregor. He was beaming at the rear of the room. He brought to mind the hearse, the prop room at the Film Loft with its coffins, rats, bats, vipers, and loathsome things of every odious description! She understood now why the film required them!

It would not require her! Judith determined abruptly. It was simply not her cup of tea, not the ballgame she thought she would be playing in. No matter what the picture's ending, the scenario was poisonous and noxious and not for her.

Judith looked around the room again. All she saw were high-spirited people, afire with new stimulation and fascination. Maybe she was only a country bumpkin after all. But she had to be true to her own reactions. Judith knew what she would be leaving behind—not only a lifetime opportunity to work with Werner Christed, but Rick Gilbert, the handsome young man beside her. Well, Rick could keep in touch somehow if they really meant something to each other, and if they didn't it wouldn't matter.

But Rick, Lena, Gregor, and even Emily scoffed at Judith's misgivings when she expressed them over coffee back in the recreation hall. Emily wondered what Judith was being so finicky about—weren't today's Hollywood movies buckets of sex, blood, and gore, she asked—with people lined up around the block to press in? Rick added that the baron's violence had little on modern television. Gregor interjected—hadn't Judith heard of the smash-hit Japanese film in which the heroine cuts off the hero's sex as final proof of their superhuman love. That film had the woman running down the street showing her lover's organ publicly! Lena added, "And what about a cult like Jim Jones' Peoples' Temple and the 900 suicides in Guyana?"

Judith almost wept in inner bafflement and frustration. The filth already in the world didn't justify more filth! she argued hotly.

Rick sided against her. *Baron of Darkness* was not

sensational or pandering, Rick insisted strongly. As Dr. Gomay had emphasized, it was a *moral* story in its total impact, and that is what mattered. In fact, Rick pressed, *Baron* actually contained more redeeming features than most of the junk violence they saw every day.

Their caring for her, and their arguments, began to reach Judith. In all honesty she had to ask herself why she alone in the room full of bright, chattering people seemed to have such powerful reservations. She wasn't some frail damsel out of another century, she knew that what her friends were saying was the truth. Maybe subconsciously she was overreacting because of her own blood-deep fears going back to recurring childhood nightmares about the Devil visiting her. Of this, she had not spoken to either Lena or Rick. It was something she wanted to bury even deeper than the drug trips, keep out of conscious memory, entirely. She shuddered. It was unhappily true that this night had stirred up the too-vivid memories of her dreams of Satan smashing through her window. In her mind's eye now, she could see the frightening demon coming implacably toward her child's bed, setting the room ablaze with his heat and lust—as Baron Gilles de Rais had done with the children he attacked!

It was Rick who brought Judith back from her lacerating remembrance. "If there is any ugliness in this project," he whispered to her, "it would be in your leaving us! Come outside with me, I want to talk to you . . ."

The storm had abated. They walked a long while, and halted finally before Judith's door. When Rick reached for her gently, Judith did not pull away. She allowed him a prolonged, passionate kiss, giving up her uncertainty. If

Rick and Werner and the others all felt *Baron of Darkness* was worthwhile, she was going to accept it! Rick's firm arms around her were what counted, his warm lips were what counted, not her childhood nightmares.

Yet, as she went slowly inside her door beside the Manor House tower, Judith Bradford had to wonder why she felt so bleakly cold on a steaming summer night.

CHAPTER TEN

Judith could not get to sleep. She was keyed up at the prospect of the decisive test to be shot in the morning. Once Rick had persuaded her to stay, the old ambition to work with Werner Christed surged in her. She checked her watch. A few moments to midnight. She would look the pits in the morning, she scolded herself.

The room was stuffy. Judith trudged from her bed to open the window. An easing wind was chasing the clouds, and the moon gleamed fitfully in the sky. Tomorrow would be clear, Judith predicted. Clear in every way. She would give Christed the audition he wanted, leave no doubt. Ah, wouldn't her mother be surprised to learn that she had run away not to disaster but to a career, and maybe even marriage to a wonderful, handsome man beyond all her dreams!

Like a muffled drum, Judith heard receding thunder, a pale echo of the earlier storm. The sense of the community around her in repose in the now-quiet night was like a soft cover of comfort to the girl.

It was then, through her open window, that she heard the lamenting. It was so faint she would not have discerned it if the breeze had been in any other direction. Her first reaction was self-doubt—she told herself that the night's disturbance might be bringing the feared drug attack. But the sound was pronounced. It was plainly a woman's voice. It was just as plainly coming from the tower. There was no denying it. Judith almost wished for the yellow signal of her sorry delusions. This reality was too heart-stopping, especially after the unsettling session she had gone through in Dr. Gomay's reading of *Baron of Darkness.*

"Help me," came piteously on the air. "Somebody please help me . . ."

Judith clung to the window. Should she disregard the repeated warnings she had received about the tower, and essay the gloomy passage outside to seek the source of the pleading voice? Who might it be? Why was the woman calling for help? Why had everyone lied to her about the tower being empty when, so clearly, someone was in there?

The voice faded as Judith stood irresolute at her window, then it rose to another entreaty. "Sick. So sick.

He-elp me, please."

Judith rubbed the back of her neck agitatedly. The woman might be dying. She was sure the feeble supplication could not be heard by anyone else. Lena's apartment was too far away, along with the director's and Dr. Gomay's. The servants were secure in their own buildings.

Grimly Judith screwed up her courage and went to her closet. Upset as she was, she still could not help a small smile as she drew on her old familiar robe. In her haste to pack back in Iowa, she had grabbed an old wrapper, a whimsical Easter gift from her mother, decorated childishly with chicks and bunny rabbits. Here on Gomay Island in the shadows of the unknown in the tower, the garment was doubly incongruous. But it was all she could slip into quickly enough, and she was grateful for its soft enfolding. She needed comfort.

Judith's smile faded when she opened a drawer for the flashlight she had seen there. Of course!—Gregor had taken that. But there was the candle, in reserve. She lit the wick carefully, away from the draft of her still-open window, and stepped into the corridor leading to the spiral staircase.

The new bulb in the hall was shining reassuringly, but Judith hesitated again. She could hear nothing now, though she listened intently. All her nerves were throbbing, tugging her to return to her door. But just *because* she had been lied to, Judith was determined now to learn the truth of the tower for herself.

Judith moved gingerly down the corridor toward the dark arch. The hall light became dimmer behind her as she went. She approached the spiral steps with a dry mouth and heaving chest. At the bottom she stopped, took a deep breath of resolution, and stepped cautiously into the deep shadow of the narrow stairwell going up into—what?

In reading her books, this had been a moment of bated breath and a delicious thrill. But now she was not safe in a hushed library or in a warm bed in the protective house of her childhood. This Urwolde reality was anything but thrilling; it was terrifying and direful with all-too-genuine suspense. Above Judith all was darkness. The blackness yielded only fitfully and grudgingly to her flickering candle. As she took wary step after wary step upward, the little light revealed repulsive cobwebs and skittering insects on damp walls spotted with a green growth. The stairwell gave off a musty smell of dankness, an unpleasant tomb-like odor. It reminded Judith of her first impression of Gregor.

In this region of gloom, Judith's blood pumped colder in her veins. She felt there was a presence above her, indefinable but sinister. It might become manifest any moment. Suddenly the girl knew the meaning of the much-used phrase—her scalp was literally prickling.

Judith hesitated once more. She told herself she was being foolhardy, ought to be back in her room getting her needed rest. Resolutely, she moved down, when the beseeching voice reached for her again. This time it required no wind to bring the sound to her ears. The moaning issued directly from nearby, just up the stone steps. Judith could not withstand the plea. She was responding not just to aid someone needing help, but also because anger spurted in her chest. The flashing signals, the weeping sounds were not her fantasies! Did Gregor and the others think she was a stupid fool that they could lie to her so baldly and outrageously? Perhaps Rick did not know about the tower, but surely Gregor and Dr. Gomay did! *If they were ready to lie about the tower being empty, what else might they be lying to her about?* She might find many answers to Gomay Island's smoldering questions just above these steps.

Judith's new resolve overcame the anxiety that had weighted her feet. Lifting her candle as vigilantly as she could, she mounted another curving flight. The stairs seemed to narrow now, and as Judith looked upward she caught her breath. Had she seen a moving figure, or was it only her agitation? Her candle flame tossed about frighteningly, came perilously close to going out. Was someone breathing down on it purposely, to take her by surprise in the dark?

Judith held motionless, listening keenly. By some instinct, she put her ear to the stone wall. Although it was cold and disgustingly clammy, she kept her face close. Yes! She heard what seemed a soft quick shuffle, as of slippered feet. Then there was a small sliding sound, as if someone were hugging the wall above her. She concentrated all her attention into her ear. Only silence now. She held her own breath to see if she could hear the breathing of another. There was nothing. She waited again. Still nothing. She had to breathe. If someone was waiting on the stairs, there should be some sound. But there was still nothing. It must have been her imagination.

Judith told herself staunchly there was nothing frightening here but her own feverish and bookish recollections. No demon was going to materialize out of the night. She was in a modern world, not lost in the make-believe pages of mournful dungeons and hair-breadth subterranean escapes from vassals of evil. Here, at this moment, the sky over the Manor House held not flying fiends but passenger jets heading for Kennedy Airport. Here, ordinary people like Lena Ludovici slept just across the building, and the actors and crew of Werner Christed's film company rested in the dormitory across Urwolde Common.

But in the tower, she was alone, where she had been warned not to go, and the silence now seemed like a looming physical shape, blacker than the darkness just beyond the small circle of her candle's tiny fire. Judith felt as if a heavy shroud were winding around her body. She stopped, unable to move further. The air became heavier. She started to gasp for breath. It came to her that she was being buried alive, that the staircase was being sealed below, and she would be entombed in this stifling passage forever. She became surer that she was having a seizure, that it was all in her mind after all. The candle trembled and nearly fell from her twitching hand. She retrieved it just in time or she would have been lost in total blackness.

Uninvited, a Latin verse came into her mind. She had memorized it once, at the time when she was fascinated with everything occult. She could not recall the author—Virgil, Ovid, Livy?—but the lines tolled all too clearly behind her eyes as she stood in Dr. Gomay's forbidden tower.

Somnia, terrores magicos, miracula, sagas,
Nocturnos lemures portentque . . .

"Dream figments, terrors of magic, spells of mighty power,/All the witches and ghosts who crowd the darkling night . . ."

That classroom was a million miles, another lifetime away. In this forsaken tower on Gomay Island the lines were no ancient poem of horror, but a real evocation of a spectral night strangling her.

No more! Judith berated herself. She had come far enough. Whatever hovered above was not her concern or problem.

Determined, Judith turned and started down the stairs. She wanted no part of whatever shade had sought her out.

Until the tremulous voice called again. "Ple-ease help me-ee!"

Judith's feet, her will, were not Judith's own. She whirled, placed a foot on another tread upward, and shifted her weight. And waited. And silence. Another step the same cautious, deliberate way, and silence still. There could not be anyone waiting on the stairs. With gathering confidence, Judith raised her candle again. She could barely see beyond another turn in the steepening steps, but there seemed to be a landing, and a glimpse of a planked door. *And the muffled wail again, closer—certainly from behind that door!*

Judith stepped up quickly now, only to stumble in abrupt, closing darkness as her light was blown out. With dismay, Judith knew at once she had not conjured up a hovering, lurking figure. Its breath was cold as it blew past her head at the candle. Long arms were reaching for her throat out of the pitch blackness. Judith realized it was a Gomay attacking—she felt the long robe and the mask on the head as she flailed madly back in the blackness.

But if her attacker was invisible, so was Judith. Although it felt as if she were grappling with a many-tentacled octopus, Judith managed to slide and elude her heavily breathing assailant. She began to strike back with furious punches in an attack of her own, knowing in her heart that it was life or death. This Gomay's grunts told her that she—*it was a woman, Judith realized with a start*—was trying to throw her down the stairs to break her neck. Oh, how convenient that would be to the liars! They could say she had been warned that the tower was dangerous, yet had trespassed, and fallen to her death in a terrible accident. Her grave would be dug next to the first dead actress! There would be nothing but the same spare wooden marker. Her mother would never know what had happened to her. She would go into eternity a ghost forever. No, she would not let herself end this way! Certainly not when she was just at the beginning of a new life with Rick, with Christed! The thoughts gave Judith added strength. Though the stairwell was so narrow that she scraped her skin bloody as she punched wildly into the darkness, Judith heard her adversary gulp with pain as blow after blow found some mark. Remembering how she had tried to knee the garageman outside the Film Loft, Judith tried to aim for the woman's breasts. They were a female's most sensitive area. If she could force the Gomay to stop for even a moment, she might win time to flee, to rush down for help, find Rick or Lena to return with her to solve the mystery behind the locked door. Even in the turmoil of her struggle, Judith realized that the Gomay was a guard, planted to keep any intruder from the tower room and its secret.

Pummeling at the Gomay's chest, Judith felt the woman's arms drop down to protect her breasts. It gave Judith a chance to grab at the Gomay's head, seeking to thumb her attacker's eyes. With a yelp of satisfaction,

Judith caught the top of the woman's mask in her grip. She yanked with all her might, exultantly looking to see what a Gomay's face looked like unhidden. But of course she could see nothing in the total dark.

The Gomay cried out in sharp consternation, letting Judith go, reaching wildly for the face cover. It gave Judith the opportunity she hoped for. Flinging the mask down the stairwell, she leaped after it to get away. But the first, coiled spiral of the steps pitched her off balance and she tumbled, just managing to avoid rolling down the rest of the stairs to certain death. Pounding footsteps came down after her, and Judith was sure the Gomay would be upon her in an instant. She could almost feel talon fingers around her neck, gripping and choking. But her opponent hurtled past without a stop. Apparently, its most important mission was to recapture its mask.

Judith got up shakily. Below her she heard the outer door slam. The Gomay was gone!

Judith leaned against the wall to catch her breath, only to be brought up straight by the weeping voice from the landing. "In God's name, please help me!"

It should be safe now, Judith panted to herself. She had come too far to turn back. Surely they hadn't set *two* Gomays at guard duty. Her shadowy antagonist might return with others, but there was surely time to open the unexplained door and help the woman inside, obviously being held prisoner against her will.

Without more thought, Judith hurried back up the stairs. A crack of light appeared, coming from the door she had marked before. She saw that she was on a small landing. She could make out a chair, where the Gomay guard must have sat. In the dim illumination, Judith also made out a heavy iron hasp and wooden beam that fastened the door from the outside. As she tugged at the lock, it made a rasping noise. If there had been any lingering question in Judith's mind about hallucination, it was banished at once. There was no doubt about the wild pounding that exploded in the locked room. The voice was a shriek of mad desperation, "Let me *out!*"

When Judith finally swung the door open she could not believe the scene that struck her eyes.

Although the chamber was high up in the tower, it looked like a dungeon. In the single, glaring bulb on a hanging wire, Judith made out a circular, low-ceilinged space. There was one window, facing the Common. On it, a wooden shutter had been nailed. The place was scarcely furnished. A spare table and chair stood near the window. There was a ramshackle bed against the rough stone wall near a door which, ajar, showed a shadowy bathroom within.

Judith saw large lipsticked scrawling on one wall: "All Thieving Whores Off My Island!"

Trays of food lay smashed along one wall, obviously flung in a fury. The room was fetid with the smell of garbage. At Judith's entrance, rats skittered squeaking from the rotting feast on the floor. No props, these rodents!

Lying in a dismal heap in the center of the horrid chamber was a figure that glared and hissed at Judith. Hidden as it was beneath a spreading black robe, Judith could hardly make out whether the creature was human or animal.

Then she saw a woman's visage. It was less a face than a mask of grief and loathing. The skin was painted stark white, a vitreous sculpture of madness. The lips were streaks of jet black. The haggard apparition was no vision of the night, but rather an animated corpse. It curdled Judith's blood. The fierce eyes seemed to shoot rays of death through the air.

The woman threw off her robe with a sudden sacrificial motion. It exposed a thin, hardly-female body, spread-eagled on the cold stone as if held by invisible wristlocks. Everything about the sight was grotesque. The woman's hair, cut close as a man's, was an impossible bright green color. Her body was nude beneath a transparent veil of golden mesh. Silver sequins covered tiny nipples of small, high breasts. The eyes were obsidian, snake-like, and funkily outlined in orange with frank sexuality. The eyebrows had been shaved away completely, giving the narrow countenance even more the appearance of a reptilian skull.

The bizarre creature sported exquisite jewelry and ornaments. From a necklace of alabaster hung an ivory-carved skull. A diamond-studded chatelaine clasped the narrow waist. Bracelets of every sort, with rubies and emeralds, covered the bony arms from wrist to elbow. On each upper arm, the woman wore a large amulet with a circle of gold. Judith caught her breath seeing the ubiquitous Gomay sign,  engraved in the gold. Judith wondered suddenly whether it was the symbol of some cultist slavery.

Altogether, the female on the floor was a flamboyant Cellini sculpture come alive, designed of malice and shaped in undissembled hatred. The bizarre woman was a Byzantine *belle dame sans merci*, Judith thought with a shiver. She was straight out of Beaudelaire's *Fleurs du Mal!*

It came to Judith that what she was seeing might be one of Werner Christed's unconventional notions about shooting a scene that took everyone by surprise. Judith looked around for a camera. Crazy as it might seem, this *could* be the director putting her to another test!

But Judith had no time to consider her hypothesis further. The figure leaped off the floor, screeching, "All you damned thieving whores! Out of my house, and off my island!"

With that, the woman flung herself toward Judith with a knife that glittered murderously in the weaving light.

Judith careened for the door. She slammed it shut against the ranting madwoman in the nick of time. This was no Christed "happening"! The woman was obviously insane! Judith rushed down the spiral staircase at such a pace that she almost fell with dizziness. To her dismay, she heard steps flying after her. She realized it would be death to try for her room, the madwoman would only trap her there. Judith raced to get out of the building, thinking she could hide in the thick trees at the side of the Manor House.

Clad only in her thin chick-and-bunny robe, Judith was drenched as soon as she opened the door. The storm had resumed, more furiously than earlier. She rushed on in fresh panic. Where could she go? Noises behind told of her pursuer closing on her. Could she make it to Lena's side of the chateau before the knife caught her back? She was strong and fast, but the knife-wielder was fueled by madness.

Judith decided to try to cross the road and hide in the church. Cold rain beat at her face, but she was hardly aware that she was wet. A bolt of lightning brought with it the petrifying image of the lunatic woman not twenty feet away.

With a cry of victory, the woman jumped at Judith, the knife high in her murderous hand. Judith spun around for the church, grateful for her years of athletics in school. But the church doors were locked, and in the time it took for Judith to find out, the woman was upon her.

The struggle was desperate—madness on one side, life-and-death on the other. Judith clawed and kicked at her attacker, scratched and punched, all the while bobbing and weaving to avoid the wild sweeps of the knife. Judith kept trying to catch hold of the madwoman's wrist, her only real chance to stave off the blade. Then she slipped on the wet grass, fell down, sure she was a goner. The heaving woman lunged down on her, the blade lifted and ready to kill. Judith rolled violently away. The woman tumbled after, still chopping the air viciously with her weapon. Again and again, lightning lit up the horrible face, the bulging eyes, the twisted mouth of total insanity.

Desperately, Judith gyrated away on the ground, cursing herself for her foolhardiness. At the same time, a great weeping of protest burst inside of Judith. She had brought this on herself, yes, but not to be slashed to pieces, murdered. She flung herself about. She had escaped the Gomay, she would escape this lunatic! Abruptly, she changed her tactic. Instead of trying to escape, Judith gathered her body tightly and then sprang forward in her own attack, like a coil exploding. Her head butted savagely into the woman's middle. There was a sharp, heaving cry as the breath went out of the thin body.

The woman dropped, holding her abdomen. The knife fell to the ground. Judith was upon it in a flash. She stood wide-stanced above her attacker, trembling with rage and outrage. It took all her strength to keep her from throwing herself on the prone body and letting the steel go in. The blade in her clenched hand seemed to have an untamed life of its own, to be demanding flesh and blood and bone. It was as if the woman's body was a powerful magnet drawing the steel irresistibly down.

Judith tried to fight the blade, to hold it back, but, almost as if she were watching someone else, Judith's eyes followed the knife as it slowly, viciously, descended implacably toward the palpitating flesh on the soaked grass. The blade was aiming straight for the woman's throbbing throat. In her mind's eye, Judith could see the sudden thrust the point would make in a moment. She could see the gash it would open, the sweeping laceration of the flesh, the wider opening of the wound. *The decapitated dog's neck pulsing blood! The evisceration spilling blood and guts!* But this was not illusion apparatus, no projection of actors in a scenario. This was a real woman lying at her feet, and she was Judith Bradford, holding a real knife an inch from the human throat!

Sick with self-disgust, Judith stumbled back. God, she prayed, what kind of violence do people harbor inside? She thought desperately, *I could have killed that woman!* I could have murdered her and been *glad* to see her blood pouring out on the grass! What kind of person am I? It doesn't matter that she tried to kill me! Yes, I had a right to defend myself—but I was ready to kill her because I *wanted* to! *Horrible!*

At the same moment, Judith knew her self-flagellation was not warranted. She vomited with the agony of her very different emotions. Her impulse to kill had been only a fury of self-preservation, nothing more. What she felt for the woman was *pity*, if anything. What she felt for herself was mortification, and endless reproach for having trespassed so rashly and blindly. What she felt about her situation was total confusion. She could not know whether Gomay Island's ways were evil, or whether the jailing of the woman, as an example, was a kindness. She could not know, Judith told herself in final self-defeat, whether she was not in a nightmare. Her spells had always seemed as accursedly real as these trees, this pouring rain, this unimaginable figure on the ground, this knife she so improbably held—which she now flung away with a shudder. She thanked God it was not bloody. The terrible murder could so easily have happened.

The woman was stirring. Fear jolted Judith. It was no time for philosophizing! Where had she thrown the knife? That was stupid! She looked around frantically. At least it was nowhere to be seen. But the woman would be coming after her, with or without a weapon. She had to find a hiding place. Judith knew one thing certainly now. She could not risk another bout: if she felt her existence threatened again she knew now she would not hesitate to kill. And it was the last thing she ever wanted in her life. She flew from herself as well as her assailant.

Judith headed for the forest. Fast as she went, she heard the woman following again.

Judith plunged away into the sanctuary of the trees, only to skid to a stop. In the distance she saw a moving torchlight and heard, heart-stoppingly, a ferocious barking. She remembered Rick telling her there were guard patrols all around Urwolde at night. *The rabbit being torn to pieces, its shreds of sinew and flesh whipping bloody in the air as the dogs ripped it savagely. Maybe this very dog!*

Again Judith whirled around. Where could she go now? The madwoman was thrashing through the trees behind her. The deadly dog was searching in the trees before her. Judith cursed the night. *Why had she ever left her room!* she lamented to the storm beating the treetops over her head.

Wretchedly, Judith sought another shelter. Leaving the trees, she saw the cemetery near by, but it offered no comfort. There was no place else. She heard the madwoman's cries coming closer once more. In despair, Judith thought she might as well give up and let the horrible night have its way with her. She could not possibly reach the dormitory building, and Rick, before the lunatic would be upon her. Judith burst into tears, but she kept running. Her lungs were heaving for air. Her attacker's steps were right behind. The woman must have fantastic strength, Judith thought miserably. Blinded by her tears, Judith stumbled on a rock. Now she was caught! But Judith miraculously found her outstretched hands pulling her up along the side of a solid—what? There was no building near the cemetery, nothing except—the car shed! And the hearse. She had run into the back of the hearse! Here it stood real and solid, no dream or vision. Her fingers were turning the latch. Without a second thought, Judith yanked the door open and vaulted inside. She flipped the handle Gregor had installed to keep street thieves out.

There was a fierce crashing against the door, and a crescendo of frustrated screaming louder than the peals of thunder that were shaking the sky. It was an endless time before the attack stopped, and Judith fell to the floor in a sweat.

It was grisly to be in the blackness of the hearse, but

Judith was thankful to be safe from her enemy, and out of the storm. It was awful to be lying where corpses had been, but Judith forced herself to put the shadow out of her head. She had to get some sleep before the morning.

As Judith yawned and stretched, her hand knocked against a box. Her heart jumped to her throat. Was she in the hearse with a *coffin?* That would be more than she could stand. Cautiously, she extended her hand, fingers sensitive to what they might find.

Oh! The wooden box beside her was unmistakable!

With clenched jaws Judith tried to tell herself that it was only another delivery of props at worst, a dummy corpse like the one she had seen before.

But that recollection of the body rolling to the ground was more than Judith could handle in her overwrought state. It exploded all the premonitions she had been bottling up. All the day's suspicions and the night's lurid chase erupted into an hysteria she could not control. Her teeth chattered uncontrollably, and her eyes burned in an abrupt billowing of yellow smoke that filled the hearse. Judith felt the acrid smoke penetrate her eyes, her ears, her brain, and she knew that the coffin beside her did not contain a mannequin. Through the yellow mist, she could see right through the coffin, and there was a corpse in it, a living corpse scratching to get out and get at her.

Even as she watched, paralyzed with terror, the cadaver pushed open the cover, sat up, got out of the coffin slowly, glaring at her, its skull's teeth bared, and started for her throat, to drink her blood.

Judith swayed in anguish and shock as the cadaver touched her with icy fingers and put its bony mouth to her neck. She heard her mother's voice calling from the coffin then: "Judith, come home. Come home now, Judy!" Her mother calling, calling, calling, as plainly as she had called from the kitchen window when Judith was a child playing outside. Her mother's voice, as clear as when she had scolded Judith for spilling her milk. Her mother's voice, as close and familiar as her scent, the overpowering sweet perfume she used, the honeysuckle smell that was filling the hearse, flowing over Judith's head, going in her mouth, up her nose, into her ears, covering her body like a sticky syrup that would congeal into her death shroud.

The last thing Judith remembered before the corpse out of the coffin had its suffocating way with her was the vivid yellow odor of her mother's unmistakable scent filling the fainting night.

The sound of the hearse motor starting woke her. In the morning light oozing through the curtained window, Judith clearly made out a coffin beside her. Mindlessly, Judith screamed out in fresh terror, and fumbled to open the door.

The motor stopped abruptly at her scream. People around Urwolde Common were astounded to see the girl drop from the back of the hearse. Weeping beyond control, Judith saw Lena and Rick hurrying toward her as voices called out all around, "Here she is!"

Gomay servants came running out of the woods. Apparently, search parties had been looking for her.

Judith dimly heard Rick's anxious question as he ran up. "Are you all right, Judy?"

Lena puffed over, shouting scoldingly. "Where in the world have you been?"

Judith clung to Rick. She sobbed, "There's a body in there!"

Lena kept scolding, "What are you ever doing in the hearse!"

Judith went on witlessly, "A body, I tell you!" Why wouldn't they listen to her?

Lena snapped impatiently, "For goodness sake, Judy, it is microphone stands! Gregor and I brought them out last night!"

Judith swallowed dumbly. The night began returning to her memory—the damnable yellow fog, the suffocating perfume that had overcome her at the end. *Had she been hallucinating the whole time?* In the tower as well as in the hearse? Obviously there was no cadaver. Lena was impatiently tossing out metal stands to show her once and for all. Was the madwoman, too, only a figment of her sick head?

Judith shrank against Rick, weary, wracked, and baffled. "I'm sorry, Rick. I don't know what's happening to me!"

He said, "Maybe I'd better take you to Dr. Gomay . . ."

But Lena was grabbing at Judith. The girl had never seen Lena like this, in a fury. "We have no time for any more of your nonsense! Werner is waiting!" Shouting irascibly, Lena unceremoniously yanked Judith away from Rick Gilbert. "We have to get you in costume!"

Judith felt foolish and a laughingstock. People all around were whispering and gesturing at her childish bathrobe. She had never been so embarrassed.

Lena called to Rick. "Go up to the cliff and tell Werner we have found her! We will come as soon as I can fix her up!"

For the first time in her wrought-up state, Judith

became aware that Rick had his face powdered dead white. His lips were painted cardinal red. He was wearing a tight courtier's doublet of a shining golden cloth that showed off his thigh muscles. There were starched white ruffles at his shoulders and wrists. His legs were encased in tight-fitting hose of court velvet. He had stepped out of the pages of a ballet or of Shakespeare. Before Judith could take him in fully, he was hurrying away with Lena's message to the director.

Lena headed Judith to the company dressing rooms, admonishing her without stopping for breath. "Do you realize what time it is? No one keeps Werner waiting! You knew he wanted to do the scene with you first! And you look absolutely awful, terrible, ghastly. I doubt you will have a chance against Emily now!"

Lena went on unhappily as she dressed Judith, who stood numbly like an obedient child in the wardrobe room. "I had a premonition this morning!" Lena fussed. "Yes! I could not find my bracelet! Imagine! It finally turned up, but I have never, never misplaced my bracelet since the day Robina gave it to me!" She scowled. "And my Gregor is furious with me, because now Werner is angry with him because of you!"

Judith was hardly aware of what Lena was saying or the costume Lena was putting on her. All she could think of was that she was glad she had told Rick about the drug visitations. At least he might understand when she told him about her vision of a demented female in the tower. The episode in the hearse had been all the proof she needed that she had been on a trip! How could there have been a living corpse to attack her? More to the point, how could she have heard her mother's voice or, irrefutably, have so plainly smelled her perfume? *It had all been in her head!* She had to keep saying that, to keep remembering it over and over. It hadn't been necessary for Lena to bring out the evidence of the microphone stands. All of last night's terror had been pure phantom, brought on by her upset over the horrible recital of *Baron of Darkness.* Obviously, it had shocked her more than she had realized, beyond her capacity to accept.

She knew the bottom line of her experience now, Judith groaned miserably to herself. Only in her own deformed imagination was there a madwoman roaming Gomay Island seeking to kill "all you thieving whores . . ." Only in her imagination all her woeful doubts. What was to become of her?

CHAPTER ELEVEN

Death Point, the highest of Gomay Island's crags, rose nearly two hundred feet sheerly from the sea. To fall off would be like plummeting from a twenty-story building. There was a local tale that in the time of the eighteenth century fishing settlement, a son of the Gomays, forbidden to marry the beautiful daughter of a poor family, leaped to his death from this point. When the girl learned of his suicide, she followed him tragically.

Below the legended height there was a circle of jagged

rocks, like a gaping maw of a leviathan shark waiting with murderous teeth.

This summit was about a quarter of a mile eastward of the grove frequented by Judith and Rick. The trail from the formal gardens up to Death Point had been widened to move film equipment. Now the cliff held a complete movie set that would be used for many separate shots. It represented the terrace of a coastal castle of the middle ages. A false front formed the seaward wall of the stronghold, with colorful pennants flying from battlements and turrets. The terrace was painted to look like marble blocks. It extended to the very brink of the precipice, but a stout balustrade ran protectingly along the edge.

Technicians were swarming over the set in the brightening sun, making last-minute adjustments. Everywhere there were grips, carpenters, electricians, prop handlers—the people who had come to the island more than a month before the cast. Moose had not needed the finished script to prepare the basic sets.

There were separate cameras at each end of the terrace. Spotlights and reflecting screens were at ready. Werner Christed, dressed in farm overalls, was talking animatedly to one of his cameramen. The director's decisive gestures emphasized that he was the command center. Dr. Gomay was on a canvas stool taking in every motion with shining eyes that relished the scene. Gregor was striding about shouting orders with grandiose flourishes.

The acting company, present today only as spectators, waited on camp chairs well beyond camera range. A few were chatting, but most were watching the familiar preparations quietly with professional eyes.

At the mock castle wall, Rick stood in his medieval costume. His eyes were closed in his whitened face. He seemed to be praying, or meditating. Near him waited Emily, barefooted in a French peasant's work pants and blouse made of rough blue material. A distinctive kerchief of red polka dots on white muslin made her look even younger than she was.

All this Judith took in at a glance when she came hurrying, late, out of the trees into the clearing with Lena. The experiences of the unnerving night were marked deeply on her face, but the morning's first confusion was giving way to a new decision. After hard second thoughts, it came to Judith that there might have been two separate aspects to the horror she had suffered. True, the events in the hearse had all too clearly been of her own conjuring—but that did not necessarily mean that she had been in a yellow fog through the earlier misadventure in the tower! She had now determined to speak to Lena and Rick about what had happened, or what she thought had happened.

If she were wrong, she would simply have to depend on her friends to understand and help her get past her weakness. But if she were right, they badly needed to know that a murdering lunatic was loose somewhere on the island—needed to know it badly indeed!

Judith saw Werner Christed turn with annoyance when Lena went to him. He shook his head negatively and pointed emphatically to Emily, in costume, on the set. His meaning was clear and, returning, Lena confirmed it in an unhappy whisper to Judith. "Werner is furious that you would dare to be late! He will hear no excuse. He has given Emily the part, definitely. He does not want you in the picture even as an extra!"

Judith's heart died.

"You will have to stay on the island, as we told you, but it will be as my assistant in the wardrobe room!"

Judith wanted to cry out that it wasn't her fault. She wanted to tell about the tower at once. The director would not be so unfair if he knew the truth. But did she know the truth herself?

Christed was commanding Gregor Ludovici urgently: "All set! Let's get this one right into the can. The weather is perfect right now, so hit it!"

A tingle of excitement ran across the clearing. To Judith it brought only a knife-thrust of disappointment. Even the sight of Rick and the knowledge that at least she had not lost him was little consolation.

She fought tears, remembering her grandmother's advice: "Never expect life to be fair and you won't be disappointed." Wise old lady! But wisdom did not ease pain.

The company script girl stood at ready before the main camera with a clap-board carrying the scene identification.

Judith was caught up in the cinematic activity despite her hurt. Moose was shouting, "Get those bottle stoppers off!" "Bottle stoppers," Judith knew, were coverings that had been placed over lenses for protection. A "grunt"—an assistant to the "gaffer," the head electrician—was calling for a "clam shell," which Judith knew was a special clamp used to hold a cloth. The familiar technical names and routines of film making began to ease Judith. They solidified the present, the normal, the real world all around her. Gregor was exhorting, "Carry the mail!"—speed it up. The gaffer was calling for a "pickle"—a small spotlight; the cameraman was adjusting a "blackboard" to shade his lens. Moose shouted for a prop man to "put a beard on it"—referring to a cover for a microphone that might be in camera range when they started to shoot. Watching the matter-of-fact workers, Judith was comforted, more ready to accept that the night before was a bad dream.

On the set, Christed was talking softly to Rick and Emily, with his arms around their shoulders. Judith recalled Rick's enthusiasm for the director's method—the *verité* of actors plunged cold into a scene. She remembered: "Werner wants to surprise the audience . . .he does it by surprising his actors!" Rick had told her how this approach boosted his own energy, and inspired performances he could never achieve under more traditional direction.

"Lights!" the director ordered. Judith bit her lip as a white brilliance sluiced down on the stage. The great spots high on their metal towers seemed like tilted buckets pouring molten silver out of the sky.

Gregor called officiously, "Marker! Okay, ready! Quiet, everybody!"

And Werner Christed: *"This is action!"* Magic words in Judith's ears, wondrous words not now to be for her! "Roll 'em!"

The hinged top of the clap-board was slapped down crisply and the filming began.

The scene of the baron and the peasant girl told itself to Judith as it did to the cameras. The nobleman's servants were tugging the village girl into the baron's presence. The girl was terrified. No words were needed. Emily *was* the young, ignorant woman who had heard evil rumors about the castle, and at the same time could not keep a youthful curiosity out of her eyes. For the first time in her life she was in royal surroundings, in royal company.

When she saw that the young lord was handsome, and gracious in manner, she grew easier, and even a little flirtatious.

Judith told herself, without reservation, that Emily was a fine actress and suited the part beautifully. Credit where credit is due. She was not at all sure she could get across as many moods and inflections without a word being spoken. Glancing at Werner Christed, Judith saw that he was openly pleased with Emily's performance.

Off camera, a sound man was following the actors with a long microphone boom. Judith was too far away to hear anything, and the scene before her unfolded like a silent movie.

After greeting the girl pleasantly, Baron Gilles de Rais wheeled about suddenly and dismissed his retinue. Without warning, he made for the girl and embraced her savagely. When Emily struggled against the attack, Rick's countenance was transformed. Judith could not believe her eyes. Rick Gilbert changed from the kind, loving man she knew into a fiend, his face disfigured with vicious lust. His hands were like talons gripping the girl.

Judith shivered. Rick was too good an actor! He projected this fury and venerous lechery as if they were his true character. What was it the great Russian director Stanislovsky had taught? An actor should experience as much as possible in order to portray emotions convincingly. But that did not mean that only a murderer could play Othello!

Something in Judith was repelled as she watched Rick playing the role of Baron Gilles de Rais. Could anyone portray such vileness unless he hid such foulness in his own depths?

Unless, Judith forced herself to go on—unless Rick was indeed a far greater actor than she had expected.

As for Emily, the girl did not have to act her fear, Judith saw at once. Emily's face was twisted with actual terror as Rick, following direction, pressed her backward relentlessly, inching her toward the balustrade edging the cliff. Emily's scream was so piercing, it galvanized all the actors watching. "Don't! *Please don't!*" Judith had to suppress a strong impulse to run on the set and free Emily from the bestial rapist.

Werner Christed's hands were fists pistoning up and down beside the camera as the scene mounted to its climax. His eyes were gleaming—clearly he was getting what he wanted on film, a harrowing distillation of terror that would set the mood of the entire production.

On the set, Rick and Emily were moving perilously closer to the railing above the sea. Rick pressed the girl against it, showing the camera a visage inflamed with implacable, obscene desire.

Watching spellbound, Judith and the other spectators were totally unprepared for what happened next.

From the camera, Werner whipped a hand signal at Moose. The crew chief tugged a rope and a section of the balustrade fell away with a rending sound. With a screech of sheer, unrehearsed panic, Emily went sailing into space over the edge of Death Point.

Judith and others screamed aloud. Judith could not believe her eyes or ears when, instead of a bedlam of horror at the cameras, Werner Christed was on his feet applauding and shouting, "Cut! That's a take! Beautiful! Beautiful!" Then, to Moose, "Bring Emily up!"

The company quieted. In a rush of understanding,

Judith realized that a platform must have been rigged just below the top of the cliff, so that Emily had dropped to it safely, though the screen would give the impression that she had gone to her death.

But everyone was immobilized when, in the silence following the director's order to Moose, there came through the air a thin, receding wail of ultimate terror.

It was followed by a broken cry from Moose: *"The scaffold gave way!"*

Dr. Gomay was waving his arms violently at a group of Gomays. "Down to the boats! Quickly! Quickly!"

Rick had dropped to his knees, a rigid figure of horror staring over the crag's edge.

At the same instant, Christed was shouting to crew men who were poised off camera with rifles aimed below. "Hold the gasoline! Don't shoot!"

Earlier, a special-effects team had anchored containers of gasoline in the ocean. They were to have exploded on cue to set the sea afire for another camera shot, which would show a dummy falling from the height into a blazing ocean.

Judith's head was pounding. She prayed she was having another spell. She cried to herself that she was still asleep in last night's nightmare, now taken a new, unspeakable turn. How could Emily, dear Emily, be gone over the terrible cliff, crushed and drowned?

Judith's eyes took in Moose hauling up a rope. Her ears heard him cry out in disbelief, *"It's cut!* Werner, some damn body sliced this bloody rope halfway through!"

Judith rushed for the woods to be sick. Her mind flashed before her stomach turned over: "It was supposed to be *me!*"

CHAPTER TWELVE

Dr. Gomay returned to Death Point from the boats below. It was impossible to find Emily's body, he reported. The tide was ebbing, and the girl had undoubtedly been washed out to sea.

When police arrived from the village of Gomayville, the island's owner showed the rope, and insisted that it had not been cut. He theorized that the night's storm winds had abraded the strands against the sharp-edged rocks of the cliff formation. It had been an unfortunate, unforeseeable, tragic accident.

Judith noticed that the policemen spoke to Dr. Gomay more than deferentially. They went through the motions of examining the rope, observed the film equipment with a gawking curiosity, and agreed with Dr. Gomay that no one could be held at fault. They would report an Act of God to the local Justice of the Peace and the State Police. There would be little trouble at the inquest, they assured Dr. Gomay. They descended from Death Point to join the boatmen searching for Emily's body.

Still in his extravagant costume, Rick steered Judith to the refreshment tent that had been erected earlier. They had coffee but found it difficult to speak. Finally Judith needed words to ease the spreading pain in her heart—searing pain compounding her many confusions. "Emily was such a great person!" she cried. What a feeble epitaph for the bright girl now shattered and lost in the endless waters.

Beneath his makeup, Rick's expression showed his sympathy and concern for Judith. He echoed the thought that had struck her when Moose shouted that the rope had been cut. Rick said hoarsely, "*You* were supposed to be doing the scene!"

His giving it voice sent a lightning of suspicion through Judith. Might the loony woman of the tower have come upon the terrace set, and cut the rope out of her distracted malice? "*All you thieving whores, off my island!*"

The idea opened Judith's floodgates, and she poured out all the night's ugliness to Rick without restraint. Several times she almost stopped. Her story sounded too improbable to be accepted by anyone. She clenched her fists and forced herself to continue until she had spilled out everything.

"It *wasn't* the drug thing, Rick!" she begged him to believe.

It helped her regain some of her composure that Rick was patiently hearing her out. His belief in her shone as clearly as the tenderness in his eyes. He showed none of the quick skepticism and doubt she expected and feared.

At the end, his response surprised her, yet it made obvious sense. He said they ought to tell her story to Dr. Gomay. If it was the drugs, the doctor might help with medicine. If the story was true, he surely ought to know it. That paralleled Judith's own previous thought.

Dr. Gomay responded as decisively as Rick. He said at once, "Judith, there could not be anyone in the tower I did not know about, but now we must go there and see for ourselves!"

Judith acquiesced eagerly. She wanted to know the truth—morbid mirage or wracking reality—whatever it might mean for her.

Dr. Gomay, Rick, and Judith left the film company still churning in shock on Death Point.

At the Manor House they went directly to the tower, and mounted the side staircase leading to the spiral steps. When they reached the landing at Judith's room, the servant Lilia greeted them with a melancholy bow. She had been changing linens, and stepped back deferentially when she saw Dr. Gomay. Judith wondered suddenly whether Lilia had been the guard of the misadventure.

Dr. Gomay asked Judith to mount the spiral stairs first, to be sure everything was the way she had supposedly seen it the night before. Though it was daytime, the only light came from narrow apertures in the tower wall, and Judith could observe little more than her candle had revealed. It was still a spidery place, and the skittering insects she remembered were still loathsome on the walls; some cracked horribly underfoot.

At the dark landing, Judith halted, afraid to open the door before her, afraid not to. At least there was a real door! as she remembered. Rick read her anxiety and stepped ahead. Judith gasped as he pushed the door open easily. There was no iron bar, *and* no sign that anything had been pried away. "That door was barred!" she cried out.

Unless.

Unless she was about to find that she *had* imagined it all, or most of it.

Inside the room, silence greeted the three of them. Silence and emptiness. The chamber held no furniture, no trays, no garbage smell, no shutter nailed over the window, no lipsticked slogan on any wall. Lipstick was not so easy to remove; if the wall had been washed, Judith considered, the cleaned section would show in contrast to the years of neglect on the old stones.

But there was no indication at all of washing or scrubbing or scraping.

Rick's hand was gentle on Judith's shoulder. "Well, Judy, you see it with your own eyes . . ."

Judith searched the space again. There was no mistake. This was not the room she had seen last night. Not seen—hallucinated. *Hallucinated.* The word echoed fearsomely in her head. But could the room have been altered somehow? Had Lilia been working here? Might the madwoman yet be real, and still threatening?

Rick's voice interrupted her jumbled questions. He was saying gravely, "I think you ought to tell Dr. Gomay about your problem now, Judy."

When Judith finally got it out, the old doctor proved surprisingly sympathetic. He arranged for Judith to come to his library later that day. He would mix some medicine, he said, and see if he could help her.

Rick, noting how exhausted and upset Judith was, took her to her room. He was sure Werner would close down the day's shooting. There was nothing anyone could do now. Judith fell into a deep sleep.

It was late afternoon when she was awakened by a sense that someone was hovering over her. She cried out when she saw a hooded figure by her bed. Had the crazy woman materialized? Would the hideous knife flash at her throat now?

Then Judith realized it was her servant standing there, with Lena coming up quickly behind her.

Lena quieted the girl, understanding that her nerves were raw. She explained softly that Lilia had come to help her move. Werner was assigning Judith the roles Emily was to have played, and Judith was to live with the other actors and the crew in the dormitory over the dining hall.

Judith turned away. The only dormitory space would be Emily's. She protested to Lena, "I can't do that!" Much as she wanted to leave the malign tower, she could not possibly take over Emily's room. It was too grisly. How could she lie in the same bed, put her clothes in a chest that had just held her friend's things? It would make her feel a murderer herself.

Lena consoled Judith again. She had anticipated her feelings, they were natural enough. They had arranged for another actress to shift to Emily's room.

Judith followed Lena and Lilia out glumly. She still felt like a ghoul, and was consumed with inner guilt because she had wanted the part so much and was so devastated when Werner had shut her out that morning. Since the accident was working out to her benefit, it was almost as if she had caused it.

With a shock it occurred to her that others, knowing she had been out in the night, might suspect just that.

Despairingly, trudging along Urwolde Common behind Lena, Judith asked herself whether she was ever to have peace on Gomay Island.

CHAPTER THIRTEEN

Gregor Ludovici brought orange juice and coffee to his wife in bed the following morning. To his amazement, she motioned him away angrily. She demanded, "Where were you last night? I couldn't sleep after everything that happened, and you weren't in bed at all!"

Gregor pretended surprise. "Why, Lena, I told you I would be working. Werner wanted a crew to set up the next scene. He is going to skip the terrace beat for now, to rebuild the scaffold and wisely give people a chance to get over the accident. But he wants to start in the church this afternoon . . ."

"I don't understand!" Lena ejaculated, but her husband cut her short with, "And you had better get your girl ready on time!"

Lena's tone was incredulous. "Do you say Werner is going to shoot this afternoon?"

"Yes."

"On the day of Emily's funeral?"

"Funeral?" Lena saw that Gregor was genuinely taken aback. He asked, "How can there be a funeral without a body?"

It was Lena's turn to show a perplexed expression. "What do you mean, no body? Surely *you* must know the Gomays found poor Emily!"

Gregor Ludovici's answer was a gruff, threatening bark. "I have told you! They found nothing!"

Lena Ludovici started to dress hurriedly. "I know what *I* saw!"

Her husband's face twisted into steely suspicion. "What did you see?"

"The girl! Emily!" Lena challenged him.

"Have you gone mad, like the crazy girl with her talk of lights in the tower and all that nonsense?"

"I am not blind, Gregor! Last night I—"

Her husband cut her off with a shout. "Felix told me again this morning—not a trace of the body!"

Lena shouted back, "Then Felix Gomay has lied to you!"

"Be careful what you say, woman!"

"Be careful what *you* say, Gregor!"

"No one calls Dr. Gomay a liar on this island!"

"Or what happens?" Lena thrust. "Do I fall off

a cliff, too?"

The man went ominously quiet. "I am sure you do not wish to find that out . . ."

"Do not threaten me, Gregor! I am not one of Felix Gomay's servants!"

"We are all his servants, and it behooves you not to forget it! Felix helped me when I had nothing, he brought us to Werner, we have work and money and a future, thanks to Dr. Felix Gomay! You will not call him a liar!"

Lena turned on Gregor Ludovici, her eyes spitting fire. Her hands were strong athwart her broad peasant hips, and her head jutted forward with unintimidated defiance. "For your information, Gregor, I saw the girl's body late last night! I saw it with these two eyes!" The woman made an exaggerated poking gesture with two fingers. Her face was tortured with her mounting distrust.

"You are out of your mind!" Gregor growled. "I know better than anyone everything that happens on this island! It is my business to know!"

His wife snorted. "You do not know that I went out looking for you. The moon was so bright I could see every twig on the trees, *and every hair on Emily's poor broken head!*"

"You were having a bad dream!" her husband thundered. "Nothing more!"

Lena shook her head positively. She would not be checked. For too long on Gomay Island, she considered, she had dismissed rumors, whispers, allusions, intimations. She had put them down to the old-time religion Gregor participated in with his kin. She herself went through some of the motions when they were unavoidable, as with the rabbit ritual at the guardhouse. She had never let her husband see that it sickened her. She had wished there was a way she could have let Judith know she was not truly part of the disgusting scene. She went on, speaking very deliberately now.

"On my walk looking for you, Gregor, I thought you might have gone into the garden behind the dormitory. I know how you have enjoyed being alone there. But instead of you what I came upon was the lights of torches moving through the forest—the pine torches the servants use when they hold their services up at the abbey . . ."

"A bad dream," Gregor Ludovici muttered. But he was listening intensely now, not trying to stop the woman.

"Of course I was curious. So far as I knew, it was not the calendar for any of the Gomay observances. What was the whole Gomay clan doing out of their quarters so late at night? I hid in the garden maze to watch as their procession came out of the woods close by. Oh, your friends came as quietly as ghosts, and in their robes and masks in the moonlight they looked like phantoms from another world—a darker world, I may say. *They were bearing Emily's body on a litter!* It was uncanny, for not even their footsteps were making a sound, as if they were spirits, funereal spirits, not flesh and blood . . ."

Her husband burst out at the woman, "Spirits! You only prove you were dreaming!"

Lena continued as if Gregor had said nothing. "At first it came to me that Werner might be making a shot. But where was the crew, where were the spots? Even Werner Christed cannot take pictures with only the moon's light. No, it was no part of the movie. It was something else, something I wish I did not see, something I did not dream last night, and do not forget this morning!" Lena's voice lifted. "They took the poor girl's body down into their basement and God knows what they are doing to it down there if Dr. Gomay has to lie about finding her—*because it was your Felix Gomay himself who was leading the procession, Gregor!*"

Gregor went white. His great fists clenched as Lena grew more vehement. "Do you really believe the old man, then, if he says there is no body for a funeral? Or were you there, too, Gregor!"

"I was not there!" the man bellowed.

Lena spat her words at him. "You were waiting for them in the basement? Getting ready for them, preparing? Tell me, Gregor, where were you last night when you were not here in our bed?"

The man sputtered, "I don't know what you're talking about. If you weren't dreaming, I don't know what the devil you are raving about!" He wiped his perspiring forehead with a heavy hand. "I am as puzzled as you by what you say you have witnessed!"

The woman sighed unhappily. "Are you, Gregor? Sometimes I do not know you. You have changed since we came to Gomay Island!" It was true, Lena Ludovici thought sadly. In many ways she could not identify, her husband was a different man since his work began on *Baron of Darkness.*

Gregor slapped Lena's dressing table crudely. "It is you who have changed, forgotten your place! You are obsessed!"

Lena fumed with rising exasperation. "Why is the old man lying? I say he has reasons I do not like!" The woman's tone quivered with an unspoken suspicion that had been growing in her since the reading of the film script. "Maybe Felix Gomay is not too clear about where his unholy movie ends and real life begins!"

Gregor said testily, "Even if it should happen that they found the body, it is common sense that Felix does not wish to upset everyone with a funeral! It can't bring the girl back, can it?"

Lena said triumphantly, "Ah, then you admit they have the girl!"

"I admit nothing!"

Lena said grimly, "Listen, Gregor, something here stinks now! I am saying that you and I should get off this island right away, because I do not like the smell of the whole damned business now! Including what happened to that first actress, Roberta Leslie!" she added forcefully.

Gregor's body shook with his anger. "My work is here with Werner! You know that! How long we have waited for this kind of success . . . !"

"We are leaving, and taking Judith!" The woman flung at him. "Don't you realize *Judith* was the one the murderer was after!"

Gregor pounded her dressing table, sending bottles flying. "It was an accident! How many times must you be told? The police said—"

Lena laughed sarcastically. "Dr. Gomay's police! You know he has them in his pocket!" Then fiercely, "Now stop arguing and go warm up that damned hearse. I will get Judith and we will go!"

"*The movie . . .*"

"To hell with the movie!" Lena Ludovici erupted into a fury her husband had never witnessed before. "After last night, I would not be surprised if this *is* murder you are fooling with, blockhead! I think we are all in over our head! I think Werner does not know what is really going on here! I am sure of it!"

The man scoffed. "And what does the all-knowing Lena Ludovici think is 'really going on'?"

The woman vented her suppressed outrage. "Ask Emily Lawrence!" Her frustration made her shrill. "I have not told you that I followed the procession last night! Yes, I sneaked behind them, and saw everything! Since you say you were not there, let me inform you what I witnessed through a basement window." The woman broke into sudden weeping. "Your Gomay friends were hacking at the poor body with butcher knives! Wasn't the poor girl broken up enough by the rocks?"

Gregor Ludovici's eyes grew hooded at his wife's recital. Her voice rose to near-hysteria: "If you were not there, ask Felix Gomay why his servants were cutting up live chickens last night and squeezing the blood over Emily's corpse in the damned voodoo coffin they abused her in!" With fresh passion she cried out, "And ask your Dr. Gomay why he insisted we find a *virgin, virgin, only a virgin!* Even Werner thought the old man was off the deep end!"

Gregor flashed, "Werner agreed! You know that!"

"Oh, yes, I am sure he found it amusing! In some ways our friend Werner Christed is as loony as Dr. Gomay!" Her words were bullets at the man. "You do not need a *virgin* if you are only *pretending* to film a Black Mass! Do you understand me? Do you follow me? Do you catch my meaning?" Lena's accent became thicker with her agitation.

Gregor's heavy face was mottled with anger and frustration. "You know we are not to speak of that scene!"

Lena's chin was up in renewed challenge. "I am tired of these secrets, secrets, secrets! The girl is my responsibility! Two dead are enough! I brought her here, and I will take her away!"

Gregor tried a derisive snicker. "Next you'll be saying Felix Gomay is the Archfiend himself, and we are all in his power!"

There was new steel in the contemptuous glance Lena gave the man. "*I* am not in anyone's power! And I do not intend to stay and find out who is! They can do *Baron of Darkness* and Black Masses and anything else they wish, but without us!"

Gregor turned pleading. "Lena! For the first time we have shares in a picture!"

"Then you stay and collect them! Not me! And not Judith!"

"Let me remind you that not too long ago you were not eating too well!"

"We managed!" The woman's tone assumed finality. "Just drive Judith and me to the village. We will find a bus to the city."

Gregor Ludovici's eyes went stony. "And spread your ridiculous story to the whole world? That will help Werner finish the movie here, won't it?"

"I will promise to tell nothing." After all, Lena supported her decision to herself, nothing could help Emily Lawrence now, and the rest was only suspicion. "You know I keep my word. I swear by the memory of Robina." The woman touched her precious bracelet.

Gregor was flint. "You cannot take the girl! I do not permit it!"

"You do not give *me* orders, Gregor! Not you, not Felix, not Werner!"

Her husband seemed to grow even larger than he was, and his voice was cutting metal. "This film has been planned for years! You do not know how much depends on it, and that is none of your business! But I tell you that you will not interfere! *The girl stays here!* The film cannot be made without her now! Do you hear? Judith cannot leave until we are finished! That is my final word!"

Lena scoffed, "Get out of my way, Gregor!"

The huge man was blocking the door.

"Out of my way, please," she repeated. And allowed herself a wistful smile. "Ah, you won't miss me that much, my dear. Do you think I haven't noticed what has been going on between you and—"

Gregor cut her off icily. "You will not leave!"

Lena heard the clear threat now. She reached for the doorknob anxiously. The big man chopped at her hand with his brute fist, and she cried out with the excruciating pain of broken fingers.

"I am sorry," Gregor hissed, "but this is what you insist on!"

The man was shaking his huge head at Lena Ludovici like a wild beast ready to attack. His eyes blazed with unconcealed malevolence. He spread his log-like legs as if steadying himself on a rolling ship. His face grew fiery, as if it were mysteriously burned. Lena frowned at an unfamiliar aroma filling the room. A new after-shave lotion? Containing something sulphurous?

Gregor did not give Lena time to consider it further. "I truly regret this," he rasped. He raised his hammer fists slowly above his wife's head.

The woman backed away, unbelieving. Her eyes glazed with flooding terror. Gregor was not going to strike her? He had never done that! They had their arguments over the years, but they truly loved each other! What hidden secret in him had she uncovered to bring on this total fury, this frenzy of violence? She ran around the room trying to escape Gregor, but he kept coming like a military tank, ruthless, implacable. He was a stranger she had never known.

Lena flung at Gregor whatever her hands came upon. A small radio from her bed table caught Gregor on the cheek and opened a gash. Blood dripped down his face, but he seemed not to notice. It made him more threatening, more horrible. Lena aimed an ashtray at his eyes, hoping to blind him. It flew harmlessly by his head and smashed to splinters against the wall.

He was upon her. Lena tried to weave away. She dropped to the floor to crawl under the bed, but Gregor grabbed her roughly and yanked her upright. He held her tight against him as if in an embrace of love.

But it was no embrace. It was thick sausage fingers gripping slowly around the helpless woman's throat. Gregor was grunting, "You have left me no choice!" He shook Lena the way the dogs had shaken the rabbit. There was a stench of sulphur in the room, overwhelming her. Lena felt her life ebbing. She struggled with all her might against her doom, but her muscles were no match for her husband's. There was no one to respond to her agonized scream for help. Before the light went out of her eyes, she heard her own bones cracking and breaking under fingers that had once caressed her. With her final breath, although she knew it was useless, Lena Ludovici choked out, "I beg you! In the name of Robina, do not harm the girl!"

They were the woman's last words as she slumped to the floor with frothing blood gurgling out of her mouth.

Meeting at once with Dr. Gomay in the manor library,

Gregor was smoking a long cigar. "I do regret that I had to kill Lena," he said gruffly through a puff of smoke. "It is inconvenient for me in many ways. But her loose tongue would have ruined everything you and I have worked so hard and so long to accomplish. We are too close to lose it!" He blew smoke out of his mouth with an angry grunt. "Now our problem is your mad daughter!"

Dr. Gomay scowled. "I had Margot safely locked away after she poisoned that first actress! If only Lena's girl had kept her nose out of our business!"

"If only your damned servant had been a proper guard!" Gregor thrust back.

"With her mask gone she had no choice. You know how deeply they believe that to be seen by anyone without the mask is instant death for them."

"Superstition is to be tolerated only when it works *for* us!" Gregor declared.

"Well, on balance I am sure you will agree it does," the old man defended.

"You should have used Lilia. I want Maria punished!"

"If you say so . . ."

"It is important to make an example. All the servants are buzzing about what happened. They know no one is safe while your daughter is roaming about the island! Where did she get a knife?"

"She has many friends among the servants—they brought her up as a child, you know." Dr. Gomay spoke placatingly. "We were fortunate in any case to convince the girl it was all in her mind. Rick helped considerably . . ."

"He wants this picture made!"

"Of course. But none of us could have quieted Miss Bradford if you hadn't done such a splendid job of setting up the room." The old man's admiration was genuine.

Gregor shrugged it off, tapping his ashes on Dr. Gomay's rug. "Years of quick stage changes, to say nothing more."

"Do not be modest with me. I bow before your powers."

"Then you should have sent Margot to the old country when her madness recurred, as I strongly advised!"

Dr. Gomay held out his hands palms up. "I wanted my daughter with me until we all return. You can't blame me for that. Margot is not insane, she is jealous. She wanted so badly to be in our film. When you and Werner refused she turned on us all."

Gregor interrupted angrily. "She has killed two actresses now! She will certainly try again! It is absurd and intolerable! Where can she be hiding?"

"Oh, I know that," the old man said unexpectedly. Gregor came alert. "She must be in the old abbey. You may not know that when the pirates were here they dug secret tunnels down to their boats. Margot used to play there as a child. She knows the twisting labyrinths as no one else. It will take time to ferret her out, but I have my people searching, and I don't think she will bother the film again."

"She had better not! We need Judith Bradford, and we are running close to our deadline!"

Dr. Gomay brought a decanter from a side table. "You need to relax, Gregor . . ."

"Yes. It isn't every day a man kills his wife."

"I didn't mean that. I am talking about your tension with the film."

"Everything depends on it!" Gregor almost shouted.

"Of course, of course. For me as well as for you and the

rest. But try this port. It is from barrels that are beyond price."

Gregor Ludovici stared disconsolately at the blood-red wine. He did not drink. Words came as a kind of rumbling in his throat. "So many years of planning. So many complications, disappointments, impossibilities. So much delicate maneuvering, so many sensitive jigsaw pieces to put together, always revealing enough but not too much of our purposes. It has been an incredible task."

"And it will be an incredible achievement! The great difficulties are behind us. We have Werner Christed. We have his company. We have his equipment. We have the island."

"Nothing must stop us now!" Gregor scattered fire as he punched his cigar out in a large metal ashtray.

"Nothing will!"

"You had better make sure your servants do not upset the applecart! Last night they went too far!"

Dr. Gomay defended, "They are not used to being out of their own country . . ."

"No excuse! I have thought they should change their dress . . ."

"They would never hear of it! They would revolt!"

"I don't want to hear such nonsense! You must keep them under control!"

Dr. Gomay's tone changed fawningly. "I assure you and promise you that everything will fall into place just as it has been planned and scheduled . . ."

"It will be your head otherwise!" Gregor put his glass down without drinking and started to the door. "I might enjoy your wine if Margot were lying in a coffin like Lena! Your stupidity last night has made me murder a woman I liked, damn you!"

Dr. Gomay gave the retreating figure a sour smile. "You had better remember to show me the proper respect in public, Gregor."

Gregor flung over his shoulder. "You had better remember who is boss! And make bloody damned sure your daughter keeps her hands off Judith Bradford!"

"I hear you," the old man said deferentially.

CHAPTER FOURTEEN

After a day of depression and restlessness that even Rick could not ease, Judith slept fitfully in her new quarters. She was awakened by a faint sound of bells and chanting coming from a distance. It was two o'clock in the morning.

Judith pulled the covers over her head. No, no! She had played the fool quite enough and had quite enough adventures on Gomay Island, imagined and/or real! She was going to stay right where she was, snug in this pleasant, modern room of pine paneling, bright fixtures, and a reassuring lock on her door.

But the tug of the strange sounds drew the girl to the window. This much she could allow her curiosity.

From her new room, Judith could survey Urwolde Common looking north. Both the church and the Manor House were plainly visible without obstruction. It was clear at once that the sounds she heard were coming from outside the Gomay quarters. She could see a procession of servants moving into the basement of the building, carrying small flares of green, blue, and orange flames. They shone like great fireflies in the mild night.

Whatever the ceremony, it was obviously not clandestine. It occurred to Judith that it would be safe to witness this interesting custom of the alien folk. But again she decided to stay where she was. It made no sense to chance possible trouble, or invite another brain-splitting spell. She had the leading role in the film now. It was not only her big chance, but everyone was depending on her. She would not jeopardize herself or the company.

Judith heard voices in the dormitory hall. She recognized Moose's hearty boom, and hurried into her slippers and robe. A group of actors had gathered in the corridor, talking about the Gomays. "Is Werner shooting a night scene?" she asked. It seemed one likely explanation.

Moose shook his head. "Be a helluva time even for Werner."

A blonde actress named Rho said, "It must be one of their religious numbers from the old country." She combed at her frizzy hair with long red fingernails.

"They give me bad dreams," an actor entered the conversation. He was a lanky comic playing a rambunctious court jester in *Baron of Darkness*.

Another actress, Vicki, a beautiful, tanned girl, complained, "That freaky old doctor and his flock of vampires have given me the creeps since the day we came to this godforsaken island. I wish I'd never heard of it!"

Moose grinned at her. "Come off it, darling. Three squares, tennis, swimming, a clean bed—alone!"

"Stifle it, Moose," she said loftily. "Just because I don't make it with you—"

Judith was caught between straining to hear the chanting outside and the talk in the hall. It was a good feeling to belong to the club. Nobody seemed to resent that she, a newcomer, was the lead. It made Judith smile to herself—it was probably because they couldn't meet the virgin requirement!

Judith suggested, "Why don't we all go down to the Common and see what's going on?" There would be safety in numbers.

Moose reached for her wrist quickly. His grip was so strong that it hurt. "That's a no-no, Judy-baby!" The others were abruptly grave. One actress asked Judith anxiously, "Didn't Rick lay that on you? We *never* butt in!"

Moose assumed his take-charge voice. "Back to beddy-bye, everyone. Werner wants us up with the birds in the morning!"

An actress with a see-through nightgown asked, "How are we supposed to sleep with all that bansheeing?"

"Plug your ears, dear," Moose laughed.

"Up yours, sweetheart," the young woman replied amiably, and sashayed away to her door.

Judith kept her own door open a crack. When the

hallway was quiet it was easier for her to hear the Gomay droning as it rose and dipped in a hypnotic cadence. She felt the sound as physically as a ribbon being spun across the night to her head, tugging her outside. Here, just a stone's throw across the Common, a strange, exotic ceremony was taking place. A "far place" was near! Her obsessive curiosity was electric and irresistible. She hated to think she was a coward.

Judith stopped herself. A long-ago singsong made up by her grandmother came to her mind: "Mistake made once, learn from your bumps. Mistake made twice, you're a dunce!"

But through the window, Judith saw a Gomay come from the basement waving a pennant of some kind to the procession, which cheered at the sight. The cloth fluttered clearly in the light of a torch, and Judith recognized it instantly. The large polka dots were unmistakable even in the distance.

What were the Gomays doing with Emily's kerchief when her body was supposed to be lost?

The scarf might have been found in the water, but Judith's blood was racing again with new questions, and her resolve transformed to a different, stubborn purpose. Goaded by her need to know whether Emily had been recovered, she slipped silently out of the dormitory. She scurried along in the shadows outside, coming to a copse of heavy rhododendrons that hid her and allowed her an open view of the Gomay quarters.

To her chagrin, the last of the robed procession was passing into the basement. The door shut solidly behind the mysterious figures. Frustrated, Judith sought a way to reach a window. Could she make it without detection? Did they have guards posted?

She would have been glad for wind and thunder to mask her own sounds. She raced for the fence of the corral where she had first seen Rick, and reached a thicket that gave her access to a window. She held quiet, stopping her breath. No motion or sound. She was safe. On her knees, she crept warily toward the rectangle of light, when she was riveted by the appearance of a robed figure coming out of the building. The masked head turned in all directions suspiciously. For an icy moment, Judith was sure the Gomay had seen her. She pressed flat on the earth, praying for the moon to stay behind the clouds.

There would be no leniency or excuse if she was caught now, she knew. She wished fervently she had let discretion win over her valor.

Fortunately, the Gomay turned to look out over Urwolde Common. It gave Judith the chance she prayed for, and she skittered to another clump of bushes from which she could look into the basement without being seen.

It took Judith a moment to sort out the jumbled scene within. The Gomays were like seething bees or, she thought, more like vampire bats in great red robes they had donned. In the center of the basement—which was draped in black and purple curtains—there was a throne like the one in the Grand Salon. Surrounded by tall black candles, Dr. Gomay sat in a demon's costume. He was the only figure without a mask. Before him, on a black-draped catafalque, rested two wooden coffins. They were, incongruously, painted gleaming crimson, and each bore the symbol Judith had now come to dread,

Both coffins had their lids open, but the boxes were resting too high for Judith to see within. She seethed with inquisitiveness, but had to be satisfied watching the Gomays. They were moving around the catafalque with excited, shuffling steps, droning and chanting weirdly.

What ritual could this be? Judith wondered. Were there bodies in the coffins? *Who?* Had they found Emily after all? And who, then, was lying in the second box? Who else on the island had died? A Gomay?

Judith's pinwheeling questions were interrupted by the sight of a masked figure stamping into the Gomay circle, clearly the leader of the ritual. The man had the size and heft of Gregor Ludovici. Judith gasped. *Could Gregor be an acolyte of Dr. Gomay?*

In that case, why did he pretend not to be?

In that case, who was Dr. Gomay anyway?

In that case, for that matter, *who was Werner Christed?*

And what, really, was happening on this strange island isolated from the world outside? Was there a film production here, or was she in the midst of something too arcane and cabalistic for her mind to take in!

The questions billowed in Judith's brain like yellow smoke, but she was sure this was no Angel Dust bedevilment. She was in no way dizzy or befuddled tonight. Everything transpiring before her widening eyes in the Gomays' basement was too visibly and provocatively real.

As Judith strained closer to the window, all her fresh uncertainties were blasted out of her head by a wild barking. A snarling dog burst at her from the bushes.

Terror jumbled Judith's mind. Now she had brought disaster on herself, finally. How could she have forgotten the dogs, the patrol, the danger? There was no escape, the beast was upon her, its foul breath in her face, its ravenous snout reaching to rip her throat. Judith could not even scream, or pray. She could only hope she would die quickly, without feeling the agony of the crushing jaws.

"Call the dog off!" It was a shouted command behind her.

A whistle pierced the air. The dog dropped away, stiff-legged, in front of Judith. Its mean fangs were dripping brutally beneath ravenous eyes. A burly guard rushed out of the bushes. He collared the dog, staring at Judith as evilly as the straining animal.

Judith still did not dare to move. She heard her unknown savior coming near, but feared to turn. He spoke again. "It is all right. This girl is new here. I will take the responsibility."

Breathing again, Judith thanked her fate that the guard recognized the Gomay authority, whoever it might be. She started to turn, when the voice commanded her, "No! You have seen too much already! Go back to your room! Do not speak of this!"

In fresh bewilderment, Judith was certain all at once that she knew the voice, though it seemed impossible. She cried out in wonderment, *"Rick!* What are you doing with the Gomays? What's going *on?"*

"Back to your room!" the voice commanded.

With an eruption of anger of her own, Judith pivoted around to see the man. She was weary of being a pawn knocked about by strange events. She could take charge of her own emotions and wishes. Defiantly, she searched the masked figure for a clue. The height and posture were Rick's, and the voice. But in the night she could not make out the eyes behind the mask.

The man said sternly, "I am not Rick!"

Judith's gorge rose. There were too many denials all

around her in a place filled with too many riddles and enigmas. Fear gave way to resentment and resistance. "Don't lie to me!" she exclaimed. Then, in a surge of self-determination, not caring for the consequences, Judith asserted herself by reaching out abruptly and jerking the mask off the man's face.

She choked with consternation. The person revealed was Rick Gilbert! The clouds had left the moon, and he was plain in the light. He coughed with guilty confoundment, and ejaculated, "Damn it, Judy!"

Judith demanded wildly, "What are you doing with those zombies down there?" She didn't care if she sounded hysterical. An earthquake was rocking the foundations of her being. If *Rick* could lie to her, the whole of Gomay Island was some kind of hell!

Rick answered curtly, "What I am doing is saving your life!"

"You know what I mean!" Judith hammered at him, refusing to be diverted.

"You ask too many questions, Judy!"

She flashed back, "Maybe not enough!"

Rick Gilbert's voice softened a little. "Listen, I know you're upset about Emily. We all are. But—"

Judith cut him off. "It's not Emily! I can't get a straight answer about anything!"

Rick made no attempt to hide his irritation with Judith's new assertiveness. "You are not supposed to be here in the first place!" he upbraided her. "Werner Christed and Dr. Gomay are running this show, and they are not accountable to you! This picture is tough enough to make without apprentice actresses going prima donna on us!"

Judith was outraged. "Prima donna? Because I ask what you are doing down there where none of us is supposed to go?"

"Because that is none of your affair!"

Judith's eyes blazed. "I'm tired of that cop-out! I expect it from a creep like Gregor, not from *you!*"

"None of this has anything to do with how I feel about *you*, Judy!" There was a quick note of conciliation in his tone.

Judith would accept no more evasions. "My questions are perfectly simple," she insisted. "You're darned right I'm suspicious of the intrigue on this island. *Especially* because even you won't tell me the truth." She turned away with her mouth tightening. "Well, I'll ask Lena! She's one person who will level with me!"

Judith was glad she had said her piece, and said it loud and clear, even if it meant losing Rick. She realized she had allowed herself to be pushed into playing a game she hated—denying her own feelings because she wanted so much to be in the movie, wanted above all to give herself to the happiness she had been finding with Rick Gilbert. But he was turning out to be a frightening enigma of his own. The whole thing was hypocrisy and phoniness, the kind of falsity she had run away from. She had left home to find her strength, not the weakness and vulnerability that Gomay Island had imposed on her.

Burning with her exasperation before Rick, Judith was resolved. If there was danger on Gomay Island, she could face it herself. If there were riddles no one else would answer, she would untangle them herself.

Rick regarded her determined face. "Judy, what the devil has gotten into you. What do you *want?*"

Judith turned away from the man. She was going to talk to Lena Ludovici, the only person on the island she trusted now. She wasn't going to look back at Rick, no matter that he was calling after her. She wasn't going to respond to the too-familiar, too-strong magnetism of his Barrymore voice.

But she halted. In fairness, she ought to give him one last chance to explain. She asked firmly, "One thing I want is to know what you're doing in that ridiculous Gomay outfit!"

There was a flicker of hesitation in Rick Gilbert's face, but his answer came smoothly. "I have been waiting to tell you, but you have kept interrupting. We are rehearsing a special shot for the film." His smile was placating. "What in the world else did you think?"

"A *rehearsal?* Moose would know if there were a rehearsal!"

Judith thought she saw the man's eyes drop again, but his reply was quick once more. "Moose doesn't know everything Werner decides to do. I am the only one of the company involved in this scene with the Gomays, so the others do not need to know."

"Is Werner down there?"

"I told you you ask too many questions!"

Judith became caustic. "And that was Gregor I saw too, wasn't it? Is he there as a 'Gomay' or as the assistant director?" She said it bitingly.

"*You* are being a nuisance, Judy!"

Judith flung her festering doubt at him. "If it's a rehearsal, as you say, then why did you deny it when I said your name?"

"Because I knew we would get into just this kind of argument!" Rick answered curtly.

Judith refused to back off. She gestured again toward the basement from which an excited babble was newly audible. "It isn't really a rehearsal, is it?"

Rick lashed out angrily now. "If you don't believe what I

tell you, stop asking me!" Then, nastily, "Go ask your Lena! She will tell you you are having your spells again!"

"Don't try to fake me out, Rick!" Judith spoke harshly, then with sarcasm: "What's in those coffins? Microphone stands?"

"I don't know. I didn't look."

"Who is Dr. Gomay?"

"You're being idiotic."

"There *could* be very different answers to my questions, couldn't there?" Judith let the implications echo around the two of them in the darkening night.

"With your super imagination, hell, yes!"

"Stop saying that!" Judith's head began to swim with perplexity replacing anger. Suppose Rick were telling the truth? Suppose Werner Christed had simply wanted a special rehearsal? It might be the only time the Gomays were free of their island tasks. Rick Gilbert's eyes were steady and honest on hers. Suppose she was being unduly quarrelsome? She was offending the one man she had ever felt close to. And being ungrateful, too. He *had* saved her from the vicious dog.

But Judith could not rid herself of the gnawing inside. She would not rest until she spoke directly to Lena in the morning. If it meant breaking up with Rick, that was what it would have to mean. She turned her back on his handsome, waiting face.

He called softly to her, in the private tone that had brought her into his arms before.

Judith Bradford refused to hear. She would not look back or say another word. Her heart was breaking, but so was the faith she had bestowed too readily.

She ran for the dormitory with tears of frustration streaming down her cheeks.

CHAPTER FIFTEEN

The next morning, Judith hurried at once to Lena's apartment. Her urgent knocking was answered by Gregor. He looked half-asleep. Judith thought grimly that she understood only too well why his fat face was more swollen with exhaustion. "I must see Lena at once!" she demanded.

The man's answer took her aback. "Lena had to leave," he said testily.

It was a blow to the pit of Judith's stomach. "Lena's *gone?*"

Gregor grunted, "Her sister . . . in Cincinnati . . . was taken very ill. I just came back from Gomayville myself. I took her to the bus to LaGuardia airport. Didn't get a wink of sleep."

"Oh, I'm so sorry. When will she be back?"

Gregor blinked at the girl with distaste, and shrugged. "When will her sister get better? Tomorrow. Next month. I do not know." He closed the door unceremoniously.

Gregor's news depressed Judith even more. With Lena gone, and Rick become a troubling questionmark, she had no one to turn to now. Werner Christed was more of an enigma than ever. And Emily was dead, so horribly dead. As Judith trudged away from the Ludovici apartment sunk in dismal thoughts, she recalled the headstone Emily had shown her in the graveyard: *Remember now that thou too may Die* . . . They had laughed together at the lugubrious thrust from the grave. Young people never thought *they* would really die. But Emily would not giggle at a gravestone—or anything else—ever again.

What a thin line there was between life and death. How true the old clichés are, Judith mused.

Yes, everyone lived with Death breathing down his neck. But that didn't mean you wanted to die before your time. Judith's chin came up slowly. Moose and his men were carrying equipment into the church studio. Life was to live, and she was alive. To her surprise, she found that, despite everything, her depression was lifting and she was again looking forward to her part in the Christed-Gomay film.

* * *

Whenever Judith's now-crowded film schedule permitted, she asked Gregor about Lena. Day after day Gregor answered with the same fixed smile. Yes, he had another letter from Lena. Unfortunately, the sister's illness continued to be serious. Lena would probably be away for a long time.

The Fourth of July had passed, without fireworks in deference to Emily's tragedy. Two more weeks went quickly, and Judith became engrossed in the filming which Werner Christed was pursuing with single-minded intensity.

Except for a few scenes together, Judith was able to keep her distance from Rick. She was glad he did not press her. He seemed to have his own preoccupations, and she wanted time to sort things out. She had spells of loneliness when she wished for his voice, his presence, his touch, but quite aside from her continuing doubts, she was determined not to be the first one to cross whatever bridge was left between them.

It helped that she was enormously busy. She worked alone with Werner Christed and Moose in the church basement, doing the special scenes the director had set aside for her to play with the private apparatus. Even after she became completely familiar with the device, she remained lost in wonder at its range and its vivid impact. Alone with the panels, prisms, and light beams, she acted full beats with a world of people, animals, and places that were magically—and sometimes revoltingly—all about her.

When she played Joan of Arc, she stood before literally legions of soldiers stretching across broad fields as far as the eye could take in—officers in magnificent, colorful uniforms on noble steeds (that reminded her of Rick), foot soldiers massed with pennants flying (that reminded her of Emily's scarf), choruses singing (that reminded her of the Gomays chanting around the inscrutable coffins). Always she was glad Moose was behind the camera.

One episode called for Judith to bathe in a forest stream after days on the battlefield. She was to undress while hidden men—projected from the machine—ogled her. When she was nude, the soldiers were to abandon all restraint and rush upon her. The director explained that he would cut the scene before the physical rape, which he would create metaphorically with shots of animals to be edited in later. But once again the equipment made everything so real that Judith felt sick when she took her clothes off. The soldiers' savage lust was like bugs creeping on her skin. She held a final garment to her. She turned to the camera with an apology. "I'm sorry, Werner."

"Cut." The director took Judith aside. To her relief, he did not seem angry. In fact he was smiling. "You're only proving that my machine makes things realer than real. Now don't worry. Relax for a minute, and we'll try again." He put his arm around her naked shoulder, and gave her a friendly squeeze.

All at once, Judith was aware of the director's touch. Standing near-nude beside the man in what was almost an embrace, she realized that her heart was racing. Perhaps if she were not estranged from Rick she would not be haying this reaction, Judith thought, undeniably a response to Werner Christed as a man and not as an artist or film director.

Judith moved away quickly. Inwardly, she believed she and Rick would come together again. Equally important, she reminded herself, there was the distance between Werner Christed and herself that she had accepted. He was an international figure of eminence and accomplishment; she was an apprentice actress. His face told of brooding thoughts and visions, of a mind proud and even defiant, even as the heros of her old-cherished stories. He was in another world. The empathy she saw in his eyes now was not sympathy for her, but a director's understanding of an actor's problem.

Besides, in a nutshell, her unbidden feelings for Werner Christed made her uncomfortable, in contrast to the easy familiarity she had enjoyed without strain in Rick Gilbert's company.

Judith did not want to dwell on her mixed-up emotions. She talked to Werner instead about the scene. "It's a horror. It's really as if the men are ready to jump at me."

The director did not respond directly. "Incidentally," he asked, "do you know the difference between horror and terror?"

Judith was surprised at the question, and thought a moment. "They're pretty much the same, aren't they?"

Christed made a negative gesture. "Your old writers of gothics knew better. You're 'terrified' when you anticipate something awful is *going* to happen—like your fear of being raped by those soldiers. You are 'horrified' when it *does* happen."

Judith found it a fascinating and useful distinction. It called for different nuances of expression as the scene developed. Once more, Werner Christed demonstrated his wisdom and his sensitivity.

They repeated the scene, and this time Judith had no difficulty completing it.

*　*　*

As days went by, Judith grew closer to the film company. She felt less strain, with her scenes going well. There were no more strange Gomay occurrences. There were no more drug episodes or yellow premonitions. Her uncertainties about Gomay Island remained, but were pushed to the back of her head by the demands of the production.

At night, talking in the recreation room, Judith found that most of the people in the Christed troupe were like her in basic ways. Most were dissatisfied with the aimlessness of their former lives. The skinny comic brought along an old issue of the *Village Voice* that described their social malaise well. Judith agreed: "Every single inhabitant has in his or her way heard the flickering voice of disgust: 'Something is wrong, something has gone wrong.'"

Someone else quoted Allen Ginsberg. "We have an international youth of solitary children—stilyago, provo, beat, mofads, nadaists, energumeno, mod and rocker—all aghast at the space age horror they are born to . . ."

Judith didn't agree at all that the space age was horrible. It wasn't all weaponry. The space discoveries were enriching man's knowledge in many fields, including agriculture, weather, the natural resources of the world. Modern society had its problems, as did every age, but life would be better and healthier, Judith optimistically believed.

She argued back heatedly that today's "product lust" was better than the *product lack* of the so-called good old days. Nor did she agree with the other major theme people quoted: "The straight world is a jungle of taboos, fears, and personality games . . ." and the way to beat it was through "bells, beads, drugs, and acid rock."

Judith turned from that silently. She knew too well that the acid way was a fraudulent promise, self-destructive, and catastrophic.

The group teased Judith, calling her "the blond square." But it was good-natured, and she did not mind.

Judith found that in the film company one did not live so much in terms of personal friendships. Especially in the confinement of the island, the group developed a sense of community in which individuals seemed to coalesce despite the vanity usual among theatre people. There was the élan of a movie company working together on the cutting edge of revolutionary cinematic creativity.

This spirit emanated from Werner Christed.

Judith felt his charismatic presence everywhere. At first, she took it to be her own hero worship of the man, but it was apparent that everyone in the troupe was personally devoted to him. It was a fresh insight into how and why people follow cult leaders. Fortunately, the director was a force for art, not evil.

Judith herself felt Werner Christed's personal attraction more every day. It was almost as if Rick's constant attendance earlier had formed a shield against Christed's personality. Now, the man's impact struck her with a new intensity. But each time she allowed herself to think of the director in personal terms, the sense of separation between them overcame her, and she put him out of her mind except as the film maker.

Judith also suppressed or evaded whatever uneasiness remained about *Baron of Darkness*. She was seeing the entire production from a new perspective. In scene after scene now she was the central character of Christed's shots. It stirred her sense of responsibility for the success of the project. It wasn't that she felt like a star, though the director praised her work gratifyingly, but rather that for the first time she had a commitment greater than her own ambition. It was a large step into maturity.

Judith Bradford was growing in other ways, more sure of her ability to meet whatever difficulties life presented. When she looked inward, she discerned less guilt about her mother than she had carried with her from home. She renewed her private promise that she would communicate as soon as her family could no longer interfere in her decisions. She found her anger at her stepfather transmuted into comparison with the men around her. What she was left with was a feeling of contempt mixed with a vague sympathy. She became content to let that mess dissolve into a past she was done with.

She was impatient to work, work, work. There was nothing Christed could ask that was too much. Sometimes the director would shoot one scene a score of times, each requiring a variation of her responses. She welcomed the constant challenges, and the exhaustion they brought at night. It made it easier to act impersonally with Rick in the beats that brought them together. There were not too many of these at this point in the production. She was grateful that most of Rick's appearances as Baron Gilles de Rais did not involve her. The atrocities were being filmed on distant sets in the forest, on the cliffs, at the abbey, and a few on boats on the ocean.

Judith wrote a long letter to Lena, describing her work with Christed. She decided not to mention the uncertainties that still came to her mind. Nor did she mention her estrangement from Rick. She considered that Lena was troubled enough with the sickness in her family.

Finishing the letter, Judith realized she did not have Lena's address. It didn't matter. All island mail in or out was handled by Gregor. Everyone suspected that he and Dr. Gomay opened the envelopes to make sure they contained no reference to the island or the story of *Baron of Darkness.* There were no complaints. Werner Christed's reasons for wanting total privacy were respected, and they understood that Dr. Gomay did not want intruders.

Judith left her room seeking Lena's husband. The afternoon was warm and joyful. Laughter came to her from the tennis court and swimming pool. A plane was buzzing busily in the distance over Long Island. Feeling better, Judith looked about for Gregor. Instead, she saw Werner Christed talking to Rick in front of the main house across the green. She was surprised. The day's schedule called for shots at the old abbey—which members of the cast described as "the spookiest joint they had ever seen."

One scene they reported was "worse than spooky"—the bloody dismemberment of a woman by the crazed baron. Judith knew it was done with mirrors like the magician's stage trick of sawing a woman in half, but the image still turned her knees to jelly. She had once seen Rick come from such an act covered with blood—ketchup, of course—and it had made her ill.

There was a second surprise when she saw the director beckoning her from across the common.

When Judith reached the two men, she was aware as never before of the differences between them. Rick was all grace; he was a lithe, swift animal like an antelope, with large eyes that held tenderness as well as alertness. Werner was the king lion, heavy-lidded, proud to the point almost of disdain, powerful and demanding. As a director he had a broad capacity for understanding and controlling others, but the relentless drive that shone in his purposeful eyes overrode everything else in his character.

In comparing the two men, it suddenly came to Judith that their physical handsomeness canceled out. What emerged was their complementary strengths. If Werner was the great director, Rick was the great actor. If Werner was removed in a world of his creativity, Rick was close in his affection. Despite herself, Judith remembered Rick's kisses. Yet, at the same moment she found herself wondering how Werner Christed's strong lips would feel on hers.

Judith turned from the disconcerting image with self-annoyance. The actresses who had been preaching women's lib concepts were right—she had her *own* talent, her own center, her own space. She did not constantly have to define herself in terms of her relationship with any man, neither Werner Christed nor Rick Gilbert!

It occurred to her that, coming upon the two together, she had a rare opportunity to settle her doubts about the nighttime ritual she had seen. She could simply mention the "rehearsal," and the director's reaction would tell her whether or not Rick had been truthful.

But the idea of such a confrontation suddenly seemed demeaning. If she still believed Rick had lied, she ought to have it out with him privately. If he had been honest, her probing would only make clumsy fools of both of them before Christed.

In any case the director immediately gave her something else to think about. "I am switching the schedule again, Judy. I want to get back to the terrace shots tomorrow. Everything is set up again." Then, sternly, "And don't be late this time!"

With a tentative smile, Rick chimed in. "We don't want to be poking you out of the hearse again." It was his first direct address to Judith since their falling out. She could not help her heart beating faster, but she still avoided Rick's eyes.

The director said, "I can't tell you not to think about what happened to Emily. That would be like saying 'Don't think of a rhinoceros for the next five minutes.'" He broke into the ingratiating smile she liked. "Of course a rhinoceros is all you would think of." His tone grew serious again. "We've taken every precaution with the railing and the scaffold. I guarantee no danger, Judy."

"I'm sure it will be all right," Judith said with her new assurance. She heard herself speaking as a professional to professionals, and was pleased. But inwardly, her heart pounded with the terrible memory of Emily sailing into space to her death.

The director went on, "I haven't had a chance to tell you, but Dr. Gomay and I are very impressed with all your rushes."

Judith felt a very nonprofessional flush mount to her cheeks. The praise brought a schoolgirlish embarrassment. It seemed she wasn't quite as changed as she thought.

Another unchanged feeling was the thrill Judith knew when Rick touched her shoulder, and said, "Judy, I think it's time you and I had a talk ourselves."

Judith hesitated. Werner Christed looked from Rick to her with eyes that suddenly seemed curtained. Then he said lightly, "We're done. Go on with Rick, Judy. This isn't my kind of scene."

When Rick took her arm and they walked along together as they had not done for weeks, Judith realized how much she had missed him. She told him she had to stop at Gregor's, volunteering, "I've written to Lena, but I have to get her address."

Inside, Gregor took the envelope from Judith with a broad smile. "Just leave it here. I'll take care of it."

Judith started out, then turned back. "Gregor, this is embarrassing, but could I use the facilities, please?"

"Why not?" he said neutrally. "Through there, past the bedroom."

Judith walked quickly through the apartment with her eyes straight ahead. She was not a snooper. She knew the type from her mother's parties; it was amazing how many pillars of society would pry into other people's drawers and medicine chests. In her own room she had sometimes found things out of place after a "social."

Coming back through the Ludovici bedroom, Judith's eye was caught by an unsought sight that made her stop in her tracks. Lena's elephant bracelet lay on the woman's dressing table, amidst an untypical jumble of cosmetic jars and bottles.

As clearly as if the woman were in the room with her, Judith heard Lena's stricken voice in the freight elevator that first day: *"You know I go no place without my bracelet!"*

It came back to Judith so vividly because it had seemed out of character for a person as solid as Lena Ludovici to be so fiercely upset about a talisman, even granting it held an exceptional sentimental charge.

Staring at the bracelet, Judith's suspicions blazed. Now she had a new perplexity to contend with. Fact:

Lena Ludovici did not go anywhere without her bracelet. Fact: The bracelet was here. Conclusion: The woman did not leave this room voluntarily. *Then what had happened to Lena?*

Judith curbed herself. There were simple answers to all her concerns if she didn't always choose to pounce on the disturbing possibilities. Example: Lena would be terribly upset about a dying sister. She would leave in a rush to make a plane. The explanation of a left-behind bracelet could be as simple and innocent as that.

Yet something in Judith now wanted to see Gregor write Lena's address on the letter. The envelope was still blank when she returned to the office. She smiled. "You *are* going to remember my letter."

"Of course." Gregor looked up. There was something in the girl's eyes that told him it would be best to be wary. He nodded. Let her see with those searching eyes that he was writing down the address of Lena's sister plainly and at once. He scrawled heavily on the envelope. Judith was satisfied. Though the handwriting was foreign-looking, she made out the Cincinnati address clearly. She studied it. She would remember it.

Returning to Rick, Judith said nothing of the bracelet. It was a time she wished to rely entirely on herself.

On Balefire Bluff, Judith stood with her arms wide, letting the wind blow her hair and her wide skirt. Rick laughed easily in his former, relaxed way. "You look like a figurehead on one of the old ships."

To Judith, it was like sailing. Sailing like the gulls, like a plane. She was on the sea and in the air at the same time, cleansed of her questions by the flowing breeze and the fresh smell of the pine trees. The grove was not an ancient bower of sweet boughs and vines. It was no enchanted arbor with flowered turf. As always, there was the harshness of rocks and of trees dwarfed and blown spare by cold ocean blasts. But she was pleased to be here again, and alert when Rick spoke in an unexpected vein.

"Judy, I am sorry, very sorry, about that stupid night outside the Gomays' place. *I did lie to you!*" He said it with emphasis.

Judith stood riveted in astonishment.

"Please sit down. I should have told you everything as soon as you asked!" Without taking her questioning eyes from the man's troubled face, Judith eased down on "their log." Rick continued, "I am not supposed to be talking about any of this, but you are more important to me than anything else. I have learned that the hard way these past days without you."

He stopped. He stared up at the vaulting, cloudless sky as if looking for a cue card to read. He turned back to Judith. "Please hear me out, and let me start at the beginning. The beginning is Dr. Gomay. He is a fascinating person. In his own way, I find him even more interesting than Werner."

Knowing Rick Gilbert's admiration of Christed, Judith realized this was no offhand comment.

"Dr. Gomay and his people have brought their own religion from the old country. It is alien and strange here. To an outsider it may seem even macabre. But when I first came to the island and the old man invited me to one of their ceremonies, I found it spellbinding. I could not dismiss it as just crackpot stuff. These people have different meanings to teach about life and death." Rick paused thoughtfully, pinching his lips with his thumb and forefinger. "Judy, you and I have talked about philosophy and religion . . ."

Judith gave an acknowledging tilt of her head. She remembered the satisfaction she had taken in their deep discussions. Rick's wide-ranging knowledge had set him off from the other actors. It was his combination of intelligence with physical appeal that had amplified her first attraction to him.

"Well, here is what happened, from the top. When Werner was first discussing an arrangement with Dr. Gomay, he came out to the island. He brought me and Gregor, but not Lena. One night the doctor invited us to one of the Gomay meetings—which they call consortiums. Werner found it of little interest. His own concepts are too strong. For Gregor, it was a welcome return to practices much like those of his own family in the past. For me, it was a powerful and heady brew—an appealing mixture of old and new."

Talking earnestly, Rick hardly paid attention to his pacing near the edge of the elevation. Judith almost called a warning, afraid he might fall in his concentration, but he turned back in time, saying, "Being a novice, I never did get their full message. It is a combination of Eastern concepts and Middle-European superstitions. I think there is nothing like it anywhere else, and it is a weird combination, I can tell you.

"For instance, part of the ritual you witnessed the other night is what they call their Life-Death Ceremony. They place dummy corpses in coffins, and pretend to bring them back to life—"

Judith could not help interrupting. "I thought it was Emily's body, and they were doing terrible things to it!"

"No! It was not Emily. But . . ." Rick stopped again, and dropped his head. ". . . It was no rehearsal, either. I did not know what to tell you! The ceremony becomes very—pagan, shall we say? I was glad they assigned me outside to guard the door. You see, it is their fertility rites at the start of the summer planting in the old country. They do things I would rather not discuss. Frankly, I have not gone back. I have told Dr. Gomay it is not for me."

Judith probed, "But it isn't too much for Gregor!"

"So you recognized him?"

"Yes."

"Well, as I say, Gregor is from that part of the world." Rick stopped again, waiting for a sign from Judith that she understood.

Judith said finally, "I appreciate your telling me."

"I wanted you to know the truth right off! But we were both upset by the dog, and then when you attacked me, to tell you honestly, I resented it."

"I guess I had my back up." Judith gave Rick a widening smile.

Gently, Rick lifted Judith to her feet and drew her into his arms. "It's still the most beautiful back I've ever seen," he smiled. Judith responded with not only her pent-up ardor, but with her relief at finding that the island's question-box was not locked impenetrably. Whatever kinky religion Dr. Gomay and his retinue practice, let it be their business, she sighed. Rick was out of it, well out of it and back with her. They would go on as they had been before. They would make *Baron of Darkness* with Werner Christed, and then leave the strange island for a future that had suddenly brightened again.

After a lingering kiss Judith moved away, saying, "Rick, I still do have questions, though."

"Ask away, if I know the answers."

"Did they ever find Emily's body?"

"No." Plain, straightforward, unambiguous.

"That night—I'd swear I saw the kerchief she was wearing."

"Yes. They picked it off the rocks."

Judith squeezed her eyes, not wanting to see the mangled form she could imagine. Then she nodded. "I thought it might be that way."

"What else?" Rick prompted helpfully.

"Well, yes," Judith said, more to herself than to Rick. Get it all out! "One afternoon, Emily and I saw you going down to the Gomay house—"

"I remember that," Rick said promptly. "I needed one of their capes for a scene, and Dr. Gomay arranged for me to pick out the proper size. Besides, at the time, I was what might be termed a novice member of their community."

Judith was satisfied, but another of her suppressed questions rose to the surface now that she had the opportunity: "Rick, did you ever see the Gomays without their masks?"

"No." He added quickly, "But I'm sure they are like anyone else!" He smiled encouragingly. "Anything else I can oblige you with?"

"What *about* Gregor?" The elephant bracelet was vivid among Judith's doubts.

"Oh, Gregor is one of their cult without any doubt. Wholeheartedly so. But he does his job for Werner very well, and that is all that matters to us, isn't it?"

"Another question?"

"Of course."

"Lena."

"Lena?" Rick seemed surprised.

"You said she didn't come out with you that first time. But did Gregor ever get her to—join the Gomays?"

"No." It was another flat statement. "You sound worried about Lena," Rick commented. Judith appreciated his concern. It was good to have someone to share her thoughts with again. She decided there was no such thing as being half-trusting any more than being slightly pregnant. In a flurry she told Rick Gilbert of Lena's elephant bracelet and her fears of some kind of foul play.

Rick's response was an open smile. "On that score I can satisfy you personally. I saw Gregor driving Lena off the island, just as he told you. I remember it especially because the hearse was being repaired, and he was driving a station wagon."

In her relief, Judith wanted to hug Rick.

He was saying, with the half-teasing grin she loved, "If you hadn't picked such a fight with me, I could have told you all this sooner."

"One last question, then?" Judith stopped. This was the most difficult of all.

"Yes?"

Judith enunciated each word as if her tongue were heavy. "The woman I thought I saw in the tower that night, the one I thought was out to kill me? Is she a figment of my mind?"

She watched Rick carefully. He was taking a deep breath, staring at her with an expression of concern, tenderness, and utter candor. "Yes," he said softly. "All in your mind."

"It was so real," she whispered, still torn.

"The doctors have told you how it happens . . ."

"You can't believe it while it's happening . . ."

"I understand."

"No, you don't! No one can. I could *touch* that woman. I could smell her, see her, feel her. I was sure she could kill me, as sure as I am that I am standing here with you now."

Rick nodded, "That's the way those damnable drugs work."

Judith smiled wanly. "How do I know you're not a delusion, then?"

Rick smiled more brightly. "How do we know all life isn't a dream?" The first question of children, the last question of philosophers.

"She wasn't there?"

"Except in your head . . ."

"The tower room was as empty as when Dr. Gomay showed it to me?"

"Yes."

Judith could not let go of it. "Beyond any other possibility?"

"Beyond any other possibility," Rick said gravely.

She nodded. She had to believe him. "Then I can only pray Dr. Willoughby was right about it fading away some day."

"Let me help it happen," Rick said tenderly. "The way we feel about each other, Judy, is the best medicine in the world. You're going to be fine."

For the first time, Judith initiated their kiss, remembering that in olden days the bearer of good tidings was always rewarded.

CHAPTER SIXTEEN

The rebuilt movie set on Death Point was waiting under heavy clouds. The night was moonless, black and damp, but not rainy. The pieces of film equipment were covered with gray tarpaulins; they rested like sleeping beasts all around the elevation. There was no wind, and no sound other than the waves far below. The bellbuoys seemed cottoned by a reaching fog, their clanging hardly audible on the cliff. The only clear sound was the snoring of the crew man Moose had sent up to guard the set.

Into this stillness a shadow crept. It slinked out of the forest, holding and starting, waiting to see if it aroused any suspicion. Inch by patient inch the stealthy figure closed toward the cliff edge where the scaffold had been reconstructed. When the shadow finally reached the balustrade, it raised an arm to saw with a long knife.

With the flash of that motion the figure uttered a muffled cry of satisfaction and swung around to race away.

But the triumphant whisper changed to a throttled breath of consternation as another hand appeared in the night—this one shooting up from the scaffold to imprison the shadow's slicing wrist. There was a brief scuffle, then a sound of cursing and a figure being dragged away.

Minutes later, Dr. Gomay stood in his bathrobe in the manor library. He stared furiously at his daughter, Margot, where his servants had shoved her to the floor before him. The knife she had carried on Death Point made a shaft of wicked light under a desk lamp. The woman's face was venomous with her sick, poisoned emotion. Her eyes glared with stark madness, her passion-lined lips curved malevolently at her father. She was a vision of night, lost in a private grief she now turned on the old man with loathing.

"You have disobeyed me, Margot!" Dr. Gomay thundered.

"You have disobeyed the family trust!" the woman lashed back. There were remnants of great beauty in the face ravaged by years of wilfulness and unscrupulous self-love. "You have betrayed our island to strangers, and broken your sacred pledge to me!"

"There was no pledge, Margot!"

"Aye!" the woman howled. Her cracked shout made even the two great Gomay guards quail. "It was my condition that none of the thieving whores could come here unless I was Joan of Arc!"

The old voice was impatient. "You have no experience of these cinema matters!"

"I *am* Joan!" Without warning, Margot Gomay threw off her cloak to pose in nakedness. The servants turned away. She was a serpent woman. Her body held the invitation of a succubus, deadly and ruinous in its open sexuality. Dr. Gomay's lost daughter was a concentrate of pure evil to make a viewer's mouth go dry, hair rise on end, the flesh shiver with apprehension rather than desire.

"I have been watching everything, you know!" the madwoman hissed. A look of cunning and virulence further darkened the sinister eyes. "I know the new whore they call Judith! She shall not escape me, as the other two did not escape me!"

Dr. Gomay signaled to the guards. "Take her to the tower! Make sure the new bars are secure. Station two guards before the door day and night! She must not escape again! On peril of your own lives!"

A defiant cackle broke from the lunatic. In one quicksilver motion, she leaped up from the floor to rush at the room's great fireplace and, pressing a secret panel, she vanished into a hidden passage before any of the startled men could follow. Her fading howls mocked their frustration as they failed to find the button only she knew.

The weather held in the morning, and Judith was up on Death Point well before the director's starting time. She was in the same kind of costume Emily Lawrence had worn. The rough blue material of the peasant blouse was scratchy on her shoulders, the rugged gray workpants felt as floppy and uncomfortable as they had the first time three weeks before. Glumly, Judith found it hard to believe three weeks had passed since Emily's accident. She strongly missed the comfort of Lena's presence, Lena's help in getting into the costume.

Judith wanted to ask Gregor whether he had mailed her letter to Lena, but the assistant director was bustling about again like a Napoleon. The only one who paid any attention to Judith was Moose. He explained that Rick was still in the make-up tent. This shot was "for the can," not just a test, and Werner wanted it right all the way.

Judith asked Moose about an unfamiliar machine she noticed standing beside one of the cameras. The man lowered his voice to her. "No, that's not part of what you worked with before. Werner isn't going to unveil his new baby until the big last scene, as you probably know. This one here is just a standard effect. It gives us a fog, by spraying out a mist of light oil. At the same time, we have a fog filter in the camera. Between the two, although you won't notice it while you're doing your scene, the film will look like we shot you and Rick in London pea soup."

Moose smiled indulgently at Judith's wondering expression. Everything about the inside techniques of film-making still captivated her.

Rick Gilbert coming out of the makeup tent was anything but captivating! He had been painted to look like a ghastly fiend from which any human would flee. His face now held a fixed, disgusting leer that reflected the craven depravity and degeneracy of Baron Gilles de Rais. His skin was pocked and disgusting with running sores. It took all of Judith's control to remember that the person beneath the horrible disguise was her Rick. She speculated with grim humor that any woman would gladly dive off the cliff to her death before she would let this foul-looking beast touch her. She wondered why Werner had altered the makeup since the first take with Emily, but it wasn't for her to ask.

She wanted badly to see the scaffold. Yes, it was solid and safe and reassuring, hanging just below the edge of the cliff, out of camera range. It was heavily-mattressed, with a firm railing all around, and held by stout ropes. She saw Moose himself climb down and jump on the platform in a last-minute test. It held, without any question. There would not be another accident. Less jittery, Judith blew a kiss to Moose.

Werner Christed called her and Rick to the mocked-up castle wall. Although Rick was pressing her hand, it was Christed's intense voice that sent a thrill up Judith's spine. "Everything is riding on you now, Judy. You've been great in your other shots, and you'll give me what I want now. You both know the blocking, so let's get this in the can the first time out!"

Out of the corner of her eye, Judith saw Dr. Gomay arrive. His gaze took in everything searchingly, as he sat down beside Gregor near the main camera. Judith was suddenly aware of the roar of the waves down below. The wind had whipped up; there was a new chill in the air, matching the chill in Judith's chest as Gregor shouted, "Quiet everyone!" The clap-board snapped. There was an instant's pause, everyone breathless in vibrant expectation as Christed called the now familiar film litany: "Lights. Action. Roll 'em!"

Judith suddenly found it hard to breathe. Her feet were

rooted, she had turned to stone. If the scene did not call for her to be dragged on the terrace, she would have been unable to move. Before the castle wall, Rick/Baron Gilles de Rais came toward her mincingly, in the gait of a haughty but effeminate nobleman. Judith hardly saw him. Despite herself, her head was filled with the picture of Emily plunging through the railing to the waiting, hungry sea. Judith wanted to turn and flee, but there could be no flight. Rick, following his part, was grabbing her in an awful embrace.

Judith did not have to act out her struggle. Her attacker was no longer Rick. The violence she felt within was not a performance, but real to her. She battled with all her strength to get away from the lecherous, diseased mouth demanding her lips. She would never be able to kiss Rick again, she moaned to herself. She would never be free of the loathing and panic that consumed her though she tried to tell herself it was only a scene.

Judith managed to stay in enough possession of herself to say the few lines that were required for the microphone that was balancing over Rick's head and hers, but she wept genuine tears as Rick forced her across the terrace to the balustrade.

"Don't! *Please DON'T!*" she shrieked in real terror. No need to pretend. Judith *was* the peasant girl scratching and kicking at the baron, beseeching him for mercy and knowing there was none, and, all too soon shoved against the railing, the fatal move and, oh, God, *impossible!* Suddenly Judith knew that the chill wind rushing up from the waves below was the breath of Death claiming her body and soul.

And, abruptly, hardly conscious, in a final gasp of horror, she was flinging out of Rick's grasp and plummeting over the edge into empty space.

The roar of the waves was a grunting of ravenous animals ready to tear out her heart, lap up her blood.

Not only Judith's breath stopped. Everyone watching congealed in a tableau of terror.

For Judith, the moment of unspeakable anguish ended almost comically with a prosaic *bump.*

The mattress of the scaffold was soft as a comfortable bed. The platform itself was sturdy as a house. It hardly shook as she landed. Sobs of relief heaved out of Judith ungovernably. Above her head, wild cheers filled the air. And Moose was standing beside her, holding her, patting her; a rock, a comforting father.

Judith heard Werner Christed's congratulatory shout: "Cut! Great! *That's a take!*"

Through the tears she could not hold, Judith smiled tremulously at Moose. It had better be a take, she thought. It was a scene she was never going to play again, not for Werner, not for anyone in the world.

She looked upward from the scaffold and saw Rick staring down anxiously. His concern was grotesque on his wicked baron's face. She waved to him, and called, "I'm okay." She could not manage a smile. The sight of him still revolted her.

The ugly, impossible contrast between Rick-as-baron and Rick-as-himself continued to be a strain on Judith as they now played scenes together day after day: Judith as peasant girl, Judith as Joan of Arc aiding King Charles VII when Gilles de Rais was a young, clean man, and then his first temptations and his first experiments with evil, going from bad to worse to unspeakable.

The two performers worked exceedingly hard each

day. It always took an interval of adjustment before Judith could accept Rick when they met for dinner, or to walk alone on the few afternoons they were not before the cameras.

The picture was going well, with more and more of the grisly scenes in the can every day. Werner remained intense, but he was pleased and praised Judith. Dr. Gomay moved about with a fixed, lopsided smile that showed his ancient gums. To Judith, the Gomays in their hoods and robes seemed to fade into the landscape. No more chants were heard in the night. The island was tranquil.

Judith kept checking with Gregor for Lena's reply to her letter. "I wonder why she hasn't answered. It's been two full weeks."

Usually, Judith got only Gregor's empty smile and a noncommittal shrug. This day he added, "There may be mail waiting in the city for you. I have to drive in this afternoon. We will see. I do think Lena ought to be back home soon."

Later, from the table where she was lunching with Rick, Judith saw the hearse start away, making for the drawbridge and the outside world. She turned to Rick, her expression hopeful. "Gregor says Lena may be back soon."

Rick Gilbert leaned across the table to say softly, "When she gets here, I would like to tell her something very personal . . ." He stopped.

"What?" Judith asked, not quite sure of Rick's meaning.

"About us." His eyes were gentle on her.

Judith heard the tenderness in Rick, and felt the warmth of the hand he put softly on hers. "What about us?" she whispered, sensing that he was expressing something deep-felt and important. They were in the midst of the dining-hall bustle, but as alone as if they were solitary on their cliff.

"About our being engaged," Rick said solemnly.

Breathless, Judith realized that Rick was proposing to her. A flooding turmoil of new emotions overtook her, sweeping away all that bad gone before. Her face broke into a brilliant smile of happiness, of acquiescence, of certainty about Rick Gilbert that needed no further examination. In her heart, Judith had prayed this would happen. Whatever uneasiness about Gomay Island and the movie characters endured in her inner mind, it had nothing to do with Rick Gilbert, the man, the handsome, strong, talented man gazing at her with open love.

Engaged! And just that morning Werner Christed had volunteered that he was more than happy with her work! Yes, her mother would be surprised at how well things were turning out after all.

Blissfully, Judith pressed Rick's hand between her palms and let him see the honest, yielding tears of happiness she allowed to roll unchecked from her elated eyes.

Judith was unaware of another's eyes that were following her every move from the dense trees of the nearby forest—snake-like eyes venomous with hatred, threat, and lunatic determination.

CHAPTER SEVENTEEN

Report to: Ursula Blake
Subject: Bradford Investigation
From: H.F.

The hearse finally showed up, late afternoon yesterday. Driver loaded cartons from loft building, and exchanged mail packages with garage attendant, as suspected. Driver 40-ish, swarthy, pockmarked face, foreign-looking. Over 200 lbs. About 6' tall.

In Greenwich Village, driver stopped at a candle factory, took large delivery, black candies, tall as a man, 6 inches thick, never saw anything like these before.

Next stop, Voodoo Store on Bleeker St., several cartons waiting. I would make out incense sticks, bags of colored powders, sacks of little idols, all unfamiliar to me. You may want to check the store yourself, card enclosed.

Hearse headed out of city, and I tailed it per your instructions. I have marked its route on the attached map of Long Island.

Hearse made another stop, on the Island, at "Century Casket Company." Picked up four coffins waiting for it. (Two plain pine boxes, two finished caskets, walnut with brass handles.) Subject paid in cash.

After loading coffins, subject headed east on Long Island, kept off expressways driving back roads. Went slow, noticeably careful to obey all stop signs, etc.

After 3½ hours, subject turned onto dirt road marked Private (see X on map). Not much used, looks to be old logging path, narrow, rutted, washed out. If you come this way, watch your springs and the marshland both sides.

NOTICE: This turn-off is easy to miss. Look for a broken-down barn on your left where I marked "Y."

On "logging road" you will run into thick forest at 2.75 miles. Ocean is on your right as you are continuing east. At 3.75 miles, hearse stopped. There is a small pier there, new or recently rebuilt.

By the map, you will see that is opposite a "Gomay Island." Map shows this about a mile long, half a mile wide, extending north-south lengthwise, looks sort of skull-shaped. The pier is at the north end at the top of the skull. The island is separated from the road by an inlet about 30' wide. (Like a moat around old-time castles!) The water looks deep, with very tricky current (wouldn't recommend boat!).

Island has high cliffs all around, looks like walled city, big fortress, no exaggeration.

Across the inlet, a stone guardhouse. 2 guards, big, tough, 6'5" at least, 250 pounds-plus, pro wrestlers (?) Wouldn't like to tangle. Thought maybe boxing camp, or secret tycoon hunting lodge, but see below.

NOTICE: The guards carry high-powered rifles, so whatever is happening on this island is No Fooling.

Also, killer dogs in enclosure. Mean customers. If you plan to investigate further, take plenty care.

Damndest contraption I ever saw came down across the water for the hearse to drive onto the island. It's a believe-it-or-not bridge right out of Errol Flynn movies (if you're not too young to remember them!)...

When guards spotted my car, they yelled and aimed at me. I followed your instructions to arouse as little suspicion as possible. I yelled back I was lost, and I got out of there but fast.

The road leads on to Gomayville Village (see "V" on map). It's 3.26 miles further east from the pier. (Deep ruts again, and more swampland--don't ditch!)

Gomayville is tiny place, out-of-the-way. Pop under 500. It's a working fish port, not a summer resort place.

ADDITIONAL FACTS:

1. No entrance to Gomay Island except over that bridge. Those cliffs lowest 50-60', no way up. Fishermen in Gomayville say there's one beach where a boat can land, but it's fenced off. Looks like nobody cares to get on the island anyway.

2. Island belongs to a Dr. Felix Gomay. He and his daughter are last of original family, rich as Rockefellers, village people say. No question they throw a lot of weight in those parts. The story is that about 10 years ago, Dr. Gomay and daughter went to live in family lands in Europe, nobody is sure where. Last year he came back to America, with a crowd of servants. Village thought they'd be good for business, but it seems everyone stays strictly on their cozy island.

3. Lots of local legends, scary, sort of. I heard of island ghosts, funny lights, weird music, screams and howls in the night. May be some basis, because this came from solid citizens who used to work in the woods along the logging road.

Some nuts, of course. One old lady says witches live in the island caves--she hears them like banshees. Could be the wind, of course. The locals are lonely, isolated, have nothing much to do all winter but make up ghost stories.

4. About 3 months ago, suddenly a lot of activity on the island. A movie company, the village

says. Excitement again, but no new business from the new people either.

5. Local police confirm. Name of film company is Werner Christed Productions, so Gomay Island is the location you're looking for, all right; and your Judith Bradford could be there. The movie people came out in 2 separate batches--the first bunch was carpenters and crew, etc. The actors and actresses arrived the last week in June, which would fit the timetable for the Bradford girl.

6. PRIME IMPORTANCE: The village police records show two recent deaths on Gomay Island, both young actresses with the Christed production. The first was a "Roberta Leslie," death attributed to food poisoning, certificate signed by Dr. Felix Gomay, the owner of the island, and a registered physician. The report says the girl got down to the island beach some way, dug clams, and took sick. I thought all you got was hepatitis or something, but assume the doctor knows better. Might be worth checking.

The second death was an "Emily Lawrence." I enclose a copy of the complete police report on that accident.

Blake lifted the attached sheet with an uneasy premonition. Could "Emily Lawrence" be Judith Bradford? The report told nothing of what Ursula Blake needed to know for identification—the girl's height, weight, hair color. But at least she had established a solid tie-in between the hearse and a Christed film production on "Gomay Island." It was time she headed for the place herself, Blake considered—and found out, among other things, why they needed so many coffins!

Blake's watch said 10:00 a.m. With any luck she could be there by early afternoon. She buzzed her secretary to get her car out, fast. Gomay Island was going to have a visitor whether it wanted one or not.

CHAPTER EIGHTEEN

Judith had a break in her shooting schedule. Werner and Rick were privately filming more of the atrocities, and Judith was thankful again that she was not needed for those gruesome shots. She was displeased that Gregor had brought no letter on his return from the city, but she wandered contentedly around the Urwolde estate, stopping to chat with her many new friends, savoring the sea air, even the gray canvas of the overcast sky this day.

She could not get used to the quick weather changes. A

day like this might begin with the brightest sun and blue above, only to draw a curtain of clouds down the sky like a great shade, and to sweep Gomay Island with a squall an hour later. Judith had known extreme weather in Iowa, but it was not normally so capricious.

With time to think, Judith pondered how far she had come in just her few weeks with the Christed company. It seemed a lifetime. Her mother's world seemed on another planet. Judith was even able to think of her stepfather without her stomach knotting. It was part of her growth that she was beginning to see the world and life through eyes other than her own. It didn't mean "everything goes," but it did call for more understanding, more tolerance of others' weaknesses—like Gregor's pomposity, she thought—and Rick's experimenting with the Gomays' religion—and the intimations of arrogance she got from Werner Christed.

With a flush that came from nowhere, Judith wondered how she would feel if it were Werner instead of Rick with whom she was emotionally involved. She scolded herself at once for a silly notion. The director was a genius who deserved the pedestal on which people placed him, not a man one thought of in terms of engagement, marriage and, ultimately, a family . . .

Judith shook her head with self-irritation. Such nonsense was like the pesky mosquitos that deserved nothing but the swat she gave them now. Even if there were no Rick in her life—and thank goodness there very much was again!—it behooved her to remember her appropriate place with relation to Werner Christed. *No* place!

Yet the thread continued to unwind behind her eyes as she strolled on. Suppose *Baron of Darkness* made her a star? Would she begin to be in Werner Christed's class then? Would the space between them shrink?

Daydreams!

And anyway, Judith repeated with growing self-annoyance, why did she want to be thinking about Werner this way when she had Rick—when their formal engagement would be announced as soon as Lena returned. Lena, whom she missed so dreadfully. Judith decided abruptly that if she didn't receive a letter soon, she would telephone Cincinnati. Then she remembered that the phone in the dormitory had been out of order from the beginning and the single working instrument on the island was Dr. Gomay's, available only for emergencies. Her desire to speak to Lena could hardly be called an emergency . . .

With her feet wandering as casually as her musings, Judith realized she had strolled through the cemetery and come to the rear, where a grotto of trees marked the boundary of the ever-present forest. Shading her eyes, Judith found herself squinting at something that did not seem right, did not seem to belong. Moving closer, she saw two graves on the floor of the grove. Two graves she did not remember. Freshly dug. No mistake. There were two obviously fresh scars in the otherwise undisturbed earth.

What did they tell of? Two new graves? Two coffins in the Gomays' basement that night?—holding *dummies*, Rick had assured her?

Judith's hands went to her cheeks. Old doubts and new jostled in her mind. The graves were like two human hands stretching up from the earth in supplication. The only thing Judith was sure of in her perturbation was that this was no yellow-fogged mirage.

Her second thought, which struck an intuitive blow she could not shield, was a dread certainty that Emily was in one of these graves—and that the other somehow held Lena Ludovici!

Judith caved to her knees, drowned in despair.

At the same instant, she felt a sudden brush on the back of her neck, as of insect antennae. Shocked again, she turned to find herself staring into the inquiring eyes of Dr. Gomay.

"I am sorry I startled you, Judith." His tone was friendly.

Her reply was to spring to her feet with an accusatory cry: "These graves are new!" If the old Merlin expected her to cringe before his skull-eyes, he was mistaken! She would not be intimidated by anything on Gomay Island any longer. "New graves!" she repeated with open combativeness.

But the surprise in the situation tilted to Dr. Gomay's side when he immediately conceded, "Yes. Of course. Anyone can see these are freshly dug."

Taken aback, Judith felt more injured. Did this old sorcerer believe he could brazen this out? She defied him, demanding flatly, "*Whose* graves?"

"Why," he answered with the same maddeningly quiet assurance, "Werner has a scene soon where the villagers come storming up to the baron's estate seeking their children. Moose has planted two coffins here for them to find." Unexpectedly, Dr. Gomay pointed upward. "You can see the camera platform the crew has constructed in this tree, for a straight-down shot. It should be very effective, typically Werner, don't you agree?"

Following the old man's finger, Judith saw raw boards in the trees. Mortification washed over her. She still had not learned not to jump to conclusions!

Dr. Gomay spoke in a fatherly manner. "Judith, you have a very important role in our picture. Your biggest scenes lie ahead. Werner and I want you to be as splendid as we know you can be. If anything is troubling you, please let me help. Is your hallucination problem bothering you?"

All at once, Dr. Gomay seemed different to Judith. Now his eyes seemed not threatening but wise and caring. His face seemed not a skull but a spare, highbred countenance. He was saying in a congenial way, "Now, Judy, I want you to see this for yourself." Before Judith comprehended the old man's purpose, he had summoned nearby Gomays and they were digging up the earth. "You will see that there are only dummies buried here. I want you to satisfy yourself completely," Dr. Gomay insisted as Judith hung her head, shame-faced. It was going to be even worse than the tower room, for now she had not even the drug excuse . . .

The coffins were brought up, despite her too-late protests. Although she believed Dr. Gomay, Judith found it hard to keep her gaze steady when the Gomays lifted the lids. Here there was a boy and there a girl, both plainly artificial. They were sickeningly slashed and broken, stained with paint to look like dried blood—exactly the kind of children Dr. Gomay had described in telling of the baron's debaucheries. The images made her shiver, and she was even more uncomfortable thinking of her shabby accusation of Dr. Gomay. She owed the man apologies and sincerely wanted to extend them, but could not bring herself to speak.

She stood silently, flushing, expecting some recrimination, but instead she heard, "It's all right, Judith. We are all jittery at this stage. *Baron of Darkness* is a fearful story, of course. And Emily's accident does not help any of us. Why don't you come along and have a cup of tea with me?"

Judith hesitated. She wanted to run off and hide her embarrassment, but she had received an invitation reserved for very few, and her abiding curiosity took over. To see the private quarters of the Manor House—it would be a rare privilege!

In a book-lined room, a servant had lit a small fire. The early August day was cool, and the stone walls of the great building made the interior even more pleasant. The tea warmed Judith's stomach, and she sat back feeling only a little out of place. Dr. Gomay was showing an unexpectedly gracious side of himself. His manners no longer seemed theatrical, but fastidious and old-worldly. He led the conversation around to the Angel Dust aberration. The doctor surveyed the thousands of handsome leather volumes lining the polished shelves. "If we only knew how the brain really works, what couldn't we accomplish? Let me say that I believe your hallucinating will disappear rapidly now that you are so solidly into a new chapter of your life. But I do have one warning, Judith. You must be prepared for the curious fact that, like a light bulb that flares up brightest just before it expires, your final bouts may well be even more vivid than those you have suffered so far. Perhaps the very next one. Your only defense is to try harder to recognize the hallucinations as illusory. In any case, if it is at all possible, try to find me at once, at the first signs of an attack."

"I will!" Judith said it genuinely. For the first time she trusted this man, and could only hope he did not guess how disloyal she had been to him and his world. Disloyal was the only word for her endless suspicions, her dark surmises, her quick distrust and plain funks. They had been her knee-jerk response to every mischance on the island. And every single one had turned out to have a harmless explanation! She had either been in the grip of her own illusion machine—as she termed her spells now with a grim humor—or she had—out of some subconscious need?—misinterpreted every event in the worst possible light, never considering the rational alternatives that had, in fact, turned out to be accurate and truthful!

She did not blame herself too stringently. Certainly the episode with Rick in Gomay robes outside the basement ritual had been seriously unsettling. Indeed, now that she thought of it, Rick might well have explained it sooner and spared her the long anxiety she had suffered. But when she added it all up, as with today's unforgivable charge of murder at Dr. Gomay, she had been wrong, wrong, wrong! That first broken coffin *had* held a mannequin. The jail in the tower *had* been a figment of her imagination—she had seen the real room with her own eyes the next day. The fresh graves just now *had* held not Emily—or Lena, what a wild notion!—but dummies Werner Christed was using. There *had* been only microphone booms in the coffin in the hearse.

If she needed a clincher, Judith had only to recall her absolute *conviction* that there had been a corpse trying to get out of that casket. And, she asked herself again, what about her mother's voice, so clear, and her mother's perfume, so plain! There could be only one conclusion. It was all, all of it, her fallibility—all phantoms of the phosphorescence still flickering in the disturbed convolutions of her brain.

She was brought out of her rumination by Dr. Gomay. "What are you thinking, Judith?" He asked it in a tone offering cooperation.

What could she tell the old man? Judith asked herself ruefully. That she had been ready, able, and willing to believe and accept every fantastic black possibility: that he, and Gregor, and the Gomays, were creatures out of a nether world, out of hell itself—witches, warlocks, demons, vampires, and God (Satan?) alone knew what!

Could she admit to this solicitous old man what she had not dared to admit to herself in the dark of many weeping nights—the shadows that had whisked in the subterranean chambers of her mind: that the movie-making was a sham, *and that Werner Christed himself was one of the clandestine island order, perhaps its high priest!*

Could she confess the terrible indictment of Gomay Island that had percolated in the recesses of her hidden fright: *that Werner Christed was preparing unholy rites*, even crazier than Jim Jones and his People's Temple mass suicides?

Could she tell old Dr. Gomay, who was comforting her now with friendly eyes, that in her seething depths she had even believed he and Christed had been planning to practice the unspeakable abominations of "Baron Gilles de Rais" on the unsuspected company when everyone had been lulled into a sense of false security? Who would there be to stop them on this hermetic island with its squads of overpowering Gomays?

No! Judith rebuked herself fiercely. A thousand times *No!* How unutterably stupid and scatterbrained and ungrateful she had been! She had only been proving once again that she was a child, with infantile fantasies and spooks. She had been troubled by her stepfather's attack;

it had thrown her off balance, unquestionably. But it was no reason to greet every day as if the sun itself were treasonable, as if there were no decency left in anyone anywhere. She knew for herself that these people were working hard for something they believed held an important world message as well as an artistic breakthrough. She *knew* Lena, and she did not doubt her! She *knew* Rick, and she loved him! She *knew* Werner Christed, and she honored him. She *knew* Gregor, and she respected his dedication! Now she even knew Dr. Gomay, and she found him giving of himself. Yes, they all had their eccentricities. That did not make them objects of dire suspicion! It made them the more human and fascinating and worthwhile!

Dr. Gomay smiled at Judith avuncularly. "I asked what you were thinking, my dear."

She could answer at once, honestly. "How happy I am!" she told him, simply. And she was truly happy that she meant it, meant it all the way into her bones. Judith felt lighter than air. She had not realized how much weight she had been carrying with such a load of melancholy on her shoulders. Now everything was airy and bright. All she wanted was to go to Rick and tell him of her—*renaissance* was all she could call it.

Judith's flying mood was shattered by the jangling of Dr. Gomay's phone. Judith literally jumped; not having heard the bell for so long, she felt as if her ear had exploded.

At the instrument, Dr. Gomay's voice transformed from the mildness of a moment before to a shrill, command: "Hold the woman there! Yes, let the bridge down! I am coming at once, at once!"

CHAPTER NINETEEN

Ursula Blake had stopped boldly at the Gomay Island pier. She intended her car to be conspicuous to the guards, and she kept her hand on her horn until the maddened dogs on the other side of the moat were leaping frantically at their enclosure. The two burly guards were waving Blake away angrily.

Provocatively, she left her car to call loudly across the water. "Tell Dr. Felix Gomay I wish to see him!"

One man yelled back in a strong accent, "No Dr.

Gomay here!"

The other bellowed, "Private property! Go off!"

Blake recognized that her operative had given an accurate description of the place and the gatekeepers. Both were as forbidding as he had reported. She called again, "Werner Christed! I want to see Mr. Christed!"

"Nobody here!"

"Go off!" the second guard repeated threateningly.

Blake shouted over the moat, "You tell Dr. Gomay I am looking for a girl who is a minor. He can talk to me or the police!"

At that, the men started to jabber to each other in a foreign tongue. One disappeared into the guardhouse. The other stood wide-legged, glaring across the water at Blake, as if daring her to come across. The furious dogs kept up their commotion, slamming their bodies heedlessly against the cyclone fence, trying to get at her.

Felix Gomay and Ursula Blake took each other in warily. The old man saluted the detective's beauty with a smile that masked his irritation. She returned a smile that masked her suspicions. He spoke in his most courtly manner, "You must forgive my ruffians here. You see, we are making a film on my island, and curiosity seekers are a nuisance."

Blake studied the man closely. Was he just the wealthy eccentric the village reputed him to be, or did she glimpse something she could only describe as unwholesome? Judgment should be reserved. She asked bluntly, "Do you have a Judith Bradford on the island?" She bet the girl was not using the Wayne name.

"Yes, of course," Dr. Gomay answered directly. "She is one of the valued players of the Werner Christed film company. They are doing the production I mentioned."

The old eyes were steady under Blake's. So far so good, she thought. He hadn't felt a need to lie about the girl or the movie company. Things might be aboveboard after all.

"May I inquire what you want with Judith?" The man's wrinkled smile enlarged. "You are not her mother, anyone can see."

"Just a family friend," Blake responded neutrally. "Miss Bradford's mother thought she might be working with Werner Christed and asked me to say hello if I was coming this way."

Dr. Gomay kept the smile on his face, but his muscles went stiff. No parents or anyone else had any knowledge of where the Christed troupe was. This woman was lying and could only spell trouble and vexation. "I will tell her," was his response to Blake as he swung about to end their conversation.

But Blake was not to be put off. If the man wanted to fence with her, she would choose the foils. She thrust hard at their weak spot. "The girl is a minor, you should know! I must see her. I represent her parents, and they will want to know why I was refused!"

Dr. Gomay parried, "All the actors are employed by Mr. Christed. I would know nothing about Miss Bradford's age or status."

"I would like to see her," Blake repeated.

"I would be pleased to invite you, but Mr. Christed has given strict orders that his people are not to be disturbed in any way."

Ursula Blake's dislike of the man grew. He might be the satrap of his island domain, but to her he was coming on as a mealy-mouthed ancient character making her more suspicious with every word. She took out her identification and used her no-nonsense tone. "I am a private investigator, sir. I have instructions from Judith Bradford's parents. If you won't take me to her now, I'll be back with the police. The State Police." Not his local lackeys.

Vexed, Dr. Gomay wondered angrily how the woman had traced the girl. He would have to talk with Gregor about their security system; it had seemed foolproof. This could be a serious matter! Gregor's murder of Lena made them especially vulnerable to a police search right now—indeed the very last thing they wanted. A shift in tactics was clearly in order. He fixed his lips in a smile again. "You can understand that I am only trying to protect the Christed production," he said, ingratiating now. "Please come up to my house with me, and let me see what I can do."

Dr. Gomay went into the guard building, leaving the door open, and speaking in a loud tone on the phone. He pretended to be telling someone to find Judith Bradford and bring her to the manor.

When Dr. Gomay brought Ursula Blake into the library, Judith was puzzled and quickly on guard. "This woman wishes to speak with you," Dr. Gomay said, and left them unexpectedly alone. Neither of them saw his watchful eyes appear in the sockets of a painting high on the paneled wall.

The two women, young and older, took each other in. Blake thought the locket photo had not shown the vibrancy and luminous spirit the girl gave off. It was a quality that might well bring her stardom as an actress. The question was whether there were other considerations. The best procedure was to be straightforward. Blake held up her identification card. The girl visibly winced. "Your mother hired me to find you, Judith. She's badly worried and concerned. I'm sure you can understand that."

The uncertainty remained in Judith's face. "How did

you ever find me here?" she asked in honest wonder.

Blake smiled. "Professional secrets." She wanted the girl to like her, and not to be afraid.

Judith stared at the detective with what she felt must be a witless expression. She was stunned by the unlooked-for advent of the woman, and her breathtaking beauty. She responded with her own openness. "I never knew detectives looked like movie stars except on TV." She couldn't suppress a laughing comment: "I'd better get you off the island before Werner Christed sees you, or I'll be out of a part."

Blake was glad to follow the conversation away from a personal confrontation. She asked, "Is Christed as wild a director as I've heard?"

The girl answered, with obvious enthusiasm and dedication to the artist, "Oh, I've learned more from him in a month than I could in years anywhere else!"

"I take it you're happy here then?"

Judith studied Blake, and decided she could trust her. She said quietly, "Happier than I've ever been in my life." It was true. Her misgivings were behind her.

From the glow on Judith's face, Blake sensed that the film production was not the only reason for the girl's evident well-being. This was a young woman in love. But her job had to be done, and Blake asked, "Is your drug problem bothering you here?"

"So my mother told you about that?" Judith's sigh was a mixture of resignation and annoyance.

"Obviously I had to know as much as possible. Your parents have gone to a great deal of trouble and expense because they care for you so much."

Now the girl's eyes changed. There was hurt in them. Judith turned away from Blake without responding. Blake got a new message. There was something in the home situation that the mother had not disclosed.

"Look," she told Judith genuinely, "I'm here to help, not to hurt you."

Judith kept her head turned; she did not want the detective to observe her agitation. Inwardly, she was confounded, nonplussed. How had this woman traced her? Why had she arrived now? Eighteen was only weeks away! Her mother probably had the legal right to force her back home, away from the film, from Werner Christed—from Rick! The prospect was devastating, the threatened destruction of her new hopes and dreams. And she did not even have Lena, who might confirm that she had every right to stay.

In Judith's distress, she heard Blake say, "Your mother did ask me to bring you home if I found you, but I can see that's something we ought to talk about. Perhaps you ought to show me around."

The girl turned with gratitude. Blake saw that her eyes, though alert, held no guile.

Judith held back for a moment. Dr. Gomay and Christed might not like her taking a stranger around the island, but she felt that she had no choice. She did not see Dr. Gomay's eyes blink in the portrait, and disappear.

On the tour, Blake's doubts were nibbled away steadily despite the professional skepticism she brought to bear on everything Judith Bradford proudly pointed out. To start with, there was the fact that Dr. Gomay had not hesitated to leave them alone. It was not the action of a man who might fear what the girl might say or divulge. The evidences of film-making were everywhere, and everywhere legitimate. The strangely dressed servants were an unsettling note, but the girl's explanations made an acceptable kind of sense.

At this juncture, Judith smiled to herself wryly. Here she was walking along, rationalizing and defending the Gomays, after her own long complaints about their grotesque garb and customs. How trivial all of her past qualms seemed as compared to the sudden possibility of being snatched back to Iowa, away from the production, her career, her friends! She would have to make this detective—this private eye of her mother's—see and understand that Gomay Island was her paradise, and Lomis, Iowa, her purgatory.

The best way, Judith decided, was to let Ursula Blake look around freely and see for herself.

On Blake's part, everything she scrutinized seemed positive. The film dormitory obviously made a pleasant, clean, wholesome home for Judith Bradford. The production workshop was impressive, no false front. The crew and actors Judith greeted as they passed all seemed decent, usual enough persons. The general layout was certainly attractive and luxurious. Blake saw nothing negative—except that she was troubled by the fall from Death Point.

Judith was impressed that Blake knew of Emily. She took the detective up to the cliff to see the razor-sharp rocks for herself. As they began the climb, Blake stopped at the sound of footsteps hurrying behind them. Judith uttered a little glad cry when she saw it was Rick catching up. Blake recognized at once that this handsome young actor was the spark lighting the brightness in the girl's eyes. She could not help but concede that they made a remarkably apt and handsome pair. The introductions were formal but pleasant, and the three went up the path, Judith explaining who Blake was, and her errand.

Blake satisfied herself that the local police could well be right about the rocks weakening the rope. She had no evidence that it wasn't an accident, just as reported. She had little to say when, returning to Urwolde Green, Rick asked laughingly, "So now, you want to take Judith away from all this?"

"All this," shortly included a tray of tea and cakes brought by a Gomay, who Judith thought might be Lilia. Blake clearly enjoyed the snack, remarking that it wasn't too hard to become used to the servants. Rick added to Judith's explanations of the religious group, and Blake's suspicions of a threatening cultism faded. It had been her only reservation. Otherwise she more than liked what she saw; she was impressed. Her regret was that Werner Christed was undisturbable, shooting a scene at the old abbey. She would have liked to meet him, personally as well as professionally.

But, professionally, it did not seem necessary. It was quite clear that Judith Bradford was in no danger; on the contrary, she was in quite good hands. It was clear, too, that the young woman was not a child to be yanked about by a willful mother, no matter how well-intentioned. This was a self-possessed young actress, working at a career she was good at, among seemingly reliable people. And, most important, a young lady happily in love with a fine young man. Against this, Blake weighed her memory of the clearly neurotic Mrs. Wayne.

Blake could wish that the movie described by Judith and Rick was less odd-ball, but nothing she saw supported the red beard's talk of "warlocks." As she had suspected, that was simply irresponsible hyperbole.

Judith was pleading, "Please! My mother doesn't really care. There isn't anything for me back there."

Blake countered with, "What if I call your folks and tell them I've found you well and happy—and recommend that they leave you here with their blessing?"

On an imploring note, Judith said, "If my mother knows where I am she'll have to run her act. She'll have the police and FBI after me ten minutes after you call her!"

"Aren't you embroidering that, Judith?"

"Oh, everything is so wonderful finally, don't let them spoil it now."

Ursula Blake repeated that she thought it was her duty to inform Judith's mother. She suggested that Mrs. Wayne might understand.

A wave of resistance surged in Judith. She had found Ursula Blake agreeable, even believed the detective was sympathetic to her. But now the woman sounded entirely on her mother's side. Judith lifted her head and stared the woman down. She had her own duty—to defend herself by attacking if that was necessary. She asked Rick to leave them for a few minutes and, stiffly and dry-eyed, Judith disclosed to the investigator the full story of her stepfather's assault.

Blake heard Judith out with mounting sympathy. The tale was all too familiar. There was only one answer, of course. There were times to tear up a contract. To Judith, Blake responded promptly, "I resign your case as of right now! I'll call to tell your mother as soon as I get back to the city." She held out her firm hand in unreserved support.

Judith Bradford stood straight as the young pines around them. There were tears of gratefulness in her eyes. "I know that isn't easy for you. I feel I've made a real friend."

Blake liked the girl more and more. "One condition, though! As soon as you turn eighteen, I want you to get in touch with your mother."

"I *always* intended to do that."

"Good!"

They both noticed Dr. Gomay approaching in his cart. Rick was seated with him.

Judith shook Blake's hand again. "I want you to know I appreciate your understanding, Miss Blake."

"The name is Ursula," Blake told her. "Here's my card, and you come see me when the movie is done." Her own smile was dazzling again. "I hope the film makes you a star so I can say I knew you when."

As they walked to Dr. Gomay and Rick, Judith spoke of the one matter still bothering her. Quickly, she explained about Lena Ludovici and asked Blake to phone for her. The detective copied the Cincinnati address Gregor had provided, and Judith asked anxiously, "Can you get the telephone number from that?"

"No trouble," Blake smiled. "I'll call your friend in Cincinnati tonight."

Dr. Gomay welcomed them agreeably. "I trust you two had a pleasant visit." He ushered Blake into the cart, saying, "I take it there is no reason why Miss Bradford cannot conclude her role in our production . . ."

Blake found she could give the old curmudgeon an honest, even enthusiastic, answer: "No reason at all." Everything on the island did indeed seem to be on the up and up, despite the histrionics at the entrance.

For her part, Judith, waving goodbye to the detective, was delighted she had thought to ask Ursula Blake to telephone Lena. What better way to contact her friend than through her own, personal private eye! She hugged Rick happily. The shadow of Iowa—which, somehow, she had always expected to reach for her—was dissipated and gone now without interfering.

CHAPTER TWENTY

As soon as the investigator was out of sight, Dr. Gomay sent an urgent message to Werner Christed. The director was to stop shooting immediately and come to him.

Christed appeared stormily. "Damn it, Felix, we agreed you wouldn't interfere with my work at any time!"

With an iron gesture, Dr. Gomay silenced the director. "We have a *crisis!* Sit down!"

Werner Christed remained standing, stubbornly.

"Crisis?" His nose wrinkled at an odor of exotic incense suddenly permeating the room. There seemed a vibrating in the air, a throbbing in his head that might be due to the alien odor, or to a feverish energy he felt pouring like an electric madness from Dr. Gomay's eyes. Christed smiled. He knew that the old man fancied himself a professional magician and had every kind of equipment hidden about his rooms for occult effects. But the good doctor should be aware that the tricks had no mystery for him. Still, the director observed, the old man's perturbation was real.

"The schedule is to be altered!" the doctor clipped. "*You must shoot the Black Mass tonight!*"

"That's impossible!" Werner Christed stated flatly. "We are not ready."

Dr. Gomay glared at the director, then hissed, "A *detective* was just here talking to Judith Bradford! Fortunately, the girl remained with us, but I do not trust this new development!" He shouted, "If the girl should be taken away we can have no Black Mass! You understand that!"

The director showed his bafflement. "What does a detective want with Judy?"

"*She is a minor!*" An accusing talon jabbed at the director's nose. "You should have known!"

Werner Christed waved away the charge. He had left such details to Gregor.

"Her parents are looking for her! I am quite sure that the detective will bring them back, with police, probably!" The ancient eyes now caught the director's like hypnotic metallic orbs. To his surprise, Christed was finding it difficult to breath in the incense-laden air. The old man was going on madly, half raving, screaming in the director's ear. "We will film the Mass tonight! After that, it doesn't matter—you can shoot around the girl's part or handle it any way you like. But we must have the Mass!" His voice rose with now unconcealed hysteria. "Everything we have done will be wasted and lost if I don't have that scene! You want that scene as much as I do!"

The director, trying to quiet the distraught old man, countered, "*If* Judy had to leave, I could fake the Mass with someone else—"

"*It would not be the same!*"

Werner Christed grew silent, his eyes narrowed on the old man. "Listen Felix," the director resumed quietly, "I have gone along with your notions because, if you want to know, they did add a note of mystery that helped me establish my own mood for the picture. But I advise you not to get carried away, and don't interfere with me again!"

Dr. Gomay challenged sternly, "Werner, are you with us in this undertaking?"

"Of course. You know that."

"All the way?"

The director hesitated. The old man's face was contorted with unspoken questions.

"It depends on what you mean by 'all the way'."

"I mean you are to make the picture as I have written it!"

"Yes, that's agreed. But I am in charge. That's agreed, too."

"Unless there is an emergency!"

"I said I could fake the Mass if I have to."

"And I have said it would not be the same!"

"It is impossible to do it tonight! That is my last word!"

"The last word is not yours!" Dr. Gomay's tone was at once hypnotic, a reaching force the more powerful for its sudden softness. "You will do as I say . . ."

The director repeated hotly, "Our agreement . . ." Werner Christed made an effort to keep his objection going, but the thickening air was making him dizzy. "We aren't prepared," he tried to protest. "It's the biggest scene of all to set up. Too elaborate. You know that . . ."

"My people will work with your crew! It can be done because it must be done! You will do as I say!" The voice was like a rope binding itself around the director's chest, squeezing obedience out of his throat.

Despite the untoward weakness, Werner Christed could not surrender without showing his own spirit. His large fingers drummed his thighs in his anger at the ultimatum. "I won't do the scene until I am ready!" he said through gritted teeth. If this self-important cock-of-the-island-walk thought his money could control artistic decisions, the Christed company would leave the place at once. It would be a smashing loss for all of them, but not worse than being forced to do the most important scene of the film in a half-baked way.

Dr. Gomay was stroking his sunken cheeks. His eyes were afire. The atmosphere in the room was like a hot mist, breathing was almost like drowning. Taking deep gulps of air, Werner Christed turned to go. The reaching voice coiled around him tighter, holding him against all his power. "You always say you prefer to work spontaneously. What better chance than to do the great Mass without preparation!"

The director's throat was choked, nearly closed. "Impossible," he muttered. More words would not come. His lips had been taped, his arms pinioned. His brain was suffocating. It was as if someone else were taking possession of his mind, his will.

The flowing, filling, thickening voice went on. "We will of course continue as before to outward appearances. Everyone will see you as having the last word. It is as we wish it. But you will know from this moment on that you take my orders. In everything. Without question. Is that clear?"

The director struggled against the dizziness and faintness that were overcoming him. "No!" he managed. "No! We will leave! I will take my people off your island right now!"

A quiet chuckle came across the muffled room. "You are a powerful man, Werner Christed, but not in my world. You see, there *are* more things in heaven and earth, Werner, than ever your philosophies dreamed on! Yes, I control powers greater than anything you can ever imagine! But let us not quarrel. Quarreling is for weak men. Strong men either battle—or join forces, as we have so sensibly done." The voice changed to encouragement. "We have a *great* film, Werner. I gladly bow to the genius you are. I thank you for bringing my script alive as only you could do. I know you do not want to leave our *magnum opus* unfinished!"

For the first time in his life, Werner Christed experienced helplessness. He did not understand where the overwhelming force was coming from, unless it was the sulphurous atmosphere in the room. A poison? Some kind of nerve gas? What kinds of unearthly conjurations could Dr. Gomay summon up?

The old man was continuing. "I regret you do not share my urgency, but you have no choice, Christed. Now let me tell you two things. First, *you will remember nothing of this meeting*—nothing except that you agreed with me, wholeheartedly, that the Mass has to be shot tonight. It is *you* who wish it—for your own artistic and creative reasons! Second, you will begin the filming of the Black Mass at ten o'clock precisely. You will not question this. You will not modify this. I have my own arrangements which must mesh exactly with this timetable, without fail. Is that understood?"

Werner Christed weaved on his feet. He wanted to defy Dr. Gomay, but his eyes were blinking stupidly, and his legs seemed putty. He needed fresh air, he told himself fiercely. Struggling toward the door, he felt a steel band tightening around his skull with a searing pain that threatened to burst his eyeballs. He had never felt anything like it; it was preternatural and fearsome. From the doorway, he saw Dr. Gomay swelling and filling the room like a monstrous insect. It was more than some insidious hypnosis. He must be drugged! Was the old man a warlock after all? Was there truth in the hazy, black rumors he had heard? He had scoffed at them as local superstitions, but something alien was surely loosened in this room, with a force that had snapped his own great strength like a matchstick.

Outside on the manor steps, Werner Christed tried to rub the acid from his smarting eyes. The inexplicable power still held dominion over him. He did not understand what had happened, but knew inwardly that he would shoot the Mass scene starting "at ten o'clock precisely" that night. It was as if a mysterious magnetic force had charged his blood, the marrow of his very bones, taken him over like some alien spirit. All of his own proud strength and might was insufficient; now he had to move with a greater authority to its darkest poles.

He had no choice, no will of his own. He did not see Dr. Gomay's eyes beetling at him from a manor window, nor hear the old man chanting in a sepulchral whisper: *"In the name and powers of Urwolde!"*

It was early evening when Ursula Blake returned to her office. She had stopped on the road for coffee and, out of curiosity about the Werner Christed film, had phoned her secretary, Beatrice, to check the library for a "Baron Gilles de Rais." She was interested to know whether the monster described by Judith Bradford had really lived or was a Christed-Gomay fiction.

Beatrice had not yet come from the library, and Blake rang her answering service for messages. Among them was another call from Mrs. Andrew Wayne. In her mind's ear, Blake could hear her demanding voice. It made her happier that she had respected the wishes of the young actress on Gomay Island. The girl, with an open road to happiness before her, should not be forced back to an unsettled home.

Blake's recollection of Judith and the island brought back her promise to phone the girl's friend, Lena Something. Blake did not remember the foreign-sounding name, and reached for the slip of paper in her purse. The telephone interrupted her. It was her girl, Beatrice, phoning from the Forty-Second Street Library.

Yes, "Baron Gilles de Rais" had existed. And yes, many books confirmed the man's crimes. They were absolutely unspeakable! Beatrice quoted sickening details from an authoritative piece in the *Encyclopaedia Britannica*, and continued, "Other books tell about a whole *witchcraft* thing this baron was into. Also, some scholars hint that the Devil himself had resurrected the baron's body, so the old murderer might be roaming the earth right now! It's nonsense, of course, but that reincarnation legend is popular in certain remote villages in Transylvania. This reincarnated baron doesn't come on like Dracula or one of those monsters. On the contrary, he is supposed to appear in modern guise, and could be anyone, old, young, ugly, handsome, rich, poor, my boyfriend if I had one . . ."

"Beatrice!"

"Point is, your Baron Gilles de Rais doesn't sleep in graves or coffins, and he doesn't drink blood. It's hard to separate the chaff from the wheat in the books about him, but I was struck by one statement, Ursula. This writer emphasized that the baron can only redeem his soul from the Devil and find peace if he performs a perfect Black Mass. Emphasis on *perfect.* That means, the writer spells out, that a human sacrifice must be made—must actually take place. *And* this sacrifice must take a specific form, no other. It must be a young female virgin—emphasis on *virgin*—who must be offered to the Devil and raped on an altar before the congregation. Raped, plus her heart cut out for everyone to touch. *Yech!*"

"Yech!" echoed Ursula Blake.

"There's more," the secretary said. Blake could hear the girl shuffling her notes.

"That's quite enough," Blake scowled at the phone. "Come on back."

"I'm afraid to travel in the dark now," the girl said.

Blake hung up and leaned back in her chair. The whole evil story of a crazy baron was scatterbrained superstition of course, a distillate of imbecility and drooling ignorance. It went considerably further than the film Judith Bradford had described—which had seemed screwy enough. Of course, there were always lunatics in every age who slimed around in arcane histories, even imagined themselves some devious character reborn. Most of them were in booby hatches with the Napoleons. Werner Christed might be avant-garde, but he wasn't nuts. Might Dr. Gomay be batty? She didn't think so. She could see why a man like Christed would be drawn to a movie like *Baron of Darkness,* particularly since it apparently did have the underpinning of an actual historical character. Still, there was nothing in what Beatrice had reported to change her mind about leaving the girl on Gomay Island. Who was she to judge what was "weird" in these days of license? Let Judith Bradford finish the picture, and let it bring nothing but good fortune to her and to her fellow workers, including the nice-looking friend of hers, Rick Gilbert.

There was one certainty everyone could take comfort in, Blake concluded in her mind: If indeed there had once been a Baron Gilles de Rais, as seemed to be the documented case, his mortal body was long, long moldering in a medieval graveyard far, far away, and not sashaying around on Long Island today.

Blake asked her secretary to bring her the special directory listing telephone numbers by address. The public generally did not know of its availability. Luckily, the Cincinnati book was in the agency library. Checking it, Ursula Blake was hit with consternation. The address for Lena Ludovici's sister, given to her by Judith Bradford, was *the Cincinnati Zoo!*

Every professional nerve rang alarm bells in Blake. Had a digit been transposed?—had Judith Bradford made a mistake?—*or* had the girl been handed a phony address on purpose? *If so, why?*

It seemed she had found one missing person only to lose another, Blake considered wryly. Her expert's mind began to click analytically. One: She couldn't reach Judith Bradford by phone on Gomay Island, certainly not without arousing suspicions. Two: It made no sense to drive out again at this hour. Three: The only chance of contact was a possible Ludovici apartment in the city. Conceivably, the woman might even be there, on her way back to Gomay Island. Suddenly, there was a string of questions Blake wanted to know about the movie production. This "Lena" might be a key person to check out.

There was no Ludovici in the phone books. But that wasn't quite a dead end. Blake knew that Werner Christed's company lived together in the SoHo commune. And, Blake reflected with a satisfied slap on her desk, she did know that address!

The SoHo street was deserted except for the garage. Blake could see the attendant sitting in the rear. He was not sleeping or reading, seemed to be staring off into space, as if attending a private vision. Perhaps he was stoned—Blake hoped so. She was sure he did not notice her in the shadow of the doorway as she completed picking the lock of the Christed building.

Upstairs, Blake hurriedly scanned the loft where Lena had taken Judith. At the distant end of a corridor, Blake's flashlight showed a locker room. It opened into a small, clean apartment. One room was a makeshift office. Letters were addressed to "Ludovici"! All the drawers were unlocked but one. Blake smiled knowingly. It was amazing how unthinking even the shrewdest people were. Of course, she would hone in on the locked drawer first. In a desk like this, she, herself, would put her important papers in the unlocked compartments, and her trivia in a locked box.

The drawer came open easily under the practiced twist of her tool. A letter, conspicuously on parchment paper, lay on top of a pile of folders.

As Blake gathered its import, she dropped to the floor, reading it alertly by the light of her small torch.

> Gregor!
>
> From the city you must now bring all that is finally required for our coven's Mass.
>
> I congratulate you again in providing us with the ingenious cover of the film production. You shall have your reward, as I have pledged. By this document I affirm that you, Gregor Ludovici, are granted the right of selling our stupendous film to our brethren around the world. They are already clamoring to use it as part of their own rituals in the glorious name of Lucifer.
>
> The girl you selected is perfect for the sacrifice I require. As you know, I have watched her most closely, and I am convinced she is chaste. Thus, at last, will our Rites be consummated. Thus, at centuries last, will the Curse be lifted from my head, and my Eternal Reincarnation be completed!
>
> I hail you in The Name and Powers of Urwolde!

There was a clear signature, in angular gothic script: **BARON GILLES DE RAIS.**

And a large red wax seal was sharply stamped with a symbol:  Blake had to think a minute before recalling where she had seen that obscure, arcane mark in old books of occult history. It was the Runic sign for Death. Runes, she remembered from her own interest in esoteric symbols, were connected with the invisible world of spirits, used as magic signs among secret cults. This "alphabet of mystery" was originally called *furthoc*, and went as far back as the third century. To come upon this ancient sign here bode no good for Judith Bradford!

So old Dr. Gomay believed himself to be the reincarnation of Baron Gilles de Rais! That would explain the weird story of the film they were making. It would also make the old man out to be a certified, bomb-ticking cuckoo. Whether Werner Christed was an innocent pawn or a conspirator for his own reasons, Blake did not know. But one thing was all too clear to her now: Her lenient appraisal of what was happening on Gomay Island had turned out to be a critical and perilous misjudgment.

As Blake rose to go, she stiffened at a sound of creaking outside. Footsteps? Had that goon in the garage seen her after all? The sound came again, pronounced, moving stealthily toward the room. Blake felt her scalp itch. No matter how many times she had faced this situation, she could not suppress the foreboding chill that clamped her jaws together in tension. Quietly, she drew her gun from her purse. The feel of the cold metal helped steady her.

The door opened a crack and held ominously. A light was swung around the room. On television shows, the flashlight often missed the detective crouching behind the desk. Not her luck, Blake frowned. The beam drilled directly into her eyes, revealing and blinding her in the same instant.

Blake ducked. The man from the garage was neither old nor frail. He was wiry as a steel cable. He lunged at Blake with a vicious curse. She fired, and missed, as he dived at her. Blake scrambled, but the man was on her back, his powerful hands around her neck. Her eyes goggled, but the move was his mistake. He had positioned himself perfectly for a jitsu throw, and Blake performed with the desperation of sheer survival.

The man went flying over her shoulder. He landed with a loud, chilling crunch of his head against the wall, slid down, and lay like dead. Blood seeped nastily from his nose and ears. It was a part of her job Blake hated.

On the street, she hurried to the phone booth on the corner and rang Carlos Rodriguez. A leather-jacketed cyclist made a fast U-turn toward her. Blake felt for her gun. If this smart-ass wanted trouble, she was in the mood to give lessons.

The macho on the bike took one look at Blake's eyes and roared into the night with rubber burning.

Blake shook the receiver. Come on, Carlos! Where the devil are you when I really need you?

When the police line finally answered, Blake poured out the incredible facts about Judith Bradford, and her ominous suspicions. "I've got to get out there right away, you see! Can you get us a helicopter?"

Carlos Rodriguez said, "Honey, you know it's out of our jurisdiction. I'll try the local police for you—"

Blake interjected, "You can bet Dr. Gomay has them sewed up!"

"Anyway, a bad storm is kicking up in that area. You can't fly it tonight."

Blake glanced at her watch. "It's eight-fifteen now. Traffic should be light, especially if the weather is bad. We could drive it before midnight, Carlos!"

"And then what?"

For the first time, Ursula Blake shouted at her fiancé.

"Stop wasting time and pick me up!" She was fuming at herself, feeling guilty that she had let Dr. Gomay-the-Baron take her in, sickened at the memory of the bleeding man in the Christed loft, and worried about the girl for whom she now felt doubly responsible. She chewed her lip in self-recrimination. Why hadn't she just done her job that afternoon and taken Judith when she had her?

"It's that serious?" the police lieutenant was asking.

"She is in danger right now!"

"Okay, then, wait for me on the corner there."

"Hold it! You people have emergency rafts, don't you? The kind that pump up?"

"What do you need a *raft* for?"

"To cross a moat!"

"A *what?*"

"Plus, stop at your church and get a holy cross!"

"Have you gone crazy?"

"I'll explain on the way!" Blake shouted, hanging up. She was only too aware of how mad her conversation sounded. But that was just the damnable trouble. Judith Bradford was obviously in the hands of madmen.

CHAPTER TWENTY-ONE

A sky-ripping storm pelted Judith Bradford's window. The whole dormitory held an air of hysteria outside her open door. People were skittering back and forth, buzzing and chattering. The announcement of the night's scene had come like a thunderclap. There had been no mention earlier of a Black Mass episode in the picture. It was just like Werner to hold back a bolt like that. Now he had everyone on tenterhooks wondering what their parts must be. Gregor and his assistants had gathered small knots of actors to cue them, but everyone was nervous and high-strung.

It was a Christed technique, the actors and actresses nodded to each other. Christed veterans recalled with pride other times when the director had sprung brand-new scenes on them, thrown them before the camera to swim or sink. They had swum, they boasted, and given the best performances of their life. To those with butterflies, the old-timers promised Christed would not let them down. "He'll be right there when you need him," they assured the doubtful. "You'll know what to do when the time comes, and if you don't, just do whatever seems called for. That's exactly what Werner wants."

Others may have been reassured, but Judith wasn't. She had jitters that felt like St. Elmo's fire all over her body. Gregor himself had outlined her part and its blocking to her, but she had trouble absorbing it. What stood out was that she would have to appear nude before the whole company. It did nothing to alleviate her mounting tension, especially after most of the cast left for their makeup and costumes. She needed neither for her nude role as the maiden to be sacrificed.

Judith wished desperately that she could be as occupied with preparations as the others were, but Gregor had given her two free hours before her call. It was hard to accept what Gregor had said they expected of her. The Black Mass seemed impossibly horrible, even for *Baron of Darkness*. But she had no choice. Her consolation was that she could trust Rick, and hope that Werner Christed would not get carried away in his cinematic inspiration. In this scene, more than any other, it was going to be important to remember what was real and what was make-believe.

She could only trust. She tried to read. Time refused to pass. The room became an intolerable cell, claustrophobic. Judith went disconsolately to her window. It was raining more heavily but despite the downpour she determined she had to get into the air and move about.

Walking alone in the soaked night, Judith tried to rid herself of the depression and trepidation the looming scene had brought. She told herself the Mass as described by Gregor was no worse than hundreds of scenes she had watched on television and in the movies. Indeed, it had a better purpose. How had Gregor put it? "Werner is using the Mass to show the world how sick its values have become. It is not sacrilege; on the contrary it is a lesson warning of apocalypse . . ."

Judith had not understood, though she nodded. Maybe it was her Catholic upbringing that made the idea so distasteful to her. She wished Rick was with her to steady her, but he had been the first to leave for make-up. He had the toughest job of all, with a plastic skin that would obliterate his own features, the way actors had been literally transformed in *Planet of the Apes*. Tonight, Rick would be like the last of the "Dorian Gray" portraits, having passed from handsome youth to the most dissolute and corrupted old age. Tonight, the cameras would show Baron Gilles de Rais ravaged and broken with the sick years of his dissipations. Knowing Werner Christed's uncanny skills at creating horror, Judith grew icier with apprehension. Now that she was engaged to Rick—waiting only for Lena's return to make the formal announcement—Judith found it harder than ever to accept him in the guise of Gilles de Rais. In that role, he became a total stranger to her, a stranger she abhorred.

Judith tried to turn her mind away, and took some comfort in remembering that the woman detective would be in touch with Lena. She would be so glad to hear from Lena Ludovici again! And Ursula Blake—odd name for a woman in an odd profession—held the promise of another good friend.

Without being conscious of it, Judith had climbed the forest path to the grove she shared with Rick on Balefire Bluff. Now she stood alone on the craggy precipice in the black, storming night. Up high, out of the shelter of the trees, the wind howled in at her bitingly from the ocean. The sea made violent sounds. The girl felt her exposure and vulnerability in the blackness around her, the boundless ocean below, the moonless sky above. It was as if the universe were a vaulting tomb burying her in the emptiness of space, and her melancholy was deepened by the mournful noises of the rain-drenched night. She yearned for Rick, down in the makeup department.

To her wind-beaten ears, the darkness became an orchestration of nocturnal instruments—the breaking surf was a relentlessly pounding tympani section, the whistling wind was ghostly flutes, the tolling buoys and distant foghorn came in underneath with a lugubrious, funereal rhythm.

Judith tried again to steer her mind to happier thoughts. She tried to daydream how it would be when the film was "in the can." She and Rick would return to New York. She would live in the Christed Loft as a full member of the great company. If the film was the hit everyone hoped and expected, she and Rick could take off on a new career. Her childhood dreams of Hollywood might really be coming true. It was a thrill to realize that now they could be more than fantasies. She had opportunity before her, and love, and good new companions all around. Her future was as bright as this night was grim and foreboding.

Uneasiness claimed Judith again. She should not have come up here alone at a time like this, Judith chided herself. Instead of easing her jangling nerves, the walk was making her feverish. She turned back to the path, and froze with the abrupt conviction that eyes, like a wild animal's, were riveted on her from the depth of the rain-drowned forest. She stared back, searching, but nothing moved except the wind-wrenched branches.

As her eyes circled the trees, Judith gasped. She saw not an animal or human, but torches. They were barely visible in the distance, and flickered constantly as the trees and shifting leaves shuttered her view. But they were plain in the night, westward from where she stood. They were coming from the old abbey, the forbidden taboo place where she had never been.

Judith's inner torch of curiosity flared at once. Who else was up on the cliffs on this wild night? Everyone in the company was supposed to be preparing for the shooting of the Black Mass.

Judith cut off her questions even as she asked them. There was to be no more imprudent adventuring for her, she reminded herself sternly. Werner Christed and Rick and all the others were waiting for her on the set. It was nearly time for her to go down, and that was where she was headed, no matter what magnet was pulling her through the trees.

At the same moment, it came to Judith that Werner Christed might have made one of his spontaneous changes. What if those torches were the filming of the procession that began the Mass? The director might have decided to start at the abbey to take advantage of the stormy night. It would certainly set the demonic atmosphere he wanted, Judith judged.

If she was right, she considered, they might want her immediately, might even be looking for her. She ought at least to check.

Hurrying on the unused path that led to the abbey, Judith saw the lights grow tantalizingly brighter. She could hear chanting on the wind. There was an ululation of voices in a foreign tongue, marked with tinkling bells. The rhythm was of a slow dance. Like a pavane, Judith thought. What was the piece of Ravel she had once practiced on the piano?—*Pavane for a Dead Royal Infant*, something like that.

Judith stole furtively into the trees surrounding the abbey. In front of her was the crumbling stone fence that marked the off-limits. The scene before her eyes was somber, and fascinating. She had been right about a procession—though she could see no cameras. But she was too late for whatever ceremony had taken place. The line of torch-carrying hooded Gomays was disappearing into the trees, descending toward Urwolde Common in sober cadence.

Judith cowered in the wet forest without a sound. She had learned by now how hyper-quick the masked gang was to react to any intrusion. They moved away swiftly, and it was safe for her to come out. She crept vigilantly toward the abbey. Before her, two torches planted in the earth lit up the waste of the ancient structure. She remembered its chronicle. Generations back, the Gomay family had supported a small monastery on the island, with acolytes of their own imported faith. The monastery itself was now only cluttered heaps of charred stones, but the walls of the small church used by the monks still stood—the old abbey.

Its broken arches were shadowed by stark, weather-ravaged trees. In the wind-fanned flames of the torches, Judith made out dark recesses in the crumbling walls, and an outside staircase that ascended to what were once turrets.

Suddenly, the wind died and the rain faded to a mild

drizzle. In the ghostly calm, the whole scene took on the stillness of the tomb. The ruins cast menacing shadows in their gloomy grandeur. The night seemed full of retreating steps and half-seen apparitions flitting dimly among the leaning walls. Judith could imagine the whipping of swords and clanking of chains in winding galleries long gone to sand and dust. Over all there was the dankness of prolonged death and falling shades, the hush of labyrinths and dungeons. The very air breathed an odor of melancholy.

It was a setting for ghosts. It sent Judith's mind back again to her books. This was the very place where the intruder with rain streaming from his haggard visage might have sought refuge from a raging storm—only to cast aside his cowl to reveal the skull and clacking teeth of Death, striking terror into the hearts of the honest monks huddled by a blazing fire. And then they all would have been saved by a wounded knight to whom they had given succor earlier—he rising from his pallet in the corner to drive off the horrible apparition and send it howling to wander again its desolate way in the uncaring wind and rain.

Taking in the abbey scene, Judith was also remembering the "ladies bathed in tears," aghast and paling at the pall of such landscapes. Had these very stone chambers seen passion and poison droughts, soft white hands turned from caresses to graves and worms? Judith smiled at her notions. She had her romances mixed up. This was an abbey, not a castle or chateau. Here holy men—it mattered not of what persuasion—had lived prayerfully and spartanly.

And here in modern times the Gomays still conducted their own outlandish rites.

Why, Judith wondered, was there a greenish flame from the window of the one shed that seemed to have been rebuilt? What had the Gomays left behind? Surely it would do no harm if she hurried across the abandoned enclosure and peeked within for just a moment before going down to the movie set.

As Judith moved watchfully from the trees, a blast of wind nearly knocked her off her feet. Freak weather! As unpredictable as everything else on Gomay Island! The storm had veered back, more savage than before. In front of Judith's eyes, a fierce gust tore at the door of the shed and ripped it off its hinges. The wood must be rotted, Judith thought, just before her mind blew out at the sight revealed to her.

She was staring at two coffins, painted startling garish red. On each box, in large design, was the ubiquitous Gomay mark, . The coffins were open! Judith swallowed with dread as she approached to see what they contained. She told herself desperately to remember the false grave beyond the cemetery and the camera platform above, to recall the hearse's dummy corpse, to summon the image of Lena taking microphone stands out of the box in the hearse. This, too, could—would be only part of the movie . . .

But her head was corkscrewing with an alarm she faintingly knew would be genuine this time, and the horror when it came was a sledge hammer. In the lurid torchlight, Judith Bradford was gazing down at the hollow-staring eyes of Emily Lawrence's corpse in one coffin and the body of Lena Ludovici in the second. No effigies, these!

Both corpses were horrifyingly mutilated, beyond Judith's ability to take in. On each forehead was deeply branded the double-arrow sign, which she still did not understand.

Not dummies! Not mannequins! Not tricks of Werner Christed's holographic apparatus!

Judith began to weave. Were her repressed anxieties

about the Black Mass bringing on her self-horror, the attack Dr. Gomay had predicted would be realer than real? Judith cried out against it. Maybe Emily, who had drowned, might be lying here in death, *but certainly not Lena!* If she leaned over and touched the terrible figure, she would touch wood or wax or plastic! Hadn't Rick himself told her he had seen Gregor drive Lena off Gomay Island? How and when could Lena have died? No, this eye-blinding sight, this nose-searing stink of formaldehyde could only be another apparition out of the ghost machine she carried in her head! If it seemed real, so had her mother's voice, her mother's perfume, the night in the hearse!

Judith raced out of the horror chamber and skidded to her knees in the rain-churned mud outside. The keening of the still-rising wind echoed her own mindless whimpering. On hinges of sheer anguish she felt her brain flailing in her skull like the broken door banging behind her. Her head was a cauldron of yellow brew boiling into acid fumes that dissolved all her senses.

All she could do was fly from the illusion of the phantoms in the nonexistent coffins! All she could do was escape from this accursed spell, this accursed island!

Judith plunged wildly into the storm-tossed forest, trying to remember how to find the beach.

She shrieked again, and darted another way as a tree sprang to life and reached for her. In her distress, Judith accepted it as another drug phantom. But blocking her path stood *Joan of Arc!* Judith swayed and sobbed aloud. The saintly face, so plain to see, was lacquered white to a mystical purity. Beneath page-boy hair, a silver robe was fastened at the neck by a glowing jewel. But the cheeks were bloodless and the eyes were not saintly. They were livid with frenzied hate, and the pall of death was on lips snarling over bared teeth.

"Now, whore!"

A gloved hand lifted a jeweled dagger.

Judith's response was a manic screech. She made no move to run or fight, but only stood shrieking like the animal that now occupied her yellowed head.

The attacker was taken aback; the mad head of Margot Gomay came up uncertainly, eyes blinking, the knife hand faltering. She expected the victim to run . . .

To Judith, the night's horrors became all at once a huge burlesque, a staged caper of her turntable brain. She laughed idiotically at the threatening figure. Her spasms of crazy cackling confounded the robed figure for a long moment, but with a curse Margot Gomay lifted the blade furiously again.

In that instant, the woman was seized from behind.

Rick's voice came up on the sound track of Judith's roiling nightmare. *"Judy! I've been trying to find you!"* The words began to clear the clouds in her head.

As he spoke to Judith, Rick was struggling to restrain the madwoman. But she twisted out of his grasp, and caromed away among the trees. If lightning had a voice it would be the cry of frustration that ripped the night as Margot Gomay fled. With new horror, Judith realized that the woman was headed blindly for the cliff's edge. Without thought, Judith flung herself forward. The woman might have tried to kill her but there were times when you acted because, as her grandmother taught, God made you human and not a beast.

Judith's tackle was clumsy. The woman struck and grabbed Judith, dragging her along toward the cliff edge.

"Hold her, Judy!" Rick's plea was desperate. Just as he lunged to help, Judith's wet hands slipped from the scissoring legs. Margot Gomay flew back into the forest with another cry of fury.

Judith rose to her feet confusedly, and turned unsteadily to Rick. For the first time her eyes fell on his made-up visage. The scream that tore the night now was not the madwoman's but Judith's. Rick Gilbert was hideous beyond belief. He looked like an exhumed corpse, moldy and worm-eaten. Shreds of necrotic flesh hung disgustingly from his skull. Judith moaned helplessly. In the night's multiplying chaos, she fought against the arms he held wide to her. In her mind, he too was a demon out of hell, a worse fate than the murderer waiting for her in the trees.

"It's *me!*" Rick kept declaring, understanding Judith's revulsion. "Me! *Rick!* Never mind this damned *make-up!*"

Judith's heart did not stop hammering. She moaned again. "Having a bad trip. I must be having a bad trip." But her head started to clear again as Rick's voice came to her, familiar and reassuring. She felt less inchoate, and wanted to sort out the turmoil now that Rick was here. A pressing idea took shape: *Rick could come back to the abbey with her!* He could tell her there was nothing inside but her inflamed imagination. He could reassure her that it was the Devil Dust that had transformed some old planting boxes into coffins . . . !

In words that seemed wrenched from her by the storm, Judith told Rick what she thought she had seen in the shed. He said brusquely, at once, "You wait here!" and ran off through the downpour.

Judith stood numbly, not feeling the rain or the wind that buffeted her. She was in a Devil's own Catch-22. Either there was unspeakable evil around her, or the drug evil within had corroded her beyond hope.

She heard Rick's steps returning, with his message—which had to cleave her one way or the other. She waited breathless, her heart a piston of distress. *"Judy, there is nothing inside,"* Rick said positively.

Judith's prayer of thanks for Lena was jumbled with an inward lament that now she must doubt her senses every day of her life. In her wrought-up state she hardly heard Rick as he stepped closer: "Werner is waiting for you, honey! I'll take you down now. Dr. Gomay will give you something for your nerves."

But what snapped for Judith Bradford was the night itself. She recoiled into her deepest self. She could take no more of anything or anyone, real or conjured—not of Rick, or Emily, or Lena, or a madwoman, or Werner Christed, or film-making.

Like an animal hit by a bullet, Judith leaped high into the air, spun around, and sped away from Rick Gilbert.

Sick or not, there was one clear resolve that cut through all her turmoil. She was not going to participate in the Black Mass. And she was not going to go on with Rick Gilbert. He deserved better than a doomed drug-zombie who could never be a fit companion, wife, mother! *His* evil was theatrical makeup and make-believe; her scourge was all too real. All she wanted on this terrible night was to get off Gomay Island and away, it did not matter where!

As she floundered through the storm-tortured trees, Judith heard Rick's baffled voice calling after her. She plunged on, heedless. This path led to the beach, she remembered, away from guards and killer dogs. She would manage the barbed wire, somehow, and the storming waves somehow after that.

Judith tripped and slid as she ran, heedless of the

branches that whipped and slashed her face. She did not care if the assassin was hiding in the storm. She would almost welcome the knife and its final peace—if indeed there was a madwoman outside her own conjuring brain.

Thunder crashed overhead like pain, and lightning scalpeled the sky into raw wounds. To Judith, the elements were echoing her inner tempest. Her whole life was blowing away like the leaves that were being whipped from the trees. Judith sobbed miserably as she struggled on. All the promises of Gomay Island had been too good to be true.

She became aware of Rick pounding behind her, not far away. Cannily, Judith halted. She heaved a stone as far as she could. Throw the stone as she had to cast away love and send Rick off her trail, out of her life, forever!

When she heard Rick Gilbert's steps recede, Judith wept with loss. She stumbled on, falling painfully as roots snared her battered feet. She felt blood on her face, on her scraped legs, her scratched hands. In the fury of the night, she was diminished, a tiny speck, gone out of an uncaring world. In despair, she sank to her knees, ready to give up. It was all too much for her to battle alone—the storm, her sick head, the jail Gomay Island had become.

But words of her grandmother rose in Judith's mind: It's not the size of the person in the fight, it's the size of the fight in the person!

Judith stood up again, wobbly on her feet, but drawing up new determination from the well of survival. She would not succumb, she swore to herself. She plodded on doggedly.

But her resolve deserted Judith when she, finally, dragged herself out of the trees onto the beach she had heard so much about. The barbed wire fence confronted her with its steel thorns, ugly and menacing. The only possible way to the water was by digging under the barrier. Judith searched frantically for a tool, but there were only some fallen branches so rotted that they turned to worm-like pulp when she tried to dig.

Judith scratched at the sand with her fingers. The hard grains broke her nails and abraded her skin raw. When, at last, she tried to crawl under the bristling wire spurs, she found that she had not dug deeply enough. Trying to withdraw, she was caught. The barbs pinioned Judith, lacerating her back like an animal's claws. She lay motionless, trapped, unable to move forward or back. Then she realized with fresh horror that now she was at the mercy of the incoming tide. "Terror is the expectation of horror; horror is the experience of terror." Now she suffered them both! Inexorably she would be drowned!

This, then, was the final destiny she had made for herself—she, Judith Bradford, so proud of her strength and independence, so confident that she could meet and overcome any challenge in the world, so certain that her talent would take her to the heights of success. Instead, it had taken her to this hell, to this trap of her undoing.

Judith cried out in bitter defeat. Alone on a forsaken beach on a bleak, mysterious island, in the midst of a tempest that was shaking the earth, she was meeting her final doom. Judith wondered whether, when the furious waves washed over her, she would see her life flashing before her eyes. She wept with a fresh sense of loss. Her life had all been preparation, there was little to remember. Everything worthwhile—love, work, her own children—was in a future she would now never know.

You cannot remember the future.

Judith tried again to inch forward, to inch back, but the wire claws nailed her to the ground. She was helpless and hopeless, totally vanquished.

Until a new shock brought her wet eyes open. Over her head came a deep voice. Not Rick's. Not the mad-woman's. It was, beyond belief, Werner Christed!

Lifting the barbed wire gingerly, the director helped the trembling girl to her feet and embraced her protectively. She was too hurt and confused to speak. She gave herself up to the strength that flowed from the man.

She hardly made out his words, only half heard by her befuddled mind. He was saying, "Everyone's been looking for you!—Rick, Gregor, even Dr. Gomay. What in the world are you doing down here, Judith?"

She could not answer, could not tell Werner Christed she was running from her illness. She had never been able to take him into her confidence as she had with Rick.

"You need to rest!" The director said, looking about. "First things first. The abbey is the nearest shelter. Let me get you out of this confounded rain. God, we should be building an ark tonight instead of setting up a Black Mass!"

Still in a daze, Judith followed the director blindly. It penetrated slowly that he was taking her to the abbey. *Now, with Christed as a witness, she would see for herself that the "coffins" were only the empty crates Rick had described!* Maybe, with the director's strength a bulwark for her, she would be able to recover her sanity, Judith prayed.

With the resilience of youth, and taking power from the director's firm hand, Judith felt her equilibrium returning.

Rain was slashing both their faces. In lightning flares, Judith made out Werner Christed's eyes, clearly concerned for her. "What made you come out on a night like this?" he was demanding. The wind blew his words away, and he did not repeat them. The shed's entrance beckoned a few feet away, and he hurried his steps. Head lowered, Judith followed him inside.

Out of the driving rain and wind, the chamber echoed with its dank silence. Standing in front of Judith, the director blocked her view of the room. She saw the man flinch, as if punched. Facing her own moment of truth, Judith fought sudden panic. She wanted to turn and fly, but with her last strength she forced herself to step to the director's side.

Yes! Horribly, damnably yes! There before both their eyes the hellish coffins rested. *No illusion—delusion—imagined fantasy!*

Inside the garish coffins, the bodies of her friends lay in naked tormented death. They were Goya slashes of utter agony. They were real. Incontestably and terribly real.

Judith's first heart-stopping thought was the memory of Rick's assurance—his absolute assertion that the shed held nothing but empty boxes.

Why had Rick lied to her?

Could it be that Rick, with whom she had been closest of all on Gomay Island, was in league with murdering Gomays?—or, as her heart cried out for her to believe—had he lied out of his caring for her, to spare her the ghastly truth, knowing the arduous scene she faced that night.

Christed was transfixed in his own horror. Standing beside him, looking down now with clearer sight, Judith went faint. For Emily and Lena were not just dead. Judith could see now that their bodies had been sliced apart and put together again. There was a macabre gap between Emily's head and her neck. There was a gruesome space between Lena's chest and her abdomen. Thighs and legs were grotesquely askew, not matched up. What other horrible blasphemies had been committed on their poor bodies Judith could not consider. She turned into Christed's solid arms with a wail of abhorrence at the bestial malignity before her.

Werner Christed's expression transformed from disbelief to hard, raging conviction. His jaws set sternly as he comforted Judith with his strong arms around her heaving shoulders.

Before either of them could give voice to their horror, there were stamping noises outside. Someone was approaching.

The director spun Judith around and pressed her into hiding with him behind a pile of stones in the room's shadows.

Two men entered.

They were Gregor Ludovici and Rick Gilbert.

They were clearly overwrought.

Dust in the disturbed hiding place rose to Judith's nose and she had to sneeze. Werner Christed unceremoniously slammed his big hand over her face.

There was quiet in the shed for a long moment as the two intruders stood silently staring into the coffins.

Then Judith Bradford, of Lomis, Iowa, and Werner Christed, of Alaska and of SoHo, New York City, found themselves listening, breathless and incredulous, on an isle off Long Island, to the conversation that ensued between the male star and the assistant director of the film called *Baron of Darkness.* It was an impossible, unimaginable, insane, bizarre confession of pretense and dissembling that—in its distorted light—freakishly illuminated, elucidated, and explained many of Gomay Island's corkscrewing questions and enigmas.

CHAPTER TWENTY-TWO

Crouched on the earth floor, with Werner Christed's arm protectively around her, Judith saw Gregor Ludovici plainly through a small opening. She blanched as he started to move past the coffins and approached the hiding place, saying to Rick, "Margot may be hiding over there!"

Another sneeze threatened Judith. She pressed her finger hard against her upper lip, praying the man would not hear her heart banging.

Rick stopped Gregor. "Don't waste our time! I

searched here as soon as Judith ran off. Damn all this! I was taking care of the girl well enough! She suspected nothing! Never for a moment! She never for a *moment* suspected who I was, how I was testing her!"

Judith intertwined Werner Christed's fingers. The earth was rocking beneath her.

Rick was going on furiously. "It was your blasted Lilia who did not do her job! She will pay!"

Gregor said mollifyingly, "Spilled milk. The problem now is where that damned Judith has got to!"

The plastic makeup twisted with rage on Rick Gilbert's head. "You don't have to tell me what the problem is!" he shouted madly. "Hasn't it been my plan from the start?" In his anger, the man pounded Emily's coffin. Judith was petrified that the pitiful pieces of the once-lovely body would spill out. She would not be able to stand any more defilement of that poor girl. But she knew that the scorching of her blood was not the abuse of Emily, but the admissions and confessions branding like hot irons into her ears as the man she knew as Rick Gilbert ranted on.

"And I don't give a damn where Margot is! For all her interference with my plans, I wish my cousin off the cliff where she sent this one!" He struck Emily's coffin again.

The madwoman was Rick's cousin! Judith choked with fresh astonishment. She listened in mounting amazement and horror to revelations that were even more weird and devastating.

"She was my uncle's responsibility and yours!" Rick fumed. "That damned stupid old man! He relishes his part so well he has begun to believe he is the leader here!" The awful-looking actor turned on Gregor Ludovici with a mad catechism that staggered the two hidden observers. "*Who owns this island, old idiot Felix or me?*"

Gregor answered with quick servility, "You do, cousin! Of course!"

"Who is the master of the great Gomay coven, who is the Keeper of the Sacred Book of Satan?"

"All live only to serve you, Master!"

The voice rose more madly. "And who—who—*who* am I?" The figure lifted to its fullest height, and an arm rose imperiously, like a king's.

Dropping on his knees, Gregor groveled and bawled servilely, "You are the great and terrible Baron Gilles de Rais, my liege lord! Have mercy!"

Judith and Werner Christed turned to each other with confoundment and disbelief, sharing the enormity of what they were overhearing. The man they had known as Rick Gilbert was obviously insane!

The actor strode about, declaiming oratorically and striking exaggerated heroic poses as he spoke. *"Am I playing a part, or am I the true Gilles de Rais?—scholar, alchemist, Satanist?"*

"The true! Only he!" came the hasty assent.

The figure halted, sternly. "Now heed my final instructions! Keep servants searching for the girl, but go to Werner Christed and say he is to start filming at once. We must be ready for the appearance of my lord Satan exactly at midnight! Do you understand?"

"I understand, Master."

The voice turned nasty: "If our resident genius, Werner Christed, is not prepared to do as I say, put him aside! You take over! We have lost all the time we can afford!"

"It is clear, Master!"

The insanely cracking voice became an animal's bark. "But first you must find your accursed Judith! Without the girl I can make no Mass! Without the Mass there can be no peace for me ever!" There was a fierce animal shriek: "Everyone will pay with blood, I promise you!"

"Yes, Master!" Gregor rushed headlong from the abbey.

Werner Christed's fingers tightened on Judith's shoulders.

The crazed figure bellowed after Gregor into the night, louder than the thunder claps rending the sky. *"I am the High Priest of Satan! All power here comes from him through me! Never forget!"*

Panting huskily, the man stood alone. His horrible makeup was distorted with his virulence. He stared down at the coffins, and a lascivious smile twisted his plastic features. "Later, my darlings," he crooned. His lipsticked mouth moistened with evil spittle. "First I must complete my greatest work, the perfect Black Mass, then we shall celebrate my ultimate victory together!"

With that, the man stamped out into the storm, carrying himself with the air of a conquering general.

Judith clung to Werner Christed to keep from shaking apart. She suffered the agony of the barbed wire again, this time not ripping her lacerated flesh, but shredding her spirit, her heart, her brain, her very soul. *Rick Gilbert, to whom she was to be "engaged"!*—madman! He, whose soft words and loving arms had won her to his breast in "their grove"—*insane!* The slimy pieces of Gomay Island's mysteries had abruptly fallen into place only too clearly, revealing a monstrously unexpected design of hellish duplicity. The pieces now clicked together like the bones of a skeleton all too devilishly, with foulest duplicity:

. . . It was Rick who had persuaded her to stay with the company the night Dr. Gomay had recited the disgusting story of *Baron of Darkness.*

. . . It was Rick who had gone into the Gomay quarters

not to ask for a robe but because he was one of them, *their leader!*

. . . It was Rick who had lied about Lena's leaving the island!

. . . It was Rick who was obeyed by the guard the night the dog attacked her. Rick's later "confessions" had been only more clever manipulation and fabrication to lull her and keep her on the island for his own dark purposes!

. . . It was Rick who had denied the bodies in the abbey, not for the sake of her nerves, but to keep the truth from her. As he had lied about loving her, so that she would be used as the sacrifice his "perfect" mass required!

Ah, Judith saw, Rick could play the monstrous baron so convincingly in scene after scene not because he was the great actor, but because he himself was evil incarnate.

In the spasms of her frightful comprehension, Judith turned pleadingly to Werner Christed, who was staring grimly at the vacated doorway. She felt reassurance flowing from this man's inner power. Whatever "Rick" had been—quicksilver, moonlight, romance—Judith was suddenly aware of something else reaching her from the director. Solid rock. Solid earth. For all the brilliance of his artistic genius, what Judith gathered in this crisis was the man himself, the man behind the artist.

All at once, Werner Christed held for her deep and reaching roots from which she gathered a nourishment never known with the other man. It was not the sweet spice and easy delight of the hours upon Balefire grove. Rather it was her new realization of a hidden hunger she had not known she possessed. For the first time, she did not feel it as presumptuous of her—for the first time it was possible to see Werner Christed not only at a distance with respect and admiration, but as a man with whom she could share personal, intimate affection.

There seemed to be tenderness and caring on his part in the way he was holding her. Judith told herself it was more than just pity for her bruised condition and bedraggled state.

She stirred in Christed's arms. Her own inner strength began to assert itself. "What do we do now?" she asked.

The director spoke, addressing Judith as equal to equal. "I had my own doubts about these people from the day Gregor Ludovici brought the deal for this picture. When I came out to the island, I was put off by the servants and the rules but I did accept it as part of their religion." A smile eased the director's stern remembering. "After all, I'm supposed to be a pretty open-minded sort, myself." Christed stopped, pinching his chin. "They tried to interest me in their cult once . . ." Judith recalled Rick's telling her that—one truth from him, at least. "But all I cared about was making the film," the director continued. "Too much, I see now. It helped them use me!"

For Judith, it was a new comfort to feel that in her peril she and Werner Christed were in one boat together. Whatever else had fallen away, she could depend on this man to the last. But what would "the last" be, in this nest of lunatics!

She repeated, "What do we do now?"

Christed stretched. His fingers touched the ceiling. His power and intrepidity filled the chamber. "*What we do now is go down to the set as if none of this happened!* We say you went for a walk and got lost in the storm, and I found you. Then I am going to shoot the Mass exactly as the scenario says—and you will play it exactly the same way!"

Before Judith could express her consternation, the director added with a smile of self-confidence, "*Except* that Moose and I will have our own men all around to make sure no harm comes to you! *And*, when the scene is done, Rick-the-Baron is going to have one hell of a surprise in store!" Christed went on somberly, "It's our only chance, Judith. Anything else will arouse their suspicions and God knows what that crazy bunch might do. If we pretend nothing is wrong, they'll go along with me just as planned. I'll turn it into an opportunity for us to get away somehow!"

"How?" Judith persisted doubtfully.

Christed answered, "Leave that to me! Just don't give yourself away. It will be hard, but be the actress I know you are!"

Judith heard the tone of a man-in-charge. Like herself, Werner Christed had been struck by waves that swamped his ship, but his concern now was to prevent a wreck of his film. She was glad to hear the authority of his tone, but it did not allay the new fear stirred in her by the madman's speech in the abbey. She was certain now that "Rick" did not intend to use film effects to simulate the vestal sacrifice. The altar which was to have launched her film career was threatening to become her bier. Seeing the dismay, Christed drew her to him again. "Don't be afraid, Judy." He smiled unexpectedly. "Trust me. I may have as big a surprise for the Baron as he has had for us! I may have an ace in the hole, you know!"

Judith looked into the earnest gray eyes with hope. "An ace in the hole?"

"They won't hurt you, and they won't cheat me out of this picture! It's the best thing I've ever done, and it's mine, not theirs!"

It was a promise Judith wanted to accept. Perhaps powers greater than Werner Christed's were abroad on Gomay Island, but she had no choice. She turned trusting eyes to the director and murmured with a white-lipped smile, "I'll try to carry it off, Werner."

Leaving the abbey, the two stood motionless for a moment in the continuing downpour. They were suddenly conscious only of each other, eyes seeking eyes, and lips, lips. The grisly coffins behind them, and the threat of the black doings before them, slipped into the unawareness of the wind. The director turned seekingly to the young actress. With a flaring of desire, Judith embraced the strong masculinity of Werner Christed's kiss at last, taking new courage from it.

A fork of lightning lit up their pressed bodies. A clash of thunder echoed the passion the night had discovered and exploded within them.

They drew apart at once. The director breathed, "I am sorry, Judy. I shouldn't have done that."

Instead of numbness, pain, and despair, Judith Bradford felt a new woman. Unfamiliar emotions were kindling in her, out of embers of a depth of passion and self-understanding that had lain dormant in her before.

Judith lifted her lips to the man before her and her eyes were glowing. "I think I've been waiting for this from the first moment I saw you. I think I always knew it was going to happen, that I wanted it to happen. But I was too much in awe of you to ever let you know . . ."

"And I was too much involved in my work to let myself know!" Werner Christed answered, in a tone of discovery that echoed Judith's. He kissed her gravely, and they started down through the forest toward the movie set to film whatever the now-to-be-unfolded climax of their picture might turn out to be.

CHAPTER TWENTY-THREE

Ursula Blake said to her police companion, "It's after ten o'clock. We should be getting close to the turn-off to the island." The lieutenant studied the map as Blake honked a slower car out of the way.

"Will you please slow down?" he said.

"My girl is in trouble!"

"I respect your womanly intuition, but we can't help her if you kill us."

Without warning, their car jerked and veered to the

shoulder of the road. Carlos Rodriguez announced, "Flat tire!"

The car Blake had left behind passed them with a razzing horn.

In the pouring rain the two detectives opened the trunk. It was empty. "Oh, my God! Somebody stole the spare!"

Passing cars splashed them wetter.

"Show someone your badge," Blake clipped. "There must be a service station somewhere." She looked at her watch with desperate hope. The raindrops tapped a cadence of defeat at her: *"You're going to be too late!"*

But they could not move on three tires. Blake sighed dejectedly. It seemed that, whatever was happening on Gomay Island, Judith Bradford was going to have to confront it alone.

CHAPTER TWENTY-FOUR

The production began as soon as Dr. Gomay treated Judith's wire-torn back with unguents that magically erased her pain. The church had been transformed. There was an altar, with a Christ figure behind it. Torches emitted swirls of yellow smoke along the walls. Cameras were positioned everywhere. The ceiling was a mare's nest of spotlights. Most important, Judith recognized the prisms, wheels, projectors, and frames of Werner Christed's invention. The Illusion Machine was to be unveiled and play its role in the picture at last.

Judith was led to her place on the altar. Lying down on the cold marble slab, she was glad to see mirrors over her head. They enabled her to view the entire sweep of the set. The walls of the building had been plastered with ugly patches of scabrous-looking moss. Trailing, viscous cobwebs were everywhere. It did not help Judith that she knew how ingeniously they were created by Moose. A small fan was attached to an electric drill that sprayed a thinned rubber cement through a cone. By varying the opening of the cone, they created gummy strands of different thickness. The sticky webs were as disgusting to Judith as if they were natural.

Nothing was natural on this awful, astonishing night, Judith reflected. She could not even distinguish her friends like Rho, Vicki, and Bernie from the swarming Gomays. Acting as members of the baron's coven, they were all robed and masked alike. Judith herself lay nude beneath a flimsy crimson veil. The torch flames all around gave off an overpowering aromatic incense with their yellow smudge. Judith's head began to throb. She coughed in the vapors, and stiffened with her old alarm. It was no time to be rattled with a seizure! If ever she needed all her wits about her, it was tonight! Judith concentrated on the reality of the director talking matter-of-factly to his chief cameraman, on the camera grip chatting with the clapper-girl, on the lighting chief who was calling: "Hey, up there, I want a brute on Judith, and kill that inky! Move the scrim now, and hit the key light."

These people would not be proceeding so routinely if they knew what she and Werner Christed had learned! Judith could only pray that she herself would not be too unsettled when the scene called for her to confront the maniac she had known as Rick. She prayed, too, that Christed could keep her safe amid the legion of insanity that surrounded them in force now.

The director signaled Gregor Ludovici, who called out officiously, "Quiet everyone!" He rang a small bell, and a hush descended over the set. The clapper girl marked the scene in the usual way, and Christed took over. *"Rolling! Start your action! GO!"*

For Judith Bradford, actress on the sacrificial altar, the camera was rolling not film but her fate.

The scene sprang to life, and she watched in the overhead mirrors with a premonition she could not control. The marble slab was icy as death. Despite the encouragement Werner Christed had given, she felt she was already in the shadow of her end. She tried to rally her spirits, but could not remain buoyed up in the threatening presence of the now-circling Gomays. It was all the worse because she had been stripped naked before being placed on the altar, and was covered only by a too transparent cloth.

With the cameras rolling, the circling assemblage began to reach for her as the script required. Sweating fingers—of Gomays or her friends she did not know—touched her intimately. Judith wished her body could shrink to nothingness. The figures broke into diabolical, threatening barks as they stroked her lasciviously. An organ sounded unexpectedly, with crashing chords that reverberated a music of terror. Judith wished that Werner would see her tremulous worry, but he was concentrated on the death-shuffle moving dolefully around her prone body. To him now, as to the others, she was just the virgin awaiting Satan at midnight . . .

A new chanting in Latin rose in bass voices,

accompanied by funereal organ cadences:

Imparibus meritis tria pendent corpora remis, Dismas et Gestes,
In Medio est divian potestas, Dismas damnatur, Gestes ad astra levatur.

A camera swung to a side door. It opened slowly to admit a column of robed figures. Moving in melancholy pace, they held aloft black pikes on which decapitated heads were impaled—heads of children, women, old men. Were these horrible, charred death heads more plastic props? or—as Judith might now terribly suspect—might they be real? No, that would be impossible! But she shivered again on her cold stone, certain that if she were to touch one of the heads, she would feel flesh. Those blank staring eyes would be moist, not congealed; those lips would not be frozen in grimaces of torture and death, but soft and ready to speak.

To speak! To accuse this mad Gomay assembly, the unspeakable "Baron Gilles de Rais"!

Seeking support again, Judith looked toward the main camera. The director, following the scenario, was signaling Dr. Gomay to step in front of the lens. The old man was to deliver a preamble at this point, Judith had been briefed.

Felix Gomay strutted forward, costumed in lavishly embroidered robes of an ancient sorcerer and alchemist. He came to the camera with gleaming eyes.

"*Murderers!*" Judith silently accused. "Wait until tomorrow when Werner and I tell our story to the police outside!"

If they ever got off this island alive, she had to add to

herself grimly.

Dr. Gomay began: "Divine travelers, in this film we are combining the occult, the supernatural, and the spiritual. Tonight we here film a Black Mass, the greatest violation of the spirit of man and God. By its blasphemies we call out the evil in our hearts. By purging ourselves in this abomination, we shrive ourselves and open our hearts, finally, to the good. *Lustrum!* Because the world has been lost to violence, venality, vanity, and lust, the path to purification lies through violence, venality, vanity and lust!"

Judith considered that in all fairness this introduction was much like Werner Christed's own philosophy of art. She could see again why *Baron of Darkness* would have appealed to him as a film project. The terrible question now was whether that was all it would turn out to be!

Dr. Gomay spread his batlike cape before the camera. "Here is the High Priest of Lucifer himself, Baron Gilles de Rais, to conduct the terrible office!"

The creature coming forward was greeted with screeching frenzy by the congregation. Beneath her flimsy garment, Judith cringed. Moose had set giant color wheels moving above. The face approaching the altar looked like Death's skull lit by hell's brimstone fire. The fingers touching Judith were the talons of a bird of prey. Judith shook with renewed revulsion when the man leaned closer than the script required, and whispered urgently in her ear. "I'm sorry I lost you in the forest, Judy! I'm glad that you are all right! Now only play this scene with me and we will both win Academy Awards . . ."

Judith wanted to strike the foul, lying actor. What boundless conceit this lunatic possessed, whoever he was! How she would like to jump off the altar and shout out the revelations of the abbey to the whole group. It was impossible to believe that even a madman could portray such innocence as Rick had managed with her. And now he was continuing his gruesome deception as if she were not a human but a bloodless puppet he could abuse like any of their plastic props.

How could this be the man who had embraced her so tenderly up in "their grove," whispered endearments, promising of their future together!

Judith twisted in a fury of misery and bitterness she must conceal.

Her distress was amplified by a sudden swooping of bats around her head. She knew that their release was the cue for a beat she especially hated. Congregants now came to collect what was supposed to be menstrual blood from between her thighs. Sickeningly, a monk was to masturbate into the same dish, and excrement was to be added, along with ashes. This gruesome mixture was to be baked into unholy wafers, in mockery of a true Mass.

Rick-Baron-Priest was chanting malignantly: "In olden days, these ashes would be from the body of a child taken from its parents, assaulted sexually, and burned alive. The blood we pour here would be from another innocent, whose body would be chopped into fine pieces into the mixture. *Diabolus!*"

Judith knew that all of this had been historically verified, but it did not make it less revolting.

"Rick" was playing his part with increasing relish. He handed the silver dish to a Gomay. "Take this now to the oven that we may eat and do the ancient obeisance!"

Judith groaned to herself. She would not put it beyond these deranged murderers to bake and consume the filth.

Above her head, the actor was addressing the now-quiet congregation: "A Black Mass was often performed directly on a woman's body, despoiling it in every fashion. After sexual abuse by the congregation, it was usual to cut out her heart. It is written that the celebrants then raped the lifeless body, beat it, trod it, and ill-used it till it became no more than a mass of flesh, shapeless, disgusting, to be thrown to dogs."

Judith trembled with the morbidity of the words and the gloating of the voice. Was that what they planned for her tonight? *It could be so!* Where were the men Werner Christed had promised to guard her? On inward lightning, a new and more terrible doubt arrowed fresh terror into Judith's breast: *Might Werner Christed himself be one of them?*

The dread thought blanketed her mind.

The man's warmth at the abbey could have been only another ruse to bring her down for the sacrifice! They were smart; they were slick and cunning; they were tricky and guileful, all of them! Her latest suspicion made appalling sense in the nefarious logic of Gomay Island!

Judith could only weep inwardly and beg God that this insupportable experience was making her hysterically unreasonable. If Werner Christed had betrayed her, too, she was ensnared beyond all hope. All she could do was pray otherwise, and play her part as he had asked her to do.

The priest—Rick—was crying out, as if addressing the world: "We violate this woman as a token, a token that all women are the gateway of the Devil! This woman here, profaning this altar with pretense of innocence—this woman is like all female flesh, charged with lust, with the craving of the filthiest sex! So will we celebrate our lusts upon her body to bring its evil unto our power and thus exorcise it! We will here witness her rape by Satan himself, and we will rape her ourselves! We will here defile her in every way, as she defiles the world by her very presence!" There were shrieks of glee through the church.

It was gibberish to Judith, but dangerous jabber. The Gomays had moved beyond logic or reason. Tonight, Judith knew now, there would be only the lust, violence, and blood of which "Rick" chanted. It was no movie script, it was their devilish plan unfolding as hinted in the abbey. *She was lost!* Sweat glistened on Judith's forehead. Even if Werner Christed were not a Gomay, there was no way she could see that he could stop this horde.

"Terror is the expectation of horror—horror is the experiencing of terror." Judith was in such terror now that she almost wished the horror would come quickly. Let them perform their abominations and let it be over! She would be dead, beyond them, beyond this cruelty of unbearable apprehension.

But there had to be more incantations first, the Gomays had to lead up to the black ceremony of violation and murder.

"So let us bid forth the Unholy One himself!" The thickening voice no longer sounded anything like the man who had called himself Rick. It began an evocation of the names of Satan in languages: "*Arhriman! Apollyn! Eblis! Loki! Dis! Glushap! Sydni! Pazuzi!* In the name of *Tiamat*, the Babylonian goddess of chaos, I bid ye all, come to the faithful, come ye up from Sheol unto us!"

"Sheol" meant hell, Judith knew.

Alien tongues—Persian, Teutonic, Celtic, Indian, Assyrian. What a power such names have exerted over men through the ages! Even in science, Judith considered, the naming of a thing gives it reality, though its nature may remain unknown. It was no wonder that these conjurations held such sway over illiterate, ignorant primitives yearning to believe in God—in God or the Devil. Or both. And why should people not believe in demons and witches and Lucifer? Were not the promises of saints always broken, prayers unanswered? Did not God and his priests have only the promise of a distant heaven to answer the present sufferings of life on earth? For Judith, these reflections became a central message of the Gomay rites.

A wand, a cup, a sword, and a pentacle were lifted in order. Judith recognized the four magic symbols used by sorcerers in olden times. "In the name of Michael, Gabriel, Samael, Raphael, Sachiel, Buael, and Calliel, I, holder and possessor of the seals of the earth, and in preparation for the evocation of Satan to take this virgin, so do I conjure thee, spirits, by these holy names of God—*Tetragrammaton, Adonay, Algramay, Saday, Saboath, Planaboth, Panthon, Craton, Neupmaton, Deus, Homo, Omnipotens, Sepiturnus, Ysus, Terra, Annennus, Unige, Itus, Salvator, Via, Manus, Fons, Irogo, Filis . . .*"

The names of God were forbidden syllables, here meant to unleash the unholiest passions of the congregation. The response was immediate. The organ pounded out frenetic rhythms; the robed figures went wild with writhing, stamping, whirling dervish dances. The Gomays howled and growled, clicked and clapped as they gyrated.

The priest figure stood by the altar, shouting above the din: "We conjure thee, Sibylia, O, blessed and beautiful virgin, to appear before us visible and resurrected in the form and shape of this beautiful innocent we have brought for your incorporation—" Here the priest stopped and pointed at Judith threateningly. Judith looked wildly to Christed. *This was the cue for the start of the rape scene!* The director's eyes were intent on the chanter. He was paying no attention to her, Judith saw. She sank into deeper despair.

"Come now to us, Sibylia! Come into possession of this virgin we have prepared for thee. Come then, Sybilia the Cumaean, the Babylonian, the Libyan, the Delphic, the Cimmerian, the Erythraean, the Samian, the Trojan, the Phrygian, the Tiburtine—come with thy prophecies and foretellings that we may know our Sovereign, the Devil, has chosen this chaste vessel to have common copulation . . ."

Judith had been instructed by Werner Christed how the rape was to be faked. The appearance of Satan would be simulated with hologram projections. Superimposed porno shots would be added later in editing. Judith's role was to struggle with all her might, but slowly succumb to a creeping lust within, and then lose all control in a wanton surrender to the infernal's sexuality.

Still without a sign from Werner Christed, Judith realized she was abandoned to live the scene, whether it was to be faked or real! She could depend only on herself. But what could she possibly do?

Judith saw that already the "priest's" eyes were gleaming fanatically at her. He threw aside her veil and drank in her nakedness. The moment she had once dreamed of as a loving and supreme ecstasy—*with this very man*—was to be a leering, sneering assault. Judith wanted to strike the vicious mouth with her fist, but she had to lie still and wait. Christed might still come to her rescue, as he had promised.

Judith's mental perturbation was distracted by a loud bleating. Startled, she saw a small goat being dragged to the altar, followed by men carrying butchering knives. No one had prepared her for an animal's slaughter. For a moment, hope sprang in her chest—the kid might be a substitute sacrifice. A shout went up. The men hung the young goat by its hind feet directly over Judith's body. She could not imagine what they intended, until she saw a blade flash across the throat. The flesh opened in a thin line of red bubbles, then the black curly hair stained with a crimson froth, and a shower of blood poured down over Judith. It was sticky and hot and smelled of death. It choked her nose. Convulsed with disgust, Judith tried to squirm away, but powerful hands held her. To her added horror, the assemblage, chittering like wild animals, descended upon the altar. They leaped to reach her bloodied flesh with their tongues. From Judith's face and breasts and belly and thighs they licked and sucked up the hot blood of the twisting goat.

Men slit the belly, and let the entrails fall on Judith's nakedness. The steaming organs and fascia coated her glutinously, bathing her in excrement and vileness. It took all her strength to keep from adding her own bile to the stinking mass that blanketed her with foulness. And still the congregation cavorted about her, seizing like hyenas at pieces of the still-living goat flesh to chew and gulp with barks of gluttony. Some Gomays scooped blood up in their palms and swallowed avidly, slobbering and staining their masks luridly.

In the midst of the orgy, Judith berated herself again, calling herself to final account. How she had scoffed at Chicago friends who had warned her about ambushes and freaks! *She* was smart enough not to be taken in. *She* would recognize danger. But she hadn't, had she? "The one sure thing about a swindler is that he never comes on like one!" She had let herself forget that axiom of experience. Now she was getting what she deserved for being too sure of herself!

But how *could* she have known? Lena Ludovici had put to rest her first misgivings. Werner Christed had a worldwide reputation. The seductions of Rick Gilbert had been so subtle, so seemingly genuine. If a person couldn't trust her senses and her heart, what kind of a world was it? Maybe it was just as well not to go on living in such a world!

But even as that surrendering frailty insinuated itself, a wave of resentment and rage geysered up in Judith. She may have been unwitting before, but she was knowing and alert now! With or without Werner Christed, she had to find some way to save herself!

The goat's head was hacked off and, oozing its brains, was placed beside Judith's cheek. She shut her eyes against the death stare of the pitiable skull, and held her breath against the reeking malodor directly in her nostrils. Close to fainting, Judith held on to the saving grace that at least it was not her blood the Gomays were siphoning, not her flesh they were shoving into the mouths behind their masks.

If only she had seen the face of the Gomay guard whose mask she had ripped off!

If only she could free her hands to rip off the masks leering down at her now!

If only someone would come to clean her off! Surely Werner Christed could see how terrible it was to have this living garbage heaped so disgustingly on her body!

But Christed was conspicuously directing his attention to everything but her, and Judith had to accept that her thread of hope was thinning to the vanishing point. All expectation of help from any direction was fading. She was falling into an abyss.

New cries filled the air: "Take her now!" "Have her now!" "Know her now!" And one stentorious voice, plainly not a Gomay but one of the Christed troupe: "Fuck her now! *Fuck her now!*" Ah, how thin is the veneer of social restraint, Judith thought jaggedly. The man calling for her rape so avidly was probably somebody she had played tennis with, swum with in the pool, danced and laughed with in the evenings.

But Rick-Baron de Rais shouted back raucously, "First comes the Violation of the Nun!"

Another cheer resounded. This was a new promise of salacious excitement. The Gomays hooted and buzzed with glee.

The organ shifted its register to a pious hymn's sound, and a woman in a nun's habit was carried in. She was fastened erect, like a crucified Christ, on a large cross, which was set up beside the altar. Judith could see all too plainly the savage acts that followed. She was able to take some small comfort from the fact that the attention of the Gomays was diverted from her for at least a time. She wanted to shut her eyes against the scene, but could not help being fascinated as Rick Gilbert approached the bound nun with a fierce-looking, knotted whip. *Would Werner Christed permit the man actually to flog the woman?*

Or was the woman another of the damnable wax effigies? The riddle was almost harder for Judith to bear than certainty would have been.

Rick Gilbert's eyes were coals of evil desire as he

approached the cross. Slowly, to the salivating moans of the congregation, he lifted the bottom of the nun's habit. Little by little, he exposed her naked flesh, provocatively, at first just her legs, then the habit was lifted over the woman's knees and halfway up her thighs. The Gomays hooted and stamped in expectation, but Rick dropped the cloth teasingly. The crowd whined and croaked until he responded with a further slow-motion revelation of the nun's body. He inched the habit up over her thighs, mature but innocent, and the Gomays barked encouragement: "More! Higher! *Show us her cunt, her holy cunt!*"

"The filth!" Judith cursed the man silently.

She saw Rick Gilbert's face working nastily beneath his make-up, his mouth twitching with his arousal as he tormented the nun, exhibiting her in a humiliating strip tease for the cruel and wanton voyeurs. He prolonged the indecency by dropping the woman's habit to cover her again. Another sibilance of disappointment hissed through the church, but Gilbert appeased his coven immediately. He reached to the nun's throat and, with soft motions lowered his hands to stroke her chest voluptuously. He drew aside her habit until the swelling breasts and red nipples were revealed. Sighs of pleasure ululated from the spellbound viewers.

Gilbert leaned forward and put his voluptuous lips to the nun's breasts. He made slurping sucking noises that brought a pounding, mocking laughter from the depraved audience. The mortified woman flinched and writhed, shutting her eyes in shame. The man's hands continued to separate the covering of her body. Teasingly again, he let the cloth fall back once or twice, but each time he opened more of the nun's flesh to view, until finally all saw the pink skin of her narrow waist—and at last her mound of curly brown hair below, the nun's soft undefiled mound of Venus covering the sacred privacy between her thighs, her sex.

But not private now. The fingers of her attacker reached knowingly for the unwilling flesh, and parted her. His fingers stroked and rotated gently, but the crowd knew the lascivious violence the skilled foreplay presaged, and they cried out for it. The woman moaned and shuddered.

Judith saw the innocence of the woman's face, the misery in her eyes. If the figure was not alive, it was a marvel of imitation, beyond belief! But the head was lifting, tears were real on the woman's cheeks. Oh, God! Judith groaned—they actually did kidnap a nun, they were not pretending! She wanted to go to the woman's rescue, but she was helpless, and worse. She could only watch.

Rick drew back his whip. It lashed out mercilessly, and opened the woman's flesh just beneath her swelling breasts. She cried out in agony.

Judith could not bear to see more. It was inconceivable that Werner Christed would be accepting this barbarism, no matter what he wanted on this unholy film. Her mind turned over. The only possible answer was that she was wrong, that Werner was performing one of his miraculous illusions. There could be no other explanation. It was small comfort, but it made it possible for her to go on witnessing the scene.

Each lash of Rick's whip brought more blood and higher screams for mercy, until the nun was reduced to a piteous whimpering. Her tears themselves seemed globules of pure red, the blood squeezed from agony beyond endurance.

Gomays brought forward a platform on which Rick stepped up to the naked nun. Shamelessly, he spread his costume and exposed himself. High yelps of delight sounded all around as Rick used his hand, with obvious pleasure, to help ready himself. The nun kept twisting her head from side to side trying to avoid her immolation, but to no avail. With a brutal grunt, Rick threw himself upon the beaten flesh and thrust his body into the bound woman. She could not resist, could not fight back. She screamed her excruciating pain, but her tribulation only served to excite the rapist more. He mounted and thrust into her like a rutting beast, plunging and rearing, plunging and rearing, until the woman fainted as he reached his raging, polluted climax.

The congregation went crazy. The Gomays thundered their hysteria. Judith wished only that she could faint out of consciousness as the wretched nun had done. What she had witnessed was, she knew, a frightful preview of what lay in store for her.

To grotesque applause, Rick came down from his abominable performance, bowing and greeting his acolytes with upraised arms and widespread fingers, as if he had just triumphed in some great cause.

As Judith was wracked with new spasms of fear, the monster turned to her and began to babble more of the ritual of the Black Mass. She heard the imminent threat to her own innocence in the foreign names he invoked—demons and succubi out of the depths of hell, she was sure. "I say Satan's will be done!" Rick was bellowing to the morass of bobbing Gomays. "Come now to the violation of the virgin here, *oh, Kasam, Ob, and Nahas!*"

The celebrants responded, "*Fiat! Fiat! Fiat!* Amen!"

Another organ chord crashed through the church. "In

the name of Manicheism, we call thee forth, oh, Satan, our Lord!"

Judith heard the climax in Rick's tone and knew her time was running out. *When, when was Werner going to act?*

"We have done everything as it is written. We have partaken of the green lion, of the serpent, of the milk of the virgin. Of the pontic water we have drunk, and with arsenic, tin, and the salts of vitriol, saltpeter, nitre have we sprinkled the altar for thy coming! Here we offer thee the juices of spurge and poppy and purslane!"

New billows of orange-brown vapors billowed around the altar. Judith could stand the suspense no longer. She wished the attack would come, be finished, kill her!

"We have eaten of the bellies of toads and have drunk the human urine mixed with the fluid of the menses, and of the milk of virgins, and the excrement mixed with the holy semen of Onan taken from a horse, a dog, and a man!"

Judith saw that the man was foaming at the mouth. He roared. "*De Operatione Daemonum! Maleus malifactum!* We offer this bride to thee, oh, *Ioth, Aglanabrath, El, Abiel, Anathiel, Maazim, Sedomel, Gayes, Heli, Messias, Beatriches, Tolimi, Elias, Danieli, Ischiros, Athantos, Imas!* By thy holy names we do call upon thee . . ."

Judith's brain swelled with a hypnotic buzzing. The names, the organ music, the crowd's moaning and chanting reached to some mystery in her own spine to claim a primeval acquiescence. Despite herself, it wrought a bubbling creepy response in her head.

"Claim now thy bride! oh, *Adonay, Amay, Horta, Vege dora, Mitai, Hel, Gregon, Surunat, Ysion, Ysey,* and by all the devils that Salomon did bind and shut them up,

Elhrach, Ebanher, Agle, Alrama, Goth, Ioth, Petra, Dougal, Othie, Venoch, Nabret, I beseech that thou congregate all they spirits thrown down from heaven! *Fiat! Fiat! Fiat!* Amen!"

The congregation knelt and was abruptly silent.

"He comes now! The great one comes!" Rick cried.

A pandemonium of twisting lights and shrieking bodies filled the church. Judith struggled to jump from the altar in the confusion, but she was pinned at once by arms she could not see. Looming before her was a hideous figure—*the Devil himself.* He appeared in a great blast of flame and thunder. Judith could not tell whether the explosion and the figure were real, or Christed's wonder machine. Or both, as had been the case when she had worked with its illusions. All she knew was that she was dying inside, shriveling to ashes before the ghoulish demon. Her skin was seared by fire that shot from its nostrils. Judith saw the Christed apparatus lighting up, but knew the figure before her was the Satan of her nightmares, real upon her now with its sharks' teeth in spreading jaws, ready to swallow her into its scaly belly. Her nose was filled again with the sulphurous stench that had contaminated her room at home when the monster broke her window to come at her.

This *was* the drugs, Judith choked to herself in new turbulence and demoralization. It *had* to be! Nothing so abominable could really be happening in even the most diseased mind! The Gomays were screeching obscenities with fresh delight as the Satan figure lewdly displayed his sex above Judith's aching body. He was turning around and around so everyone could see his priapus, fearfully enlarged and engorged.

The assembly was mewing, neighing, cackling, whistling. The organ keyboard was thumping and squealing. Gomays tumbled about the altar foaming at the mouth. Others were leaping upon each other, ripping clothes off hysterically, copulating without restraint, uttering frantic incantations in tongues.

The Devil capered more closely to Judith. His hooves struck sparks from the altar as he cavorted above her bloodied, aching body.

In utter despair, Judith thought this was not her old nightmare becoming reality, but reality becoming the nightmare. It was no film simulation, she cried inwardly. Why didn't Werner Christed see it and move before it was too late, too fearfully late!

The gigantic Satan pranced closer, taking goatlike hops, and continuing to flaunt its raunchy organ above her head. More of the celebrants became inflamed with sex and fell upon each other in abandon until the church floor was a snake-like mass of writhing bodies. Cries of orgasmic climax tore the very air apart profanely.

Judith tried with all her will to see the Satan figure as only an actor or a Christed projection of the kind that had terrified her during her first test. But everything was too complete and authentic all around—the shrieking noise, the sexual odors of bodies rutting, and the goat stink of the obscene sex organ approaching her thighs.

Burning with trepidation, Judith remembered that the script now called for the final cue before the actual rape. And, yes, coming toward her, with cameras following, was a Gomay carrying the wafer Judith was to swallow.

Judith gagged at the prospect—but another blow swept that horror from her head. There before her eyes, on the Gomay's wrist as she lifted the tray, was Lena's bracelet!

And on the marriage finger, Lena's wedding band! In how many ways had the miserable Gregor been faithless to her friend! Everything on this night was miserable sacrilege!

As the abhorrent wafer was shoved against Judith's compressed lips, she saw Moose looking from his perch among the spotlights, seeking a signal from Christed. But the director was impassive at the camera. Judith's suppressed doubts about Werner Christed caught hotter flame and fused into molten terror. Her last, dying hope was that he was giving the coven as much rope as possible in order to get as much evidence as he could on film. That remained a possibility, though remote now that her moment of ultimate crisis was at hand. While she gagged on the rancid wafer, the Devil was bearing his body down directly on Judith.

The moment of her ravishment was inescapable now!

The screeching in the church was shaking the roof.

The girl wept helplessly. Now she would die, and worse!

Except that there came a curt command from Werner Christed: "*Cut! Wait!*"

There was consternation, snarling and barking from the celebrants. The Satan-figure rose up from Judith's spread thighs with a bellow of frustration. Christed shouted back, "I have to adjust the projectors! It will only take a minute . . ."

The Devil actor turned to curse the director, and Judith seized the moment to squirm free of him. In the extremity of her desperation, she reached up violently and ripped his mask away.

It was Gregor!

Inwardly, Judith was not surprised. And well she might prefer death to ravishment by this beast of beasts!

This brute did not need to wear movie make-up or costumes to be satanic.

At the same moment, in the pandemonium. Rick Gilbert was reviling Christed with a stream of profanity. "No waiting! Go on! Go on! This is *my* film! Keep the damned cameras rolling!"

On the altar, an enraged Gregor grabbed Judith and began to pound her head mercilessly on the marble. "You killed Lena, didn't you!" Judith heard herself scream as pain splintered her skull. Judith went dark just as Moose and a band of his men fell upon Gregor and dragged him off.

But swarms of Gomays fought back. Their numbers overcame Judith's rescuers. With violent curses, Gregor Ludovici was upon the altar again. In a frenzy of sex, he imprisoned Judith in his giant arms, forcing his hugely erect phallus against her once more. In indescribable anguish, Judith felt the giant sex beginning to enter her as Gomay hands again yanked her legs apart.

As stunning as it was unexpected by anyone in the church, salvation came from another quarter. A piercing scream rang out behind the altar, and the silver figure of Joan of Arc leaped into the spotlights. As improbable as a Christed projection, it was Margot Gomay! With the super-strength of her madness, she hurtled directly at Judith and, ramming through the Gomays, she hit and shoved the bewildered girl off the altar.

But powerful Gomays fell upon Judith where she landed on the stone floor.

In the same instant, Rick Gilbert seized the madwoman's knife and slashed at her crazily. He cut her to shreds and stamped on her torn body as it fell, pouring out blood. There were confusing croaks and growls all about. Gomay hands roughly lifted Judith back to the altar. She heard Rick command in a hysterical shout free of all pretense now: "*Go on, Gregor!* It is midnight! Take this miserable virgin now, damn your unholy soul! *Take her or I am still cursed!*"

Judith was a pool of pain, but the death she yearned for did not come. It was ironic that it should have been the insane woman—her would-be murderer—who had almost saved her, but now Gregor was upon her again. He would rape her now, and then the Gomays would cut her open and take her heart for the rest of their ceremony. They would slice up her body and put the sections together in a bright red coffin like Emily's and Lena's . . .

Vaguely, Judith saw Christed and Moose fighting their way toward the altar, cursing at Gregor and Rick. For a moment hope flared in Judith, but there were too many of the Gomay people. Judith saw Christed and Moose fall, and she gave up her soul. She closed her eyes and waited for it to be over. It was the end.

But instead, gunshots sounded.

A silence of dumbfounded paralysis spread over the movie set. A voice of authority blasted: "Police! Freeze! Hold everything or we'll shoot!"

Judith was too stunned to take it in. All she knew with a sobbing prayer of thanks, was that Gregor and his foulness fell away from her in time, just in time.

Catapulting free of the altar, Judith caught the incredible sight of Ursula Blake, accompanied by a policeman.

Judith's relief swirled to dismay as she saw what Blake and her companion could not observe. A gang of Gomays, hiding up in the church rafters, dropped down to seize the two strangers before a warning could be given.

In the turmoil of the reversal, Rick grabbed Judith and roared again to Gregor. *"There is still time!"*

What none of them saw in the new commotion was that Werner Christed had pulled loose of the Gomays and was lunging for his control board. Furiously kicking Gomays out of the way, the director called with a great shout to Moose. *"Now!"* His fist hammered at a red lever.

New pandemonium! The church reverberated with a rending explosion that brought the roof down. The screech of ripping wood filled the air, and stone walls collapsed sending up huge clouds of choking dust. Great beams flew through space. The cave-in threatened to bury everyone in the falling building. Yelps of panic came from the Gomays scurrying ratlike to escape. There was a bedlam of pounding feet caroming toward the doors. The stampede was led by Dr. Gomay.

But Rick obdurately and single-mindedly held Judith prisoner on the altar. He kept screaming for Gregor to complete the rape, and the monster-devil started for Judith still again.

Werner Christed careened to the altar. He slammed Rick Gilbert with murderous blows to the man's head and gut. Gilbert doubled over howling with pain. Judith thought she had never heard a more satisfying sound! With "the baron" beaten to a pulp, Christed turned on Gregor Ludovici. Though Gregor was a heavyweight, Werner Christed seemed to tower over him, his anger adding to his natural power. He beat the ugly man to his knees. Christed's great fists pummeled the fat belly with the fury of the director's outrage for himself and for Judith. Gregor's wild gasps for air were music in their ears.

Judith began to laugh, in a hysteria of relief and

understanding. *Bless the Illusion Machine!* Bless genius Werner Christed! Bless the secret effect he had shared with no one! The cave-in of the church was so real that Judith, though she knew better, could swear the stones and timbers and glass were actually shattering all around.

Outside, later, walking hand in hand with the director, Judith saw Ursula Blake keeping the Gomay crowd at bay with a crucifix held high before them. Her companion had his gun on them while he called for the State Police on a walkie-talkie. The storm had passed, the moon was bright in a clearing sky and the scene was etched in the night like an outlandish tableau against the silent, witnessing forest.

Judith heard Blake call to her anxiously, "Are you all right, Judy?" Judith smiled and waved at the woman reassuringly. It was hard to realize that her dire peril had somersaulted into rescue and safety—thanks to her mother's concern! Her mind filled with new gratitude as she stared at the sullen, beaten faces of the wicked cast of plotters—Rick Gilbert, Felix Gomay, Gregor Ludovici, an evil crew hardly to be matched in history! And she was not only free of them, but of the drug cloud as well! It came to Judith that she had this night faced a murderous sequence of agonizing shocks, and had not once surrendered reality.

Judith was certain that if she could pass this ordeal, she would never again have to fear the yellow dominion that had haunted her so miserably.

Around her nude body Judith Bradford tightened the crimson veil she had snatched from the altar. She was secure and clothed in the armor of her new self-knowledge.

As she viewed the cowering group of Gomays on Urwolde Common, she knew there was one last contact she wanted to have with them. Leaving Werner Christed's side, she went directly to the Gomay woman named Lilia. "*The bracelet and the ring!*" she demanded, brooking no denial, speaking for her friend Lena Ludovici.

Sulkily, the Gomay woman obeyed.

Judith returned soberly to the director. At least Lena and her cherished possessions would have a decent burial, as would Emily Lawrence—in whose coffin she might herself be lying but for the grace of God, Ursula Blake, and Werner Christed. Unfortunately, the punishment to be suffered by the wicked would not bring her friends back.

Judith was grateful for Werner Christed's firm grip on her elbow. Despite her determined show of self-control, she was quivering inside with the fearful ordeal of the night and the narrowness of her eleventh-hour escape. Werner Christed's touch transmitted a bolstering strength she needed badly. She felt again the deep tenderness that flowed beneath the man's power, almost belying his masculine forcefulness.

"Let's get you cleaned up!" the director took over. Quickly, he led the befouled girl away from the church and the confounded and stunned crowd. Hurrying along to the dormitory, Judith found her knees wobbly as fresh waves of relief surged through her sore body. It was hard to take in that she was truly safe, not doomed, finally out of the cauldron of Gomay Island's revealed viciousness and endless duplicities. Island of lies! Island of betrayal and corruption! Maze of maniacal chicanery!

Werner Christed's voice came through the night as a

reassurance of reality, welcome reality: the horror was finally overcome, finally dissipated. The director was asking, with a gesture toward Ursula Blake, "Judy, who is that woman? She obviously knows you—" His curiosity was unconcealed.

Judith explained at once about her mother's search for her. The director halted on the path and faced Judith gravely. "You know, I have wondered about your age all along." Then, "Lucky for all of us that your detective showed up when she did!"

Judith added, "But it was your machine that did it, Werner! God, you had the whole world tumbling down!"

Nearing the dormitory, Christed spoke again, his tone almost apologetic. "Judy, I knew the agony you were in, but there wasn't anything I could do that wouldn't make things worse. I realized that you must be suspicious of me." His face was drawn with concern. "I couldn't blame you if you took me to be one of them—"

"Yes, Werner." Judith's eyes were silver pools of honesty in the brightening moonlight. "I did have to think that tonight. But deep down I never truly believed it." It was good to have this in the open, aired and settled between them, and so put out of their minds.

"I'm glad." The answer came with what sounded like a sigh of relief.

At the door of Judith's room, the director told her, "It was as if they had me hypnotized." He shook his dark-browed head in continued puzzlement, scowling: "It took every last ounce of strength to pull myself free . . ."

Judith smiled at Werner Christed. In a reversal of roles, she was the one to give reassurance now. "It's over, Werner!" She squeezed his hand. "All's well that ends with a good hot shower!"

The director's face uncreased. He returned Judith's smile and stretched his lean body out on her bed, relaxing for the first time. "I'll wait for you right here."

Judith said quickly, "Yes, please. I don't want to be alone."

When she came back into the room, clean and refreshed, her skin scrubbed and shining, Judith was wearing her Easter bunny bathrobe. It made her self-conscious, and she felt her cheeks redden. "It's silly, isn't it?" she blushed for the juvenile garment.

Werner Christed rose slowly to his feet, his eyes steady on Judith's glowing face. His voice was low and tender. "From the first day, what reached me was your innocence. And your promise as a woman." Judith waited. She might be in a child's dress, but she didn't feel like a little girl. The director reached for Judith's shoulders. In doing so, he inadvertently parted her robe. The man whirled around at once, his back to Judith.

Judith was deeply touched. For all his worldly experience, Werner Christed was conventional and considerate of her when it came to this personal intimacy. For herself, Judith considered, she had posed naked for Werner scores of times—why should a fleeting glimpse of her body now leave them both flustered and flushing?

Warmly, she knew the answer. It was the difference between impersonal acting and their new closeness. Judith fastened her robe, and lifted her hands to Werner Christed's broad shoulders. Turning him back to her, she whispered, "I thank you, Werner. For everything." And, of her own will and direction, Judith Bradford stood on her toes, lifting her lips forwardly and without reserve to kiss the man she now knew beyond all doubt she had been waiting for.

In the confession of their ardor the two felt without more words that they were pledging themselves to each other, starting a new life already distant from the evil that had surrounded them both so malevolently.

Safe and happy in Werner Christed's arms, Judith Bradford considered that Gomay Island had brought her not only grief, pain, and suffering, but love. For that she would always be thankful. The island's dark shadows would linger and hover over her life always, yes—she would never forget Lena Ludovici or Emily Lawrence. Nor would she forget the terrible Rick Gilbert, or Gregor, or Felix Gomay, or the pitiful madwoman and her horrible end. They were a lesson to heed well in a complex, difficult, and often perilous world. But she was tempered steel now, and no longer alone. The blackness of Gomay Island would only make the contrast of her happiness more luminous and radiant as she and the man embracing her built their future, in love and in work, together. That was all that mattered now.